GW01376841

About the author

On retirement, after a career in language teaching and linguistic research in a number of educational establishments, the author took up creative writing. His keen interest in European history in general – German in particular – led him to write this, his first novel, which has a historical background.

Innocence Unbound

DEDICATION

To the memory of my wife
Margret

To Michael & Jennie
Kindest wishes
Andrew

Andrew Richardson

INNOCENCE UNBOUND

AUSTIN MACAULEY

Copyright © Andrew Richardson

The right of Andrew Richardson to be identified as author of this work has been asserted by him in accordance with section 77 and 78 of the Copyright, Designs and Patents Act 1988.

All rights reserved. No part of this publication may be reproduced, stored in a retrieval system, or transmitted in any form or by any means, electronic, mechanical, photocopying, recording, or otherwise, without the prior permission of the publishers.

Any person who commits any unauthorized act in relation to this publication may be liable to criminal prosecution and civil claims for damages.

A CIP catalogue record for this title is
available from the British Library.

ISBN 978 1 84963 072 6

www.austinmacauley.com

First Published (2011)
Austin & Macauley Publishers Ltd.
25 Canada Square
Canary Wharf
London
E14 5LB

Printed & Bound in Great Britain

ACKNOWLEDGEMENTS

I owe a debt of gratitude to Emily Lacika and Brende Hawkes for their suggestions and encouragement during the writing of this book.

In writing this piece of fiction, I found the following books most helpful:

The Austrian Mind, by William M. Johnson (University of California Press, 1972)

In Search of Jewish Community, Eds. Michael Brenner & Derek J. Penslar (Indiana University Press, 1993)

The Silence of Pius XII, Carlo Falconi. Trans. By Bernard Wall (Little, Brown and company, 1970)

A Moral Reckoning, by Daniel Jonah Goldhagen (Alfred A. Knopf. New York, 2002)

Jewish Vienna 1860-193,. Eds. Helfried Seemann and Christian Lunzer (Album. Vienna, 2006)

Prologue

Vienna 1945

A man walks up a tree-lined driveway towards the house. He looks about. Everywhere are the lethal armaments of war: an acreage of parked columns of heavy T34 Russian assault tanks, their guns silent now, half tracks and transport trucks with red Cyrillic markings painted on their sides. Heedlessly, they have churned up the parkland and wiped out the flower beds. Large, green military tents cover the once carefully manicured lawns, the playground of his childhood. Soldiers in their shabby, sandy-coloured uniforms, some with blue caps bearing distinctive red bands, are smoking, lounging and sitting about: the besetting idleness of an army with no enemy to engage. It is late spring but a chilly eastern wind enwraps the city. The remnant odour of burnt diesel oil hangs in the air. Slavonic voices mingle with smoke from the wood fires they have lit to keep warm.

As he makes his way forward, he is not challenged until he comes to a forbidding roll of razor barbed wire strung across the gravel drive. A surly-faced guard, pointing his rifle menacingly, shouts at him in Russian, the language of the vanquisher. He tries to explain in German what he wants but the defiant look on the soldier's face tells him that his words are having no effect.

'It would be rash to try to get to the house,' he says to himself. 'Is all this not theirs by force of arms? Aren't these men the real winners of this tragic war? Only a fool would oppose them.'

Eerie phantoms, lurking in the background of his brain and long suppressed, take form and speak to him in ghostly tones as the trees and stones awaken the haunted labyrinths of memory. His disquieted mind goes back to the day when life, his new life, had begun. Withdrawing a little and through a gap in the trees, he can just make out the dark form of the house.

Chapter 1

Vienna 1932

Ulrich Dreher paid off the taxi and ran up the steps into the house. The imposing sandstone dwelling had been designed by his great grandfather Ahren, a wealthy Viennese small-arms dealer and manufacturer. A rounded tower at one corner, a steep mansard roof and tall mullioned windows gave it the appearance of a medium-sized French chateau. It would not be out of place in Normandy or Anjou. If you were to look up, you would see, carved into the central span of the granite-pillared portico, the family coat of arms, the emblem of a lathe, representing the name Dreher, and the motto 'Arma virumque cano' - 'I sing of arms and the man'. A witness in stone of the wellspring of the Dreher fortune and success.

Ulrich strode through the hall and drawing room then into the attached atrium-styled orangery where he found his mother. The Viennese press, the social columns to be exact, described Frau Elke Dreher, even now in her middle age, as 'a strikingly handsome woman', once comparing her pale complexion to a fine piece of Viennese porcelain. They extolled her position as Vienna's leading society hostess and elegant guide of fashion. The proof was there to see, for she was wearing a rich, silk fabric with a corded effect, what her Parisian dressmaker called *pou-de-soie*. She had an extensive, not to say expensive, wardrobe. Ulrich's father Dieter sometimes complained about her expenditure on clothing, but to no avail. Extravagant was the word he used.

"Ulrich, what brings you home so early?" she exclaimed, taking off her spectacles and looking up from her embroidery. Her voice was filled with surprise. She spoke to him in English, a legacy of having spent several formative years being educated in an exclusive convent school in southern England. The nuns had excelled in her case for she spoke with the accent of the English gentry, mainly Catholic, who sent their daughters there to be schooled for a life of privilege.

"I've got some really good news," he said. His face betrayed his youthful excitement. "Professor Felbiger has told me in confidence that I've passed my practical test. He said my design for the sub-machine gun impressed the examiners."

"I'm not at all surprised. You've worked very hard for this."

He went over to this mother and kissed her on the cheek. She was his confidante. He held nothing back from her. Well, almost nothing. Small intimacies, he told himself, are best left unsaid, and there had been a few of these in his young life.

"Your father will be pleased, when you tell him."

He sat down on one of wicker-basket chairs.

"The results haven't been published yet but father probably already knows. Professor Felbiger was his fellow student at the Polytechnic. I wouldn't be the least surprised if he hasn't already phoned him. When it comes to information Vienna's just a big village," he laughed.

"My dear Ulrich, I've had a lifetime of Vienna's incestuous manners. Betraying a confidence is treated as a social grace. Take that Frau Dorfmeister, or is it Buchleitner? I can never remember the wretched woman's name. Only last Sunday she was telling me that the Cardinal intends to open a soup kitchen for the unemployed. What rubbish. His Eminence himself told me he doesn't want his name being personally associated with some kind of socialist charity. She's got no discretion at all. She's like a loud-mouthed union leader. And we've enough of them these days."

She paused. "Do you think you'll be seeing Bernerdina again?" she asked. She gave him a knowing look. Bernerdina had been an emotional minefield.

"She gave up on me. I wasn't prepared to take time off from my design project. I don't blame her for finding someone else." He didn't really believe this but he had to approach the subject with a certain delicacy and circumspection for he knew from experience that his mother had the uncanny ability to unravel his adolescent excuses. Ulrich, I can read you like a book, was her constant catchphrase.

Inwardly he remembered. I was slightly tipsy and I propositioned her. 'I'm a virgin,' she'd said, 'and shall remain so till I marry.' She slapped my face, and ran off in silly tears. I felt humiliated and stupid. Foolishly, I told the priest in the confessional. He upbraided me and said fornication, where on earth do they get these words from? even in thought, was a mortal sin. Celibate priests. They know all about sin and nothing about sex. I've never been back to the confessional.

"It's over. I don't think I'll be seeing her again."

"What a pity. She was rather a pleasant girl. Most suitable. Such a pleasant family."

He knew what his mother meant by the word 'suitable'. The term oppressed him, much like the interior of the confessional.

He stood up, took off his tweed jacket, casually placing it on the back of the wicker-basket chair and sat down again. He liked to think of himself as casual, liberated, at ease. It put distance between himself and his father whom he regarded as a stern parent. He then put his feet up on the oak coffee table in front of him.

"Darling, I do wish you wouldn't put your feet on the table," she said, "it's not becoming."

"Sorry mother, it's the fashion. American. You see it in the movies."

"We're Austrian not American. Anyway, I'm glad you're here. I must talk to you about your twenty-first birthday party. According to my diary, there aren't many days left for preparations."

His mother's diary. She chronicled all the details of their family and social life in fine morocco leather bound notebooks and called them her diary. He knew the social season was his well-connected mother's life, organising and planning of family gatherings, soirées, balls, concerts and festivals. For the analytically-minded Ulrich, it was all too tediously boring, though curiously this did not lead him to miss any such function.

"Can't we postpone it?" he said. "The planning I mean. Not the party."

"I need to know how many of your friends you want to invite. I shan't be able to do any planning until I know the numbers coming.

Don't forget Gerda comes home this evening," she added, "you must tell her your news."

"I'm not so sure. My dear sister is more interested in the latest jazz and not guns."

"She's doing well at school. The Ursuline nuns tell me she's good at languages and art."

"Quite the little painter is she?" He really did not want to be told how clever she was at art. Leaving childhood behind, he had gradually grown further apart from his younger sister, prone to bouts of unexplained silliness and giggle fits.

At that moment, the butler, a middle-aged man, in evening tail coat and formal striped trousers came into the orangery.

"Madame," he said.

"Well, Saracco?"

"Father Kiesl has arrived."

"Show him in."

Saracco turned to go.

"Saracco, bring us some tea. Father Kiesl prefers Earl Grey."

Sarraco returned with Father Kiesl in train. The priest had a noticeable tonsure-like bald patch on the crown of his head, giving him a monkish appearance but, otherwise, there was nothing monastic about him: well-groomed, exuding an aroma of eau de cologne, pince-nez, white gloves and carrying, in one hand, a hawthorn cane with a silver knob and, in the other, a black homburg. He had the air of a sacerdotal dilettante.

This obnoxious priest, Ulrich thought, I hate it when he leers at me with those lecherous eyes. I've heard from some of my friends that he's got a dubious reputation. Choirboys in the sacristy. The Church authorities must be turning a blind eye for he's obviously not been defrocked. Yet.

"How nice to see you again Frau Dreher," Father Kiesl said in a high-pitched, effeminate voice. He articulated every word as if it were an organ note.

"You're always welcome here, Father Kiesl."

"I've come to tell you my good news. His Eminence has just offered me the post of Diocesan Master of Choristers and I've also been asked to give an organ recital of Buxtehude at Herzogenburg Abbey."

"Congratulations. Heavens, this is an afternoon of good news," she laughed.

Father Kiesl gave her a surprising look.

"Ulrich, has just passed his exams," she told him. "Most pleasing, don't you think?"

"Of course," he conceded, in a barely disguised vexed tone, objecting, it would seem, to being upstaged.

Standing up, Ulrich greeted the visitor. Good manners and reserve. Those were the virtues his mother espoused, herself a lady of impeccable manners. You keep your dignity that way, she would tell him. But he could not get away quickly enough. It's a pity, he thought, that creatures like Kiesl exist but they do.

"If you don't mind, mother," he said, "I'll go into the garden, I need some fresh air and give the matter of your list some thought." Making a half-hearted apology to the newcomer, he gave a high pitched whistle which brought a West Highland terrier bounding into the orangery.

"Let's go for a walk, Charlie," he said to the dog.

* * *

With Charlie running in front of him, Ulrich walked out of the orangery and down into the rear garden. Ornamented with finely clipped box hedges, this had an extensive parterre, a medium-sized pavilion, whose design was loosely copied from the Petit Trianon at Versailles, several terraces, a topiary and a fountain with a statue of Ares, the Greek god of war, sculpted out of white Parian marble. Ulrich's smoothly working and logical mind found it difficult to believe that the geometrical patterns in the symmetrical squares, the precise rectangles and the octagon were of French rather than German design.

He entered the pavilion, which his mother kept filled with indoor plants, and settled down on one of the lounge chairs. Ringing in his ears were his professor's remarks, 'Your design is original and simple. The idea of a sub-machine gun is one of those things that's engaged the armaments industry for decades. The Thompson sub-machine gun is just too heavy in close military combat.' In researching the subject, Ulrich had discovered that the American police used it, calling it the 'tommy gun' but their military had not yet adopted it. He would never forget the professor's final comment, 'I shall recommend you for first prize.'

What would my great-grandfather Ahren have thought, he mused, if he could have known about my design for a gun?

He rose and went across to an antique English mahogany serpentine-shaped chest of drawers. Opening one of the top drawers, he took out a medium-sized notebook. It was Ahren's journal.

He had started to keep it as a young apprentice in an iron and steel foundry where he designed the pistol that was to make him famous. Ulrich returned to the lounge chair, sat down and opened the journal. The more he read, the more Ahren's handwritten neat German gothic script and fine turn of phrase appealed to his discursive cast of mind creating a particular bond. He felt he was being filled with his ancestor's infectious enthusiasm.

'Today is a day of wonderful joy,' Ahren had written. 'I've found someone who has agreed to help me. I know my handgun will be a success because of its original design. Last week I went to one of those Viennese high-ceilinged, marble shrines, where Mammon keeps his treasure, to ask for a loan to build a workshop. When they saw my dress and cap, the sacred guardians of capitalism turned me down with haughty disdain. So yesterday I went to see Max, a Jewish moneylender who has a reputation for shrewdness. He wears thick spectacles, for he's myopic, has a green skullcap and speaks with a coarse Galician Yiddish accent. He's my saviour. 'I'm always willing to lend money to those making and selling arms' he told me, 'for, like death and coffin-makers, arms and their dealers are certainties in an uncertain and even poor world.' I slapped him on the back and said, 'Max you're a fellow cynic'.'

The journal described how Ahren set himself up in business and called it the Vienna Small Arms Company. At the outbreak of war between Russia and Turkey in the fifties and in the Austro-Prussian war of the sixties, he clandestinely sold arms to both sides. It proved a shrewd move. Soon Serbian nationalists, Polish exiles, Greek insurgents, Ruthenian rebels, Italian and Russian revolutionaries, desperate expatriates and every type of Balkan anarchist came knocking at his door. They were an unsavoury lot but Max had been right, there is always money to be made from selling arms even to the poorest of beggars.

As well as supplying arms to the Austrian Imperial Army, he was one of the first to do business with the newly formed German Empire under von Bismark. The journal recounted that the Kaiser himself possessed a Dreher pistol and his military officers of all ranks boasted to owning one. Once he had made his fortune, his financial affairs were handled through a leading Viennese Jewish investment bank. 'Jews', he wrote, 'are the only people I can trust with my money'.

He then built his chateau-like house, the Dreher family home.

'I admire the French for their light, elegant architecture and artistic originality and, in designing the house, I was much influenced by visits I made to the chateaux of the Loire in the aftermath of the Franco-Prussian war. I'm grateful for that war, for it provided the foundations of my fortune. This house symbolises my prosperity and marks my ambitions.'

The journal then went on to describe Ahren's difficulties with his fellow citizens.

'Snide remarks, obviously motivated by piqued jealousy or wrathful envy, have followed my swift rise up the rigid Viennese social ladder. I've been told that high society, in their aristocratic salons naturally, where imperial society balls are organised, proclaim with hauteur, 'Dreher's little palace is too French, it's not Austrian', and 'Dreher is a nouveau riche upstart Bavarian'. Such expressions of noble disdain are often, so it would seem, embroidered with exclamation marks and Baroque gestures. But I know them for what they are. The disagreeable truth, which of course they refuse to admit, is that my house reminds them of the humiliation of Austerlitz, Napoleon's crushing defeat of Austria. I ignore them. Let them scoff. Money has no class. I'm German and the Austrian tiara set are fickle.'

Ulrich closed the journal, leaned back in the lounge chair and closed his eyes. The delicate bouquet of fragrances, suffusing the pavilion, brought an evocation to Ulrich of childhood and adolescent memories, lodged in his mind like daguerrotype snapshots. His mother taking him to Scotland to visit distant relatives. She was proud of her Scottish roots. 'My maternal great-grandmother,' she told Ulrich, 'married a Scotttish laird, a certain Angus Gunn, the Third Marquis of Badenoch and Strathnethy in the Central Highlands.' Another incident came vividly to his mind. Playing in the French garden and then coming to this very place to find his mother crying. On asking why she was weeping, she replied that she had just learned of the death of her elder brother, on the Western front. He had cried with her, not for her loss - he couldn't really understand that - but the fact she was filled with sadness and sorrow. Then, much later, there was a brief affair with the Czech housemaid, consummated in this very pavilion. His mother somehow must have found out and summarily dismissed the hapless girl but said nothing. At least not to him. He felt sorry for the girl but the experience left its mark. He knew the impossibility imposed by their social differences.

Charlie gave out a sharp bark and, jumping from his wicker basket, ran to the open door. Ulrich's uncle, Claus, his mother's other and older brother, came up the steps into the pavilion. Dressed in a white linen suit, a panama hat and pink paisley silk bow tie, he sported two-tone white and black shoes, giving him an affected air. He once told Ulrich that when he was being baptised, according to family history, his own mother insisted that the parish priest spell his name in the register with a 'C' in the English fashion and not a 'K'. The elderly pastor was not going to refuse a lady whose family name began with a 'von'. The von Juggardts were a minor aristocratic family, remotely linked to the House of Hohenzollern. The Catholic branch, of course.

"Ulrich," he said in a strong melodic voice.

"Claus, how wonderful to see you." Ulrich, when alone with him, always addressed his uncle by his first name. 'Don't call me uncle, it makes me feel old,' he once charmingly chided his adolescent nephew.

He sat down on another of the lounge chairs.

"I didn't know you had got back from London," Ulrich said.

"Yesterday."

"I see you've found your panama. I thought you said you'd lost it in Cannes."

"I did. This is a new one. Bought in London."

"So what were you doing there?"

"Met up with people I knew at Cambridge. Went to a cricket match."

"The mystery game."

"You could say that. The language of cricket can't be translated. Certainly not into German. Not with all our compound nouns and verbs." He smiled. "The game lasted five days, all the players dressed in white, naturally. Like most things English, class conscious. Gentlemen and players. Restrained clapping and laconic cheers. I joined King's junior team when I was at Cambridge. I'm afraid I wasn't a great success."

He took out a silver cigarette case and proffered it to Ulrich who took a cigarette while Claus handed him a light. His uncle held his in a long, gold cigarette holder.

"So, what brings you down here?" Claus said. "Philosophising or romanticising?"

Claus had a lambent wit. Ulrich loved him.

"Neither. Mother wants me to make up lists for my twenty-first birthday party."

"Ah! Twenty-first birthday parties. Heady days. Did I ever tell you about mine?"

"No."

"I'm afraid I misbehaved myself. Or, as my father said afterwards 'you brought shame on the family.' Well, he would know all about shame. He inherited the family's high-class leather business but gambled away the profits. He didn't seem to care a damn about the von Juggardt family's good name. The party was a success as far as I'm concerned. All my friends who came were more interested in your mother than in me. Of course, she was quite the alluring beauty in those days. Had a magnetic attraction all of her own. She had a crush on her music teacher at the time so she was able to ward off the unwelcome propositions of several of my friends."

"So what happened?"

"Parties in those pre-war days were very formal. Overexcited girls dressed in white, huddled together like shy deer in a forest glade. Viennese society was made up of glamorous but neurotic young ladies."

"I never thought mother could ever be neurotic."

"She was an exception. Girls of good family were hardly allowed over the door without some kind of chaperon. Sexual ignorance was widespread. Part of the hypocrisy of the society as it then was. Under the old regime, you had a society of philandering young men and repressed young women. Little wonder Vienna created psychoanalysis."

"Sounds exciting to me."

"I'm not so sure. Anyway, I got drunk. Broke a lamp and made myself thoroughly objectionable. After all I had just become twenty-one." Claus puffed his cigarette.

He paused. "Thank God the past is over."

"What have you got against the past?"

"It's all that nostalgia. I'm talking about prewar. We'd go hunting while the ladies made plans for the coming season for masked balls, art shows, concerts and festivals. We were mad about hunting. Once I was with this friend when we saw a peasant funeral cortege at the other side of a field and we jumped our horses over the hearse. I feel ashamed of that time. I take no pleasure in what we did. After the war, the social pyramid that was Viennese society, of which we were near the top I might add, simply collapsed and vanished. Good riddance I say."

"Things weren't so bad, surely. I remember the day - I was only a small child at the time - when mother and father took me to the famous Corpus Christi procession. It was very colourful."

"For heaven's sake, Ulrich, do spare me religion."

"No, listen."

"I don't have to listen," Claus insisted and slightly irritated, "because I remember the ridiculous show myself. An endless procession led by the imperial troops in battle-dress accompanied by military bands, followed by the clergy, dressed up in their various religious habits, bishops and then the Cardinal, robed in fine, red watered silk and wearing a red tasselled hat. They looked like a bunch of superannuated, fancy dressed tarts. However did we put up with it all?" Claus rose up and taking hold of the brass rod used to open the upper windows, put it over his shoulder like some medieval weapon and pretended to march round the room. "Finally came the Emperor flanked on each side by members of his elite regiment of Spanish Dragoon Guards carrying halberds. The procession appeared grand and stately but for our senile Emperor overseeing a decrepit Empire, it was supposed to remind the unwashed masses of the splendours of the former Holy Roman Empire, the mighty union of crozier and sword, a Divine blessing of a secular throne. It was neither holy nor Roman nor an Empire. The whole ramshackle edifice came down when our Methuselah of an emperor died and the allies carved up his empire. *Deo gratias*, thanks be to God, say I, for that." He replaced the rod and sat down. "

"You should have been an actor, Uncle Claus."

"Now that you mention it, the whole ceremony, part religion part state, was play-acting. The Emperor, the Cardinal, the clergy, the soldiers. What do you think they were doing if not acting? In any case, why have you remembered that?"

"Because there was an attempt by a Serbian anarchist to assassinate the Emperor. At the moment his carriage was passing where we stood, a young man tried to jump on the open carriage but was savagely cut down by an officer of the guard. When I returned home, I came here to the pavilion where I played being an officer of the guard."

"Well, there you are then. The whole thing was merely children playing."

A relaxed silence fell over the two men.

"I understand that congratulations are in order," Claus said.

"My exam results?"

"Your mother mentioned it to me when I arrived just now."

"I shouldn't say so myself, but I'm pleased."

"By the way, does your father know?"

Ulrich hesitated.

Long angled sunlight broke through the windows casting shadows everywhere.

"Mother will tell him."

"Why don't you?"

"I've never been comfortable telling him anything. He was always too distant for me. In any case we've never really got on well."

"As small children it's difficult to think of parents as human. We see them as special minor gods, what the Romans called '*Lares Familiares*', the deities that cared for the welfare of the household. Then when we grow up, though it comes as a kind of mystery, we realise they're human. Of course they haven't changed, we have."

"You're in a philosophical mood."

"You get like that when you're trying to explain things to a young person."

"Point taken."

"Your father is a complex man. He disapproves of me. He thinks that being a stockmarket speculator, I'm a parasite living off hardworking industrialists like himself. It's not far off the truth, I suppose. But that's how the world is. The stock market is only another form of stage magic. On the other hand, you could argue that the arms trade is another word for a goldmine. He nearly had a fit when I told him that not only had I read *Das Kapital* but I've made plenty of it."

Ulrich laughed.

"Your father," continued Claus, "has a host of things to think about, running one of the largest arms company in Austria. The Austrian Krupp of small arms, if you like. He's a very busy man."

"When we were young he didn't have that much time for us children."

"In the immediate post-war period when you were growing up, the devastating result of reparations, imposed by the allies, and the consequent hyperinflation had catastrophic effects on businessmen like him. It made him angry and bitter. That's how it was. I remember once he compared himself to the captain of a sinking ship, 'The ship is flooding and I must bail it out'. They were bad days for him but he did save the company."

Claus took a draw on his cigarette.

"Quite popular as far as I know," he continued. "The Union of Viennese Industry elected him their chairman. The business community admires his sound critical judgement, his ability to appraise and evaluate a business opportunity, negotiate a contract and patience to carry it through. Mind you he can be, excuse the language, bloody-minded and, when necessary, coldly ruthless."

"He thinks I've let him down. You seem to forget, he paid for special private lessons for me but I failed to pass the entry exams to the Polytechnic, my obligatory Latin let me down, and I had to do with second best at the Technical Institute. He went into such a rage. 'I was hoping for a first-class skilled engineer,' he screamed, 'what I'm going to get is a second-rate tool-man.' I'm sure the whole of Vienna could hear him. I felt so humiliated. If it hadn't been for mother, I don't know what I would have done. I feel a certain shame even now."

"You can't resent him forever."

"I won't. I'm determined to prove him wrong that I'm no mere second-rate tool-man. I want to be like my great-grandfather and be a precision engineer."

Ulrich reached forward and knocked the ash from his cigarette into a cut glass ashtray.

Claus stood up. "It's time we went back to the house. I need a drink. Let's go."

* * *

The two men and the dog made their way back to the house accompanied by the rays of a dying sun. The orangery was ablaze with lights. Father Kiesl had gone, much to Ulrich's relief, but his sister Gerda was occupying his favourite basket chair, much to his annoyance.

His father, Dieter, a man of about fifty, was sitting in a lounge chair. Of medium height, heavily built, with keen quick eyes, balding and greying, he carried a careworn expression.

"Congratulations, Ulrich," he said, "Professor Felbiger told me that you've passed your exams. I think this calls for a small celebration." He sounded in a buoyant mood.

Ulrich said nothing.

"Well, young man, aren't you going to say something?" he said. There was an irritable note to his voice.

A indecisive silence followed.

"I shan't be happy until I've produced a working model from my design," Ulrich said.

"You mean a prototype. It's called a prototype," his father corrected him.

Ulrich stayed silent but he could feel rising anger. How was it my father could turn congratulations into correction?

"What about the champagne, then?" Claus said. "This is what my American friends call the cocktail hour. A very civilised custom. It's the only reason I ever go to the American Embassy."

"Is it? I thought," Dieter said, "you might have other interests there."

"Is it possible," Elke said, intervening, "that you gentlemen could stop the banter and get on with celebrating Ulrich's success?"

A housemaid brought in a tray with bottles of champagne and set it down on a sideboard. Claus took it upon himself to open a bottle, pour out the champagne into wide-brimmed glasses, which the maid took round to the others.

"Ulrich have you given your party list any thought?" his mother said.

"I'll have it ready for you tomorrow."

"I'll hold you to that Ulrich," she said with a laugh but there was a stern tone to her voice. "I really must have the list," she repeated. "Without it I can't make arrangements. There's a whole host of things that I must think of, catering, flowers, music..."

"Ulrich," Claus said, "you're seeing the frivolous side of our dear family."

"Claus!" Elke exploded, "I do wish you would stop being so rude, you're hardly the one to talk about frivolity. As long as you don't get drunk then the family's honour will remain."

Claus merely shrugged his shoulders.

"I'll do my best to get the list ready, mother," Ulrich said.

"I shall engage the Hofburg ensemble, then you youngsters can dance the night away," she said.

"Can't we have a jazz band?" Gerda said. "that would be fun. There's this new band coming soon, they play ragtime and blues. They've just returned from America."

"Jazz," Dieter said. "I don't understand why you young people seem bewitched with all things American. It's played by black men. Negroes. Not the least bit Austrian. Even the clergy in America call it jungle music."

"What your father is saying," Claus said, addressing the two youngsters, "is that you shouldn't mix our dearly beloved Strauss with Louis Armstrong. Though I dare say they've a lot in common. Their music is pretty erotic."

"I think you're wrong Claus," Dieter said. His face was contorted with barely disguised scorn. "The German race has produced Bach, Beethoven, Mozart, Hyden, Strauss and our own Gustav Mahler. What has American ever given us? Jazz. It's a bastard race. They've even ruined their own banking system and are making us pay for it."

"I'm not an authority on music like you Dieter," Claus said. There was a playful edge to his voice. "But Strauss. It's intoxicating. All that whirling around holding hands with a stranger. The flirtation. You can't tell me that it doesn't fan the flames of passion. In New Orleans and Chicago they play jazz in bars and brothels. Mind you, I can't somehow imagine old Strauss being played in a bordello."

"Father," Gerda pleaded, "don't listen to Uncle Claus. I'm sure there are lots of Ulrich's friends who would like a jazz band. After all it's his birthday party."

"Well, Ulrich," Dieter said, "is that what you want?"

"I suppose Gerda is right. I haven't really given the matter much thought. It seems a good idea."

"Oh for heaven's sake, Dieter," Claus exclaimed, sounding exasperated, "they're no longer children. For once let them be. Things have changed. The way you and all the others go on you'd think the old Empire still existed. It seems you can't let go. Can't you see that the Emperor is dead and with him his ramshackle court. Anyway it was filled, excuse the language ladies, with befuddled old farts." He stood back and drew on his cigarette. "It's time we all danced to a modern tune."

"Claus, I really can't take you seriously," Dieter said, twisting his glass as if looking for a way out. He paused. "However, if your mother agrees, Ulrich, then I'll go along with her."

"Ulrich's going to be twenty-one only once," Elke said, "so I agree. And since you, Claus, seem to approve, I'll expect you to foot the bill for any jazz band." She paused and smiled. "There's one proviso. Only Strauss before midnight."

* * *

On a warm summer's evening, the birthday party was held in a large marquee on the lawn next to the pavilion. Ulrich, for once, pleasantly found himself the centre of attention. Elke fulfilled her usual role as society hostess. The Cardinal Archbishop and two of his suffragan bishops put in a brief appearance: the Drehers were generous donors to the church. The six-part ensemble opened by playing the old imperial national anthem. The jazz band was made up of white and black musicians. A dark young woman in silver sequins and feathers sang in a deep husky voice and then did an impromptu erotic dance. 'Les Folies Bergeres has come to Vienna', quipped Claus. Ulrich loved it. The youngsters and some of the adults danced the Charleston and the tango. Claus taught them how to do the Lindy Hop. Dieter was in an expansive mood making a speech extolling Ulrich's virtues. As the night wore on, Ulrich got slightly drunk and made a pass at several of the younger women. At the end of the party, in the early hours of the morning, they all sang 'Happy Birthday to You' and 'Auld Lang Syne' in English.

Chapter 2

Vienna 1933

Late one Friday afternoon, as he rushed along the passageway linking the Technical Institute workshops with the lecture rooms, Ulrich collided with a young woman. Carrying a small stack of books, she stumbled and fell in front of him. He stooped down and, helping her to retrieve the books scattered on the parquet floor, quickly appraised her. Slim and of medium height, she had raven hair done up in a chignon, wistful deep-set eyes, almond-shaped and golden brown, clear skin and was wearing an olive cotton frock and flat shoes. He noticed her long, delicate tapering hands like those of a pianist. 'Judge a woman by her hands,' he recalled his Uncle Claus saying.

"You clumsy idiot," she cried.

"I'm really sorry about that. May I help you to carry the books?"

"Oh, I suppose so." There was irritation in her voice. "I'm on my way to the library and I'm late."

"The library, that's not far, is it?" he said, in a teasing sort of way.

A mild sardonic grin met this statement.

"You're a student and you don't know the library? Go on, away with you."

"My name's Ulrich," he blurted out.

She didn't say who she was. He stayed with her as far as the library. When they arrived, she showed him where to put the books and, without a further word, disappeared. In his four years at the Institute, he had hardly been near the library and never seen her before. There was something about her, he couldn't say what, that struck a sensitive chord deep within. Then he remembered an English sonnet his mother had taught him:

> *'Shall I compare thee to a summer's day?*
> *Thou art more lovely and more temperate....'*

He could not recall the rest.

* * *

A few days later, on his way to the cinema, Ulrich glanced through the window of a city centre coffee house and noticed the same young woman he had encountered in the Institute library, with another girl.

It started to rain. Abandoning social discretion, he went in. The midday coffee house was crowded and a haze of cigarette smoke hung over the customers, hiding their indiscretions. The two women were sharing a red velvet banquette, eating Linzertorte with jam and nut fillings, and drinking coffee. Such coffee houses had the reputation of being places where affairs of both kinds were conducted in what was familiarly called 'cuddling corners'. She looked at him with surprise, her face suddenly lighting up, making him feel pleased with his decision.

"I was only passing." It was a lame explanation, but caution had already been thrown to the winds. "May I join you?" Without waiting for an invitation, he pulled up a chair to the table and sat down. She gave him an inquisitive frown.

"This is Ulrich," she said, turning to her friend. "He's a student at the Institute."

"You have me at a disadvantage," he said to the young women with whom he had previously collided.

"What do you mean?"

"You know my name but I don't know yours."

"It's Ruth and this is my friend Erika."

"Pleased to meet you, Erika."

He gave her a slight, polite bow.

Erika stood up.

"Sit down, please," he said with a laugh, stealing a sideways glance at Ruth, "don't leave because of me."

He produced a packet of cigarettes and offered it to the two others.

"We don't smoke," Ruth said with pursed lips.

"Do you like working in the library?" he asked Ruth. It was the only thing that came to mind. He felt a pleasurable tension in speaking with her.

"It's alright except when you're knocked over by clumsy students who don't know where the library is."

"I'm really sorry about that." He put his hand over his heart in mock apology. "It won't happen again."

Having the two young attractive women to himself raised his expectations.

"Do you work in the library?" he asked Erika.

"No. I work in a drapers shop. I sell ladies clothes."

"Haute couture?" He'd heard his mother and sister use this term but he wasn't quite sure what it really meant.

"We sell mainly prêt-a-porter, but it's a select shop so we do have up-to-date Parisian fashions and attract younger and not so young women."

"I've no doubt my sister or even my mother may have patronised your shop."

"Patronised my shop! That's a fine thing to say. Well, let me tell you, sir," Erika said, her eyes on fire, "it's not my shop and if there's any patronising going on, you appear to be the one doing it." Her eyes were aflame with anger.

Ulrich tried to hide his embarrassment.

"Look, I'm very sorry. I didn't mean it that way. I do apologise."

"Students! They ought to work for a living, instead of poncing about." Snapping up her coat and handbag, she stormed out.

Ruth remained sitting. The ensuing silence was confusing.

"Why do women always walk away – or run off when faced with a problem or hear something they don't like?" he asked.

"Do they? Maybe you've forgotten this is the nineteen thirties. It's not the last century. Don't you know that young women are sensitive creatures?" Her engaging face belied her annoyance, making it seem affected.

"I didn't intend to be condescending. Maybe I should've said, 'shop'. You think of a word when it's too late."

"'*L'esprit de l'escalier.*'"

"What's that?"

"It's French for what you've just said. Thinking of a word when it's too late."

"You speak French?"

"Schoolgirl level. I seemed to have picked up phrases." She paused. "This city has too many rich women who treat shop assistants as if they were servants. You touched a raw nerve."

"I'm sorry I offended your friend. I'll have to make up to her, I suppose."

"Don't worry. I know her well. She can be a bit touchy."

Ulrich felt himself being pulled towards this young woman, wondering what her hair would look like falling over her neck and shoulders. Those dark eyes, very alluring. A look so intense. Her voice caught your attention. Something rather Italian about her, he thought.

"You don't fancy a trip to the cinema do you?" he asked on impulse. "I like American films, there's this Buster Keaton movie on just now, *Free and Easy*. It's a talkie."

"You're rather forward. I hardly know you."

"It's to make up for my clumsiness."

"I thought you students wouldn't have time to waste going to the cinema."

"We don't, but I submitted my project last month so now I feel free."

"What project would that be?"

"A prototype for a sub-machine gun. It's based on a design of mine I made last year."

"My you are a clever boy!" She laughed. "So you've finished with the Institute? Now what are you going to do? Jobs are so hard to come by these days. Lots of my friends are unemployed."

"I've got to do my military service first. When that's over I'll probably get work in my father's factory. I hope so." He paused. "I know I will."

"A factory. What does it make?"

"You are persistent. It's, it's," the words stuck in his throat as if what he was going to say were criminal, "...an armaments factory.

It makes all sorts of guns and such like but trade is pretty dire. It's all these international restrictions. We've, I mean my father, had to lay off workers."

"Would that be the Dreher factory?"

"Yes."

"Half the workers in this city seem to work there."

"Not quite."

"If you were to make more useful things maybe you wouldn't have to lay off so many workers."

"Not really. It would entail re-tooling the whole factory. We'd be out of business before we started."

She put her hand in front of her mouth and gave an illusory yawn.

"I'm sorry I must be boring you."

"Students tend to do that. They either talk shop or else spend their time joking."

"So you know lots of students?"

"Have you forgotten? I work in the library."

They fell silent for a moment.

"Do you play tennis?"

"You must be joking. Working girls like myself don't belong to the tennis-playing class. For us tennis is a luxury."

"Don't worry. I belong to this club and I thought you might like to have a game."

"Well, if it's like the other clubs in Vienna I shouldn't think they'll allow a Jewish girl in."

He was taken aback by this news.

"You're Jewish?"

"Yes." There was a hint of defiance in her strong voice.

"My father," Ulrich said, regaining his mental composure, "is chairman of the club committee. I shouldn't think there'll be a problem."

"You mean you hope not."

"No problem," he said, waving his hands in a dismissive gesture. Inwardly he told himself, there's a problem. She's Jewish and she won't be so easily misled. She probably thinks I'm being naïve. But I've given her my word.

"Please, don't bother. I wouldn't want to cause you any trouble," she said with a dismissive toss of her head.

"There'll be no trouble," he said, with hope draining from his voice like rainwater from a roof down a waterspout, "my parents are pretty broad-minded. Quite liberal in fact. I'm sure some of their friends are Jewish. My father is in business. He must meet Jewish businessmen. Our bank is…"

He got no further for she quickly cut in.

"Stop," she said, holding up her hand. "Forgive me for saying so but I'm not stupid. We Jews know our place in… in this country." Were there tears in her eyes? He couldn't really tell. But her distress was obvious in her face. Clearly agitated, she stood up. She went to pick up her coat.

"Please," he said. He was now pleading. "Please don't leave."

He reluctantly helped her to put on her coat. In doing so he touched her shoulder.

"I really am sorry. I wish you wouldn't leave," he said. It was in vain. She left.

He watched her leave, then sat down.

His mind, preoccupied the whole of the previous year, suddenly realised his project, his prize design and his sub-machine gun, were not so important. He felt like a man coming out of a dark cellar finding himself blinking into a bright, luminous sunlit sky.

In the days that followed, the image of Ruth, her deep brown eyes and subtle beauty, possessed his waking day and his nightly dreams.

* * *

Ulrich and his father found themselves dining alone together. They sat at one end of the long rosewood dining table. It was a coincidence of events whereby neither his mother, engaged in one of her social events, nor his sister, away at school, were there. Dieter being a confirmed cigar man seized his wife's absence to light up. Pipe smoking, he would derisively say, was a dirty habit, blowing out the spittle when the pipe becomes blocked.

"Ulrich, I'm impressed with your sub-machine gun," he began, puffing on his cigar. "To get a good profit we need to sell it to a big buyer. Which means Germany. The time's not yet ripe. They're forbidden to re-arm. But sooner rather than later they will." He paused to draw on his cigar. "It's time you knew but as soon as you've done your military service and return home, I intend to take you into the firm as a junior partner."

Ulrich was surprised at his father's statement. The irony of the situation was not lost on Ulrich. His father was giving him the news that he had desperately wanted to hear for so long, instead he was looking for an opportunity to introduce the subject of Ruth.

His father was clearly in a relaxed frame of mind. An unusual occurrence. However, he knew his father well enough not to expect any favours.

"The first thing we must do is take out a patent on your gun," his father said, pointing his cigar as if it were a weapon.

"I'm really grateful for your faith in me, father, but..." he hesitated for a moment, searching for the right word. Instinct told him to proceed with caution. A wrong word here, an inapt expression there, could just as quickly change his father's mood. "Shouldn't I be taking out the patent? After all it's my design." He felt a shiver of disquiet down his spine. He had surprised himself with his own boldness.

"Naturally, but who's going to pay for the patent? Patents, as you must have learned from your time at the Institute, don't come cheaply."

"Mother..."

"Will do exactly as I say. She's mistress in this house but when it comes to business, I give the orders. Under no circumstance would she gainsay me. The matter of the sub-machine gun is strictly business."

"What about the banks? Wouldn't they help?" Ulrich persevered yet felt he was at the edge of defiance.

"I'll be candid with you." His father gave him a long measured look. "Once you're a partner, you'll be able, legally, to sign contracts on behalf of the company. The patent will be in your name as the inventor, but we'll draw up a legal agreement so that the Dreher Company has sole right of manufacture. That way we all benefit. What belongs to the company is yours and mine and this family's. The family's name is Dreher, the company's name is Dreher, and you're a Dreher. The world of finance, as your Uncle Claus will confirm, is interested only in success. The Dreher name means success. The banks wouldn't touch you if you tried to act alone. I hope I make myself clear?"

Ulrich turned his father's statement over in his mind. This is not going well, he thought. He's going to lay a cold hand of rejection on me.

"You do, father."

"Look, son," his father said with unusual familiarity, "a dozen years ago this company faced bankruptcy. Through no fault of its own. It was a victim like all German peoples of the most deceitful injustice ever done to a whole nation. Don't forget, we're German. I managed to save the sinking ship. I'll do anything to keep this company and family together and so should you."

They both sat, unspeaking, looking at each other until Dieter broke the silence.

"Let me tell you something I've never told you before. Just after the war, I came back from the factory one day and was confronted with the sight of my own father, your grandfather, hanging from the high wooden balustrade here in this house. I rushed to the kitchen, took hold of a knife and cut the rope. I held his limp body in my arms and wept. By the time your mother, Gerda and yourself had returned from a short stay in Salzburg, father's remains were already deposited in one of the city's funeral homes. I put my own grief to one side to manage everyone else's. Despite the shock of this tragic death, I defied the despair that had caused my father to end his own life. Instead I vowed to get even with those I blame for this tragic blow to our family. Those damned statesmen who disabled our family's armaments business by their senseless decrees at Versailles." There was stinging anger in his voice.

Ulrich felt stunned to learn for the first time that his grandfather had committed suicide. Although the two families had shared the same house, his grandfather had always appeared a remote figure to the young boy. During the war he hardly ever saw him. His first instinct was to feel compassion towards his father but his mention of the family's armaments business as a reason for his evident anger made Ulrich loath to express his initial feeling.

"I've no intention, father, of deserting this family," he said. "It's just I must find my own way. I want to follow in great-grandfather's footsteps. Surely that's not too much to ask."

"When I was your age I wanted to do the same. Believe me, outside this family you would be nothing."

Ulrich decided to change the subject. He was getting nowhere about the patent.

"There's something that I wanted to ask you, father."

"What?"

"I've met this girl, she's a librarian at the Institute. I'd like to invite her to a game of tennis. Could she come to the club for a game?" He didn't mention that she was a Jewess. His courage only stretched so far.

"The club has strict rules about female members or guests for that matter. No doubt you already know that. I'll think about it," he said.

Ulrich indeed knew that membership was strictly limited to a tight social elite. Jews were outside this circle. There must be some way he could circumvent the restrictive rules. But how? Despite his father's tentative assurance, there was a certain finality in his voice. He decided not to pursue the matter for the time being.

The conversation lingered on in a desultory fashion. After dinner, his father retired to his study.

Ulrich wandered into the large drawing room. When he was a child, it was normally out of bounds. He sat down on one of the Biedermeier padded sofas and looked around the room, thinking what the working-class Ruth would make of this exposure of his family's wealth. In was in this room, with its high ornate ceilings, four crystal chandeliers and tall windows, curtained with gold fleur-de-lis designed brocade and lined with silk damask, that his parents lavishly entertained Vienna's fashionable society, its cultural, political and ecclesiastic elite, such evenings imbued - his mother saw to that – with a hint of pre-war high culture and aristocratic manners. Furnished by his forebears, their eclectic tastes were shown in glass display cases filled with delicate vases, statuettes and other precious objects, with a rare piece of Medici porcelain and other pieces from Vienna itself, Sèvres, Meissen and pottery from ancient Greece and Rome, a collection of antique arms, including a fine sixteenth-century south German single trigger, long wheel-lock, holster pistol. To one corner was a suit of armour in burnished steel, crafted in Spain, when it was part of the Hapsburg Empire. One cabinet contained scientific instruments and several natural history specimens collected by his grandfather on his journeys overseas. A rare Savonnerie carpet and several fine hand-woven Aubusson rugs covered the mahogany floor. Against one wall were a rosewood pedestal games table and an antique Augsburg walnut cabinet. In another corner stood a bronze statue of the Virgin by Aristide Maillol. Around the walls hung a Claude Lorraine and a Pissarro. Among the other paintings were those of previous Drehers, including one of the family black sheep Volkmar, Ahren's own father, a bankrupt Munich landlord who had fled Bavaria to Vienna to escape wrathful creditors, chasing him to recover gambling debts. The expression on Ahren's face as it stared down on him was one of victorious arrogance. His grandfather – the one who committed suicide – had ironic and rheumy eyes. His father looked down at him half-smiling, the painter vainly disguising the careworn expression. One portrayed his great-grandmother, Ahren's wife, a woman of stern, delicate beauty who, it was said, became the most influential social hostess in Vienna. Another one showed his mother as a young woman. He admired her refined, grave elegance and noble features.

He got up and strolled across to the Bösendorfer grand piano, atop of which were several framed family photographs. One depicted his parents on their wedding day, as they came out of the cathedral, where they had been married by the Cardinal Archbishop of Vienna. His mother looked radiant and beautiful in her long, white bridal gown, handed down from her own Scottish great-grandmother. A diamond tiara encircled her veil, once worn – so he was told – by Marie Antoinette.

With quickly vanishing hope, he sat down on one of the armchairs to await his mother's return. Would it be right for me to bring Ruth here, he wondered. It would be like showing off or worse, patronising. She's working-class. That's one hurdle. But the bigger problem is she's Jewish. He tried to recollect his thoughts. He had not knowingly made the acquaintance of a Jewish girl before. How could he? His upbringing was in a devout Catholic household. He himself was not particularly devout, but his mother attended mass several times a week. Weren't the Jews named 'perfidious' in the Good Friday service? In his family and social circle, Jews were always referred to in derogatory terms. His father would never employ a Jew in a managerial position. His parents never mixed socially with Jews. At his private elementary school he and his classmates were always taunting a particular Jewish boy by calling him 'greedy Jew', 'dirty Jew' and 'filthy Jew'. They often sang popular anti-Jewish songs.

The Jews. What is a Jew? What is it like to be a Jew? Memory transported him back to his high school. Father Hahn, a German Jesuit from Ulm, a gangly man with rimless glasses and woeful features, was standing in front of the class of thirteen-year-old boys. He usually taught Latin and Greek to the Upper School, but he also took the younger pupils for religious instruction. He had once been a missionary in south China and would recount with agonising words, how the Yellow River ran red with the blood of Chinese Christians, martyred by the evil pagan Chinese during the Boxer rebellion at the turn of the century. It was known that he was the confessor to several of the country's bishops and gave spiritual guidance to a number of eminent people.

'This is Holy Week,' the priest reminded them in solemn tones, 'and, above all else, you must keep in mind the Passion, suffering and Crucifixion of our Lord Saviour. This is central to the Catholic faith. You, Dreher, who do you think murdered Our Lord?'

'Was it the Romans, Father?'

'No, Dreher, it was not the Romans. Yes, they crucified him physically but who were the real culprits? Fuhrmann?'

'The Jews, Father.'

'Correct. The Jews killed Our Lord. They are what we call the Christ-killers.' He spoke slowly and deliberately, pausing between each sentence. 'The Jew is a devil worshipper. Never forget, Christ was betrayed by the Jews. Always keep in mind the Jews are very sly, very crafty, full of guile. So what did they do? They persuaded the Romans to scourge, torture and then crucify Him. 'We're not allowed to put another Jew to death', the Jews insisted. They were lying, of course, but to appease them Pilate did what they asked him.'

There followed a detailed, graphic description of Christ's excruciating pain and suffering: how during the scourging the skin was ripped from his back, how they had pierced his skull with a crown of thorns, how they had driven long spikes into his wrists, causing every nerve in his body to shake with agony.

'This was,' the Jesuit said, 'the most wicked thing that anyone had done in the whole of history. And to the Son of God.' He paused. 'Why,' he rhetorically asked his wide-eyed and impressionable audience, 'do you think there are Stations of the Cross in every church? Not only to remind the faithful of Our Saviour's sacrifice but also to ensure they know who to blame for this horror. The Jew. The crucifix, too, is everywhere. Not only the huge vivid lifelike crucifixes in churches, in our schools and faithful Catholic homes, but small crucifixes hanging around people's necks on silver and gold chains. Every time you see a crucifix never forget the real culprit.'

The next subject was the Jews 'in our midst'.

'Some Jews,' he said, 'are known to murder good Christian children and then use their blood in the baking of the Passover bread. This is well-known in places like Poland and Russia. That's why the Jews have been expelled from those countries, and rightly so. The majority of people in Europe are Christian, whereas the Jew is different. The Jew is a fanatic about his religion. He doesn't want to be like us Christians, he doesn't want to be sorry for what his people did to Christ, doesn't want to turn away from his false books and convert to the true religion. Holy Mother the Church tells you,' he pointed a solemn finger at his young audience, 'the Jew must bow down before the cross, repent and be saved. All Jews are condemned to hellfire if they remain stubborn in their refusal to see the light. Every Christian has a duty to ensure the Jew is cast out of our community. We are told to hate the sin but love the sinner. In the case of the Jew you hate both the sin and the sinner until repentance.'

Ulrich leaned back in the armchair.

Ruth doesn't look like a Christ-killer to me when I touched her shoulder that day in the coffee house an electric charge went right through me. Could I be wrong about the Jews? All that hatred. Could the Church be wrong? It's easy to hate someone you don't know, people you don't know. When I look back and think about what the old priest was saying. Good Christian children murdered and their blood used to bake bread. It sounds like a lot of rubbish. How could I have believed it?

He heard the front door opening. He went out to the front hall to greet his mother.

"Good heavens, Ulrich, still up? Do you think I've just come back from Argentina?" she said in a jocular way. The reference was to the occasion when his parents had gone off to Buenos Aires on business. The children were left in the care of their paternal grandmother, a grim and austere lady who could not get over the death of her husband. Nor the dissolution of the Empire. She did not hide her bewilderment, at seeing her fellow citizens, just after the war, in an angry, bankrupt city, full of disabled war veterans in threadbare lederhosen, scavenging in the Vienna Woods and living in Vienna's massive sewers.

"I must speak to you, mother."

"Can't it wait till tomorrow? It's rather late and I'm tired."

"It won't take long."

"If you say so." She spoke in a gentle tone.

They adjourned to the drawing room. He briefly sketched out the conversation with his father about Ruth.

"The problem as I see it has to do with the tennis club rules. I'm not against rules but after all, it's only a game of tennis," he said.

"You might not think them important but rules hold society together," his mother said. "That is how I was brought up. And in these uncertain times even tennis club rules guarantee our place in society. It's a private club and that's how the members like it."

"Are you saying we must keep out the revolutionaries from the gates?" He laughed.

"You might laugh but put it like this. You've now reached the age when you can apply to the club for full membership. Something *I* can't do on my own behalf. Not yet at least. How would you feel if the hordes from the Karl-Marx-Hof, those hotbed tenements of Jewish communists and socialists, descended on the club demanding admission? I know your father would most certainly not want them in. Nor you for that matter. However, my darling Ulrich, I shall have a word with him and see if he can get Ruth an invitation as a guest." She picked up her coat and made to leave.

"There's one other thing," he said with foreboding.

"Which is?"

"She's Jewish."

She gave him a baleful look. He felt guilty as if he had struck her.

"I wondered when you mentioned her name." She paused. "I think it best you don't see her again. Your father would be upset and angry. In any case, it wouldn't be acceptable in our social circle. You must understand that. You know how we all feel about those people. Jews are trouble. I'm really too tired to argue with you now. Ulrich dear, please forget we had this conversation." With that, she left him and went upstairs.

He stood for a few moments trying to control his feelings. He shook with anger and frustration. At himself and at his parents. He made his way through into the orangery. He opened the large double doors giving on to the French garden. On the distant horizon just above the outline of the pavilion lay the thin crescent of a waxing moon, cold and white, obscured every now and then by black clouds. The shapes of the hedges and bushes shed faint shadows that seemed to reflect his agitated state. He wanted to shout Ruth's name out loud. He hesitated, not wanting to disturb his parents. He recalled a German literature lesson at his school. He had to recite by heart to the class a short poem written by the Austrian poet Reiner Maria Rilke. It was called 'Evening Love Song'. He still remembered it.

> 'Ornamental clouds
> Compose an evening love song
> A road leaves evasively
> The new moon
> Begins a chapter of our nights,
> Of those frail nights
> we stretch out which mingle
> with these black horizontals.'

He had blushed as titters ran round the class of adolescent boys. Deep within himself, he wanted to possess Ruth, own her, keep her for himself. Could Ruth feel for him what he felt for her? The dilemma facing him: on the one side, his mother, his father, his family, his friends; on the other, Ruth, a Jewish girl he scarcely knew. Beset with a profound sense of loneliness, a tide of emotions engulfed him.

The sky clouded over, obscuring the moon and leaving everything in the dark. An early autumn chill-wind blew over the garden. He could hear the far-off bark of a dog and from the distant trees came the hoot of an owl. The sleepy summer days and cosy winter nights of my childhood have gone forever. He turned and went indoors.

* * *

He wrote Ruth a letter but promptly tore it up and wrote another and another. Letter writing was not one of his accomplishments. He had an attack of nerves and, in a panic, found it difficult to express himself. He wanted to see her and explain things. He went to the library but she wasn't there. Eventually he managed to scribble a note which he left with one of the assistants. Soon he would be away from Vienna doing his military service. He did not receive a reply.

Chapter 3

Vienna 1935

Ulrich saw her from a distance. She was skating alongside a tall young-looking man. Two years had passed since last he had seen her. Despite the lateness of the season – it was one of those crisp and dazzling mornings in Vienna, a gripping icy wind, down from the distant Carpathian Mountains, kept alive the city's open-air rinks. She was wearing a brown astrakhan hat, a long fox fur coat and her hands were enclosed in a fur muff. As he followed her around the rink, watching her skate with grace and elegance, the image came to him of a ballerina on ice and his deep ardour for her resurfaced. He thought it had faded during his two years of military service but it dawned on him that he had been subconsciously nursing it all along. Emotional turmoil welled up inside him. A gnawing jealousy made him want to skate forward and push the man out of the way. Suddenly, she noticed him. She said something to her companion and they made quickly for the exit. Ulrich, filled with hope and energy, skated towards them as they struggled to unlace their ice-skates.

"Ruth, what a pleasant surprise to meet you again," he said in a breezy fashion. He gave the other man a disapproving look.

"Ah! Ulrich," she said. There was sudden disquiet in her voice, as if she were afraid of her own emotions. "This is my brother Reuben."

Was that a blush on her cheeks or the effect of the chill wind, he wondered.

There was a brief unsettled silence.

He turned to Ruth. "Do you still work in the library?"

"No."

"She works with Doctor Goldstein," Reuben blurted out. Ruth gave her brother a mildly reproachful look.

"Ruth, I would like to see you again," Ulrich said. "Catch up on the news. I've been away. Military service, that sort of thing." The words tumbled out.

"We're in a hurry," she said. "I'm sorry but we must be off." The verbal feint was transparent.

Nonetheless he noticed her tone had softened.

"I'll see you about," Ulrich said as he watched them disappear into the darkening twilight.

Ulrich was not dispirited. As a youngster, he is camping with friends somewhere along the Ziller valley. It is a chilly early morning and his turn to prepare breakfast. The overnight fire appears to have gone out. Amidst the embers, he detects a tiny, almost imperceptible, smouldering red glow. He gently blows on it and a thin wisp of flame leaps up. As he feeds the flame with small twigs then larger ones, a fire takes hold. It warms him and brews the coffee. He breaks into song. Ah the memory! Meeting Ruth once more, he felt an inner glow.

* * *

Several Doctor Goldsteins, lawyers, medical doctors and university professors, were listed in the Vienna telephone directory. After a number of vain attempts, he finally heard her voice.

"Ulrich here. Is that you Ruth?"

"Yes."

"I was so happy to run into you again. Can't we meet? I'm not a monster you know."

"You're being melodramatic." He smiled to himself at her overcoloured reply. He loved her chiding him. "You shouldn't be phoning the surgery unless you want an appointment. If Doctor Goldstein thought his telephone was being used like this he wouldn't be pleased." Her voice was quiet and gentle.

"Can't we just meet then?"

She paused before answering.

"Do you know the Museum of Fine Arts?"

"Of course!"

"I'll be there around midday. Saturday." The phone clicked.

Ulrich had visited the museum only as a child when his mother had taken him there. The long-fronted building in sandstone on the Maria Theresien-Platz was offset by a stately central cupola and two smaller ones. The Italian Renaissance style edifice was conceived, so the story went, as a memorial to convey a sense of the Imperial glory of the art-loving Hapsburg dynasty and a fitting setting for their vast collections. He wondered why Ruth had chosen this sombre venue for their meeting. He would have preferred the intimacy of a coffee house.

Arriving early, he walked up and down in front of the main entrance. A chilly edge to the early spring wind made him pull up his collar. It was that inconstant period between the harsh cold of winter and the welcome early warmth of spring. He craved some sun and blue sky and would be glad to see leaves again on the still-bare trees. Ruth's image filled him with a nervous tension and a strange feeling of guilt. The weight of his family and the Church bore down on him. He wanted to lift the burden but he realised it could not be dissolved in a moment. Am I doing wrong? Maybe I shouldn't be here at all. The family wouldn't approve. I can hear them now. 'Our social class is against Jews.' Father would be thinking of the consequences for business. 'If my business colleagues thought my son was consorting with a Jewess, they would wonder what kind of control I had over you.' Then there's the Church. In our catechism classes the nuns never concealed their utter contempt for Jews. 'Jews are Satan's children, they're a brood of vipers, contact with Jews is to be avoided,' Sister Agnes had said. Am I even committing a sin meeting a Jewish girl? I know nothing about Jews except the Church's voice telling me they're Christ-killers.

He saw her advancing gaily towards him, her face lit up, eyes sparkling. He caught his breath. His inner anxiety and self-tortured questioning about Jews, suddenly evaporated like dark clouds burned by a summer sun. Before he could utter anything, she greeted him. "Let's go inside," she said, darting up the steps to the entrance with energy and purpose. He willingly followed her. Once inside, she led him to a small side alcove where they sat down. Shafts of sunlight streamed through the tall Norman-arched windows, highlighting the marble pillars ornately decorated in various colours and rich gold-leaf. The interior of the building had a pseudo-ecclesiastical air, its exuberant baroqueness reminding him of Stephansdom, Vienna's great cathedral. Ruth did not remove her coat for the museum was not warm.

"You know this place?" she asked.

"Not really. I used to come here with my mother when I was young. I haven't been for some time. I don't remember much about those visits."

"You should renew your acquaintance. You could say that this place is a jewel box, symbol of the old Empire. Its soul if you like."

"I hope you didn't bring me here to… to give me a history or art lecture."

"Do you need one?"

He looked directly at her. This friendly shadow-boxing must end.

"Ruth, I would like to know more about you. Here we are, more than two years on and I don't know even your family name.

"It's Gitelmann."

"Gitelmann?"

"Yes. My family came originally from Galicia."

"That's part of Poland, isn't it? Are you Polish?"

"No, Ulrich, I'm as Austrian as you are. As you probably know or perhaps don't, it used to be part of Russia. The French promised it to Russia in the middle of last century, when there was some kind of threat of war between France and Germany."

"So what brought you here?"

"My people fled from there to get away from Russian pogroms. The Czar hated the Jews and every now and again he would send in his savage Cossacks to put fear into the poor people. It was to ensure they didn't foment revolution. The Austrian Hungarian Empire was always an enemy of Russia so we came here. My grandfather settled in Leopoldstadt."

"That's the…" He hesitated.

"Yes. The Jewish district. I seem to be giving you the history lesson you hoped to avoid."

She laughed softly and her eyes sparked. For some moments they didn't speak. Their silence was tense with potential. He took her hand and she let him.

"Ruth," he said, "I did try to get in touch with you after we met two years ago. Knocking you over in the corridor." He laughed. "During my military service I couldn't get you out of my mind."

He spoke slowly and deliberately. "Ruth, I love you."

It was a poignant moment for him. He had never uttered these words to anyone other than, as a small child, to his mother.

"The Russians used to burn the houses of Jews and cut off their heads," she said, as if feigning disinterest in what he had just said. "At least here in Austria they might not love us but they don't do that."

"Ruth, you're not listening. Are you? I said I love you." He gave her a wounded gaze.

"I did hear you. It's just that I hardly know you."

"I hardly know you. That doesn't mean I can't love you."

"That's what I'm afraid of."

"Afraid of what? Not of me I hope."

"Of course not, silly. It's just that Jewish girls don't go out with Gentile boys." She spoke softly. "I'm not sure if my family will approve. I've been brought up to believe that Jewish girls only go out with Jewish boys."

"I've never thought of myself as a Gentile," he said. "I'm a Catholic."

She laughed a silvery laugh.

"Ruth, do you love me?"

She brooded over the question. At length she said, "I don't know. I can't give you the answer you want. Outside my family, I haven't loved anyone. Not in the way you mean." She took hold of his arm. "Let's walk a little."

They walked up the Grand Staircase and stopped on the landing. Facing them was a large marble statue of a naked man raising his club in his right hand ready to strike while kneeling on the chest of the half-man half-horse, arched backwards and lying on the ground, and gripping him by the throat.

"That's *Theseus and the Centaur* by the sculptor Antonio Canova," Ruth explained. "Quite a turbulent struggle, don't you think?"

What, he thought, am I supposed to think?

"Interesting."

"It's really symbolic," she said. "It's reason overcoming the primitive forces of nature."

On reaching the top of the wide staircase they found themselves in the picture gallery. As they wandered from room to room, Ulrich wasn't really looking at the pictures. It was enough to have Ruth beside him. They stopped before one painting. It was a country scene.

"That's *A Country Wedding* by Pieter Brueghel the Elder" Ruth said, as if Ulrich wouldn't know it. He didn't.

He gazed at the painting. What he saw was a group of country yokels. They appeared to be figures of fun. Even the bride had a doltish grin on her face. The groom was gobbling his food unaware of his surroundings. One of the musicians in the corner had a hungry, forlorn look about him as he watched the food being carried to the table.

"When I look at this painting I usually think that my ancestors might have been like that. My family originally came from a rural Jewish shtetl. A close Jewish community. For the main part they were farmers."

"You seem to know about all these paintings."

"I should. My sister works here. She's a picture restorer. I come here often. Besides, I'm interested in fine art."

"Is your father an artist?"

"Of course not. He's a tailor. My brother Reuben, whom you met, is a lawyer. I would like to be a painter but my family couldn't afford the fees for me to go to art school. I do a bit of embroidery and tapestry."

"I suppose you're going to tell me that you play the violin or piano," he said in a slightly mocking tone.

"As a matter of fact, I do play the piano." She gave him a chiding smile. "Ulrich, if you want to keep your friends you must stop being so whimsical. You'll become tedious and we can't have that."

Thank you Ruth for the lesson. It makes me love you all the more, he thought.

They progressed from one room to another, Ruth unabashedly commenting on a skeleton embracing an erotic nude, appraising a grotesque self-portrait, pronouncing on a handsome cavalier or an ugly child. Several portraits reminded him of the paintings of his forebears hanging in the drawing room at home. Struggling to understand, he looked unseeing at the paintings, unable to find words to express himself. Compared with her, he was, he realised in a moment of self-knowledge, inarticulate. While he was tongue-tied, she spoke a language he knew little about. Hers was a vocabulary of colours, textures and gestures, a grammar of light, shadow and shade. The soft cadences of her voice whetted his curiosity.

Her life is more interesting than mine, he thought.

"The only way to judge the quality of a painting is to have an open mind, you must come to the work with a fresh outlook," she said.

He was being lectured, he knew, but he was a willing pupil and beginning to enjoy it. She explained to him how artists worked. "You see that old man," she pointed to a black-framed self-portrait by Rembrandt, "there's an honesty about him. He isn't afraid of painting himself as he sees himself. He did it using a mirror. Would you like to have your painting done looking old and ugly? Look at that penetrating gaze, it's sincere. He bears his soul to us." As she was speaking Ulrich was trying to look into her soul. The realisation came that he was seeing her as she was. A young, attractive, well-informed and intelligent woman.

Pointing to a painting of a man having a crown of thorns rammed down on his head by a couple of torturers with the butts of their staffs, she asked "Do you recognize who that is?"

"It's Christ."

"It's a painting by the Venetian, Caravaggio." She paused. "How do you feel about that pain and suffering he's undergoing?"

What came to mind was Father Hahn's hostile censure of the Jews. He found himself fighting his own jaundiced eye.

"All that about Christ, the Crucifixion the Crown of Thorns," he said, "it took place two thousand years ago. It's not so important."

"I'm afraid you're wrong. The Crucifixion goes to the heart of Christianity. Without it, there would be no Christianity."

He stopped and turned towards her.

"Ruth I meant it when I said I love you. I'm sorry about how we think of the Jews. If I can get to know you better, I might see things differently." He paused. "I will see things differently."

"Ulrich you don't have to explain anything." She spoke in a gentle way.

There was a silence. "We all give pain and feel pain," she said enigmatically.

Her statement confused him. What is she referring to? Is it personal?

As they continued their way, she pointed out the devices used by various painters to portray the absurdities and follies, the vanities and pride of mankind. She did not hide her sympathy for the procession of leprous outcasts, starving beggars, and ugly cripples. She censured the pretentious elegance of Velazquez's Spanish grandees and their scornful and self-satisfied arrogant looks.

"How do you know so much about all these paintings?" he asked.

"Looking, thinking. Then there are evening lectures. Books. Such things as libraries exist though I believe that you already know that," she said, with a tantalising smile.

As they left the gallery, he turned to her and said, "whatever happens Ruth, I really want to see you again. Why don't we go for a walk in the Vienna Woods. We'll be away from prying eyes."

She waited for a moment before replying.

"Alright. I look forward to that."

She suddenly came forward and kissed him on the cheek.

He watched her as she made off towards the Ringstrasse. His mind was filled with a host of images, Leopoldstadt, Breughel's painting *A Country Wedding*, Rembrandt and Caravaggio. Above all it was filled with Ruth. *'She possesses me and one day I'll possess her.'*

* * *

Claus had invited Ulrich for lunch at a discreet wood-panelled restaurant, where, from the upstairs dining room, one had a fine view of the Graben, the city's main shopping thoroughfare.

"Ulrich," he said in a strong melodic voice.

"Claus, how wonderful to see you."

"How's the arms trade, these days?" Claus said with a caustic smile.

"You may joke, but it's my bread and butter."

"Talking about which, I recommend the seafood, it's excellent. Brought up from Trieste on the overnight train. It goes well with a fine white Grüner Veltliner."

"So what news do you bring me?" he said with prescient eyebrows and a frown.

"I've fallen for a girl." Ulrich surprised himself at his sudden rashness.

"Good Lord, you've become a romantic. This town's full of men and women falling in and out of love. You thought you were a sturdy self-sufficient man, and now you've been hit with what the French call a *coup de foudre*, a thunderbolt."

A waiter brought a large platter of seafood.

"This," Claus gestured to the large lobster on the serving dish, "is just the thing to clear your brain."

"You may jest, but I'm serious this time."

"From the look on your face I'd say you probably are."

"I really love her."

"Let's drink to that." They clicked glasses. "So what do your dear parents think?"

"Ah. A slight problem there." Ulrich hesitated. "She's a Jew. Her name is Ruth."

Claus gave him a pensive look.

"I guess you haven't told them? Am I right?"

"Yes. And if you don't mind I would prefer they didn't know. At least not yet."

"If at some future date I can win mother over about Ruth, father will do what she wants."

"I wouldn't bet on that." He drew on his cigarette. "Personally I see nothing wrong with the Jews. Much put-upon, in my not-so-humble opinion. When I was at Cambridge, before the war, I met a lot of clever Jewish scientists. When I worked in New York in a Jewish-owned investment bank, I soon learned if you make a deal with the Jews they keep their word. I never had a problem with them. It goes against the general trend of things these days but I really like them." He paused.

"So when do I get to meet this young maiden who's stolen the heart of my dear nephew?"

"Can I trust you?"

Claus laughed. "Don't worry, dear boy. I'm a confirmed bachelor."

"She's very attractive. I thought she might be Italian when I literally bumped into her."

Ulrich retold the incident at the Institute.

"I'm not surprised she appears to be from the warmer climes of the south, if your description is right. After all, the Jews are a Mediterranean race. A race blessed with brains and hallowed with blood. I'm going to drink to your wise choice."

* * *

After lunch one Sunday, his father took him aside into the orangery. "You and I must have a little talk." He went forward and opened the French doors on to the summer sunshine. "Can't have your mother complaining about cigar smoke." Dieter's tone was suspiciously conspiratorial but he was in a serious mood. One of his business moods.

"It can't have missed your attention, Ulrich, that our little corporal, Herr Schicklgruber, won power for his Nazi Party in Germany, a couple of years ago." Dieter always referred to the German Führer with patrician condescension, somewhat in the manner of Elke talking about a housemaid. He sometimes referred to him as 'the agitator'.

"It's no longer a secret but he's embarked on a massive rearmament programme " he continued. "A half a million conscript army. The Führer owes the army's senior generals for their support in his election campaign. I see many opportunities for us, from a business point of view, that is. I'm not much interested in his politics. He says that he is going to crush the communists and tame the unions. Perhaps he might like to come here. Personally, I don't want to see a return of the social democrats and the communists with their Red Vienna. I don't want a repeat of what happened at the end of the twenties, when the factory had to close and there was social unrest, fighting on the streets, death even of some of my workers. The stupid men thought they could bring about social change by revolution."

Dieter lit a cigar. "There's a member of the tennis committee who can blow rings with his cigar smoke. Did I ever tell you that?"

"Not that I can remember, father."

"Perhaps not. Very working-class habit. Clever, mind you." There was a pause.

"I didn't think the working classes could afford cigars."

Dieter gave him a sour look.

"We're going to Berlin next month," he said.

"What, both of us?"

"Yes, both of us. I'll leave my senior manager, Herr Billig in charge. I want you to come and learn how to deal with politicians. No one is more avaricious than a politician. I understand from my contacts that the Führer is an outstanding exception. However, those around him most certainly are not. And those are the ones we'll be dealing with. So brace yourself for plenty of double-talk, deceit and hypocrisy. I want to profit from this new climate in Germany. It will ensure our future. The company's future. In any case this country's future is tied to that of our powerful neighbour. It would suit our business to be part of the greater Germany that the Führer talks so much about."

"What about his National Socialist Party, the Nazis? I read in the papers about murders and killings by the Führer's followers. I'm not sure what it was all about but…"

His father held up his hand.

"You mustn't believe everything you read in the papers. Germany is dealing with its communists, its socialists and its union troublemakers and of course the Jews. Sometimes these things get out of hand. I only wish our own government would act as firmly. The Führer was democratically elected. He's supported by his people." Dieter paused and drew on his cigar. "And the Church. He's made a concordat with the Vatican which brings it into line with Nazi policy. I'll be happy to deal with his government. I'm convinced our sub-machine gun is something they'll be interested in."

Ulrich inwardly objected to his father's reference to Jews.

"Wasn't it Nazi Party members who murdered our own chancellor?" he said.

"Those were Austrian Nazis but we've got them under control. They've no chance of taking over here like they did in Germany. People like me will see to that."

There was a pause.

"First we must find out what the Czechs are up to. At the present they're our only real competitors."

"What about Krupp?"

"I never underestimate the German opposition. It's the Czechs I fear. That's why I want you to go to Pilsen and find out what they're about."

"To the Skoda factory?"

"Precisely. It's one of the biggest munition factories in the whole of Europe."

"I don't know anyone there."

"No, but I do. It's a fellow called Kirschner. Hans Kirschner. He's a Sudeten German and an old friend of mine. He's in top management and knows more about armaments than anyone I know. He will be able to give you all the information I need. The sooner you go there the better."

* * *

Ulrich's room in the Penzion Adler in Pilsen, lay behind the metre-thick walls of a medieval town house. The tongue-twisting Czech language baffled him, but, fortunately, this was the German speaking part of the country. There were only a few others in the hotel who seemed to be mainly commercial travellers. The adjacent restaurant had the strong odour of a German beer hall, and served traditional Bavarian wurst, dumpling and roast pork.

The day after arrival, on the way to the Skoda factory, he walked through the main town square, overshadowed by an enormous Gothic cathedral and high tower which he reckoned, with his engineer's eye, must be over a hundred metres high.

It was not difficult to find the Skoda works, for it seemed to dominate this industrial town of myriad glass and porcelain factories. Herr Kirschner, a thickset man, with a mop of black curly hair, flecked with grey, was waiting for him and they embarked on an extensive tour of the factory on a small battery-driven buggy. 'We imported it from the United States', he said to Ulrich. The huge steel rolling mills, the vast machine workshops with their high heavy lifting gantries, hydraulic presses and the enormous foundries where massive gun castings were being forged impressed Ulrich. The intense heat of the blast furnaces and the incessant noise of the giant jackhammers were overwhelming. It was a triumph of steel and manual labour.

"The Versailles Treaty closed off a lot of our traditional market so now we make sixteen-inch guns for the British Royal Navy," Kirschner said.

Later, during lunch at one of the city's more elegant restaurants, Kirschner talked about his native country. He praised Pilsen's famous beer. 'France has its wine, Scotland its whisky, Russia its vodka and Czechoslovakia has its ice cold, golden beers.' However, he reserved his most eloquent praise for the country's greatest strength, its engineering prowess.

"This western part of Czechoslovakia was the real Austro-Hungarian workhorse of the industrial revolution in Central Europe. Even today this country is one of the most economically advanced and industrialised countries in the world. It's an engineer's paradise. You should come and live here." He laughed.

"I dare say my father wouldn't agree to that."

"How is your father? I haven't seen him for years. He's a first class engineer and businessman. He came here several times in the old days with *his* father."

"Times have been difficult for him. There's been no end of political trouble and industrial strife. Red Vienna and all that. I think he worries a lot."

"I suppose that's why he sent you here."

"What do you mean?"

"Ulrich, my friend, and I hope you don't mind my calling you Ulrich, I know your father well enough to surmise that he's a bit like me. He doesn't really think of himself as Austrian. He thinks of himself as German. It's like this. When the French and British broke up the old Austrian-Hungarian Empire they created all these independent states, this one, Yugoslavia, Hungary, and so on. But the old Hapsburg regime was essentially German. That's why nearly everybody here speaks German. Your father looks across the border and sees the rising power in this region. The Führer's got great ambitions."

"Why am I getting this little history lesson?" Ulrich smiled.

"Because your father sees re-armament in Germany as a business opportunity."

"So?"

"So you're here not merely to have a tour of the Skoda works but to find out what we are making and whether what we're making we are selling to the Germans. I know I'm right. The answer to the first is that we still concentrate on heavy armaments and small arms and the answer to the second is no, we are not selling arms to the German government. Besides the armament restrictions imposed by the Versaille Treaty on Germany, the government here is not much in favour of the Führer. So we don't do arms business with them. We sell them locomotives, steam turbines and equipment for power stations and water treatment works. That's about it."

Kirschner leaned back in his chair and sipped his beer.

"Any more questions young man?"

"Yes I do have one. Do you make any sub-machine guns?"

"Again, the answer to that is no. We tried to buy the patent for the Thompson gun from the Americans but didn't succeed for one reason or other. We lost interest." He paused. "Look, I must get back to the office. Before you return to your lovely Vienna you must visit some of this city's attractions. Pilsen used to be the capital of the Holy Roman Empire. Ah past glories! There's the cathedral, and, of course, the synagogue, which is the largest in Europe. They say it's the largest in the world outside Jerusalem. Give your father my regards."

Ulrich stayed on and ordered another beer. He wasn't interested in the cathedral. However, mention of the synagogue reminded him of Ruth.

* * *

Ulrich sat with Ruth on the noisy tram as it trudged out of the city to the northern suburbs in the direction of the Vienna Woods.

"I'm going to Berlin next month," he said.

His arm was entwined in hers and he felt a tremor pulsate through to his.

"What on earth for?" Her tone and a look in her eyes told him that she was not pleased at this piece of information.

"Business. I'm going with my father. Hopefully and if we're successful, it'll provide more work for everybody." He realised that he had treaded on a sensitive issue. Despite his efforts to excise the subject from his mind, the Jewish question was never far away. Reports of the Nazi treatment of Jews, particularly in Berlin, were rarely out of the pages of the liberal section of the Viennese press.

"I don't know why anyone should want to go there."

"I'm sorry Ruth. I shan't talk business or politics."

"Good. If you want to talk politics then I suggest you have a chat with my brother Reuben. He's the family politician. He's not really a politician but he likes to think that he knows everything about the subject. It's a common male delusion. The girls find him boring. If he continues like that he'll end up being an old bachelor."

"Well, I hope *I* won't." He gave her a sideways glance. "I know I won't."

They alighted at Heiligenstadt, the terminus, alongside the mixed sandy and light brown painted Karl-Marx-Hof. Ulrich remembered his mother's words referring to it as a hot-bed tenement of communists and socialists. Had she ever seen the kilometre long block, he wondered, erected by the Social Democrat council, the majority of whose members were Jews, to house working people? He didn't think so. From some of his fellow students at the Institute, he learned that for the first time the workers had subsidised rents, running water and toilets in their flats. Privately-owned apartments for workers were expensive yet had not been equipped with such amenities.

"It's ironic," Ruth said, looking up at the flats.

"What is?"

"The council built these flats in what is essentially an upper-class residential area."

"Working votes to keep capitalists out of the city government."

"That's a cynical view. It didn't save the workers from last year's pounding by the police and army, on the orders of the clerical fascists."

"I thought you didn't want to talk politics."

Ruth gave him a wry look.

At Heiligenstadt they mounted an open-topped charabanc which took a steep zigzag course on the narrow road up into Kahlenberg.

"Have you been up to Kahlenberg before?" Ulrich said.

"Of course. It was more fun when I was a little girl. We used to come up here on the cog and pinion railway with its single carriage, through Grinzing and Krapfenwald. The line was shut down after the war. After that we used the bus."

At Kahlenberg, arm in arm they strolled along a well-trodden footpath through the extensive woods leading to an open space with a southern panoramic view of the city, the Danube and the Danube canal. A line of high hills to the west were etched against a milky blue sky. Hanging over the city, like a blanket, lay a thick beige cloud created by the thousands of smoking chimneys from the city's houses and factories, obscuring the sun for its hapless inhabitants. Continuing their walk, they passed the white and magnolia painted chapel of St Joseph. Ruth insisted they stop to read the plaque on the front wall, commemorating in German and Polish, the defeat, in the late seventeenth century, by a joint Polish and Austrian army, of the Muslim Ottoman forces, then laying siege to Vienna.

"I'm sure there must have been Jewish soldiers among the Polish forces," Ruth said.

Winter had suddenly given way to spring. Recent rain left a subtle aroma over the wooded landscape. A confirmed city-dweller, Ulrich saw the beauty of the countryside only through urban lenses. The birds, the plants and the flora were, in reality, little known entities for him. At that moment however, he was scarcely interested in nature. His attention was on Ruth.

"I'm glad to be out of the city," she said, giving his arm a squeeze. "Though I wouldn't come here alone."

"You've been here before with other boyfriends, I mean."

"I've never had a boyfriend. What about you? Have you had other girlfriends?"

Ulrich thought he detected a slight note of jealousy in her voice.

"I've had other girlfriends. Just in passing you might say. Temporary. All we ever did was go to a dance or go to the cinema and hold hands in the back seat. Boring really."

"Am I boring?"

"I don't think you could ever be boring Ruth."

They walked in silence for some time then he said:

"Do you know what I think? I think the best word to describe you is fiery. Yes. That's the right word. You're fiery."

"That makes me sound devilish. Why do you say that?"

"Because behind that well-controlled exterior lies a passionate soul!"

"You've been reading too many romantic novels Ulrich." She gave out one of her infectious chuckles.

"Come on I'll race you to the next corner," he challenged her. He set off and was soon ahead. He was a boy again playing in the garden at home. She was having difficulty in keeping up with him. He stopped, turned around and walked back to meet her.

"I'm wearing the wrong shoes for this sort of lark," she said with a laugh.

"I'll have to get you a pair of army boots," he quipped.

"Look, let's go and sit on that log over there."

When they had sat down, he looked at her.

"Do you like it here?"

"I'm really glad to get away from the city," she said. "I love the sound of the birds, the sight of the beeches, the oaks, the smell of the pine. Did you know there's more than forty different species of birds in these woods?"

"You sound like a naturalist."

"I'm not really. It's just that when I'm here I feel a kind of freedom you don't get in town." She paused for a moment. "Listen. Can you hear that woodpecker?"

"I wouldn't have noticed if you hadn't told me."

"You would have to be soulless not to love this place. When I was young, I used to come here with my mother, sister and brother during the war. Our father was away at the time, in the army on the Western Front."

"Were you happy then?"

"You mean coming here on a visit?"

"No. I meant as a child."

"Yes, I was. We're a very close family. Very Jewish. Times were hard for us during the war. Especially with the rationing. It was even worse just after the war. Food was so scarce. Often we ended the week with only half a loaf of bread in the cupboard. That seems impossible now but that's how it was. Everyone was in the same situation. Some were even worse off."

"I believe what you say is true but I find it incredible."

"You probably would." But there was a kindness in her tone.

"The Drehers' sole sacrifice to the war effort was my father complaining loudly that he found it difficult to get his favourite Havana cigars."

She laughed.

"What did your Uncle Claus give up?"

"I don't know. His favourite cognac, I suppose." He paused for a moment. "Why didn't you go to art school? Your brother went to the university."

"Reuben was very bright and won a scholarship. That's the only way ordinary working-class Jews could get to university. I left school at fifteen and was fortunate to get a job in the Institute library."

"All the better for me. I wouldn't have met you otherwise."

"One of these days I shall have to tell my parents about you. I would love you to meet them." Her voice trailed off. "Maybe your parents will relent and then I could go and see them?"

"Do you like working for Doctor Goldstein?"

"You are avoiding my question."

"Because I don't have an answer, Ruth. I just don't know." He looked deep into her eyes. "Right now, you're the most important person in my life. Everything else is secondary. I intend it to remain like that."

He waited some moments and then said, "Ruth, may I kiss you?"

He embraced her and held her very close. He caught the subtle fragrance of her perfume and a sensuous urge welled up deep inside him. Suddenly she began to weep. He didn't say anything for some time. He held up her face in his cupped hands. "What is it Ruth? Please tell me." He spoke with tenderness.

It was some time before she replied. She made no attempt to wipe the tears from her eyes. It was as if they were symbols of something deeper. Like the sounds of a great swelling organ that vibrates for minutes after the organist has stopped playing.

"Right now I feel so happy. I think I'm falling in love with you." She gave him a distraught look. "I just don't see how it could possibly work."

"Of course it can. It must. It will."

"How? There's an impenetrable wall between us. I'm Jewish and you're a Christian. Between our families between our backgrounds. If I could get rid of the past two thousand years I would. But I can't. Don't you see?" She hesitated. "Ulrich, I shall want more out of life than walking in the Vienna Woods." She hid her face in his shoulder and gently sobbed. He held her more tightly.

"Ruth, darling, there is no wall between you and me. Invisible or otherwise. Our love will prevail."

For once, he thought, I'm going to take charge of my life. I can't and I won't let her go.

Chapter 4

Vienna 1935

On their journey from Vienna to Berlin, Ulrich and his father made a detour via Munich where Dieter, as president of the Bavarian Association of Vienna, had business to transact. He did not confide in Ulrich what the nature of this matter was. 'Those Bavarians used to have their own tinpot king,' Claus once derisively remarked to Ulrich, 'reigning over a kingdom of priest-ridden peasant farmers.'

Returning to Munich's gloomy central railway station for the onward journey to Berlin, Dieter ordered a sullen-looking porter with a shaven square head to take their cases and find them an empty first-class compartment. The two men settled into the window seats. Dieter opened the *Volkisher Beobachter,* a Munich newspaper, and was soon absorbed in its political pages despite the fact that he was self-avowedly non-political. Ulrich looked through the carriage window and wondered why so many *Schutzstaffel*, commonly referred to as the SS, were milling around on the platform. Their sinister black uniforms, scabbarded daggers and brooding presence conjured up visions of the Black Knights of his childhood legends.

The door to their compartment was suddenly opened and a tall, middle-aged man entered. He had a sour magisterial demeanour, a raptor-like nose, dark brown hair severely brushed back and wearing a well-tailored SS uniform, looking as if it had just been fitted. Through round steel-rimmed spectacles, which give him a slightly academic air, his cold blue eyes gazed superciliously around the compartment.

"Are these other seats taken?" he asked in a polite, aloof tone.

"No," Dieter said.

He nodded to the younger man also in SS uniform and carrying a leather case, who had followed him into the compartment and now placed the case on the luggage rack and left. Stretching out his hand to Ulrich's father, he introduced himself. "Colonel von Wartenberg."

Dieter stood up. "Dieter Dreher."

"Of the Dreher gun?"

"Yes."

"I've one myself. I inherited it from my father. It came in handy on the Western front. There's many a poor Frenchman who was on its receiving end. Were you in the war?" he asked in a casual tone of voice.

Dieter had been asked before, during the war. "I failed the medical," he said. He did not elaborate. At the beginning of hostilities, Dieter had suffered a mild form of tuberculosis. This, however, had gone by the middle of hostilities. His father had insisted that he stay to help in the business. 'Without us,' he reportedly said, 'the military wouldn't be able to fight.' Ulrich often wondered if the real reason was his grandfather's concern that his only son would be killed. Being well-connected, he had pulled strings and Dieter stayed at home.

"Indeed," von Wartenberg said, giving Dieter a wintry-eyed look.

Ulrich had heard of von Wartenberg's reputation of being one of the most powerful men in the Führer's entourage, whose personal story had been well publicised. His family, aristocratic landowning *Junkers* from East Prussia, had apparently, on the eve of the Great War, lost a considerable sum of money when the building of the Baghdad railway failed to materialise. His father blamed British opposition to the German plan for his family's considerable financial loss. German industrialists pointed an angry finger at Lloyd George, at the time British Chancellor of the Exchequer, who was hostile towards The Baghdad Plan stating it was a threat to British interests in the Middle East and India.

The express train picked up speed as it hurried past the Munich suburbs on its way north. Ulrich became absorbed in his own thoughts as he gazed out at the passing Bavarian farming countryside, a colourful patchwork of agricultural small holdings.

Foremost in his mind was Ruth. He could still feel the touch of her lips on his, feel the sensual throb of her soft breasts pressing against his chest, see her eyes filling with hot tears and still hear her soft voice as she told him she loved him.

At some stage, I'll have to tell my parents, but not yet. They're not ready. We don't have to hate the Jews. Hate is one of the cardinal sins. That much I remember from my catechism lessons. What have the Jews ever done to me? Nothing. Ruth, the most beautiful thing in my life is Jewish. The Jews are as good as us, maybe better. Why should I have to believe all those stories about the Jews that the Church tells us? They could have made them up. Probably did. The family will have to accept her. I only wish I could see the future.

"I notice, Herr Dreher" von Wartenberg said, "you are reading our Party newspaper. Are you a member of the Führer's party?"

"No. As a businessman, I try to keep out of politics."

"That's a pity." The colonel sounded condescending. "Here in Germany most businessmen and the traditional social elite support the Führer and his message. Many princely families have flocked to the party en masse. Nearly a fifth of my senior SS officers are titled nobility. All over Europe top industrialists support the Führer's views. Take England. The Prince of Wales, the heir to the English throne, came here to see the Führer. He told me himself, the Prince that is, he wished the Führer would come to England and rid it of her Jews. He said that many of his friends look with envy at Germany."

Dieter raised his eyebrows. "Indeed."

"You should reconsider. After all, like yourself, the Führer is Austrian. He wants Austria to become part of the greater German people. Several of the top people in the party are Austrian. Indeed, some of my most enthusiastic officers are Austrian. They consider the SS as much an Austrian force as German."

The train pulled into Nuremberg station. The compartment door opened and a young man entered followed by a porter carrying a large case. Without addressing anyone in particular and speaking German with a strong foreign accent, he introduced himself. "The name's Thompson. William Voolen Thompson. People call me Bill. I'm American."

Dieter looked up from his paper without saying anything. Von Wartenberg gave him a tight-lipped grimace.

"You guys going to Berlin?" Thompson asked.

"At least my father and I are going there," Ulrich replied, as if wanting to break the Trappist silence of the other two men. "I can't speak for Colonel von Wartenberg," he said, nodding in the direction of the colonel. "My name's Ulrich Dreher."

Ulrich marvelled at the easy familiarity of this Thompson, a man of his own age.

Thompson sat down and made himself comfortable. After a while, he addressed von Wartenberg.

"I wonder if you can tell me, Colonel, what way is Germany heading?" The sudden question sounded provocative.

"Why do you ask?" The colonel's tone, that of a man accustomed to subservient respect, suggested he considered the question an impertinent interruption.

"Well, sir, it's my job. I'm a journalist."

"Perhaps you might tell me who sent you here?" The colonel spoke to him as he would a brash junior officer.

"No one. I'm what's known as freelance. I gather information and sell it to whoever will pay."

"You being American, I'm not surprised money would come into it," the colonel said.

"In fact, money has much less to do with this than you suggest, Colonel. Americans today are not much interested in Europe or in Germany for that matter. They've too many problems of their own. So, I've got to write stuff that will make them interested. But, it won't be easy. Hence my question. This guy who calls himself the Führer, where's he leading Germany?"

"That's a big question," von Wartenberg said.

"The reason I ask is that since coming to Europe, I've been reading up about the Versailles Peace Treaty. Was that a good move?" It sounded more like a challenge than a question.

Ulrich watched von Wartenberg's face carefully to see how his expression might change.

"The Versailles Treaty," the colonel said, fixing Thompson with a withering gaze," imposed humiliating terms on Germany. Germany didn't surrender unconditionally. I fought in that war. My men and, indeed, the whole of the German Army fought honourably and gallantly. They were just as heroic and brave as any American, French or English soldiers. They were prepared to suffer and if need be die for it. Patriotism doesn't have borders. I was there at the end of the war when the Armistice was signed at Compiegne. It could easily have been the other way round. It wasn't our generals who surrendered, they played no part in the senior councils of the war. It was the politicians, aided and abetted by a weak-kneed Kaiser who brought humiliation to the German nation. But Germany is rising again."

Von Wartenberg took out a thin gold cigarette case and lit up. He smoked slowly and deliberately. He eyed Thompson with the visual acuity of a hawk.

"Sir," Thompson said in that known polite manner which is a mark of the American attitude to older people, "you've still not answered my question".

Ulrich was a bystander to this exchange between the German and the American. He looked at this young American so full of self confidence and arrogance. Yet his demeanour harboured a healthy openness like a current of fresh spring wind. I can't imagine any young Austrian journalist being so bold, he thought.

"Before I answer your question," said the solemn-faced colonel, "I should like to remind you that Germany lost the war not only to England and France but mainly to America. Your president declared that the United States would take no part in this European war. Your Congress passed a Neutrality Act. However, the United States did enter the war. We would have beaten the English and the French if it hadn't been for the intervention of America on their side. Now why would America disregard its own legislation? Can you tell me that?"

"I'm afraid not. I guess you know the answer otherwise you wouldn't have asked."

Thompson gave von Wartenberg an unwavering look.

"Indeed that is so. The answer is simple. America was dragged into the war by Jewish big business interests which had grown fat on supplying the allies. They made it impossible for your country to dispense with this trade. The World War enriched America and its Jews and impoverished Europe. I blame the Jewish bankers in Wall Street. They're the ones who caused the recent financial crash and depression and the ones who really stoked the fires of the last war."

"Don't you have Jewish bankers in Germany? Why America?"

"We have indeed. What concerns us is the international Jewish conspiracy against the rest of the world. These Jewish bankers belong to the same families wherever you go. Berlin, Paris, London, New York. Where these people are makes no difference. They belong to the same families, they share among themselves the confidential information they possess about their governments. They'll betray their own country when they can make financial gain for themselves."

"If that's the case, the Jewish bankers in America won the war for us. Nothing treacherous about that."

"That's a cynical view. As far as this country is concerned, the Führer is determined to punish the Jews for their treachery."

"Not all Jews are bankers," Ulrich intervened, spurred on by Thompson's apparent lack of deference towards this senior officer of the Third Reich. "In Vienna there are Jewish doctors, lawyers, shopkeepers, blacksmiths, horse-dealers. Many Jews are just manual workers. They're not bankers. I can't think a Jewish butcher or baker has confidential information about the government." His father glowered at him.

Von Wartemberg did not answer. Instead a sullen silence descended on the compartment. The colonel took out a large, white handkerchief which had a black swastika woven into each corner.

"Germany will recover its pride," he said, after blowing his nose. "You can tell your readers, young man, that our Führer is backed up by the people, industrialists, by landowners and by the churches. The Vatican was not only too willing to sign a concordat with the new Nazi Government, it actually initiated the process. In fact, the Cardinal Secretary of State whom I met and who signed on behalf of the Pope is most supportive of the aims and policies of the Führer towards the Jews."

"So you've got God on your side," Ulrich asked.

"When we strike against the Jews, yes."

"So what's Germany's next move?" Thompson said.

"Seventeen years after the war we're still being humiliated." Von Wartemberg's voice struck an irate tone. "The French still occupy the Rhineland, the English tell us how many soldiers we can have, how many naval vessels, how many planes. This is intolerable. But, we're a resourceful people. Germany will not allow itself to be dictated to by the English and the French. Under the Führer's leadership we will defeat our enemies."

"Who are your enemies?" Thompson said.

"The Jews. They remain a permanent threat to Germany. Communism is Jewish, most communists are Jews. They want to import the Jewish-Bolshevik revolution here. We will not allow that to happen. Just after the war, I commanded an army brigade that crushed a communist attempt to take over Berlin. It was led by a notorious Jewish woman, Rosa Luxemburg. My men shot her and threw her body into the Landwehr Canal. Had we let them succeed, this country would have been ruled by Jews. I can't think of anything worse. I'm going to make sure the communists and their allies don't try again. That's why I've joined the Führer in his campaign to restore Germany as a great power."

"We had the same trouble in Vienna not so long ago," Dieter remarked. "There was an uprising of workers and trade unionists. The communist press called for the killing of judges, politicians and others. Dreadful situation."

"There you are," the colonel said. "The Jews are not just trouble here, they're trouble everywhere."

"My father didn't say Jews were trouble," Ulrich insisted, "he said the trouble in Vienna was caused by an uprising of workers and trade unionists." His own natural deference had evaporated.

"I think," Dieter said, his face distorted as if he had swallowed a poisonous herb, "my son was too young to remember those days. I'm sure the Jews were behind the troubles."

"How do you intend to defeat your so-called enemies, Colonel?" Thompson persisted, "when you add up the numbers, Jewish bankers, communists, workers and trade unionists, that's a lot of people."

"Indeed," von Wartenberg said, "but we'll defeat all of them but not in the same way. We'll start by getting rid of the social criminal Jews and then convince the others. That's where the Führer's genius lies. I shall harbour no guilt if ordered to get rid of the Jew."

"Genius?" Thompson said with a laugh. "Sir, in my book a genius is someone with exceptional intellectual talent. Do you really believe your Führer has that?"

"You might smirk and laugh but let me tell you he's a genius. The future will prove that. He knows people. He knows the mind of ordinary workers. We Germans are an intelligent, hardworking people. The war left Germany with a legacy of dispossession. Our people have suffered more than most from the war. Two million dead. I can't accept that such a sacrifice was in vain. Then there was the inflation, or rather hyperinflation, the Depression, unemployment. Haven't you ever seen the pictures of honest German people taking wheelbarrows of worthless paper money to buy simple things? That was not caused by us. It was caused by the Jews."

"You sound bitter, Colonel. Are you bitter?" Thompson said.

Ulrich could not but admire the probing, forceful insistence of the American, undaunted by the superior air of this German aristocrat.

"No, I'm not bitter. The Führer has started to make changes. You don't even have to be an intellectual prodigy to work out that if you give people work, give them money to spend, build them good housing, schools and hospitals and roads and railways they will support you. When they see that Germany has a strong army and navy and air force they will feel safe. The Fuhrer has begun this task of rebuilding Germany, of restoring its moral fibre. He's finally broken the shackles of Versailles. Once the German people realise that the Führer puts Germany and the German people first, they will follow him, they'll fight for him and be ready to die for him."

"If you don't mind my saying so," Thompson said with a smile, "that sounds like socialism to my American ears." He paused for a moment. "You appear an unlikely socialist to me, Colonel."

"But, that's where you're wrong. Yes, it's true the Führer leads a socialist party. The difference is that it's national socialism we are talking about. This is not the revolutionary socialism of the Marxist kind. Take me. I'm a patriotic and loyal German. I put nation above all. That defrocked priest Stalin is an idiot. He thinks in terms of world revolution but he can't even feed his own people. He massacres millions of them and lies about it. Most of his nation live in dire poverty. He wants to export Jewish-Bolshevik communism to Germany. We'll not allow him to do that."

"Colonel," Thompson said, "I must thank you. I owe you one, as we say across the Atlantic."

Von Wartenberg gave him a suspicious look. "What do you mean?" he said.

"When I got up this morning I wondered what story I would file this evening. You've given me that story."

At this, the colonel stopped talking. The conversation petered out. A brooding silence overtook the compartment. Dieter had already fallen asleep. The colonel closed his eyes. Thompson read a book. Ulrich looked out of the window

He's not bitter, so he says. If that's not anger, I don't know what is. Why make the Jews a scapegoat for everything that's wrong with society? It's Father Hahn all over again. Only in a political garb. If Ruth were here, how would she feel in the face of this torrent of hate? How would I feel after a torrent of racial hatred were I Jewish? What worries me, it's got deep religious roots, like noxious bindweed.

Later the four men shared a table for lunch in the first class dining car. The conversation was banal and desultory. Von Wartenberg was no moneyed parvenu. He talked about his ancestral lineage, the large estates his family owned in East Prussia, the exciting boar hunts in the forests. An obsequious head waiter fawned over him while taking the orders. The talk rarely strayed far from the colonel's own favourite subject, namely, himself. Dieter was vague and discreet about the reason for their journey to Berlin. Von Wartenberg ordered champagne, insisted the others drink but drank most of it himself.

* * *

Ulrich and his father on their arrival in Berlin made their way to The Reich Ministry of Defence and Armaments, a limestone building near the stern Brandenburg Gate. As a functionary in a grey uniform led Ulrich and his father up a wide marble staircase, Ulrich remembered his high school history lessons. 'Whereas elsewhere in Europe,' had declared his history master, a small Jesuit of Hungarian origin, 'the state had an army at its disposal, in Prussia the army disposed of the state. The Prussian army was not a state within a state, it was the state. This military monarchy turned Prussia into a major European power.' He went on to explain how it was a superior army in a warring continent, that the ruling classes all took great pride in military service. 'What the world saw' he said, in a certain tone of disapproval, 'was a fierce amalgam of martial music, parades, spiked helmets, jackboots, barracks and staccato commands. The political masters of Prussia wore a military uniform.'

Dieter and Ulrich were shown into a large room and told to wait.

"I used to come here with your grandfather," Dieter said, "to sell arms to the Kaiser's army." There was a nostalgic tone to his voice. "The Army had its armaments procurement ministry in this same building. Even the secretaries wore uniforms. We would pass generals, colonels and other senior ranks in the corridors and business was conducted in these palatial-sized offices. Portraits of the Kaiser and his Hohenzollern forebears were carefully placed in the rooms and the walls of the wide staircases. I suppose you could truthfully say it reflected the regal spirit of the Prussian Germanic Empire. It resonated to the sound and drumbeat of power."

"The sound and drumbeat of power," Ulrich said, in parrot fashion. "Father, you ought to become a fiction writer."

"You might deride all this, but I remind you it provided many jobs back in Vienna. And," he emphasised, "the house you live in."

"I'm not unaware of that, father. I just thought your phrase was a flight of the imagination."

"Well, it wasn't. All this didn't appear out of nothing. It was the result of the scientific and technological work carried on at the Friedrich-Wilhelms University, here in Berlin. As a precision engineer, you should know that. As a result, the German army gained technical superiority over its rivals, and accounted for its astonishing success. Its catastrophic defeat in the Great War changed everything." His father was in one of his rare lecturing moods. "The terms of the Treaty of Versailles castrated an army that had been the most efficient fighting machine in Europe since the days of Napoleon. Nonetheless, the present German Army is still controlled by the same General Staff who are powerful people and belong to the same elite landowning *Junker* class. They intend to restore its past glory. And we are going to help them do it.'

Dieter pointed to a photograph of General von Hindenburg, the aged, white-haired former president, whose craggy face seemed the epitome of Prussianism. "This man," he said, "represents the old defeated and discredited imperial Germany and," pointing to that of the Führer, "he *is* the new Germany."

A side door opened and a tall, clean-shaven man entered. He had grey, sharp and serious eyes, was wearing a dark pin-striped suit and appeared to be in his late thirties. He bowed when shaking hands with Dieter.

"I'm Herr Doctor Engineer Otto Giersberg and represent the Minister of War." He gave them a searching look. "So, gentlemen I meet the famous Dreher family," he said. "I've read through the correspondence between yourself and the minister. Naturally, he has left me to conduct any negotiations with you. And this young gentleman," he nodded in Ulrich's direction, "is the designer of the gun?"

"Yes, I designed the gun and made this prototype."

"I must congratulate you."

The three men gathered around a large design drawing of the sub-machine gun that Dieter had brought with him. Also on the table was the prototype. They discussed its technical merits, its firepower, accuracy and reliability. Giersberg's comments showed he was an expert engineer, especially knowledgeable about guns. He picked up the gun and drew his hands over the barrel, stroking and caressing it in a sensuous way as if it were a woman's body.

"This gun is an unusual design Herr Dreher. I admire the simple, open bolt, blowback mechanism and the distinctive curved detachable box magazine." Giersberg spoke as if he were addressing a class of students. "This, I presume, prevents the nine millimetre ammunition from getting dirty and of course," he held the gun in a firing position, "its range of more than a hundred metres."

"It will be most useful in close combat," Ulrich ventured.

"Indeed?"

"It requires," Ulrich said, "a minimum amount of machining by using simple pressed metal components and minor welding."

Giersberg turned to Dieter. "Have you shown this design and the prototype of this sub-machine gun to any other party either here or elsewhere?"

"No. I prefer that the German government has first refusal."

"That is most thoughtful of you." He paused. "Does anyone outside your company know of the existence of this gun?"

"The patent office in Zurich. Otherwise no one else."

"We can rely on the Swiss to be discreet about this matter. They're a friendly government. We have good relations with them."

"I'm only interested in coming to an understanding with your Government. For the present moment, at least."

"As you will understand Herr Dreher, we have a number of other designs to evaluate. Most don't come up to our rigorous standard but yours has definite possibilities." He sounded as if he were reading from a Ministry script.

To Ulrich's knowledge, there was no other sub-machine gun on the European market. The Thompson model was unavailable. The American authorities would not allow it to be sold to the Germans. Giersberg is bluffing, he said to himself.

Dieter looked at Giersberg with scarcely suppressed anger.

"Herr Doctor Giersberg," he said, with steel in his voice "I think it's time for a little candour. It's an open secret that the Führer wants to rearm. He wants to bring Germany up to the same level as France and England. He has said so himself. I understand that, in addition to the usual army regiments, you're forming a parachute unit. No other country has such units."

"Herr Dreher, I see you're well informed." His tone was non-committal.

"In this business you have to be." Dieter paused for a moment. "This gun is precisely the sort of weapon they'll need. I didn't come all the way from Vienna to discuss possibilities. I'm here to make a deal."

"No doubt. There is one aspect that you must consider. If we were to conclude a deal, the minister has made it clear that the manufacture of the gun would have to be done here by a German company. I don't think he would move on that."

"Herr Giersberg," said Dieter, deliberately dropping the title 'doctor', "I'm as German as your Führer. He was born in Linz, I was born in Vienna, he went to school in Linz and I went to the Polytechnic in Vienna, which has an international reputation." This was an inferred comparison that the Führer failed to get into the Vienna School of Art. "Most German Austrians would welcome union with the German Reich but we're forbidden by the Treaty of St Germain. Most of my fellow countrymen are well disposed to the new Germany. Austria has become a mere rump of a once great empire. A large head on a small body, if you will. You perhaps don't know but when Austria was created as a separate state in 1918, it was called German-Austria. My family is German. I don't consider myself as anything but German." His voice took on a supercilious tone. "My factory only employs those mainly of German descent. My factory is German. What more do you want? If necessary, I'll make representations to the Führer himself. Directly."

There was a silence while Giersberg absorbed Dieter's verbal onslaught. He looked hesitantly between Dieter, Ulrich, the drawing and the gun. Finally, he said, "That will not be necessary, Herr Dreher. You've made your point. I suggest that we test-fire the gun tomorrow. We have a facility in the basement here in this building. If your gun passes the scrutiny of our experts including myself, of course, I'll be making my recommendations to the minister. If he agrees with my decision, the contract papers will be sent to you. I must impress upon you the need for absolute secrecy about this gun. We will, of course, insist on putting our own inspectors in your factory, to oversee the manufacture of the gun and that the workforce observe total confidentiality."

Just as the ministerial group were about to leave the room, Ginsberg turned to Dieter. "From our government's records of dealings with the Dreher company in the past," he said, "it would appear that a Jewish bank in Vienna handles your financial affairs. Is this the current position?"

"That is so."

"As you know, in this country it is illegal for Jews to own or run companies. This holds especially true of banks. It would be illegal for us to deal with your company through a Jewish bank, no matter where it is registered."

"Are you saying that I must change my bank?"

"Herr Dreher, it's not for me to presume to advise you how to run your affairs. It's up to you to make such decisions. However, I'm obliged to explain to you the legal position of the German government. If you wish to accept a contract from this government, you'll have to comply with German law. I'm sure we understand each other."

In the taxi taking them back to their hotel, an exhilarated Dieter turned to Ulrich.

"Forgive the pun, Ulrich, but always stick to your guns". He rubbed his hands together. "We've just won ourselves a wonderful contract. It guarantees years of work."

"So are you going to change banks?"

"If it means a contract with the German government, yes. You must learn that when it comes to business, loyalty to self comes first."

Ulrich gritted his teeth, but kept silent.

* * *

After dinner that evening Ulrich made his way to the Excelsior, a luxury hotel, built in a neo-classical style, located in the city centre. He found Thompson in the bar, talking to the barman, who was wearing a Nazi Party pin in his waistcoat, and a young, long-legged woman in a suggestive dress, perched on a bar stool.

"Say, it's great you should come." He spoke English. "The barman tells me Berlin is a haven for insomniacs. The night life must be something."

A young man in the uniform of an SS officer appeared, went up to the young woman and they both left arm in arm.

"Well," Thompson said, "there goes my hope for the evening. I wouldn't want to compete with the guy in the black uniform."

Ulrich and Thompson went and sat at a corner banquette. Thompson called the waiter and ordered drinks.

"Did you file that report of yours?" Ulrich asked.

"Hey, I've hardly arrived. I must see the night life before that." Thompson had an infectious laugh. He offered Ulrich a cigarette and then lit both. "You didn't say what you're doing here."

"My father runs a company in Vienna and we've come here to try to get a few contracts."

"Sounds interesting. Contracts for what?"

"Metal manufacturing. That sort of thing."

"Say, what do you think of that guy von Wartenberg? Those black uniforms give me the creeps."

"He harbours a big grudge, blaming the Jews for Germany's woes. What does he know about American Jews?"

"Everyone likes to give Uncle Sam the Bronx cheer. Do you really believe what he said about everyone supporting the Führer?"

"I don't know. I can only tell you what I read in the Viennese papers. They say he's popular."

"He uses strong-arm tactics."

"Like what?"

Thompson went silent.

"I spent some time in Munich," he finally said, "getting the feel of the place. A friend back in New York told me that it's where all this Nazi stuff started. You know, the party, the movement, that kind of thing. It's where old Adolf found his feet, as it were. Why does the guy call himself the Führer, the Leader? It's crazy. Can you imagine Roosevelt calling himself that? People would only laugh."

"It's no laughing matter here in Germany. They take him very seriously. Look around. There's huge posters of him everywhere. Don't make a joke about him because they'll probably lock you up."

"Don't worry, I won't be doing that. Not after what I've seen."

"What have you seen?"

Thompson looked around the large lounge and over to where the barman was drying glasses. He lowered his voice.

"That New York friend I mentioned, well, he gave me a good contact in Munich. This contact is a pretty influential journalist and he enabled me to visit a concentration camp at a place called Dachau, about ten miles north of Munich. It's run by the SS. One of the senior guards took me around. I couldn't believe what I saw. You can't even start to compare it with a normal prison. They're holding thousands of emaciated prisoners in dilapidated buildings, under terrible conditions. The camp is secured by high, electric barbed wire fences. The guards go around holding whips in one hand and German shepherd dogs on leashes in the other. When I asked the guard what kind of crimes these men had committed, he told me they were Jews, communists, homosexuals, Jehovah's Witnesses, all sorts of people, who are deemed political enemies of the state. They're there to be re-educated. If that's re-education I'm the queen of Sheba."

"We hear rumours of that place but I didn't believe them. If what you say is true..."

"Believe me what I'm telling you is what I've seen with my own eyes. You couldn't make it up. When I was studying law, I once visited the infamous Sing Sing prison up the Hudson River from New York. It houses about fifteen-hundred pretty serious criminals who've been convicted of serious crimes. I can tell you, their conditions are palatial compared to those of those poor guys in Dachau who haven't been convicted of anything. It's just that the

Nazis seem to hate them. So they just lock them up. No legal process, no court hearing. I wouldn't like to be a German."

"You'd better not let my father hear you say that. He'd have a fit."

"The guy who started all this concentration camp setup and now intends to build more is our old friend von Wartenberg. He's head of the SS. You heard him on the train. All these people, especially the Jews and the Bolshevik communists are criminals. You can see where his anger is coming from. He sees them as traitors who made Germany suffer. So now it's payback time. No wonder the Jews are fleeing this place. I would if I lived here."

"Why's that?"

"I'm Jewish on my mother's side. According to Jewish rabbinic law, you're Jewish if your mother is Jewish."

"My girlfriend is called Ruth and she's Jewish."

"What does your family think about her?"

"I've not told them except my mother, and she said the Jews are trouble."

"What are you going to do? Ditch her?"

"Absolutely not."

"You've got a problem big-time, my friend. My father's family only really approved my father marrying my mother because she was an only child and came from a wealthy New York family. As for me, I've been brought up a Christian so I can see things from both sides. Lots of the big banks and companies are run by Jews. They also run the theatre industry in New York and the movie industry in Hollywood. There's envy and anti-Semitism in the States, but what's happening here is pure madness. Hey, we're getting too serious. Come on, let's go and find a nightclub and get us a couple of dames."

They were to be disappointed.

Walking along one of the main streets towards the Alexanderplatz, the nightlife district, they saw on the opposite side of the street, three men in brown uniforms, kicking and shouting at a bearded elderly man lying on the ground.

"Come on," Ulrich urged, "let's go and help that old man."

Running across the street, they came up to the assailants and confronted them. Ulrich had seen the police in Vienna attack striking workers and even beating them up. Usually it was a confrontation between young men in large groups with even larger groups of police and militia. This looked different.

"Are you police? What are you doing?" Ulrich demanded.

"Who the hell are you?"one of the men shouted at him in a rough Berlin accent. "Are you some kind of Jew lover or what?"

Ulrich and Thompson were in a dangerous position. They were two to the other three. The other two men in uniform stopped kicking the victim and turned to face Ulrich.

"No," Ulrich said, "I'm not a Jew. I'm from Vienna and the police there don't treat anyone like that." He felt his blood rising.

"Oh, yeah?" one of them said. "Then why don't you two just clear off back to Vienna and let us get on with our work here."

One of the three, a podgy type with an achned, porcine face gave him a fat defiant smile. "Are you two poncies come to save the Jews? We'll have your lot locked up with this lot, I can assure you. The Führer himself has given us orders to clear Berlin of the scum Jews, homos and gypsies that pollute this good city." Another, whose uniform was too big for him, looking as if he had just left school, joined in the chorus of disapproval, cursing and swearing. The three carried batons and looked threateningly at Ulrich and Thompson.

Thomson turned to Ulrich. "Shall we hightail it out of here or have a go at these thugs," he said in English.

"I don't think attacking them would be wise," Ulrich cautioned. "They've probably got the law on their side. If they blow on their whistles we'll be outnumbered. Leave this to me."

"I know your chief," Ulrich said, addressing the three assailants. "Colonel von Wartenberg. He's a friend of my father. I shall tell him what I've seen you doing to this old man. You'll have to deal with him not me."

At the name of von Wartenberg, all three looked at each other. They were uncertain what to say or do. Slowly they moved away leaving Ulrich and Thompson with the elderly man. When the uniformed men had gone some distance along the street, Ulrich and Thomson approached the man. He was in a high state of agitation, shaking, his eyes filled with tears and fear, his breath came in short spurts. His long flowing beard was covered in spittle and blood was coming out of a cut above his eye. He was breathing heavily. It was obvious that he was in some pain and distress. He had difficulty in getting up. Ulrich and Thompson took him by the arms and helped him to his feet.

"We must get you to a doctor," Ulrich said.

"No, no! No doctor." He stammered in an anguished whisper. "I want to go home. I must get away from here. Those young brutes will be back. Even if they kill me, no one will care."

"We'll help you home," Ulrich reassured him. "Where do you live?"

"Not far from here. I'll be alright." He sounded nervous and confused.

"Please allow us to help you. Those fellows won't attack you again as long as we're with you."

Picking up the old man's broad-brimmed black hat that had fallen in the gutter, Ulrich took one arm and Thompson took the other and together they made their way slowly along the street. After a short distance, the old man led them down a side lane and stopped in front of an apartment block.

"I live here. You've been very kind to me. Thank you, thank you." He spoke in nervous staccato sentences. He clearly wanted to get away as quickly as possible. "I shall see myself upstairs. My wife is waiting for me." He pulled out a key, had difficulty in inserting it into the lock of the door, eventually succeeded and disappeared inside. The heavy door slammed noisily behind him.

Things did not get any better for the two young men. When they arrived at an ill-lit venue and descended some steps, they found themselves in a boisterous atmosphere filled with men in brown-shirts yelling out Nazi songs and leering at a young woman performing a striptease. After a few drinks and two other clubs, where they met the same uniformed clientele, Ulrich's appetite for a night on the town had evaporated. They returned to the Excelsior, where they exchanged addresses. Ulrich didn't think he would see Thompson again.

* * *

The next morning at breakfast Dieter was in a buoyant mood. "Well, today's the big day. We're going to show Herr Doctor Giersberg a thing or two."

He looked across the table at Ulrich.

"You're looking a bit glum, young man. Last night not go well, then?"

"It was an interesting experience."

Chapter 5

Vienna 1936

On a day of blue skies and sunshine, Ulrich and Ruth stopped at a small *Heuriger* in Grinzing on the edge of the Vienna Woods. The little wine tavern, just off the main street, had the usual green wreath hanging over the door. They sat down on one of the wooden tables, surrounded by laughter and the sound of clinking glasses, evidence that the customers loved the tart white wine made – so attested the bottles' labels – by the tavern's owner.

"I've told my parents about us," Ruth said. Ulrich had become accustomed to her occasional knack of making a laconic statement.

"How did they react?"

"They were surprised and intrigued. I suppose they took it for granted when I said I was meeting a friend, it was one of my female friends."

"Did you tell them that I wasn't a Jew?"

"Of course. I also told them that you were a Dreher."

"And?"

"They equate the name with an armaments factory."

"Is that all?"

"When you think of Krupp do you think of Herr Krupp and Frau Krupp and all the little Krupps?"

He smiled faintly.

"This little Dreher is now a big Dreher."

"They want you to come to the flat to meet them. If you join us for the meal on the eve of Shabbat, it might give you some idea of Jewish family life."

Although not far from the city centre, the Leopoldstadt district was not entirely uncharted territory for him. He remembered passing through it on the tram, when his nanny had taken him to the Volksprater, the huge amusement park, where he had gone up on the giant Ferris wheel. His recently acquired knowledge of Jews, however, gleaned from his growing close relationship with Ruth, made him muse that he was seeing the area through new lenses. Now on his way to meet Ruth's parents and family, he saw crowded workers' tenements, rows of small Jewish shops and Orthodox men, conspicuous in their trailing black coats, full beards, hanging sidelocks and wide-brimmed hats. Others were wearing yarmulkes, the traditional Jewish skullcap. He knew the district by its familiar name as the Mazzesinsel. Ruth told him that Mazzes was a kind of bread that Jews ate. What it had to do with the island formed by the Danube and its canal, was a mystery to him.

Despite the fact that it was early evening, the streets still bustled with activity, the numerous baker, kosher butcher, and greengrocer shops were still open. As the tram passed along Taborstrasse, he was impressed by the architectural magnificence of the fruit and flour stock exchange. Carters were shouting at their horses, young delivery boys, carrying baskets on the front of bicycles, wended their way among the crowds, some young boys and girls were picking up the horses' droppings and filling zinc buckets.

He knocked at the door of the Gitelmann flat. He hoped his inner agitation would not be obvious. Ruth answered it. Her eyes lit up at his arrival. She showed him into what appeared to be the sitting room and introduced him to her father, called Mati and her mother, Miriam. Miriam, a tiny lady with greying hair, made her excuses and disappeared. A gentle aroma of cooking pervaded the apartment.

"Mother's busy in the kitchen, getting the Sabbath meal ready," Ruth said as if reading Ulrich's mind.

The apartment's modest size took him by surprise, the pavilion at home was much bigger. There was an upright piano in one corner, on top of which were family photographs, a bookcase filled with books, a small writing bureau and a nondescript cupboard.

"I'm curious," Ulrich said. "The small oblong box fixed to the right-hand doorpost, what is it?"

"That's a mezuzah," Mati explained. "I put it up myself when we first came to this flat."

Mati was a small man with thinning auburn hair, a short beard, moustache and wearing a pair of thick spectacles. He could scarcely have reached his half century but appeared older. Ulrich noticed that Ruth had her father's eyes and his long tailor's fingers.

"Are you really interested?" Mati said.

"Dad, he wouldn't ask if he weren't interested," Ruth said.

"It's made of wood," Mati said, "and inside there's a small piece of parchment containing quotations from the Bible. It tells us that we must obey God's laws. 'Write the laws on the doorpost of your house.' It's one of our customs. That's from the Torah."

"The Torah is what Christians call Deutoronomy," interjected Ruth. "It's the fifth book of the Old Testament. It's a set of three sermons, delivered by Moses reviewing the previous forty years of wandering in the wilderness, and a detailed law-code by which the Children of Israel are to live in the Promised Land."

"Excuse my ignorance," Ulrich said, "I suppose I ought to know all that but I don't."

"The parchment is prepared by a qualified scribe," continued Mati, "and the verses are written in indelible black ink with a special quill pen. The parchment is then rolled up and placed inside the case. Come with me and I'll show you."

The two men, followed by an apprehensive Ruth, went back to the front door. Mati showed Ulrich the contents of the mezuzah.

"We fix the mezuzah to the doorframe to fulfill the mitzvah. This is a biblical commandment."

He picked up the delicately inscribed parchment.

"The verses comprise the Jewish prayer Shema Ysrael beginning with the phrase 'Hear, O Israel, the Lord your God, the Lord is One.'"

The little group returned to the sitting room.

"I'm afraid I'm totally ignorant of Jewish customs, Ulrich said. "They don't…"

"Teach you at school?" Mati said.

"It's just that we're brought up to think that everyone's like us. Christian, that sort of thing."

"What my father means," Ruth said, "is that we Jews know all about your religious festivals, Christmas, Easter and Pentecost, but

Christians know nothing about our religion and beliefs. After all, you can't read the history of art without some background knowledge of Christianity."

"I must admit I couldn't name any Jewish festival," Ulrich said.

The door of the apartment opened at that moment and four people entered, two men and two young women. Ulrich recognised Reuben. One of the women, however, bore a close resemblance to Ruth and he guessed that it might be her sister. Ruth made the introductions. It was her sister Rosa. The other two were introduced as David and Sharon Katz.

Ulrich felt self-conscious as if he were an intruder in the midst of this family chatter. To his surprise, they did not appear to be embarrassed by his presence. Silently he listened to their playful, friendly banter and laughter.

Turning to Ulrich, Ruth said, "David and Sharon intend to emigrate to Palestine with their young son Benjamin."

"Palestine? Why would they want to do that?" There was genuine astonishment in his voice.

"Because," David said, "that's our homeland."

"I thought the Jews left Palestine a couple of thousand years ago." Ulrich said. He vaguely remembered this from his classes in religious history.

"They did," Reuben said. "The Romans expelled the Jews and since then it's been the desire of some Jewish people to return. Especially among those living where they're being persecuted. Zionists want to found their own Jewish state where they won't be victims of religious and racial hatred."

"But Jews aren't persecuted here in Vienna," Ulrich said.

"Not exactly persecuted," Reuben said. "However, the anti-Semitism that's always existed is now being used by our own Austrian Nazis to make people hate and discriminate against Jews. Unless you're a rich banker or such, you feel you're a second-class citizen. Even doctors and lawyers are not exempt. Then there's the fear that the little monster over the border might take it into his head to swallow up this country."

"You really believe that could happen?" Ulrich asked. "Isn't that just a lot of talk?

"I might be a Jew, but I'm not a prophet." There was a noticeable tone of frustrated hostility in David's voice. "The

German Führer has said he wants to create a greater Reich, a Germany that will include Austria. Bring stability to his country. He promises to get rid of the dole queues. His followers here peddle the same propaganda. It's amazing the number of people, even educated people who believe this dangerous drivel."

"I must get more customers soon or I'll be soon joining the dole queue," Mati cut in. "Business is bad enough without some people deserting this country at the first sign of difficulty. It's easy when you're rich."

"We're not rich, you know that Mati," David protested, "but we're not going to stay here and find ourselves being persecuted if the Nazis take over."

"When you've all finished," Miriam said with a hint of frustration in her voice, "perhaps we can go to table and begin the Shabbat."

The table was covered in a white cloth, on which there were two candles. The other three men all wore black scull caps. Mati filled a silver cup with red wine and then spoke words in a language that Ulrich did not understand. Everyone poured water over their hands. Mati cut up one of the loaves which Miriam had brought in from the kitchen and gave a slice to each one including Ulrich.

"It's called challah bread. We eat it at Shabbat," Miriam said.

Mati passed the cup around the table. Ulrich took a sip of the rich red wine.

Family talk was the main subject of conversation during the meal. Then Ulrich spoke up.

"What are you going to do in Palestine?" he asked David.

"I'm not sure but the Yishuv, that's the Jewish community, are building a new garden city called Tel Aviv, just outside of the ancient city of Jaffa. They need architects. And I'm one."

"I still don't see why you want to go to Palestine if you want to escape anti-Semitism," Ulrich said. "You could go to England or America."

"Anti-Semitism is everywhere," Sharon said, "except in countries where there isn't a Christian majority. You don't find anti-Semitism in Muslim countries. Jews and Muslims lived happily together in Spain until the Christian Queen Isabella waged a war against both communities and threw them out."

"But Palestine isn't a Jewish state," Ulrich said.

"No, but the Balfour Declaration…"

Mati suddenly raised his voice.

"Oh for heaven's sake, I do wish you youngsters would stop going on about Palestine and Zionism and all that doom and gloom. All I want is to be left in peace and get on with my life. My two brothers fought in the war. One was killed, the other wounded, both in the Carpathian Mountains fighting the Russians. Miriam's brother and two of her cousins fought in the war. I fought in the Western Front in the same unit as that Führer fellow. Now he's the high and mighty Chancellor of Germany. So what? We've been part of the old Empire for hundreds of years. All this talk about being Jewish as if we don't belong here. Well, I belong here. I'm an Austrian citizen by birth and as much Austrian as anyone else. Jews have been in this part of the world since Roman times. In the old Imperial army there were at least a dozen nationalities, Hungarians, Czechs, Serbs, Slovaks, Slovenes. We got on alright together. Everybody tolerated everybody else. Now everything has changed. It was a bad day when they broke up the old Empire. They've never liked us all that much here but at least they don't persecute us like they do in Poland and Russia."

"You're right Mati," David said, "but things are changing. We've got these fascist bullies roaming the streets shouting anti-Jewish slogans. I'm sorry to say this Ulrich because you're the guest here, but Jews have become a target for all those who want to join Germany. They're the Christian majority. We're only a minority. I don't want to join the new Reich. I want Austria to remain separate but that's not going to happen. The Führer is Austrian and he's determined to annex this country as part of some kind of greater Reich."

"As for going to Palestine," Mati said, "it's not on, as far as I'm concerned. I'm a Jew and I'm not changing that, I'm Austrian and I won't change that. The Zionists and their friends think they can fix our problems by some kind of fanciful idea of becoming farmers in Palestine, a desert country. They're deluding themselves."

Silence descended on the table for a moment.

"My family," Ulrich said, "originally came from Bavaria but I don't think of myself as German. I'm Austrian. I don't want this country to be joined with this so-called Reich. Not everybody hates the Jews. I don't. Yes I did once but no longer. Then I met Ruth."

He looked across the table at her. Was she embarrassed? He didn't care. "Let me tell you something else." He then went on to relate his experience in helping the old man in Berlin. "I didn't come to his rescue because he was a Jew. I helped him because he was a fellow human being. Even if I'd known he was a Jew, I would still have helped him."

"That's most laudable of you," David said, but he made no effort to disguise a sceptical note that had crept into his voice.

"If only it were as simple as that." Reuben said. "The truth is a lot harsher. Although the Social Democrats have had a majority on the city council since just after the war, the state government is dominated by the clerical fascists. That is what they call themselves, and are proud of it. Two years ago, as you'll no doubt recall we had a minor civil war. Our clerical fascist government stripped the Social Democratic mayor of Vienna of his powers and gave them to the chief of police, who ordered his forces to attack the workers, who tried to defend themselves. The clerical fascists then called this a revolution when all that the workers were doing was defending themselves. When the army was called in and started to shell the workers' flats, it was all over. When a government calls in the troops to kill their own fellow citizens who only want to recover their civic rights, it has lost all moral authority, in my opinion."

"Reuben," intervened Ruth, "Ulrich is our guest. He's not here to listen to a political sermon."

Reuben looked at his sister.

"I apologise," Reuben said.

"Rueben does go on," Ruth said.

Ulrich was beginning to like Reuben. He was talking a language that he'd never heard in the Dreher household. The give and take of political argument was new to him. While he was listening to Reuben speaking, he remembered his meeting with Ruth in the Fine Art Gallery. Her brother had her passion and enthusiasm.

"It's alright," Ulrich said. "Perhaps I should take more interest in what is going on."

"You'll have to learn, Ulrich," Ruth said, "if you put eight Jews in a room, you'll get ten opinions. We are an argumentative lot."

"The only people to solve our problems are ourselves," David said.

"Problems? What problems?" Ulrich asked.

"He means the Jewish problem," David said. "There are two versions of the Jewish problem. The first version is that the Jews per se are a problem. That's the view held by the majority of our dear fellow citizens. Then there's our version which goes something like this. For the past couple of centuries, especially here in Austria, in Germany, France and the rest of western Europe, Jews have tried to become part of the society in which they lived. Did you know," he said, speaking directly to Ulrich, "that although we're only a small percentage of the total population, almost half the doctors, dentists and lawyers in this city are Jewish? That three out of the four Austrian Nobel Prize Winners for medicine were Jewish? We've always paid our taxes, taken part in the social and professional life and become good patriotic citizens. In other other words, we've integrated. Or, so we thought. Now, we see the rise of a nasty and dangerous anti-Semitism, which threatens that cosy picture of ourselves."

"Like you, Reuben, I'm a lawyer," Sharon said, "but I see Zionism as the only solution." She spoke with a lawyer's dispassionate conviction. "You're right. For the past hundred years or so, we've integrated or tried to integrate into the societies in which we live. Jews didn't think of themselves as being other than Germans, Hungarians, Poles, French. I agree with you. They were loyal citizens, paid their taxes, fought and died for their country. We knew that many people didn't like us, but at least we felt they respected us as fellow citizens. Now the time has come for Jews to waken up to reality, for things are changing. Jews have become the scapegoat – now there's a fine biblical term – for everything that has happened: the war, the deaths, family losses, the food shortages, inflation, the depression, poverty, unemployment, you name it, it's there, the list is endless. Do you think I like it when I see day after day, newspaper cartoons of balding, potbellied Jews with the huge hooked noses, bloody fangs, smoking fat cigars, portrayed as greedy bankers or money lenders? Do I look like that? Now we have this Führer, promising to wipe us all out. He's started in Germany. Opened these concentration camps. He said he's going to put enemies of the state in these camps. So who's first to be sent? Jews of course. The fascists here in Austria have made no secret about what they want. And they'll get it. That's why I'm leaving for

Palestine. We aim to create a Jewish state there. At least there we'll be safe."

Ulrich interjected to relate what Thompson had told him about Dachau.

"So it seems the reports we are getting from the Jewish Agency are true," David said.

"Excuse me, but what's the Jewish Agency?" Ulrich said.

"It's an organisation that's recently been set up to rescue Jews at risk and resettle them in Palestine. That's where we're going."

"I'm like you, dad," Ruth said, "I want to stay here. We can make a difference. We shouldn't try to mollify those who hate us. You don't have to be a Zionist to be a loyal Jew. I've been going to these groups where they are teaching children about our history and faith. It's amazing how many don't know much about their Jewish traditions."

Ulrich looked at the group around the table. He kept his gaze on Ruth. At that moment he decided that he would ask her to marry him. She was going to stay. She wasn't moving off to Palestine.

* * *

After dinner one evening, shortly after his meeting with Ruth's family, Ulrich summoned up the courage to confront his mother, feeling if he could win her over, his father's opposition might be weakened. They were in the orangery, which, with its colourful flowers and vibrant indoor plants, his mother preferred to the formal atmosphere of the drawing room.

"There's something I must tell you," he said.

"I hope you've not been following your Uncle Claus's bad example." She inevitably equated wrongdoing with her brother.

"You mustn't judge Uncle Claus so severely. He's my best friend."

"You know what your father thinks about him."

"I want to talk to you about Ruth."

"Ruth? Who's Ruth?" his mother asked. Her face was screwed up in genuine puzzlement.

"It's the girl who used to work in the Institute library when I was a student."

"Now I remember. But that's some years ago. Has she died or something?"

"No, of course not."

"I've a feeling that you're going to tell me something I don't want to hear." She paused. "Now I recall. She's a Jewess."

"Mother, you mustn't use that word. It's offensive."

"I'm sorry to displease you, Ulrich, but if that's what she is then that's what she is. So what are you going to tell me?"

"I've been seeing her since I finished my military service."

There was an uncomfortable silence.

"I was wondering why you were being so reticent these days."

His instinct told him his mother had already divined what he was about to say.

"I want to marry her."

"You what?" A gasp of astonishment accompanied this question.

"Want to marry her."

"Have you asked her?"

"Not yet. But I would like father and yourself to meet her."

"Ulrich, this is not good. Not good at all. I think you're being rather foolish. I did warn you. The Jews are trouble."

There was an ill-boding silence.

"You mean inconvenient. It's not going to look good socially. Is that it? It's not what she does that makes this awkward for you, it's what she is. Isn't that so? We Drehers and all our friends consider the Jews as second-class citizens. Father's moved all the company's accounts and investments out of the Bernstein bank, at the behest of the Nazi government."

"I don't like your tone, Ulrich. We've never fallen out and I don't want to fall out with you but if you persist in what I think is a very unwise decision I believe that's what's going to happen." She sounded hurt.

"If I ask her to marry me she may not accept."

"You delude yourself if you think she's going to refuse. What age is she?" Without waiting for an answer, she continued, "Young women of her age are looking for a husband. She won't refuse. I was just twenty when I pursued your father. My parents opposed it but I went ahead despite them. They eventually agreed. What we have here is a totally different matter. Jews are a separate race, a different religion. You're right. I admit, we don't like them. Our friends don't like them. Ulrich you can't do this to us."

"Father banked with a Jewish bank." Ulrich said, raising his voice. "He didn't think it wrong to take their money. This family's fortune began with money borrowed from Max, the Jewish money lender. Our so-called friends nearly all bank with Jewish banks. They invest in Jewish banks and put their savings in Jewish banks. If she were a Bernstein banker's heiress, I've no doubt father and yourself would approve."

"Stop, stop, for heaven's sake. Keep your voice down. If one of the maids hears, it'll be all over Vienna tomorrow."

"I'm sorry, mother, you can't see it my way. In any case, I don't really care what the rest of Vienna thinks or says. I'm going to ask Ruth to marry me and if she accepts then it'll make me the happiest man in this town."

"You'll be cutting yourself off from your family and all your friends. Has that occurred to you? You're going to give great pain to your father. He looks forward to the time when you'll take over the firm."

"I'm a partner in the business and I really don't see how my marrying Ruth, if she accepts, is going to change that situation. I've considered everything. Ruth is a Jew and she can't stop being a Jew. I accept that so why can't you?"

"Well, it's not just me, you know. There's the Church to be considered. If she were to take instructions from the nuns and convert to Catholicism there would be room for compromise."

"So my love for her has to be conditional? Is that it? Ruth hasn't put any conditions on my love for her."

"I'm sure she hasn't. She knows a good catch when she sees one."

"Mother, I pursued her not the other way round. I love her and want to marry her."

"If you continue in this way you'll pay a high price for your obduracy. You can't defy the Church."

"I'm wasting my time trying to convince you, mother. I really am."

He abruptly got up and walked out.

* * *

After a midday concert in the State Opera House, Ulrich and Ruth made their way by tram along the Karntnerstrasse towards the Danube Canal. Ruth talked about Mahler whose music they had just heard.

"He was a tortured soul, you know."

"Who was?"

"Gustav Mahler. Are you listening Ulrich?"

"Yes, but I really don't understand this kind of music. Strauss, yes. Mother plays Brahms and Beethoven. They've got some great tunes. I can whistle those. But this Mahler. I find him difficult."

"You'll get to like him. You might even whistle his tunes," she said with a laugh.

They reached the canal, sat down on a bench and watched the long barges, from which the barking of dogs could be heard. Smoke rose from the factories in Floridsdorf on the far side of the canal and river. It was a simple everyday event as if life could never be shattered.

Life has been good to me, he thought, but I'll not let my family stop me from marrying Ruth. I'm determined to have my own way on this. Come what may.

"What are you thinking Ulrich?"

"Ruth will you marry me? I love you and I can't think of life without you."

"I love you Ulrich and I want to marry you but there are many obstacles."

"The biggest obstacle are my parents. They'll have to put up with my decision whether they like it or not. I don't really care now." He paused. "I love you and I'll make them understand." There was a firm hard edge to his words.

She turned and held him tight. She kissed him firmly on the lips and he could feel her hot tears run down his own cheeks.

"We'll run off to America or Palestine," he whispered into her ear.

"You're a big silly." She laughed.

"Ruth, you and I are together now and no one is going to separate us. Not my parents and not the Church. No one."

Chapter 6

Vienna 1935

Ulrich's steely resolve was soon to be put to the test on an anvil forged between family and Church. The setting was a family Sunday lunch around the elegant oak dining table. There were only a few guests among whom was Monsignor Alfred Kirchmann, an auxiliary to the Cardinal Archbishop of Vienna, a well-known figure in the Drehers' social circle. The Monsignor had a Freudian habit of twisting his silver pectoral cross as if he were proclaiming he had two sides: one, the devout and pious; the other, worldly and secular. Middle-aged and prematurely bald, his red piped and buttoned cassock hanging loosely from his tall, lean frame, he had sharp, dark blue eyes and a prominent forehead. A semi-scowl and sardonic smile hovered on the sides of his mouth. He had written a critically acclaimed book about papal infallibility and ecclesiastical authority. Some spoke of him as a future Cardinal and, it was whispered, even considered him 'papabile', a possible candidate for pope. He had once tried to persuade an adolescent Ulrich to enter the diocesan seminary. 'With your family background,' he had said, 'you'll make a good priest.' But the young man politely refused the offer, the sterile fruits of a chaste celibacy being no substitute for the secret delights such as that offered by the Czech housemaid.

"Monsignor, how is his Eminence's health these days?" Elke asked. "I understand he's not been too well. Prayers were said for him this morning at High Mass."

"Indeed," the Monsignor said, "we're all praying for him. His heart has been troubling him for the past year."

"He must be sick with worry about all this civil unrest," Dieter said. "Take the events at Floridsdorf. If the workers had their way we'd all be followers of Stalin and his Jewish communist hordes,"

"You're right," the Monsignor said. "For the workers to plunge this country into a kind of civil war was unforgivable."

"What you're really saying, Monsignor," Claus said, "is that we've exchanged democracy for a fascist state. This city was the most democratic in all of Europe until the clerical fascists took over." Claus had just turned up uninvited to the lunch.

"Claus, I must disagree with you," the Monsignor said. "The Church has always considered democracy a dangerous concept. So-called democratic states act against the Divine interests of the Church. They do the work of the devil. France is a warning example. Thirty years ago under Emile Combes, France made a law separating Church and State. What was the upshot? Secular education. Thousands of Catholic schools were closed. The law put an end to the funding of religious groups. At the same time, it declared that all religious buildings were property of the state, it forced many religious communities to flee France. It was an open attempt to turn the people of France against the Church. The pope at the time issued an encyclical letter condemning this flagrant attack on the Church."

The Monsignor was an inveterate preacher.

"Fascism is hardly compatible with Christianity," Claus said in a nonchalant way.

"On the contrary, fascism recognises the Church's rights and authority." The Monsignor warmed to his theme as he proceeded. "I personally know His Holiness is aware that the greatest threat today is the Jewish Bolshevik threat. He sees that fascism brings order and progress, it unites the people against a common enemy. So-called left-wing intellectuals deride fascism. It's not the Church's business to interfere in politics but it's necessary for her to safeguard her position. When the workers take to the street shouting anti-clerical slogans and singing chants of hate against their fellow citizens, the Church can't and won't stand by and do nothing. Little wonder his Eminence has a bad heart!"

"I hope you don't believe your own propaganda, Monsignor," Claus said.

"Claus, please," Elke cut in. She looked at the Monsignor. "Monsignor, please excuse my brother's manners." Turning back to Claus she said, "Monsignor is our honoured guest so I think it wise we stop talking politics at table."

After lunch, the other guests left, Dieter retreated to his study with a close business friend and Gerda went off to play tennis. Elke, the Monsignor, Claus and Ulrich went into the orangery, which was full of sun and light, with large pots of hydrangeas and vases of lilies giving off a subtle aroma. Elke gave Claus hints to leave, which he ignored. A maid brought in coffee.

"Ulrich," Elke said, "have you come to a decision about that young woman, what's her name…?"

"Mother, she's not a what's her name. She's called Ruth. I've already told you." Ulrich raised his voice. There was defiance in his eyes. "And, yes, in answer to your question, I have come to a decision."

"Well?"

"I've asked her to marry me."

"You can't be serious!" His mother said with disbelief.

"I am and she's agreed."

"Does she intend to convert to our faith?" the Monsignor said, addressing Ulrich. His tone made the question sound neutral and innocent, as if he were asking Ulrich whether he was going to play tennis that afternoon.

Mother must have told the Monsignor that Ruth was a Jew.

"With respect, Monsignor, I really don't think that's any of your business," Ulrich said.

"Ulrich!" Elke exploded with anger.

"It's alright Elke," the cleric said in a soothing tone. "Ulrich is merely defending himself." He faced Ulrich. "However, I'm afraid, young man, that it is my business. As a senior member of the archdiocese, it's my duty to counsel and guide. When it comes to marriage the church has absolute power over its members. It's even enshrined in our state constitution. I should know. The Vatican appointed me its representative to draw up a concordat with the Austrian state, giving the Church a privileged position in the Austrian constitution. Besides, I'm sure that you must be aware that a Catholic cannot marry a non-Catholic. That's Canon Law, the Church's own law, which is above any state law. There's only one thing for it. This Jewess must convert or else there can be no marriage. I can arrange for the nuns to give her instruction."

"Jewess, indeed," Ulrich said. He was angry now. "You spoke those words as if Ruth were a tart."

"If you mean some kind of seductive biblical figure, a bewitching man-killing Salome, you exaggerate. The thought was far from my mind. I'm merely trying to help you to see a way out of your problem. If she abandons her false beliefs then all will be well."

"Why should Ruth abandon her own faith to become a Catholic? Would you abandon your faith, Monsignor?"

"You know the answer to that." A scowl creased his face.

"Right. So why should she? I don't see why Ruth should give up her faith just to satisfy the Church's laws, she's not bound by them,"

"No, that's true but you are."

"Am I? I was baptised without being asked. I didn't have any choice in the matter. You're caught in the net as soon as you're born. I want to marry Ruth and nothing is going to stop me." Ulrich's tone was defiant.

"Elke, do you mind if I smoke? It helps me think," Claus said.

"Yes, if you will." She sounded annoyed.

"As a semi-detached member of this family," Claus continued, blowing his cigarette smoke in a languid manner, "I've got some ideas about this matter."

"What are those, may I ask?" There was a supercilious note to the Monsignor's voice, but the lines around his eyes had sharpened.

"Bluntly speaking, Monsignor, I think you're wrong. You've just used the word absolute. But, the Church treats it like a piece of elastic in the interpretation of its own laws. It forbids divorce but agrees to annul a marriage. Annulment is merely a convenient euphemism for divorce. You know yourself, if people have money they can find a clever lawyer who'll argue their case before the Church authorities in Rome. The larger the sum of money the easier it is to get an annulment. There's a recent case where a member of the Italian royal family after a marriage lasting ten years got an annulment on the ground that the marriage hadn't been consummated. Yet she had three children by the marriage. It's called Jesuitical casuistry. Maybe that's because the celibate clergymen running the Church will sacrifice their so-called absolute principles when it's profitable or expedient." He smiled as he brought his cigarette back to his mouth.

The Monsignor sat glowering at Claus and twisting his gold pectoral cross between his thumb and forefinger. He ignored Claus and turned his attention to Ulrich.

"This woman is a Jew and I would like to remind you that Judaism continues to be hostile to Christianity. Let me explain the Church's official doctrine on the Jews." The Monsignor's voice took on a condescending tone. "It's based on the Bible or more precisely the New Testament. Matthew chapter twenty-seven, verse twenty-five, *'and the whole people said in reply, His blood be upon us and upon our children.'* The whole people here means the Jewish people, His blood means the Blood of Christ. It could not be clearer. It is a core doctrine of the Church, and has been for centuries, that imputes to the Jewish people a burden of collective guilt. The present Holy Father, his Cardinals and the hierarchies all over Europe hold firmly to this teaching. Only recently the Archbishop of Warsaw, Cardinal Hlond, whom I know personally and highly respect, issued a pastoral letter to be read out in all the churches of Poland in which he wrote that the Jews are waging a war against the Catholic Church, that they're in the forefront of Bolshevik forces, they perpetrate fraud, practise usury and deal in prostitution."

"Monsignor," Claus said, interrupting the cleric's flow, "I think you missed your vocation, you have unlimited talents for a stage career. I'm no biblical scholar and theologian, like your good self I did not attend the esteemed Gregorian University run by our dear friends the Jesuits, my theology has no God, but I think you're being cavalier with the facts. Correct me if I'm wrong, but weren't the Gospels written several decades after the events they portray? The small Christian community was made up of Jews who had chosen to break away from the main Jewish community and set up their own. So they were written with the aim of demonising their former co-religionists with the stigma of being to blame for the death of their leader and founder Christ. To my agnostic ears the words sound crudely anti-Semitic." Claus lifted his head in a gesture of careless defiance. "I think," he continued, "that the Church would do well to cut those verses out of the Gospels."

"You sound more like a religious philistine than a heretic," the Monsignor said, his eyes blazing with indignation.

"I prefer to think of myself as a rational onlooker. One doesn't have to subscribe to the Nicene Creed to be a good person. What really worries me and other right-thinking people is that the Church's position is dangerous as well. Simple-minded people and not so simple-minded could easily conclude that Jews should be punished for this. That could and has led to violence. Does the Monsignor, then approve of the recent violence being used against Jews in Germany?" He gave the cleric a searching look. "The Church should look into its soul and take responsibility for this climate of hatred against the Jews. When some poor Jew who has committed no crime, is battered to death on the streets by a vicious mob, the Church can't raise its hands in horror and say 'not my fault'. *'Qui tacet consentire videtur'* as the Romans said, silence is consent. The Church will have as much blood on its hands as the perpetrators of the crime."

The pectoral cross was given another twist.

"You're being melodramatic." There was venom in the Monsignor's voice.

"So why haven't the bishops and clergy in Germany forbidden their congregations from taking part in the burning of synagogues, the boycott of Jewish shops? The Jews haven't broken any laws, still less been convicted by any judicial procedures."

"The Church wants," the Monsignor said, "our Christian communities to be rid of the Jewish threat. Jews must be made to purge their guilt. As a Christian, I've an instinctive repugnance of Jews. I see them as the enemy, a Trojan Horse within. The Church could not allow a Jew to go through a marriage ceremony without converting. For a Jew to take part in a Christian act of faith would be blasphemy, a sacrilege, a mockery of the Catholic religion and of its holiest articles of faith. The Church is the Bride of Christ. Christ should not be defiled by a Jewess." He paused. "From a quite different angle, I would say that by marrying a Jewess, Ulrich will be adulterating his German blood."

"At last," Ulrich said in derision, "I'm glad you've mentioned my name. I'm not some passive bystander here. I love Ruth and intend to marry her." He threw the Monsignor a baleful look. "I know the Church likes to think of us all as children. Even calls us its children. Well, I'm no longer a child. Nothing you do or say will stop me."

"I'm inclined to agree with Ulrich," Claus said. "The difficulty is the Church itself. It preaches freedom of conscience but it's never been comfortable with personal freedom and liberty. By its very nature it's undemocratic. Monsignor, you've admitted yourself it doesn't like democracy. No doubt that's why it's much more comfortable dealing with dictators like Il Duce and his new found friend the Führer and our own lately deceased Chancellor. His predecessor as Chancellor, a Catholic priest no less, spent most of his time undermining this country, the most democratic state in Europe. As far as the Church is concerned the state can do what it likes as long as it respects the Church's privileges. That's what your precious concordat was all about, wasn't it Monsignor?"

"That's a most cynical view, Claus," the Monsignor said. "The Church was founded by Christ himself and, I repeat, is above any state laws. That's why we run the schools and why the clergy can't be prosecuted in a civil court. The Concordat means this state agrees with the Church's position. Ulrich cannot marry Ruth and nothing is going to change that." He waved his hand in a gesture of dismissal.

"It's seems to me that the real reason for your opposition, Monsignor, is that she's Jewish," Ulrich said. "If she were a rich Protestant princess, the Church would soon enough accommodate her. But, she's not. She's Jewish. You've just told us the Jews must purge their guilt. What for? Oh yes. Now I remember. They were supposed to have killed Christ. That was two thousand years ago. Even if it were true, which personally I don't believe, it would mean that blame for a criminal act can be passed down from one generation to the next ad infinitum. That in my opinion is an insidious and dangerous ethical principle. Yet, as you've just said, that's precisely what the Church proclaims as a fundamental moral doctrine." He paused for a moment. "How strange that in the most devout Catholic countries, such as Poland, our neighbour to the north, where the local clergy literally rule their congregations, Jews are regularly persecuted and burned out of their homes. And, what does the Church do? Nothing. Christ preached love but when it comes to Jews the Church makes an exception."

"Can we please get back to the main point," Elke intervened. "Ulrich, I beg you. Please rethink your decision," she pleaded. "If you're so determined about marrying her, you could ask her if she's willing to convert."

"I've made up my mind, mother. I really don't care what the Church thinks."

"I'm afraid that's not the end of the matter," interjected the Monsignor. "Even if she becomes a Catholic, she'll have to give her agreement in writing that any children of the marriage will be baptised and brought up in the faith."

"I've no intention of changing my mind," Ulrich said, bristling with anger. "If we have children they'll not be baptised. I'll make sure of that."

He stormed out of the orangery muttering to himself, *'they will not do this to me'*.

* * *

His head throbbing with anger and frustration, Ulrich found himself on a volatile afternoon wandering the city streets, without aim, oblivious to people and places, carts and horses, cars and trams, the noise and bustle, the squally rain soaking him to the skin. The monumental edifice of Stephansdom, Vienna's great Gothic cathedral, rose in front of him and some power, like a magnet, drew him in. Entering through the Giant's Doorway, he walked slowly down a side aisle of the immense cathedral. He sat down and looked around. The statues glared down at him from their high plinths above the baroque altars. The aroma of incense from the midday High Mass still hung in the air. The choir was practising Verdi's 'Te Deum' but Ulrich did not feel like praising God.

Hearing a baby's cries, he turned around. At the baptismal chapel near the south tower he saw a group around the stone font. A newborn, unaware of what was happening, was being initiated into the Church. *'Extra ecclesia nulla salus,'* Father Hahn once said, 'outside the Church there is no salvation.' What an intolerable thing to say, thought Ulrich.

Although it was not ringing, he could hear the peal of the great Pummerin bell inside his head. It awakened the past.

It was in this cathedral I was baptised, made my First Communion and first confession, been confirmed by the Cardinal himself, attended Christmas midnight masses, took part in the grim

Holy Week penitential services, when the faithful were enjoined to feel remorse for misdeeds and sins, and on Good Friday to pray for perfidious Jews. As a child, I didn't know the meaning of the word perfidious. A priest had told me that it meant treachery.

The Church rules my life. It controls my very secret inner thoughts through the confessional. I can't do what I want to do, to say what I want to say, read what I want to read unless I fall in line with what the Church tells me to think, do, say or read. I've fallen in love. Now it's opposed to my marrying the woman I love. Why is the Church so unbending? In my catechism classes they taught me that love is the greatest virtue. Now I'm told that I should not love Ruth because she's a Jew. The Church seems to want us to hate the Jews. Well I won't. I love Ruth and I'm going to marry her. If the Church expels me, so be it. I won't be dictated to."

Gradually an inner peace and calm possessed him. He wiped tears from his eyes. He got up and, without looking back, left the cathedral.

* * *

Later that day, without returning home, he went to see his Uncle Claus. Claus was in evening dress. He was going, he explained, to a performance of Strauss's *Die Fledermaus* at the Volksoper.

"Uncle Claus, what's wrong with them all?" Ulrich protested loudly. "They act as if I'd murdered someone. I've fallen in love and want to marry. Is that wrong?"

"Your mother worries about you, Ulrich," Claus said. He went over to his drinks cabinet, chose a bottle of wine and poured two glasses. "She's devoted her life to the family. And especially you. No one has given you more support. It's this Jewish matter." He raised his glass. "Here's a toast to Truth." He sipped his wine. "The Church doesn't help. That Kirchmann is so self-important. He deceives people. Behind that ascetic and imposing figure lurks a scheming and worldly careerist, consumed by his own dissimulated ambition. He's got a reputation for being cunning. On becoming an auxiliary bishop, he ruthlessly manipulated the removal from office of a popular archdiocesan Vicar General, who had opposed his appointment. The word pontificate must have been coined with him in mind. If only he mouthed dreary platitudes that he didn't believe in, like some little shifty politician, it wouldn't be so bad. Except he's deadly serious. Which makes him dangerous. In this matter he says what he means and means what he says."

"You mean they'll excommunicate me?"

"No doubt. It's in the rule book. All that nonsense about racial purity is political gobbledygook. The Church should steer clear of politics. Its founder said so. Render to Caesar, and all that."

He paused.

"When the Church wants you to do something right, it asks for your integrity, when it wants you to do something wrong, it asks for your loyalty. The Church does more harm than good. Like Janus it faces both ways."

"What do you mean?" Ulrich said.

Claus gave Ulrich a long measured look. "I once fell deeply in love." He stopped and drew on his cigarette.

"I thought you were the eternal batchelor," Ulrich said, a surprise in his voice.

"It wasn't a young woman but a beautiful Italian man. He was a writer and poet. He wore his hair long and openly scorned 'manly sports'. As a well-known figure in Rome and Florence, his published work was first ridiculed then condemned by the Church as being immoral, effeminate and would have an evil effect on young men, making them into dandies."

He looked firmly at his nephew to gauge the effect of his words.

"You mean..."

"Yes, I do mean. I'm homosexual. Don't be shocked. It a great deal more common than you think. Especially among the higher social ranks. I should know. In any case, class doesn't exist among us. You take your friends where you find them. The general with the corporal."

"Uncle Claus I'm not shocked. As far as I'm concerned, it's your own personal business."

"That's very tolerant of you, Ulrich. Very liberal. What really troubles me is the hypocrisy. The Church preaches a high moral code. Moses coming down from the mountain. Yet it lives with ambiguity. The Church condemns homosexuality yet I know some members even of the hierarchy who are active homosexuals. One of them once laughingly remarked to me 'I'm celibate but not chaste'."

"Tell me this Uncle Claus. Why can't two people of different religions marry and have children? Why does the Church have to interfere? Surely both can practise their beliefs without harm. What the children believe should be a matter of bringing them up and letting them choose."

"I agree. There was a time when the Church would have burned you at the stake for saying that." Claus laughed. "It might be a joke now but, by God, it's not so long ago that they actually did that. I'm an agnostic when it comes to religion."

"Uncle Claus, all I want to do is marry the woman I love. I'm no threat to the Church. I don't dispute any of its dogmas or its doctrines. I'm not denying Eternal damnation, the Holy Virgin, Armageddon or the Hereafter. I'm not some kind of sixteenth century reformer like…" He hesitated while he tried to remember a name.

"Like our dear Martin Luther or that gloomy Swiss, John Calvin, perhaps?"

"So why does the Church act like this? Telling people how to lead their lives?"

"It's called social control. The Church uses people's faith to ensure obedience. For the Church, truth is an artefact of the will. One of the departments of the Roman Curia is called the Holy Office. The Holy Office of the Inquisition to give it its full title. The ghost of Torquemada still stalks the Vatican corridors. The Church uses it as a tool to silence dissenting voices. That tells you everything you want to know about the Church's attitude to truth. The parable of the shepherd with the flock of sheep is not wrong. The clergy treats its laity like sheep. Conformity is a virtue, dissent a vice. This present clerical fascist state here in Austria is the model that the Church feels most comfortable with."

"I don't care a damn about the Holy Office." Ulrich's voice rose. "The Church can go to hell for all I care. I'm going to marry Ruth whatever the Church thinks. My family had better get used to the idea. I told her I would marry her in a synagogue if necessary. Why should she be made to change her faith because of me? She hasn't told me to change mine. Where does it say in the Gospels that I can't marry a Jew?"

"It's ironic. Christ was a Jew, he was circumcised as a Jew, died as a Jew and was buried as a Jew. His mother was a Jew, all his disciples were Jews. Peter was a Jew, Paul was a Jew. All the first Christians were Jews. They thought of themselves merely as another Jewish sect." He paused and lit a cigarette. "If I keep talking like this I might become one myself."

There was a long silence.

"I've made up my mind," Ulrich said, his face taking on a determined expression. "I'm going to marry Ruth."

"I'm glad. It's your life. Don't let the Church boss and bully you about. I'll always take your side."

* * *

The next morning in his office in the Dreher company headquarters, Ulrich was reviewing the plans for the new extension to their Vienna factory that would hold the special lathes to mass-produce his sub-machine gun. The builders were due to begin work in the next few days.

The inter-office telephone rang.

"Ulrich, can you come through." It was his father. "I must have a word with you."

His instinct told him what the likely reason was for the call. In vain he tried to recall the previous afternoon's ill-natured verbal exchanges. He picked up the plans but then put them down and went along the corridor to his father's office. As he entered, the signals were all there. His father's taut expression, the twitch in his left eye, always a sign of strain and stress, the arched eyebrows, tight lips, the furrows on his forehead more deeply etched than normal, the way he was sitting rigidly with his hands clasped in front of him. All bore evidence that this was not going to be the usual business matter.

"Sit down," his father said in a surprisingly affable tone of voice. There was a long pause. "Your mother has told me about your idea to marry this young Jewish woman. Perhaps you would like to give me your version."

"I don't suppose my version is any different from mother's."

"Perhaps not but I would still like to hear yours."

Ulrich felt like a pupil in the headmaster's study, endeavouring to give an account of a playground fight. His mind the previous afternoon had been so full of turbulence and agony that his present recollection was confused. He gave a vague and discordant outline of what had transpired.

"You realise, of course," his father said, "any personal decisions you make will, one way or another, affect this business." He sounded like reason itself.

"I can't see what my love for Ruth has to do with the company."

"Let's leave love out of it for the moment, shall we? It's an emotional word. Let's focus on the matter of your intention to marry her. I take it, that's your intention, is it not?"

"Yes."

"Ulrich, you're my heir. Besides a lot else, you'll inherit this company. So what you do is of importance to me. Your decision to marry comes top of the list. It's not the 'what' that counts but the 'who'. In this case a Jewish woman."

"I can't see the relevance of that."

"That's the problem. So let me explain. If you marry a good Catholic girl there's no problem. She would be the same religion, have the same values we have, she would be acceptable to the family, our friends and, most importantly, the Church."

"I thought you might get around to that. As I told mother and the Monsignor, I'm not going to allow the Church to dictate to me."

"You don't seem to understand. The Church is not only important, it's everything. You cannot, I repeat, cannot marry this Jewish woman. That's final."

"I'm still not going to be controlled by the Church. Falling in love and wanting to marry a good woman, and Ruth is a very good woman, has to be the most wonderful thing a man can do. Father, please I beg you, invite her to the house, meet her. Judge her for yourself."

"I don't have to. My mind is made up for me by the Church. There's lots of things that I would like to do but is forbidden by the Church. If you're a Catholic you belong to the Church. There's no escape. You can't be partly Catholic any more than you can be partly pregnant. It's all or nothing. I'm not a theologian nor am I devout like your mother but I'm one hundred per cent Catholic and I do exactly as the Church says and demands. And that applies to you as much as me. So forget this marriage plan of yours. You'll never get the Church's blessing." He fell silent.

"Is that everything, father?"

"Look why don't you take a few days off. A few weeks if necessary. Go to Munich or Berlin or Switzerland. Even Paris. London. New York. Anywhere, but just give yourself time to think. You've got to change your mind. That is certain. You can't persist in this crazy idea to marry this Jewish woman. If you do, I don't want to think of the consequences."

Ulrich left his father's office, his mind made up. 'I'm not going to give up Ruth. As for the consequences, I'll have to live with those. My great-grandfather Ahren arrived in Vienna with nothing and succeeded. I'll do the same. Ruth is my future.'

Chapter 7

Vienna 1935

The uncared-for condition of the staircase leading to Rabbi Levitansky's flat made Ulrich feel ill-at-ease. An ancient lift out of order, missing wall tiles, peeling wallpaper, a broken gas light mantle on one landing, all spoke of a venal landlord thinking only of rents. The stairwell smelt of fried onions, stale tobacco and penury. Cathedral House, where the clergy lived, suitably staffed by liveried servants, was, reflected Ulrich, a palace compared with this rundown apartment block.

Together with Ruth, he was on his way up to meet the rabbi.

"I've been to see the rabbi," Ruth had told Ulrich at their previous outing.

"What did he say?"

"He wants to meet you."

"What shall I say?"

"As little as possible."

They arrived on the fourth floor. Ruth knocked gently at the door to the rabbi's flat, which was opened by a small, elderly lady dressed in black, her grey hair done up in a severe bun. Introducing herself, she said she had an appointment and asked to see the rabbi. They were shown into the study. Ulrich, looking around, was impressed by the scholarly atmosphere of the room with its shelves of books in German, English and other languages and scripts. The range of subjects told an elequent story, bibles, religion, literature, history, politics, biography, a host of reference books and encyclopedia. Despite their wealth, the Drehers had hardly invested in books. In his home, there were two bookcases, one with English novels, the other with German, both of which belonged to his well-read mother.

Rabbi Samuel Levitansky came into the room. Ulrich saw a countenance that exuded an aura of spirituality. He was a fine-looking, grey-bearded man with a powerful jaw and deep-set, dark, keen eyes, a deeply furrowed brow, and stooped shoulders as if he were burdened with the weight of two thousand years of Jewish diaspora. The rabbi came across as a man of religion wholly different from the senior prelates invited by his parents to lunch and dinner parties who had made little impression on him. He recalled their talk, mainly men's political gossip, support for the clerical fascist government, asking Dieter advice about investments, boasting of their ten year, *ad limine,* visits to the Pope, dropping names about this cardinal or that, telling risqué tales that, he surmised, could only have been gleaned from the confessional. They could all take their drink.

The rabbi's eyes, animating his penetrating gaze and peering out of the strongly carved head, seemed to be searching into Ulrich's inner being, weighing him up, seeking to understand what had brought this young 'gentile' into his study. His expression spoke of one who instinctively knew the human condition to be tight, narrow and fragile. He came straight to the point.

"Ruth tells me that you want to marry her. Do you?"

The enquiring voice was gentle yet firm and reassuring.

"Yes, sir."

"Don't be afraid. You can call me rabbi. I would prefer that. I must tell you, as I've already told Ruth, that mixed marriages, by that I mean a marriage between a Jew and a non-Jew, are not always a blessing."

"The Catholic Church forbids them," Ulrich said, "that's why I'm here."

"What I mean is we Jews don't encourage people to convert to our faith," the rabbi said, ignoring the reference to the Catholic Church. "Unlike the Christians and Musulmans we don't proselytise. We don't send missionaries out to Africa, Asia or India to convert the natives."

"I've not thought about conversion," said Ulrich.

"Rabbi, I'm sure everything you say is true," Ruth intervened. "My question is, are we allowed to marry in the synagogue? I don't want to marry him outside our faith."

"I'm happy to hear that. Yours is not an unknown problem. Regrettably, a number of Jews do marry outside the faith. In Germany alone a quarter of those getting married choose a non-Jew as a partner. That's a very large percentage. Unfortunately, many Jews have become secularised in order to feel more integrated into the society in which we live, wearing their religion like a comfortable fur coat in winter. The Jews in this city are no exception. Instead of practising their faith, some indulge in these meaningless arguments in which Zionists, Liberals and Orthodox spend their energies and money on political struggles. The problem is deeper than you might appreciate. I don't accept the Zionist contention that Jews constitute a separate political nation, that we must all go off to Palestine and occupy it in the name of Judaism. Yes, as a biblical aim it's understandable. However, as a practical proposition, as far as I'm concerned, it's unworkable in this modern world. We can't put the clock back two thousand years. Nor do I accept the notion that we're merely a religious community. Being Jewish transcends religion and includes being a member of the Jewish people. As a people we transcend borders. Regretfully, we're a divided community and I'm afraid that the forces of fascism will overcome us unless we gather around our faith."

"My question still is," insisted Ruth, "can I marry Ulrich in the synagogue?"

"The short answer is yes. In theory. In Judaism, marriage is basically a civil contract. This is unlike the position of the Catholic Church, which regards marriage as a purely religious contract. From our point of view, I can see no hindrance between yourself as a Jew and Ulrich as a Christian getting married as long as the 'I do' is given in mutual free will. However, mixed marriages often tend to weaken our community, which is becoming beleaguered every day. Our fellow Jews in Germany at this moment are suffering as never before. The Nazi persecution of our people is destroying the efforts of centuries of trying to integrate in the societies in which we live. I fear for our future. Dante's *Divine Comedy* tells us where we are, namely, in the vestibule of Hell. I must warn you Ruth, that being married to a Christian will not save you if the worst comes to the worst."

"What do you mean?" she said.

The rabbi stood up and took a book from one of the shelves.

"Look at the title of this book. It's called *The Handbook of the Jewish Question*. It's so unbelievably anti-Semitic. Yet it has gone through numerous editions since first published. It's read by many of our own fellow countrymen. It's become a Nazi handbook. It drips with pure racial hatred and it points to one group of people only. The Jews. Although it does not state it in as many words, its deep historical origins are based on the proposition that the Jewish people are Christ-killers. It talks about eradicating us as a people. This is so… so incredible in these modern days. I fear the future and so should all of us."

"I'm very aware of the anti-Semitic feelings of many in this country," Ruth assured him, "but I want to become Ulrich's wife because I love him and he loves me."

"I understand that. Love is the cement that holds a marriage together. But life is going to get difficult for us here in Vienna, with the clerical-fascists and their friends ruling."

"Surely marrying Ulrich will strengthen my life not weaken it?"

"Perhaps." The rabbi turned to Ulrich. "Have you told your parents? I can't think they will approve."

Ulrich described his relationship with his family and their objection to his proposed marriage to Ruth.

"You might think that my concerns have to do with religion," said the rabbi. "In a way they do, but my own objections have little to do with religious dogma or rules or regulations. It goes much deeper. Someone who doesn't know our people, Ulrich, cannot properly understand the difficulties that Ruth and you are letting yourselves in for. There was a time, before the Great War, when I thought we Jews were fully accepted citizens of this great civilised country. Germany and Austria have not been like Poland or Russia where honest old Orthodox Jews lay on the streets of their shtetl with their black hats and long pigtails intact but with their brains battered out by mobs seized with pogrom madness." The rabbi paused. "Anti-Semitism is woven into the very cloth of Christianity."

The rabbi's words reminded Ulrich of the old Jew whom he had helped in Berlin.

"What we're seeing in Germany today," added the rabbi, "is another chapter in our bloodstained history." He picked up a piece of paper lying on his desk. "Here's a letter I received only a couple of days ago from a dear friend of mine in Berlin. It tells of the horrors and crimes being committed against our people, of synagogues being burned to the ground, the Torah bells and scrolls defiled and smashed on the ground, cemeteries being vandalised. For what? Death is now commonplace and suicides take place on a daily basis. Yet not a single Christian voice is raised in their defence."

Ulrich held up his hand.

"With respect, Rabbi, why are you telling me this? This is Vienna. Not Germany. I've no intention of living in Germany. If you agree to our marriage, we'll be living here not across this or any other border."

The rabbi shot him an anxious look.

"You may think that but history is against you. Before I returned here to care for my one surviving elderly parent, I was the rabbi of a synagogue in Berlin, so I know the German mind and what kind of people they are. I'm not referring to living in Germany. I mean that Germany will come here. The Führer has said he intends to bring Austria into what he grandly calls the Greater Germany. Everything he ever wrote or said he would do, he has done and made legal. No one has opposed him."

The rabbi stopped speaking and looked out of the window at the rain and the drab tenement building on the other side of the street. "When I was young," he continued, "I had a cousin, an engineer, who worked in German East Africa, building the railway from Dar-es-Salaam up to Lake Tanganyika. He told me about a place called Serengeti, a vast plain where every October millions of buffalo, wildebeest and zebra travel from the northern hills, crossing the Mara River in pursuit of the rains. These animals merely follow their instinct. They can't do otherwise. In the same way the German people have lost a mind of their own. They're blinded by a herd instinct. The Führer intends to wipe out the Jewish people one way or another. The German herd is supporting him in this." He spoke in a firm but gentle voice without any recrimination.

The rabbi sat down and there was a grim silence as Ulrich and Ruth absorbed what he had just said. Ulrich looked at the Rabbi and saw centuries of suffering in his deeply lined face. He wanted to reiterate that Austria was a free independent state and the rabbi's fears were unfounded but he refrained. So anxious was he to get his permission to marry Ruth, he held his peace.

"It's better you marry within the faith, Ruth. You both have my blessing."

* * *

Some weeks later, with rabbi Levitansky officiating, the marriage ceremony took place in the Norman-arched synagogue on Pazmanitengasse. The whole Gitelmann family and a host of Ruth's friends were present. The Dreher family stayed away. Dr Goldstein and his wife were there. Ulrich's fear of being isolated disappeared when Claus turned up, wearing a tan herringbone linen suit, looking dashing, debonair and sporting a small but richly embroidered skullcap. Nervous and fearful of making a mistake, Ulrich was intimidated by the strange surroundings, the arrangement of the seats and the chuppah. Standing under this bridal canopy and wearing a white skullcap, he listened to the unfamiliar language of the prayers, the music and the cantor's singing.

Later both Ruth and himself signed the Ketuba, the beautiful ornate marriage contract. Ulrich followed the Jewish tradition of stepping on a wine glass, symbolising the fragility of human happiness.

"Religion is theatre," Claus whispered to Ulrich at the reception party afterwards. "If you have to play a part, do it well." Much to Ulrich's relief, he also charmed the gathering, joined in the dancing of the Hora with graceful skill and agility and made himself popular, especially with the ladies and the children.

* * *

The train arrived late in Venice. The young couple, however, were heedless of time. Claus, who saw them off, had paid the journey and the honeymoon in advance. "The famous bronze horses were stolen," he remarked to Ulrich, who didn't understand what he was talking about.

As the train passed through the Eastern Alps, Ulrich gazed out of the window, seeing not the Austrian and Italian countryside but rather revisiting in his mind the painful, noisy, angry break with his family.

I seem to have died and been reborn again. Yet how can I not feel pain and sorrow at my mother's begging tears, at my father's unmistakeable mixture of anger and frustration? The Monsignor was present at our final meeting, a version of Rasputin, lurking in the background and exercising, an evil influence. He soon let slip his pastoral mask and changed his once solicitous words into dire forebodings.

'I think that you're being very foolish. You realise, of course, if you carry out your intention to marry the Jewish woman outside the Church, you'll be committing a mortal sin. You will cut yourself off from the Church.'

I wasn't fooled by his sanctimonious smile nor intimidated by his menacing tone.

'The Church does not tolerate dissidents. I warn you to remain anchored to Mother Church. If you cast your moorings, you'll find yourself drowning in a sea of troubles.'

I'd heard his florid and dramatic language before, when he delivered the Lenten Sermons at the cathedral. Claus remarked, 'Vienna has now its own Savonarola'.

I can still hear my mother's voice. 'You'll be cutting yourself off from your own family, friends and the Church. Don't be foolish and throw everything this family has given you for the sake of some dreadful Jewess. It will be some weeks of joy followed by years of ashes.'

Mother, please don't speak like that of the woman I love. I'm part of this family and don't want to break with it. My decision gives me great pain but I don't regret it. I love Ruth and I want to share my life with her. Besides, I'll not have my life controlled by the Church, being told who to marry and what to believe. The Monsignor here is trying to frighten me by saying I'm not free to leave the Church without dire eternal penalties. I'm not as well-educated as he is but I know when my personal freedom and liberty are being taken away from me.

So I walked out of the house built by my forebears from the proceeds of the sales of guns. Now I'm an outcast from my own family. What really riles me is that I've been a faithful Catholic all my life yet the Church would not accommodate me. When I told Claus this he remarked, 'the Church's blanket is too small for your bed.'

Venice became a week of great happiness for Ulrich. He had Ruth to himself every day and night. He made love to her with great tenderness. They joked, laughed and played childish games in the intimacy of the hotel bedroom. They took trips on gondolas. They went to the opera and a concert. As usual Ruth proved a reliable and thoughtful mentor. She had brought a notebook and made sketches of several of the palaces and churches. He was astonished: she had read the guidebook with admirable thoroughness. When they visited the Basilica of St Mark, she pointed out the four bronze horses over the central portal, remarking that they had been looted from Constantinople during the Fourth Crusade.

As the week passed, Ulrich began to realise how circumscribed his own inner life really was. Compared with his new wife, he felt he was an ignorant Christian peasant. His young Jewish wife was not only knowledgeable but enthusiastic about the architecture and sculpture of the imposing churches, the splendid palaces, the slender and elegant bridges. The red and gold interior of the Levantine synagogue, with its intricately carved wooden pulpit, impressed him. Ruth told him that Jews were only allowed to settle in Venice at the end of the fourteenth century when the city was at war with a neighbour and needed money from Jewish moneylenders.

"They had to get permission to leave the ghetto by day," she explained, "and were obliged to wear a yellow circular piece of cloth stitched on the left shoulder of their cloak in the case of men, and a woman had to wear a yellow scarf."

"So anti-Semitism existed even then."

"It's taken us centuries to win our emancipation."

"It looks threatened again."

"Only if we don't stand up for what is ours by right."

"If you want, we could always join David and Sharon in Palestine," he said.

"I hope you're not serious," she said, "I don't want to go to Palestine. Can you imagine me working on a farm every day picking oranges and tomatoes or whatever they grow out there? I'm Austrian and remain Austrian. I don't have any other country. My ancestors saw their fathers, husbands and sons fight bravely and die for Austria." Ruth was in one of her fiery moods now. "And I'm still determined to stay there."

Ulrich quickly put his arms around her waist, picked her up and swung her round several times. He kissed her.

"Ruth, I love you even more when you're like this," he said with a laugh.

* * *

One morning they were sitting sipping coffee outside a small café.

"Hi there!" said a voice in English. It was Bill Thompson, the American journalist. Ulrich stood up and introduced him to Ruth. Thompson eyed Ruth with absorbing interest.

"I'm always pleased to meet a beautiful lady," he said. "So what brings you to Venice?"

"Always the journalist asking questions," Ulrich said. "We're here on our honeymoon."

"Wonderful. Congratulations."

"What brings you to Venice? I thought you were in Berlin."

"I'm still based in Berlin but I'm on my way to Rome to interview Mussolini. I thought I'd stop over here for a short break."

"Do you like it in Berlin?" asked Ruth in her halting English.

"That depends. For me as a journalist it's the centre of things politically. The Führer is making all the news. Then I'm scheduled to cover the Olympic Games. So it's sure good to be in the right place."

"I couldn't bear to be in the same city as that Jew hater of a man."

"That sounds a personal comment," Thompson said.

"It is. I'm Jewish," she retorted.

"No offence meant, ma'am."

There was an embarrassed silence for some moments.

"Look, why don't you two come to dinner with me this evening. Catch up on the news. Celebrate your marriage."

Ulrich agreed willingly but Ruth was more reluctant. Bill Thompson got up and left them. When he had gone, Ruth stood up and just walked away. Ulrich ran after her. She pushed him away.

"Leave me alone Ulrich. I want to be alone for once."

"I'm not going to quarrel with you Ruth but..."

"There are no buts, Ulrich. I just need a little space."

With that she left him, standing gazing into the waters of the Grand Canal. He spent a miserable afternoon, full of remorse, cursing Bill Thompson. Their first unspoken quarrel. The time passed slowly and not even the appearance of Mussolini would have caught his attention. He wandered through the city not knowing where he was going, crossing bridges and nearly missing his footing along the narrow walkway along the side of some unknown canal. He thought he might get drunk or throw himself into a canal. He finally reached the hotel where they were staying and made his way up to their room. Ruth was lying on the bed. She was asleep but he could see that she had been crying. He knelt on the floor and gazed into her face. He took her hand and gently kissed it. She woke up and put her arm around his neck.

That evening, Thompson, exuding American charm, met them in the hotel lounge.

"I must apologise for this afternoon. I forgot my good manners. I'm a journalist not a diplomat and my job is to tread on other folk's toes."

"If that's your job then I suggest you stand on the Führer's toes, if you can get near enough," Ruth said with a gentle laugh.

"That's not so easy. This guy is surrounded by so many armed guards you wonder what's he afraid of."

"Our own chancellor was assassinated recently by Austrian Nazis," Ulrich said, "so I suppose he might even fear his own people."

"In America we've got anti-Semitism. All sorts of clubs exclude Jews. But it's an individual choice. Jews don't have to join such clubs. In Germany the state itself is making war on the Jews. The Führer has made the country a legal no-man's-land for Jews. They're barred from teaching, journalism, radio, theatre and movies. They're not even allowed to work in the public services. They've had their pension rights taken from them. Worst of all, the state has withdrawn their citizenship. A Jew is now a mere subject without rights. Fundamentally if you're a Jew you're literally stateless. Speaking as a lawyer and not as a journalist I would say that's a very dangerous position to be in."

"What exactly do you mean?" Ruth said.

"Let me explain. Back in the States we've got what's called the colour bar. Negroes are segregated from whites, this is legal in the South. They're not allowed to share the same parts of a bus as whites. Even education is separated into schools for whites and schools for blacks. Restaurants, bars, hotels and a host of other places, and would you believe it, drinking fountains, are reserved for whites. A black man can be lynched for stepping out of line, and risks his life if he tries to do something as brazen as voting. In the North we don't legally exclude a Negro, except de facto, we do. But that could change if there were a challenge in the federal courts. The federal law still upholds the Negro's right to be a citizen. In New York and Chicago and elsewhere, a black man has the right to have recourse to the courts. He may or may not win his argument but he's got the right and the American constitution will uphold that right. In Germany, and that's the crucial difference, the Jew has no legal rights or protection at all. The consequences of that are frightening. If I were you Ruth, I'd be praying that the Germans don't annex Austria because if they do…" At this he drew his hand across his throat.

"Is this what you're telling your readers back in America?" Ruth said.

"Afraid not. America has become isolated from Europe. Most Americans don't really care a fig what's happening in Europe. Except that is for a few, a very small group, who can't understand how the nation that produced Beethoven, Goethe and Schiller could elect such a thug as their leader. For the majority, Europe is far away and they're much more interested in what comes out of Hollywood. Movies counteract the worst aspects of the Depression. They give people an escape from daily life. Folks don't want to hear about Hitler and the Jews. So I write travel articles about the beautiful regions of Germany, especially the wine producing areas, the progress in building new highways and houses for the workers. That's how I get published. Every now and then I can pen a political piece that might attract attention. Such as interviewing Mussolini."

"What do the Americans think about the Führer and Il Duce?" Ruth asked.

"They admire them."

"Admire?" Ulrich said, his voice full of astonishment.

"Of course. They believe that fascism is the great bulwark against communism. The majority of Americans don't like Jews, they see them running Wall Street. They believe Jewish bankers are responsible for unemployment. So when I write about the persecution of the Jews in Germany, editors just throw the copy in the trash can."

"I hope Austria stays independent," Ruth added. "I think that people are foolish to think that the Nazis will bring an end to poverty and unemployment in Austria."

"The French have a saying." Thompson said, '*un ventre vide n'a pas d'oreilles*', 'an empty stomach has got no ears'. Whoever promises the unemployed work and food will have their votes." Thompson looked at his watch.

"Sorry you guys, but I must be off. I've got a train to catch first thing tomorrow. Lots of packing to do. You must come to the States sometime. If you decide to come, I'll give you letters of recommendation."

"I'd like to go and watch Babe Ruth and the New York Yankees," Ulrich said. "Uncle Claus says that baseball is a great game."

"And big money. Some of these players earn thousands of dollars a year. More than the president."

"Why is it that men are so obsessed with sport?" Ruth said.

"It's better than war and fighting each other," Thompson replied.

* * *

On their return to Vienna, Ulrich found a flat for Ruth and himself and settled into married life. The social columns of the Viennese papers had ignored his marriage. Being socially ostracised did not disturb his sleep or peace of mind. There was, however, a dark cloud. Much as he tried, finding employment was difficult, having turned his back on his own family. Other doors, too, were closed to him. It was clear that the business community in Vienna was reluctant to offend his father, one of their most important members, by offering his estranged son work. The Jewish community hardly knew him. With his Institute diplomas and record as a prize student, he knew that, had he approached any of several German companies, one would probably snap him up. He realised he could not follow that road. This period of soul-sapping idleness had started to undermine his self-confidence. Most of his friends politely shunned him. He went to see Claus.

"You're job prospects aren't so good then?" Claus said.

"Closed doors. Ruth must worry she's married an unemployed gun-maker."

Claus let out a chuckle.

"A day out in Graz is just what you need."

Fine rain was falling as Claus's red Italian sportscar burned up the distance to the capital of the Styrian province. The landscape of deep ravines and dark forests suited Ulrich's present mood. He did not doubt that he had made the right decision but worried about being isolated.

They arrived in the city in time to have a stroll around the Old Town with its numerous gabled houses with their stucco decorations. Crossing the main square, they sat in the late summer sunshine outside a restaurant within sight of the Town Hall. Claus ordered a bottle of local red wine. It was served by a bald-headed young man with a small moustache.

"Arms are coming into their own these days." Claus poured out two glasses of wine. He lifted his glass. "Here's to some good luck for you."

"What's this about arms?"

"There's a war started in Spain, as you no doubt realise. General Franco is a fascist. He wants to topple a democratically-elected government. Il Duce has his eyes on Africa, wanting to ape the British and build a colonial empire, except his will be a fascist one. Sending in his army to defeat a bunch of ill-armed natives in Abyssinia. He's a blustering imbecile. But a dangerous one. The Germans have re-occupied the Rhineland. Wars all over the place. Everybody needs arms these days."

Ulrich eyed his uncle suspiciously.

"Unfortunately, Uncle Claus, I've plenty of time to read the newspapers so I'm well-informed about what's going on. I would prefer to be earning my living. Why have you brought this up?"

"As I see it, Europe is dividing into the fascist states and the democratic ones. Sooner or later there's going to be a clash. The Führer has grandiose plans for his Third Reich. No overseas colonies for him. No. He wants to conquer the world."

"How do you know that?"

"It couldn't be clearer. He's said so himself."

"So what has this got to do with me?"

"I went to a reception at the British Embassy the other night. And, it gave me an idea. Of course, the embassy is not what it used to be. I remember the old one. During the time of the Empire when an invitation was a social must. Our great city was the cultural, economic and political heart of central Europe. A very important place in those days. Britain was the world's greatest and wealthiest power and naturally its embassy occupied a prominent position. It was a grand and elegant Gothic Revival masterpiece and, obviously, the British wanted to affirm their might and self-confidence."

"A proud lot the British," Ulrich said with a laugh.

"It was very impressive to see statesmen from all over Europe foregathering in the magnificent, well-appointed rooms, to discuss, deliberate and debate important international affairs and treaties. I can't count the diplomatic functions, dinners, balls and receptions I went to. That's what I admire about the British, it was all meticulously organised and carried out with punctilious observance of protocol. The British always surpass everybody in that sort of thing."

"Did my parents go?"

"Quite a lot. Your father always had an eye for business opportunities."

"Interesting was it?"

"In a way yes. The displays of pageantry were designed to impress the rest of Europe with Britain's imperial power and dominance. A First Secretary once boasted to me *'We're the modern heir to ancient Rome.'* I got to know the diplomatic staff. London, by that I mean the British Foreign Office, set the regal tone that pervaded the embassy. There was an underlying kind of boast about the place. The British never stopped telling us continentals how impeccably honest and incorruptible they were. Which I must confess was more or less true although it appeared a little condescending. They used to brag in a diplomatic way that Britain only intervened in European affairs to keep the balance of power between the warring factions. One ambassador told me that Britain was very much the European nanny keeping the peace between her quarrelsome and unruly charges. The word Waterloo was, metaphorically, carved into the very fabric of the embassy."

"Thanks for the history lesson. Now what's your big idea?"

"A little touchy are we? My idea may yet save your financial skin young Ulrich."

"Well, what is it?"

"Your sub-machine gun. Remember you told me you'd made some kind of deal with the German government and there was no other gun like it on the market?"

"As far as I know."

Claus sipped his wine. "I was thinking that there might be another opportunity. My proposition might let you off the unemployment hook. There's only one country that would be likely to stand up to the Führer. Britain. Look at it like this. Russia is out of the question. In any case, Uncle Joe would probably double-cross you. I'm not sure about the French. Politically, they're very unstable at the moment. Now the British. They've begun to rearm and I think they may well be interested in your little gun. It's worth a try."

"Wouldn't that be treason?"

"Of course not. Have you forgotten you're partly British. More even than the British royal family. One-eighth or is it one-sixteenth, I can't remember. You've got Scottish blood in your veins. Not much, but just enough to salve your conscience."

"I don't know anyone at the British Embassy."

"You don't but I do."

Chapter 8

Vienna 1935

Ulrich rang the front door bell of the British Embassy, now housed in a former insurance building down a side street close to the Ringstrasse. This was but a shadow of the opulent building of the former imperial era as described by his Uncle Claus. It was answered by a uniformed commissionaire.

"I've an appointment with a Mr. Henderson," Ulrich said.

He showed Ulrich into a grim, unwelcoming room off the main hallway and told him to wait. The room contained a row of old-fashioned chairs with faded red covers and on the wall were framed photographs of a balding and bearded George V, wearing a scarlet military uniform, with his stiff, generously-bosomed and superbly bejewelled Queen, as well as pictures of Buckingham Palace, Windsor Castle, Balmoral, the Canadian Rockies, Sydney Harbour Bridge and the India Gate in New Delhi. The setting and the scene exposed the delusion of the imperial flummery, a case of shabby clothes underneath a faux fur coat.

Ulrich sat down musing to himself.

Should I be here? Am I being disloyal? On the other hand what is loyalty? Father didn't think he was being disloyal when we sold my design to the Germans. Then again, he considered himself as much German as Austrian. I'm Austrian not German. I've no loyalty to Germany. It was a business deal and this is a business deal. The English aren't our enemies. We aren't at war with them. In any case, I've got some Scottish blood in me. Mother's rather proud of her Scottish blood. I wonder if I should let Mr Henderson know my British connections? No, I suppose not.'

The door opened and a middle-aged man entered. Although tall, he walked with a slight limp, had dull grey eyes and was bald. He gave an impression of being tired of life, of someone who had expected higher things but found himself in early middle age confined to the diplomatic backwater that Vienna had become.

"I'm Henderson," he announced in a non-committal tone. "I'm sorry, Herr Dreher, if you've been kept waiting. I was in a meeting. Perhaps if you might follow me, we can go somewhere more convenient to talk."

Henderson led the way up to a first-floor room. He ushered Ulrich into a small office, where they sat opposite each other with a desk in between. The desk top was bare and gave no hint as to Henderson's exact position. He gave Ulrich a fixed look that said, 'you have my attention but not for long.'

"Herr von Juggardt," Henderson said, "gave me a little of your background and your reasons for wanting to see someone here."

"Have you known my Uncle Claus long?"

"Several years, in fact. We met at a function when I was posted to Washington. That was in the late twenties, before the Wall Street crash. Later we lost touch but when I came here as First Secretary we renewed our friendship. So, what can I do for you?"

Ulrich was struck by Henderson's use of the word 'friendship'. Henderson and his Uncle Claus were friends not just acquaintances. He related briefly his time at the Technical Institute, his design for the sub-machine gun and the making of the prototype. He quickly glided over the breakdown in relations with his father and leaving the company.

"The reason I've come here is to find out whether the British government would be willing to buy my design for a sub-machine gun. I've brought a copy of the design with me," he said, pointing to the briefcase.

"I'm not an engineer," Henderson said, "so I'm not in any position to judge this matter. However, a number of questions of a general nature spring to mind. Who actually owns the patent?"

"I do. But, I made over the legal rights of sole production to the Dreher company."

"That of course is not an insoluble problem. Speaking as a layperson in these matters, I venture to suggest that anyone wanting to manufacture this gun could approach the company to get a licence from them. Has this design and the prototype been bought by anyone else?"

Ulrich then spoke of his visit to Berlin and the meeting with Giersberg. He stressed the secret nature of the contract between the German government and the Dreher Company.

"I've made modifications to the original design," he added. "I could resubmit the design to the patent office."

"Herr Dreher, I'm not familiar with the subject of patents and legal rights of production. I'm sure there's someone in this embassy who is. However, I would be less than candid if I didn't tell you that HMG…"

"HMG. What does that mean?"

"His Majesty's Government. You must excuse the abbreviation. It's the term we employ. The British government has obligations under a number of treaties to further the process of disarmament. We believe that arms and war will not solve the tensions in the world." Henderson's eyebrows went up and down, and the furrows on his forehead appeared and then disappeared as he spoke. "Hence, I think that we would not be interested in your design for a gun – even modified. I'm sure you'll find your own government is officially of the same view. When countries fail to adhere to their treaty obligations they lose credibility." He paused for a moment.

"Britain never fails its treaty obligations," Henderson continued. "We've no intention to rearm. On the contrary, there is a strong popular voice in Britain against rearmament. I would like to be able to help you, Herr Dreher, but I can't."

Henderson gave Ulrich a polite smile, shook his hand and led him back to the main door. Outside, Ulrich bristled with anger at being so peremptorily rejected. He hardly gave me five minutes of his precious British time, he said to himself.

* * *

A week later, an envelope was pushed under the door of Ulrich's apartment. Inside was a short typewritten note in English asking him to be at the Stephansdom, at the tomb of Emperor Friedrich III. It gave a time and date. The note was simply signed 'S'. The note had an aura of mystery that intrigued him.

Ulrich had not visited the cathedral since the day he had confronted his family with his decision to marry Ruth. A black-cassocked priest wearing a biretta was walking up and down a side aisle, his lips moving silently as he recited his breviary and a nun was arranging flowers on the High Altar. Ulrich passed a white marble statue of Our Lady with a beatific countenance, head encircled by a halo of golden stars and at her feet lay a crushed serpent. He remembered singing the Sicilian Mariners Hymn, '*O sanctissima, O piissima, Dulcis Virgo Maria!*' O Most Holy, O Most Pius, Sweet Virgin Mary. The saccharine words stuck in his throat. His religion, he thought, was now reduced to faded memories.

He approached the Apostles' Choir, where the Emperor's tomb lay, a large creation in pinkish Salzburg marble. As he stood gazing at the misshapen hobgoblins attempting, Ulrich mused, to wake the emperor from his eternal sleep, he heard a voice behind him

"You must be Herr Dreher," the speaker said in English. "I'm Jim Smith."

Ulrich turned round to confront the newcomer.

"I was expecting Mr Henderson," he said, surprised.

Jim Smith, was middle-aged, of medium height and build. He was casually dressed in a dark brown suit and old, well-worn black shoes. He ignored Ulrich's reference to Henderson.

"I was told I might find you here," he said. He didn't say who had told him. "It's odd how we must lower our voices in a church. Are you a believer?" The tone in which the question was asked suggested to Ulrich that Smith was indifferent as to the answer.

"I suppose so."

"I'm Presbyterian myself. Sorry, that should be 'was'. Church of Scotland. You like this rococo style?" He pointed towards a nearby altar, invested with statues of chubby, naked angels.

"You mean the decorations on the altars and tombs?"

"Just so."

"I've never thought about it. I've been brought up with it. It's always been here."

"I don't like all these fancy elaborate embellishments, stained-glass windows, pretty statues, altar paintings. My Presbyterian soul recoils from all this frivolous rococo, it's too papist, too foreign to my strict kirk upbringing and way of thinking. I prefer the stark austerity of the gothic structure rather than the flamboyant and ornate opulence of this Papal Roman Baroque interior. It smells too much of absolute power and wealth. I understand it was inspired by the Jesuits." He waved his chin around in a gesture taking in the whole edifice. "The Reformation wasn't just a reform it was a revolution. Then again, I suppose I'm prejudiced."

"I'm sure you haven't brought me here to talk..."

"Church architecture? You're right. I haven't. My apologies. Why don't we go and have a coffee. I know just the coffee house not far from here."

Jim Smith looked relaxed as he sat sipping his coffee. He lit up a small Havana cheroot but did not offer one to Ulrich.

"You're a designer, so I'm told." Again, he didn't say who had told him.

"Mechanical engineering. I've designed all sorts of things."

"I'm into books myself. In fact, I run a small English language bookshop here in Vienna. You'd be surprised the number of locals who speak English. It's not much of a living but I get by. I like books. You read much? German I suppose."

"Books, I mean novels don't interest me much. I'm a precision engineer. I prefer working with machines and engines, that sort of thing."

"Well, every man to his last as the old cliché goes. As a matter of fact, I'm on the lookout for a book on machine designs. You wouldn't have any would you? In German, I mean." He picked up his cup. "I say, the Viennese do make damn good coffee. I've found that the further east one travels the better the coffee."

"I've a few books on mechanical drawing and designing, if that's what you're looking for."

"The thing is, I've a client who's willing to pay well for an engineering design even if it's not in a book. You get my trend?"

"Mr Smith what exactly are you looking for?"

"I'm on the lookout for the design of sub-machine gun."

"Did Mr Henderson tell you about me? He's the official I saw at the British Embassy."

"Henderson? Don't know anyone of that name. No, the fact is, old boy, my client actually lives in England. He mentioned that I'd find you here. You wouldn't have the drawing with you, by any chance?"

"No. I didn't know what this meeting was about."

"Of course not. Silly of me really. Look, if you like you could come to the bookshop and we could discuss matters. I might interest you in a book or two. I stock serious books but on the whole I sell mainly novels. Most of my customers are students and women. They've more time on their hands I suppose. The women I mean. Poor husbands have got to earn the daily bread. They like romance. It's amazing how Jane Austen and the Brontes go down a treat."

Ulrich was finding it difficult to keep up with the way Smith switched from one subject to another as if to throw off balance the person to whom he was speaking. He couldn't quite get the measure of Smith, who gave an impression of easy-going affability and charm.

"I don't think I'll be buying novels. Can we discuss the matter of the sub-machine gun?"

"Well, not quite here. It would be better at the bookshop."

"Is there anything else you would like to know?" Ulrich said, a little irritated.

"Sorry, old chap. I tend to go on a bit. A bad habit of mine. Part of the patter I use to get customers interested in books. Here's my card."

Smith pulled out a leather wallet and produced a small business card. Ulrich looked at it and noticed it only carried his name and the address of the shop. No telephone number.

"Do you speak German?" Ulrich asked.

"Sort of. I prefer to speak English rather than bad German. Most of my customers prefer to speak English. Must oblige the customer." He pulled out a hunter watch. "Good heavens is that the time? Must run. See you at the shop some time."

Smith suddenly stood up, picked up his coat and was gone before Ulrich had time to say goodbye. Ulrich ordered another coffee and sat for some time retracing his conversation with Smith. *Was that his real name?* Smith's offhand manner and denial of being acquainted with Henderson made him suspicious. The fact he did not say who his client was, bothered Ulrich. He thought he should have questioned him more closely about his shadowy client and his obvious knowledge about the existence of the sub-machine gun. The next time they met, he was determined to be on alert and vigilant.

* * *

Some days later, Ulrich decided it was time to pay Jim Smith a visit. The English language bookshop was situated near the university. He looked round and hesitated before entering. The door gave a peal of bells when he opened it.

"Ah, Herr Dreher," Smith said, with a welcoming smile, "like the bells? The sound's based on Big Ben in London. Though I dare say you already know that."

"I don't. I've only passed through London and that was when I was a small child. I would like to visit. Perhaps some day."

"Jolly good. Why don't we adjoin to my office?"

The office, at the rear of the bookshop, was small, smelling as much of cheroots as of books, and consisted of a table, two decrepit chairs and shelves crammed with books and magazines. There was an out-of-date calendar showing a picture of the Thames and the Houses of Parliament. The atmosphere of the room reminded Ulrich of Rabbi Levitansky's flat.

"Excuse the mess. I've got to check these books over. People read them and bring them back for sale. Sell more that way. Keeps the money coming in. Take this," he held up a well-worn book. "Now this is by a fellow called Maugham. All the rage. Been in and out a dozen times."

He faced Ulrich and gave him a long measured look.

"So you'd like to visit London? I think the opportunity might just have arisen. The client I mentioned when we last met, would like you to go to London. Take your drawings with you. It's safer than the post. All expenses paid. So, no problems on that score. What do you think?"

"I'll have to consider it." Ulrich remembered the previous meeting with Smith, who had outwitted him.

"I wouldn't wait too long if I were you, old sport. Those Czechs in Prague are a pretty smart lot. You wouldn't want them to steal the march on you. Would you?"

"What do you mean?"

"Get there before you."

"No."

"That's it then. Look here's an envelope." Smith opened a drawer and drew out a brown envelope. "This has got rail tickets, English money and instructions for when you get to England. Oh, by the way, you go via Switzerland and France. Avoids Germany. Can't have the old Hun peering into your affairs can we?"

"Who's your client? I must know before I accept this envelope." He was determined not to be caught out again by Smith. "I don't want to get myself involved with some kind of gunrunner."

"No chance of that, old chum. My client is of the highest reputation."

"I would still like to know who this client is. I don't want to undertake a fool's journey. I'm not prepared to hand over my drawing just to anyone." There was a firm tone to his voice.

"Good for you. I like spirit in a young man. Bit like myself actually. The fact is, you'll find out when you get to England." His voice took on a sharp edge. "You'll have to work things out for yourself, if I may say so. You didn't come to this bookshop by accident."

Ulrich stood looking first at the envelope then at Smith. It was clear that Smith was not going to venture much more. He realised that he was treading water much deeper than he had anticipated.

"When would you like me to go?"

"It's not me, old chap, who wants you to go. It's the client. As soon as possible. I guess you can manage that."

"I don't know London."

"Not a problem. My client will take good care of you. You'll enjoy London. Coffee's not so good but then you can't have everything can you? I say, can I interest you in a book? No, I suppose not." He held out his hand. "Good luck. I'm sure you'll not regret this."

Later, Ulrich realised that his days of political innocence were over. He was nervous and uncertain. When he told Claus of his encounter with Henderson and Smith, his uncle's reaction was simply to advise him not to say anything to anybody. 'Not even Ruth. Especially not Ruth. If you tell her anything, you inevitably put her in possible danger. For people like Smith and Henderson, the seal of secrecy is as sacred as it is for the priest in the confessional.' When Ulrich told Ruth he was going to make a business trip to

England, she gave him a perceptive look. 'Going to sell your design to the English?' she said.

* * *

It was a warm day when Ulrich arrived in London. The two-day journey from Vienna was broken by a short overnight stay in Paris. He had no trouble passing through the customs examinations in crossing the several border frontiers, the Swiss and British officers were strict but courteous. Only the French were rude, confirming his schoolboy prejudices. Arriving at Dover after an uneventful Channel crossing, the boat train - he had the compartment to himself – wended its way through the gentle English countryside. He felt himself being seduced by the soft and beautiful landscape, filled with laden apple trees, so strangely different from the dramatic mountains and thick, dark forests of Austria. His own history lessons at school often painted the British as a nation unable to be revolutionaries.

Suddenly the compartment door opened and a man came in followed by a woman and two children, an adolescent boy and a younger girl.

"Is here empty?" the man asked in a hesitant voice.

"Yes," Ulrich replied.

The man turned and spoke to the woman in German.

"Pardon my intrusion," Ulrich ventured, speaking in German, "but are you German?"

They all looked at him with silent fear in their eyes.

"Yes," the man said. "I take it from your accent you're Austrian," he added, more as a statement than a question.

"Yes. That's true. So what brings you to England?"

"We're not coming here to England. We're on our way to the United States. We're going to Liverpool to catch a boat."

"Why didn't you sail from Bremen or Hamburg?"

The man looked at him suspiciously and did not reply. Ulrich surmised who these people were.

"My wife's Jewish," Ulrich volunteered in a breezy manner, "although I'm not. We were married in the synagogue in Vienna."

Neither the man nor the woman said anything. Ulrich began to feel embarrassed. He wondered what to say. It was clear that they did not trust him and given the circumstances he didn't blame them. The two children sat rigidly quiet, gazing at him, fear in their eyes.

"Have you been to Berlin?" the man finally asked.

"I was there last year," Ulrich replied. "I wasn't impressed."

"What do you mean?"

Ulrich briefly related his encounter with the uniformed thugs on the street, telling them how he had helped the old Jewish man.

"Things have become impossible now," the man said. "By the way, my name is Vogelstein. Professor Doctor Vogelstein."

"Are you a medical doctor?"

"No. I'm – I was – a professor of high energy physics at the University of Berlin. My research is in a new subject. It's called nuclear fission. And now I'm nothing. I'm German but not German. I've lost my job, my career, my house and my possessions. But I've my life, my family and my freedom." He paused for a moment. "The Nazi state has robbed me of my citizenship, declared me and my family stateless. In other words as far as they are concerned we are non-persons. My family has been German for hundreds of years. I've Berlin in my blood. Now, suddenly they don't want us. I'm one of the lucky ones. Through friends I've got a post at an American university. The Führer and his friends will come to regret this."

"Why do you say that?"

"Because most of the professorial staff at the physics faculty of the University of Berlin were Jews. We are, or rather were, researching the possibility of splitting the atom to produce power which in turn would produce electricity. It's many years away but it's certainly possible. Germany is at the forefront of this research. Now they'll have lost all those capable of achieving real results. I'm taking my talents and knowledge to America. It's a shame. It's more than that. It's a tragedy. I love Germany. I love its cities, its countryside, its music, its literature, its language, its culture, its work ethic. And now?" He held up his hand in a gesture of despair. "Madness has infected the German people. They've lost their wits. They've lost their soul. They've had their brains removed by the Führer without realising it. They think they've elected a benign Parsifal who's going to free them from their economic straits and redeem their pride. Instead, they've become ensnared by a belligerent rabble-rouser." He paused for a moment. Anger blazed in his eyes as he delivered this indictment.

"This man hates us," he continued, "burns our books and destroys our art. The Nazis have looted our synagogues and desecrated our cemeteries. This maniac has created a repressive police state and we Jews are his main victims. For us Germany has become a country of fear. We're accused of being the cause of all Germany's woes." His voice was filled with distress. "One day the German people will pay a high price for this."

His wife turned to him.

"Darling, calm down. This gentleman is Austrian not German." Her voice sounded nervous.

"I apologise," he said to Ulrich, sullenly.

Doctor Vogelstein sat glum and silent for the rest of the journey.

Arriving at Victoria Station, Ulrich bade farewell to Doctor Vogelstein and his frightened family. Any remnants of self-reproach about his present mission had long disappeared. His chance encounter with the ex-professor of physics further confirmed that he was doing the right thing for his own Jewish family.

* * *

The Water Garden hotel in Kensington was small and discreet. Ulrich could see no sign of either water or a garden. The receptionist, an elderly man with a stammer, recommended a restaurant called Gilbeys as having the very best of English food.

As he sat by himself at a corner table, Ulrich recalled Professor Vogelstein's tirade against the Nazis. He looked at the other diners. The English dined quietly, he observed. Voices were restrained, politeness obtained. It was as if he were in a church and even a faint whiff of incense seemed to hang in the air.

I wonder if these well-mannered English are capable of doing the things the Berliners have done to the Jews. Would they persecute and drive into exile their best brains, burn synagogues, smash gravestones? Would they create a police state? Would these people even tolerate one?

The next day he took a taxi to the address in London, Smith had given him. It was a nondescript building at one end of Curzon Street. A brass plate next to the entrance announced that it was the 'Department of Ancient Monuments'. Ulrich was puzzled but, nonetheless, presented himself at the reception. This consisted of a long desk, behind which stood a couple of men wearing dark-blue uniforms.

"I'm not sure if I've come to the right place," he said hesitantly to the men behind the desk.

"And who might you be, if I might ask?" one of them said.

"My name is Dreher. Herr Ulrich Dreher."

"German are we, sir?" There was a scowling tone in the voice, antagonism in the eyes.

"No, Austrian."

"I see. And what might your business be here, sir."

"As I've already said, I'm not sure if I've come to the right place."

"That, of course depends on what you want, doesn't it, sir?"

Ulrich was fast losing patience.

"Look, I've a letter of introduction. It's addressed to a Mr Lionel Jerrold."

However, he didn't hand over the letter. Instead he looked at the man and waited for his reaction.

"Mr Lionel Jerrold? You'd better wait here, sir, while I make some enquiries. Can't have any old Tom, Dick and 'Arry through these doors, can we now, as I'm sure you'll appreciate, sir."

He got up and disappeared through a rear door. The other man said nothing, engrossed as he was in a newspaper he was reading or pretending to read. After several minutes, the door opened again and the uniformed man reappeared.

"Herr Dreher, if you would follow me please, sir."

Ulrich was irritated by the man's frequent use of the word 'sir'. There was a sharp astringent sting of insolence in it. He followed him through the door and up two flights of stairs, along a corridor. They stopped in front of an unmarked door. Ulrich was ushered into a large room occupied by a long table with several chairs on each side. It resembled the boardroom of the Dreher factory in Vienna but that was where the resemblance ended. This was a soulless place with no carpet on the floor, no paintings on the wall and high curtainless windows.

A short while later the door at the end of the room opened and two men appeared. Both wore dark pinstriped suits.

"Herr Dreher," said the older of the two men. "Pleased to meet you. I'm Jerrold and this is my colleague Mr Bethell. Please sit down. I hope you had a pleasant journey from Vienna. You found the hotel alright then?"

Jerrold had a lean, handsome face with a moustache and a friendly demeanour. He gave off a slight odour of gin.

"Our friends in Vienna have informed us about your drawings. Perhaps you might tell us about yourself?" He didn't say whom he meant by 'our friends'.

Ulrich repeated most of what he had already told Henderson and Smith, including the contract between the Dreher company and the German government, but took it for granted that Jerrold knew a lot more. At the end of his explanation, Ulrich decided to do a little questioning himself.

"Are you connected with the embassy? I mean the embassy in Vienna?" he asked, addressing Jerrold.

"Not exactly. They did inform us about your offer to sell your design for a sub-machine gun. The British government is interested. Personally I'm not an expert on guns. A couple of our people who are, will be here this afternoon to inspect the drawings."

"May I ask you, Mr Jerrold," Ulrich said, "why your department is called the 'Department of Ancient Monuments'?"

"Because that's the main department occupying the building. My outfit, merely takes up one part."

"What outfit is that?"

"We do all sorts of things. Like looking after requests such as yours. You could say that we're a clearing house. Government calls on us when it has a particular problem and we find ways of solving the situation. Take your case. You approached the embassy with a request. Embassies are Foreign Office responsibility. They don't deal in guns, if you see what I mean. So they passed the request to us. I've found the right people interested in that line of work. You'll be meeting them this afternoon."

Jerrold gave Ulrich a look that made it clear he didn't like intrusive questions. He turned the conversation back to Vienna.

"Under the contract the German government made with the Dreher company, how many guns are to be manufactured?"

"Why do you ask that?"

"Because Germany has quitted the Geneva Disarmament Conference and is secretly and illegally rearming against its international treaty obligations. The Führer's economic policy is to promote heavy industry, most of which is related to rearmament."

"Even if I were to give you that information, which by the way I can't because I don't know, what difference would it make? I can't prevent your government from making it public. It could easily be traced back to me. I've a Jewish wife and that makes my position very awkward. The Austrian Nazis murdered our Chancellor Dolfuss so what's my chance of avoiding trouble?"

"That puts a different light on matters. I couldn't ask you to put yourself at risk, though to be frank you've taken a risk coming here," said Jerrold in a curt but polite tone.

"I'm not worried about any risk to myself. I must have some guarantee that my wife will not be put at risk."

"Put it this way, Herr Dreher. I can give you absolute guarantee that the British government will not divulge any information you give us. The department which I represent holds confidentiality in high esteem. I can assure you it's in our interests that no-one knows you're here, still less what you're doing here. So there has to be secrecy on your part as well. In the meantime, may I suggest that we go for lunch? Have a chat, that sort of thing."

Leaving Bethell at the office, Jerrold took Ulrich along Curzon Street into Berkeley Square to a restaurant named Les Delices de Normandie.

"Drink?" asked Jerrold.

"Not in the middle of the day. I'll have a tonic, though."

"No gin? We run our Empire on the stuff," This was said with a thin smile. "Ever tasted Normandy cuisine?"

"No. We've got our own excellent Austrian dishes."

Jerrold ordered creamed scallops in their shells and leg of lamb and recommended them to Ulrich.

"They're both specialities in that region and I'm always generous with myself when HMG. is paying."

"His Majesty's Government."

"So you know? Good. Now tell me, is the ordinary man in the street in Austria in favour of the Führer? I was just wondering if your own little Nazi party in Austria is not trying to force their extremist views on the good citizens of Austria like one forces bitter medicine down a reluctant child's throat."

Ulrich wondered what interest Jerrold could have in Austria.

"Why do you ask? Mr Smith or the British Embassy in Vienna are surely better placed than myself to inform you."

"You're right. On the other hand, they can't see things through Austrian eyes. Embassy staff don't exactly rub shoulders with hoi polloi, if you see what I mean. That's the reason for my question."

"A large number of people probably sympathise with the Nazis. The Church supports the present clerical fascist government."

"Wine?" suggested Jerrold, shifting the conversation away from Austria. "They usually drink a white Muscadet with our choice. But, I discovered a couple of years ago a most acceptable alternative. Sancerre rosé."

Despite his protestations, Ulrich did take a glass of the rosé.

"Ever think of going to work with your father? Smart engineer like yourself should be a trump in his pack of cards, I would say."

"It's difficult if not impossible."

"Oh, why's that?'

"I'm afraid that we fell out over my marriage. My wife's Jewish and did not meet with my parent's approval."

"Have you any brothers?"

"No."

"Well, there you are then. An only son and heir. I'm sure he'll come round."

"I don't think so. I suffer what is called in German, '*ein Kirchenbann*.' I don't know the English for that."

"Excommunication."

"The Church is involved. I'm sure you understand."

"I do. Old Henry VIII was excommunicated. Good thing too. Stood up to the Pope and cast off the shackles of Rome."

"That might be past history to you but for me in a Catholic country it's a social stigma."

"I'm sure there must be some way back into your father's good books."

"Are you trying to tell me something Mr Jerrold?"

"As a matter of fact, you could do us a big favour."

"What would that be."

"It's information really. If you were to work for your father, you would be in an advantageous position to know what the Germans are up to. Armaments wise, Germany is a bit of a dark continent, as far as we're concerned. We would be grateful if any of that information were to come our way."

"That's spying, isn't it?"

"Herr Dreher, that's not a word I would use. It's slightly, how shall I say, vulgar. We British never spy. We gather information. Intelligence if you will."

"You sound like a Jesuit, Mr Jerrold."

"Know them do you? The popes made good use of them as spies. I'm talking the Reformation period here."

"It's treachery."

"It depends on whose side you're on. Are you German?"

"No. Certainly not. I'm Austrian."

"Well then, you're in a neutral position. The best of all worlds. No burden of loyalty hanging around your neck."

It dawned on Ulrich that he was, in a sense, already committed to the British side.

"I'm sure there must be some German company that could use your talents. Think about it."

"I'll see," Ulrich said in a non-committal way.

After lunch, the two men made their way back to the oddly named Department of Ancient Monuments. A mere cover, Ulrich assumed, for something else.

When they arrived back, Jerrold introduced him to the two experts.

"Before I show you the drawings," Ulrich said, addressing Jerrold, "I would like to know what proposition you have in mind. These drawings are not the same as those which the Dreher company made the basis of their transaction with the German government. They are a modified and much-improved version. The gun manufactured from these drawings will be more accurate, take a larger gun magazine and be better air-cooled than the former version."

The three other men remained silent. Finally, Jerrold spoke.

"If, and only if, we, and by that I mean these experts here, are satisfied, shall we be able to make you an offer. We shall want full and absolute ownership of the drawings. It would mean that you destroy any copies that you have made and that you do not make further copies. In addition, we would bind you to total secrecy on this matter. That, of course, includes your wife."

"What has my wife to do with this?" said Ulrich in a sharp tone.

"On the face of it, nothing. But, as you said, she's Jewish. It's not in the British government's interest for any such drawings or information about these drawings to fall into the hands of the Haganah in Palestine."

"Haganah. Who are they?"

"They're the Jewish defence force in Palestine. Britain is the Mandated Authority and right at the moment, we're in the firing line in an undeclared civil war between Arab and Jew. Hence our insistence on total secrecy in this matter."

"So what is the deal?"

"That we place a thousand pounds sterling in an account in a bank in Zurich. You alone will have access to that account. It's almost as much as our prime minister earns in a year." He smiled as he made the comparison. "Besides," he added, "a couple of years ago the Swiss authorities enacted a law of banking secrecy to protect German Jewish money. It also protects everybody else. You'll benefit from that. Such are the little ironies of life."

"How do I know that such an account will be opened?"

"It's a matter of trust. We'll keep our side of the bargain. We trust that you'll keep yours. It's not the gun per se that matters but the information contained in these drawings that's important. We wouldn't like the Germans to know that we have a new version of this gun and a better version than theirs, and we wouldn't like to think that Haganah could get hold of a design possibly to use against us. It's as simple as that. No breach of trust by either side."

Ulrich produced the drawings and the two experts set about their work. It would be the last time that he would see them for they pronounced themselves highly satisfied. As Jerrold accompanied Ulrich out of the building, he turned and said to him,

"If you ever need any help you can always get in touch with us through Henderson at the embassy."

"What do you mean, 'help'? What help would I need?"

"The Führer has not hidden his intention to form a greater Germany. He's Austrian and wants to make Austria part of that greater Germany. If that occurs, the troubles visiting the Jews in Germany just now will transfer themselves to Austria. I admit that I'm not particularly enamoured by the Jews. They're much too clannish for my taste. But what's happening in Germany is a warning to Jews everywhere. You said your wife is Jewish. Hence my offer of help. It's an illusion to think that our German friend has renounced any of the projects he mentioned in *Mein Kampf*."

"Before we part company," said Ulrich, "I was wondering if you know my Uncle Claus. His name is von Juggardt."

"Ah, von Juggardt. Yes, we were at Cambridge together." He did not elaborate.

They shook hands. When he arrived at Victoria Station the next day to board the boat train for France, Ulrich noticed the headline on a newspaper billboard, 'Anglo-German naval accord signed yesterday. Controls on German naval rearmament removed. French angry'. Did Jerrold know something he didn't?

Chapter 9

Vienna 1938

Late February. A crisp early Sunday afternoon. Ulrich and Ruth, pushing a pram with their one-year-old twins in it, were walking in the Burggarten. The stark background of black, bare trees gave the city an air of stillness and false calm as if to mirror the febrile atmosphere gripping the country about German intentions to take over Austria. The clatter of horses' hooves on the cobbled roadways was muffled by a thin carpet of snow. The low angle of the sun's rays exaggerated the sharp outlines of the Hofburg Palace, atop of which a gilded and double-headed imperial eagle glowered over the surrounding park and buildings.

Unexpectedly, Ulrich saw his mother together with another woman coming towards them through the gate nearest Mozart's statue. Dressed in a long, sable fur coat and matching hat, she retained her upright bearing, age not seemingly to have touched her. An emotional storm overwhlemed him. Once more, as if from the back of a stage, he heard the words 'treachery', 'betrayal', being uttered – as they had been – by the sanctimonious monsignor. He ignored them. His pain of separation could not be exorcised, it was still too raw. This was, he felt, a charged moment giving him an opportunity, as he saw it, to extend an olive branch to her, for he dearly wanted peace between them. He had not seen her since he had walked out of the house three years previously. She spotted them and deliberately approached.

"How nice to see you at last, Ulrich," she said in an offhand manner. "This is my friend Frau Buchleitner. We're mutual friends of the new Cardinal. I presume you're aware that Monsignor

Kirchmann is now Cardinal Archbishop of Vienna?" She spoke as if it were her habit to meet and speak with Ulrich daily on some trivial matter. She made no attempt to look at Ruth or the children.

"Mother, this is Ruth and these are our twins," he said confidently. "I'm sure Uncle Claus has told you all about us."

"Not that I can recall," she replied. "In any case, I've hardly seen him these past two years."

"He comes to see us," said Ulrich.

"He was always attracted to people younger than himself. I suppose it reassures him as he grows older."

"These are your twin grandchildren, mother-in-law," Ruth cut in. "This is Gabel, our son, and Rahel, our daughter."

"My dear lady," Elke said, with a withering look, "I refuse to recognise these children as my grandchildren. They're Jews and will always be Jews." She snapped out the words and turned away to give her attention to Ulrich.

"Why do you hate us so?" Ruth retorted in a resentful tone of voice. "Whether you recognise them or not, these children are still your flesh and blood. If you touch them they'll not bite you. We're part of the same family aren't we? I don't hate you. I've no ill feelings towards you. We could be friends if you wanted."

"That's not possible."

"A well-educated lady like yourself seems to have forgotten her Shakespeare."

"What do you mean?" Elke said in a testy tone of voice.

"Shylock in the *Merchant of Venice* says, 'I am a Jew. Hath not a Jew eyes? Hath not a Jew hands, organs, dimensions, senses, affections, passions? Fed with the same food, hurt with the same weapons, subject to the same diseases, healed by the same means, warmed and cooled by the same winter and summer, as a Jew is? If you prick us, do we not bleed?'"

She got no further.

"I don't need to be taught Shakespeare by a Jew," Elke snapped. She turned to Ulrich. "Of course we're always at home to you Ulrich. Just don't bring your Jewish brood with you." Suddenly she walked away with Frau Buchleitner in tow.

"Mother," he shouted after her.

She turned round.

"How's Charlie?" he asked. It was, he realised, a pathetic attempt at reconciliation.

"Your father had him put down the day after you left."

She strode off arm in arm with her companion.

For several minutes no word passed between the young couple. Finally Ruth said, "Ulrich, will you take up your mother's invitation?"

"Jewish brood. If my family want to act as if you and our children don't exist that's their affair. I'm no longer part of that family. But they're not entirely to blame. The Church must carry final responsibility for all this hatred of the Jews. It pretends to be the church of peace and understanding instead it slyly foments hate among its people."

"Why blame the Church when each of us must be responsible for our own actions? Do you know what I think? I think she's angry with herself rather than me. If she would only let go of the haughty part she is playing, she might even accept her grandchildren."

"That's what infuriates me. She was a caring mother. She could be so fun-loving and even frivolous when I was a child, joining in our games. And now this."

"I find it hard to believe she can be so cruel towards you, her only son."

The walked on in silence.

"Our children are Jewish," Ulrich said. "You and they give the true meaning to my life. The past was wrong. I was the victim of the Church's teaching. Every Catholic in this country is a victim. I've broken away from the Church's shackles." His disjointed thoughts and words came tumbling out. "Look," he said, holding out his arms, "no chains. And now my mother won't even recognise her own grandchildren. How warped must the Church's teaching be to achieve that result?"

"Ulrich you mustn't allow your rancour to warp your judgement. I'm sure there must be good Christians everywhere."

"Ruth don't tease me, please."

"Don't be so touchy Ulrich. If your mother has the same feelings every woman has she can't harden her heart against her own grandchildren. After all, she made you what you are. And I love you. She'll come round one day. When she sees them walking, running and talking, these spiteful feelings will disappear."

"How's that going to happen? This is a big city. She moves in different circles to us."

"Not entirely. We've just met her. She'll be won over in the end."

"I'd like to think so but I'm not so sure."

"When you fall in love, it's a triumph of heart over head. A woman is ruled by her heart not her head. She thinks with her heart and not her head."

They walked on and Ulrich felt uncomfortable with the silence.

"I blame that Monsignor Kirchmann," he said. "He poisoned my parents' minds against me."

"You'd better watch out. He's a cardinal now. He'll hit you over the head with his red hat."

"You're being flippant Ruth. In any case, how do you know that he wears a red hat?"

"Paintings in the gallery always show cardinals wearing a red hat. Besides, the Catholic Church never changes, even in its dress."

* * *

The recently formed Jewish Action Group were meeting in Ulrich's apartment. Several members turned up. Although mainly young, there were some middle-aged among them. Reuben Gitelmann, the chairman, introduced them to Ulrich and Ruth. They sat about chatting and drinking glasses of beer and wine. The air was thick with cigarette smoke.

Reuben opened the meeting.

"The reason I've called this meeting," he announced, "is to discuss the dangers our community faces and what we can do about it. The situation becomes more ominous by the day. It's clear from information we're receiving through our own Jewish sources that the nasty little man from Linz is determined Germany swallows up our country. They call it *Anschluss*, annexation. There's no one to stop him, neither the English nor the French. They don't have the means even if they had the willpower, which they don't. I wonder who's going to be next, Czechoslovakia maybe or Poland?"

"What you mean is that soon there won't be an independent Austria," intervened Ulrich.

"Exactly. Look at it like this," Reuben continued, "I believe the Austrian Nazi gangs rampaging through this city is a pre-arranged plan so they can call in the German army to restore law and order. That way they'll achieve their goal of union with Germany. We must organise our people. They're going to need protection. So, any ideas?"

"It's a little late in the day to talk about protecting our people," said one member. "For the past several years, since the coming of the Nazis to power in Germany, I've been warning about this. Unfortunately, most of our people don't believe we can suffer the same fate as our fellow Jews in Germany. I disagree. Yet my loyalty to this city makes it very difficult for me to believe that the Viennese will allow that to happen.

"Anti-Semitism will only be beaten by standing up to it," Ruth said. "As for Nazism, it's founded on anti-Semitism. Didn't the Führer go to a Catholic school? He must have been injected with the virus of anti-Semitism. There can be no compromise against this evil. God alone knows what these people are capable of."

"The lesson from our big neighbour is clear," said a small man with a swarthy complexion. "The Nazis simply kick you out and get others to take your place. They might replace our people with second-class professionals but that doesn't trouble them. So long as they get rid of us the better it is for them. In Berlin they're stealing the properties and possessions belonging to Jews with no compensation. It's pure theft. Beatings, murder and concentration camps that's the lot of our fellow Jews in Germany. I just hope it doesn't come here."

"We form an important part of the cultural, academic and social life of this city," said one other member of the group, a man named Albert Schoenfeld. "A large number of the staff at the university are Jews, half the musicians in the orchestras are Jews and the same goes for doctors and lawyers. As you know, I'm a lawyer. A lot of the trade and banks are ours. I hardly believe that our fellow citizens would tolerate the elimination of the Jewish community. But, I could be wrong."

"It's the first time I've heard a fellow lawyer admit he could be wrong," Reuben said. Laughter followed this remark. "The Austrians, our so-called fellow citizens, are just as anti-Semitic as the Germans. However, it's not what they want that counts. It's what the Führer wants. They'll follow him like sheep."

"I don't share the general pessimism of this meeting," another protested. "I work in the Ministry of Foreign Affairs, I can tell you that our own Chancellor is totally against such a union with Germany. The Führer is not going to come here. It's all propaganda to frighten us. The German military high command, as far as I know, are not too keen on this so-called annexation either. The information our people are sending us from Berlin is that the army isn't ready to invade this country. It's one thing for the Nazi thugs to beat up Jews on Berlin's streets and another for German soldiers to invade Austria, a sovereign state, take over the government and incorporate it into Germany."

"I don't believe that," said a tall, dark-featured man with a wan expression. "My advice is to get out as soon as possible before that happens."

"You mean leave now?" Reuben said. "You can't expect people to give up everything they have and go off to some foreign country based on rumours."

"You only have to look at what's happening in this city" continued the previous speaker, "to know that these Austrians are in love with the Führer. Most think of themselves as German. As for our Chancellor. The Führer will swallow him up."

"It won't be easy to find some kind of refuge in another country," Reuben said. "A few embassies might be willing to give out visas in small numbers but that's all. The English have opened a few doors for the resettlement of Jews in British colonies but that's all."

"What about Palestine? They're always crying out for more immigrants," said one who up to that point had remained silent.

"I know the Zionist aim, is to have a homeland where the Jewish people will be safe," intervened Ruth. "I understand their point of view, but the reality is we're Austrians. You don't have to be a Zionist to be a good Jew. We share the same language and culture as our Christian neighbours, our political allegiance is to this country. Why should we be forced to abandon all this because a madman doesn't like us. We've had to put up with this hatred of the Jews for too long. We must resist them, if they invade."

"How the hell are we supposed to do that?" retorted a small, fat, balding member called Ben. "There are tens of thousand of Jews in this city alone. Of course, it's alright if you're a doctor or a lawyer or other kind of professional person and lose your job, you'll find ways to get another post elsewhere. You'll have the money to go to France or England or wherever. What do I do? I work in a factory making brushes. The great majority of our people are just ordinary working-class folk who don't have the money to abandon their lives here for uncertainty in some far-off country. Why should they? They're as much Austrian as everyone else." His voice rose in anger. "In any case, do you think the English or the French will take me in? My advice is to lie low and keep out of the way of trouble. I wouldn't mind going to Palestine and work on a farm. I couldn't be worse off than working in a factory here. I just don't have the money to do that."

"The *Kultusgemeinde* might help you," Reuben said.

"What is that?" Ulrich asked.

"It's an organisation founded to help Jewish people, mainly to do with religious practice but it also has a social function. There are poor Jews in Vienna. Many were very badly affected by the inflation – its funds were based on Austrian government bonds, which were seriously devalued. So after the war a large number of people suffered financially."

"I'm not sure if the wife would want us to go to Palestine," Ben said. "She's not the least convinced about our group or Zionism." He laughed nervously.

The meeting continued for a further hour. Ulrich was surprised. The only practical outcome was how the meeting had exposed the divisions among the members.

"We'll meet at the beginning of next month," declared Reuben by way of closing the meeting. "By then we should have more ideas about what strategy to adopt in the face of this growing threat to all of us."

When the group had broken up and the members had drifted off, Reuben stayed behind.

"You're really worried aren't you?" Ulrich said.

"Things are coming to a head," Reuben replied. "Some of my friends, mainly professionals, academics, doctors and lawyers have gone abroad, some to Switzerland, others to France, England and the

United States. However, it's not easy for others. Ben works in a factory, he's given us a view that's held by most of our people. It's not only workers who are in this situation. Bankers, department store and property owners and commercial developers have assets tied up here. They've little option. They can't sell even if they wanted to for there aren't any buyers. The leaders of the anti-Semitic movement are biding their time. They look across the border and what do they see? Nazi chiefs enriching themselves by stealing Jewish businesses, houses, property and art collections. They're praying for the Führer to invade."

"I thought that if the worst comes to the worst, we could go to England," Ulrich said, "but Ruth won't hear of going abroad. For the moment, I agree with her."

"The family is here," Ruth said. "I feel obliged to my parents to my family."

* * *

Next evening, there was a knock on the door. It was Claus. Ruth had spent the afternoon preparing a traditional Viennese meal. Claus, forever the gentleman, came armed with a large bouquet of roses and some toys.

"How's my favourite girlfriend?" Claus said in his usual bantering tone. "A beautiful woman in a city of beautiful women."

"Uncle Claus," Ruth said, "you're an inveterate flatterer."

"Where are the little ones?"

Claus loved the twins. On his occasional visits, he brought toys and played with the children on the floor of the flat. He loved them and his face betrayed a lonely sadness. Ruth often noticed this, despite his easy-going, tolerant manner, his sense of humour and his infectious laughter. For his part, he treated her with infinite respect. She went off to fetch the twins.

Ulrich described meeting his mother at the Burggarten.

"I only wish she would recognise her grandchildren," he said.

"She'll come round one of these days," Claus said.

"I wish I could share your optimism. Why should my family punish their own grandchildren?"

"Are your parents punishing them? From their point of view, not that I agree, you're the one who walked out of the family. You made a choice and now you've got to live by it."

"It was a choice forced on me. You were there."

"It's your father, I worry about."

"Meaning?"

"He's become terribly earnest about life. Mind you he's always been like that. He thinks the world owes the German-speaking peoples a great debt. The last war, the Versailles treaty, the Depression. He can't forget the past. Yet he's doing very well out of German rearmament and become very pro-Nazi."

Ruth returned with the children.

"I've news for you," continued Claus. "Next week, I'm off to Paris to an auction of Impressionist paintings. They're the only safe investment these days. You wouldn't like to come with me, Ulrich would you?"

"I'm too busy being an assistant accountant. Ruth's the one you should take. She could advise you with all that fine art knowledge she has."

"That's a good idea. What a wonderful imaginary scandal. I can hear the talk around the Ringstrasse about the more than middle aged Claus borrowing his nephew's young wife for a trip to Paris. Your parents would have heart attacks. In a more enlightened age such a thing might be possible. Unfortunately, we live in a dark age, an age of intolerance."

"We're the victims of that darkness," Ruth said. "Why can't we just be allowed to have our own customs and religion? Why can't they let us be? We're not doing anyone any harm. Some of my friends who have converted to Christianity are still looked upon with suspicion. It makes me want to weep it's so childish and stupid."

"So what do you intend to do? Emigrate?"

"Running off to England or Palestine for that matter is out of the question. I love this country too much."

"It won't come to that," Ulrich said.

"Once the twins have grown up, they must learn to ride," said Claus. "I can't think of anything more worthwhile. I'm sure Gabel will make a fine horseman. Join the Spanish Riding School."

"Uncle Claus, I think your imagination is running away with you," Ruth remarked with a laugh.

"If you're a parent you've created something in your own likeness. Not having children of my own, I use my imagination as a comforting substitute." He stopped speaking for a moment. "Heavens, I'm turning into a philosopher. Mustn't let that happen. I suggest a glass of our good white Austrian wine. It's the best cure for philosophical ramblings."

There was a sudden banging on the front door. It was Reuben. He was breathless and highly agitated. His eyes flashed and he stood with one hand steadying himself against the hallway wall. Before he could say anything Ruth said, "What's the matter Reuben?"

"It's the Germans. They've closed the frontier."

* * *

The morning after the shattering news about the closure of the frontier, Ulrich came in early to work. He worked for an accountant named Otto Siedler, who was not Austrian but came from the Sudetenland, a part of Czechoslovakia, inhabited mainly by ethnic Germans. Of medium height, corpulent, with a dark complexion, he had sharp eyes that were never still and a perpetual frown that added years to his features. A prominent red birthmark on the side of his left temple gave him a mildly repulsive appearance. He held a smoldering resentment against the Viennese, 'they're a bunch of hypocrites. They respect and use my financial skills but treat me like a Czech peasant. Well I'm not Czech. I'm pure German. In fact, I detest the Czechs.' Ulrich had never known him to smile or laugh.

Most of Ulrich's time was spent travelling to various factories throughout the country inspecting company accounts and ledgers. It was tiresome and boring work but it gave him an insight into the country's vital industries and its rich mineral resources. It provided him with a salary. He also revised and corrected the work of the other two younger assistants. Working for Siedler, Ulrich found that his mathematical skills as a precision engineer enhanced his ability to cope with accounts, for he had the gift of being able to add up in his head complicated rows of figures accurately with remarkable speed.

Ulrich found Siedler already in his office. As he passed the open door, Siedler shouted at him to come in. It was a small, tidy office filled with a large imposing oak desk, which Siedler once boasted to

Ulrich he had inherited from his grandfather. Ulrich thought this latter information was meant to impress him rather than express the truth. He knew from one of his several contacts that Siedler's father had been a railway labourer, a drunk who bullied his wife and children.

"Have you heard the news?" Siedler exclaimed excitedly. He dropped his normal formal tone when speaking to Ulrich.

"What news?"

"About the border with Germany being closed."

"I presumed, Herr Siedler, you meant a new lucrative contract."

Siedler ignored Ulrich's remark. His shifty little eyes darted about more feverishly than usual.

"It means that at last Austria will be incorporated into the new Greater Reich."

"How do you make that out? The frontier could have been closed for all sorts of reasons."

"I know from the highest authority it was the Führer who ordered the frontier closed," he said in an intriguing tone of voice.

"Why? Is he afraid we might invade Germany? I can see it now," Ulrich said, raising his arm in a dramatic gesture and pointing nowhere in particular, "the brave Austrian army taking Berlin and marching up the Kurfurstendamm."

"There's no call to be so flippant Herr Dreher. I might just as well tell you that things are about to change in this town."

"In what way?"

Siedler sat back in his chair, opened his cigarette case and took out a cigarette. He lit up.

"Take the big business people," he said, a voice full of scorn, "the bankers, politicians, lawyers and judges. They despise outsiders like me who've got where I am through hard work. They all know each other. They form cliques, belong to the same clubs and societies and social groups. Small business people like me are kept at the door."

"Hasn't it always been like that?" asked Ulrich in a mock innocent tone.

"It has and I despise it. *But*," Siedler had the habit of stressing his 'buts', "what most people don't seem to realise is that this city is really run by the Jews. Haven't you heard of International Jewry? The Jews insinuate themselves into key positions in the state then they control them. Take the communists. That Marx chap was a Jew. The Bolsheviks are all Jews. Their leader Stalin has surrounded himself with the vermin. Red Vienna was the work of the Jews. They stirred up no end of trouble here in this city. The people who inhabit the city sewers wouldn't have to live there if it weren't for the greedy Jewish bankers."

"If I may say so Herr Siedler," Ulrich said, "and no offence meant but I think you're talking a lot of rubbish."

Siedler puffed vigorously on his cigarette. "Rubbish eh? Is that what you think?" his voice striking a higher note. "Well, you're wrong. Did you know Jews encourage abortion?"

"I'm sure back street abortions are not confined to Jews."

"What about Masonic lodges? Can't deny that. Run by Jews. We all know what kind of pagan rituals go on there. I'm not the only one who thinks that they indulge in some very nasty practices. Even the Church teaches that they kill young Christian children and use their blood in their services."

"You shouldn't believe everything the Church preaches. It's all propaganda from Rome."

"Maybe. Do you know where all the best contracts and deals are made? If you want a decent contract you've got to become a Mason. Where does that leave me? I'll tell you where that leaves me. Right outside. I'm a good Catholic and so can't become a Mason. The Church is right. They're a bunch of pagans. So I'm excluded. I've had to work bloody hard to get my contracts. So I don't owe the Jews a damned thing." Siedler broke off his rant, stood up and walked across to the window overlooking the street. He remained immobile for a few minutes, turned to face Ulrich then said slowly and deliberately. "That's all about to change." A sneering grin spread over his face.

"How do you know that?"

Siedler tapped the side of his nose with this right forefinger.

"You will see. You will see." His face was suffused with a surly grin.

"Are you keeping something from me?"

"I repeat, you will see."

"Is that all, Herr Siedler?"

"Not quite. I've made arrangements for you to go to Linz the day after tomorrow. There's a job I want you to do. All the instructions are here." He handed Ulrich a green folder. "Read them carefully. It's a timber company but my inside information is they've got a sideline in specialised paper making, which they've not declared to the Tax Authorities. It's your job to find out. If they're hiding something I want to know." With a pre-emptory wave of his hand, he dismissed a bemused Ulrich.

* * *

That evening, after the children had been fed and put to bed, Ulrich and Ruth sat at the dining table enjoying one of Ruth's specialities, Tafelspitz.

"Ruth, darling," Ulrich said, "this news about the closure of the frontier is not good at all." He then related his exchange with Siedler. "I've been thinking, with money in the bank in Switzerland we could go there. Either that or France or England. I fancy the United States myself. What do you think?"

There was a long silence before she answered.

"Ulrich, dearest, I know how you feel. It's just that I can't leave my parents and the rest of my family here. Most people in our community don't really believe all the tales coming from Germany. Even if they did, what can they do? The majority are just ordinary working class, they earn a weekly wage and that's it. They don't think of going anywhere else, for the simple reason they can't afford to."

"Ruth I would never want you to leave your father and mother. If you feel strongly about this, then we'll stay. In any case, this so-called annexation might not take place. Siedler is a pompous ass and likes people to think he's so important."

Chapter 10

Vienna 1938

It was a short walk from the Linz railway station down to the Danube where the Linz Timber Company was located. Ulrich heard no sound coming from the nearby shipyard, hidden behind a long high wall, its massive entry double doors, with their dark green peeling paintwork, firmly closed. He continued further till he came to the main wrought-iron gates of the lumber yard. A jaded-looking security guard asked his name, checked his identity papers and let him pass. Enormous piles of giant logs were stacked neatly in regimented rows and squares like the formations of the ancient Roman army, portrayed in his school history books. To one side the tall, brick chimney stack of a huge building belched out white smoke. Two gigantic open sheds contained several industrial circular saws cutting logs into long, wide planks, helped by the force of massive stone flywheels. The finished planks were being hauled away on long carts drawn by teams of four dray horses. Further to one side were high mounds of sandy coloured sawdust. Everywhere was the sweet smell of wood resin, bringing back to Ulrich memories of liturgical incense.

Skirting the sheds, Ulrich made his way to the office building at the further end of the yard. He mounted an external cast-iron stairway to the main door. Once inside, he introduced himself and was told to wait by a middle-aged clerk, wearing a blue industrial coat. A door to one side opened and a man appeared.

"Herr Dreher. I'm Franz Goetschl, the assistant manager. Herr Siedler phoned to tell me you were coming. I've arranged for you to use my office. One of the clerks will provide you with our account ledgers."

"I'm impressed by your saws," Ulrich said.

"They're the largest in the country. They have to be, for we process over a hundred thousand cubic metres of fir and spruce a year."

Ulrich settled down to his examination of the account ledgers. He worked the whole forenoon but couldn't find any mention of paper making. He decided to pursue his quest after lunch. At lunch time, he made his way back into the city centre where crowds of people were milling about. Giant red banners with the black and white swastika emblem were now hanging from several buildings. He stopped a passing man.

"What's going on?" he asked.

"Haven't you heard? The Führer's crossed the border with his army and is coming here to Linz. He's going to receive a warm welcome," he said ambiguously.

Ulrich went to a restaurant he knew from previous visits to the city, on the side of the square opposite the town hall. A waiter showed him to a table but his colleagues appeared to be more concerned with what was going on outside than serving the clientele inside. He was on the point of complaining about the slow service when there was a great shout from outside. Most of the customers, followed by the waiters, rushed for the door as if the fire alarm had just sounded. Ulrich, curious as to the cause of the commotion, tried to get outside but found his way barred by the crowd. With much effort, he gradually elbowed his way outside and joined some others on the wide windowsill, giving him a panoramic view. Thousands of people were packed into the town square. Church bells started to peal, adding what Ulrich thought was a sacred note of approval to the event. The crowd let out raucous cries of, 'He's coming, he's coming.' Then in unison, as if led by some unseen conductor, they took up the chant of 'one people, one Reich, one Leader.' There were repeated screams of '*Sieg Heil*'.

A cavalcade of cars, struggling to make its way through the enormous throng, was brought to a sudden stop. Ulrich could make out the diminutive figure of the Führer, wearing a long, brown leather coat. He had descended from one of the leading cars, a black six-seater Mercedes convertible, and was being pushed, shoved and, at times, bodily carried through the tightly packed crowd towards the town hall by a group of black-uniformed SS bodyguards. The vast crowd greeted him with wild enthusiasm. The ecstatic adulation continued until he appeared on the Town Hall balcony. It was then that Ulrich noticed the brooding, menacing figure of Colonel von Wartenberg, standing at his side.

The man next to Ulrich shouted and cheered.

"Our saviour has come," he cried. "Now we'll all be part of Greater Germany. We'll be real Germans."

The Führer motioned to the crowd to fall silent. Even from his not-too-distant vantage point, Ulrich could see his eyes blazing with the ardour of a conquering hero, transfixing the massed body of people below him. He launched into his speech in a high-pitched staccato voice, carried over the square by a couple of hastily rigged up loudspeakers. One moment he screamed at his audience, the next he caressed them with flattery. He was proud to be German, he cried, proud to be a soldier and wear his Iron Cross won for bravery. 'The schoolboy from Linz has returned,' he shouted. 'Austria is now going to be part of the Greater Reich.' Each statement was greeted with tumultuous cheering, the raising of the arm in the Nazi salute and cries of *'Sieg Heil'*. With the skill of the practised orator, he manipulated the volatile emotions of the crowd below, who appeared mesmerised by his torrent of words.

At this point, Ulrich tried to escape the crowd with the intention of getting back to the timber mill, but the effort was futile. The mass of people was too dense and tightly packed. He gave up trying and resigned himself to listening to the Führer's tirade against the Jews. He spoke with messianic-like zeal, 'The Jews are a different race, odious and bloodsucking moneylenders. This criminal race has the dead of the World War on their consciences. They are the enemies of the state and must be rid of.'

The words caused Ulrich to remember similar words being drilled into him as a child, time and again by the pious and sincere nuns in his catechism classes, later by his Jesuit masters at his high school and not infrequently by priests from the pulpit. The chilling words, spat out in a tone of deep hatred, reverberated around the square like a blast of winter wind. 'Jewish Bolshevism, Jewish capitalists bandits, Jews must be removed from the state, Jews are poisonous germs, Jews are liars and cheats, Jews have done nothing for mankind, the Jew's art is pornographic filth and his music is degrading rubbish.' The vitriolic rant went on. 'I, the Führer, will destroy the menace, lance the poisoned boil, exterminate the vermin.' Strutting up and down the balcony, he waved his arms about in wild, theatrical gestures. His yelling sounded to Ulrich like the howling of the monkeys he had heard in the Vienna zoo as a child. He screamed the words from the Nazi's own anthem, the Horst Wessel Song, 'The day will come for reprisal, no forgiveness' and the heaving mass broke into united song.

'This man's a sorcerer,' Ulrich whispered under his breath. 'He twists words so I no longer understand my own language.'

His neighbour turned to him.

"What did you say?"

"Nothing."

When, eventually, Ulrich arrived back at the timber mill, he found it closed and locked up. He surmised that the workers had all gone to the rally at the town square. He would have to return later to retrieve his papers. For the moment he really didn't care about ledger books and accounts. He feared for Ruth and the children. He remembered Reuben and the members of his Jewish Action Group forecasting the storm to come. Greatly perturbed, he made his way back to the railway station and returned home.

* * *

A heavy pall of black smoke lay over Vienna. On his way to work, Ulrich witnessed gangs of Nazi thugs brandishing hunting guns and clubs wandering the streets, taking hold of Jews and mercilessly beating them. He realised the danger Ruth might be in if she ventured outside with the twins. Turning round he quickly made his way back to his apartment. Reuben was there, much agitated.

"This town has gone mad," Reuben said, "it's a Russian-type pogrom. How wrong we all were. The evil isn't months or years away, it's already burst upon us. Jews are being attacked openly on the street and the police stand by. Some are even taking part. I came round to warn Ruth not to go out. I've also some bad news. I've been told the police have arrested Rabbi Levitansky and his wife and taken them to the main police station. I'm really on my way there now to see what I can do."

"Is that wise? They might arrest you!"

"I'm a lawyer. Senior police officers can't brush the law aside."

"The Nazis are in charge now," Ulrich said. "They work to different rules. I insist on coming with you. They might ignore you but they can't ignore a Dreher." He spoke in a confident manner.

The two men left the apartment, Ulrich advising Ruth not to venture out at any cost. On their way across town to the police headquarters, they witnessed the ruthless violence of the Nazi mobs. One young man was having his shirt torn from his body while uniformed thugs rained blows on him, leaving him bleeding on the pavement. Broken glass, from the display windows of the Jewish-owned shops and stores, was scattered everywhere. Even smartly dressed men and women took part in throwing taunts, jibes and insults at Jews being taken into custody.

When they arrived at police headquarters, they noticed that instead of the usual police officers, they were confronted by men in the black uniform of the SS. Ulrich immediately caught the mood of the place and signalled to Reuben to keep quiet.

"Leave the talking to me," he whispered.

Ulrich approached the main desk. The officer behind the desk asked him for his identity papers. When he read them, he looked again at Ulrich.

"You're a Dreher eh?"

"I'd like to the see the senior officer in charge."

"Do you have an appointment? He's a very busy man."

Ulrich pulled out his wallet and withdrew his business card.

"Give this to him." He handed the card over to the officer. "Let him take the decision."

After some hesitation, the officer went to find his superior. It wasn't long before he returned.

"He'll see you," the officer said with a smirk on his face. "Follow me."

"I insist that my brother-in-law comes with me," Ulrich said. His voice had taken on a tone of authority. "You needn't ask for his papers. He's not an enemy of the state." He was surprised at his own boldness.

Ulrich and Reuben followed the officer up a flight of stairs, along a corridor and were ushered into a large office. The room contained several chairs and a very large desk. A huge swastika was draped from one wall and a large framed photo of a sullen-faced Führer hung on the other. A small man, in the uniform of a senior SS officer, stood looking out of the window with his back to them. He turned around and Ulrich found himself face to face with Otto Siedler.

"Well, well, well," Siedler said slowly in a pompous tone of voice, accentuating every syllable, "Herr Ulrich Dreher." Before Ulrich could catch his breath, Siedler continued, "Didn't I tell you things were about to change. Well now, they have."

"Herr Siedler..." Ulrich said, astounded at the black apparition in front of him.

"Herr Siedler no longer." He sat down behind the desk, opened a box, drew out a cigar and with slow movements cut the end off and lit it. "To you and the rest of this town, I'm now Major Siedler of the *Schutszstaffel*. My job is to protect the good citizens of Vienna. In other words, Herr Dreher, the Führer has put me in charge of this city. Not exactly the Führer. His right-hand man, my commanding officer, General von Wartenberg. A new Nazi dispensation has come into being. I'm going to sweep aside all that rubbish parading in the name of democracy. In any case democracy doesn't work. My job is to clean up this town and sweep the garbage into the Danube. I refer of course to our Jewish friends." He spoke in a false semi-jocular way. "I must tell you that I've closed my company. If you've come to see me about your job, I'm sorry to tell you that it no longer exists."

"I've not come about that. I'd no idea I'd find you here. We, that is my brother-in-law and myself have come to obtain the release of Rabbi Levitansky and his wife. I understand they've been brought here."

"If I may say so, Herr Dreher, what the hell has that got to do with you?" A harsh caustic note crept into Siedler's tone. "They're Jews. They're part of the garbage. They're going to be disposed of."

"I'm a lawyer," Reuben said, "and I demand that if you hold Rabbi Levitansky and his wife, you charge them or release them immediately."

"You demand. Do you, indeed? Who the devil might you be?" Siedler gave Reuben a venomous glare.

"My name is Reuben Gitelmann, I represent..." but he got no further.

Siedler held up his hand. "With a name like that you could only be part of the trash," he said sharply. "A lawyer eh? Well, well, well. Then let me tell you, sonny, that as from this moment on you're no longer a lawyer. Forbidden under Reich law. You're out of a job. A word from me and you'll find yourself joining your precious rabbi and his wife," he hesitated a moment, "in a concentration camp." He turned to Ulrich.

"Herr Dreher you never told me you had a Jewess for a wife. My God, to think I gave you a job. You'll be lucky to save your skin."

"My father is a friend of Colonel von Wartenberg," Ulrich said. He knew this was hardly true but it had an effect on Siedler.

"I hope you're not telling me a fib, Herr Dreher. That wouldn't do. The colonel, or should I now say general, has left for Berlin. I'm in charge and I intend to carry out the Führer's orders to the letter. We've already started. There is something else you might like to know."

"What would that be?"

"As from yesterday the Reich's Nuremberg Laws now apply to this country." He smirked.

"What do you mean?"

"Herr Dreher when you worked for me I always had the impression that you were pretty ignorant about what was going on in the world around you. You never even knew that I was a senior active member of the Nazi party here in Vienna. Now you tell me that you don't know about the Nuremberg Laws."

"Besides being insulting Herr Siedler…"

"Major."

"Major Siedler. Besides being insulting what have these so-called laws got to with me?"

"A great deal actually. You're married to this man's sister. He's a Jew and she must be a Jewess and you don't know about the Nuremberg Laws? They forbid intermarriage between Aryans and Jews. Lots of consequences."

"Aryans?" said Ulrich quizzically, his face screwed up. "I'm not an Aryan. I'm Austrian."

"For you Herr Dreher that means Germans. It means you. We're looking at purity of race here."

"This is madness. Aryans. This whole thing is crazy," Ulrich shouted at Siedler.

"Those Laws don't apply retrospectively here," Reuben cut in.

"You were a lawyer Jew-boy but no longer. I've already told you that. Besides, I won't take any lessons from a defrocked lawyer." He turned to Ulrich. "I apply the law here. What I say, goes. Heed my warning if you want to get yourself out of this mess."

"Mess," intervened Reuben. "You mean you've ordered your bully-boys on to the streets to beat up and harass innocent citizens just because they're Jews?"

"I would hold your tongue young man, if I were you," Siedler said, standing up. There was anger in his voice. "In any case, they've not received orders from me. We in the SS don't commit violence or disorder on the street. It's not our style. We're a respectable organisation. We use much subtler methods against our enemies. But we're not going to stop the ordinary citizens from expressing their anger against the Bolsheviks and International Jewry. They're doing what our esteemed Führer has demanded, 'let the people act'."

"I suppose violence is allowed under this new regime?" Ulrich asked.

"You could say that. Cruelty impresses people. Nothing makes greater impact on the ordinary man in the street than brute force. I'm your new politician, Herr Dreher. Terror is the most effective political instrument. I shan't be afraid to use it merely because naïve middle-class milksops like yourself take offence at it."

"So what's happened to Rabbi Levitansky and his wife?" Ulrich said. "You said they're in a concentration camp. Is that right?"

"To be candid, I really don't know, I don't concern myself with the trivial details of every person taken into protective custody."

"Protective custody," Ulrich said, "the only protection people need is protection from the Nazi thugs roaming the streets beating people up."

"Quite so," Siedler said. "You've just mentioned that Jews are being attacked in the street. We've probably taken the rabbi into custody for his own protection. His whereabouts right at this moment are unknown to me. In any case even if I did know I wouldn't tell you, Herr Dreher." He turned to Reuben. "One more thing Herr Gitelmann. You'll have to wear the Star of David."

"What for?" Reuben said angrily.

"It marks you out as special."

"Special for what?"

"It marks you out for special treatment."

Siedler sat down at his desk. "I'm a busy man so please leave. Otherwise you'll both find yourselves being taken into protective custody." He rang a bell on his desk. The young officer who had evidently been waiting just outside the door entered almost immediately. He gave the Nazi salute.

"Show these two out," Siedler snapped.

As they walked through the lobby of the police headquarters, Ulrich reflected upon his bruising encounter with Siedler. He felt a stranger in his own country.

* * *

It was early April and Ulrich was seriously worried. Public notices informed the population that their country was to be joined to the Greater Reich and would lose its name. Henceforward, it was announced, it would be called Ostmark, the Eastern province of the German Reich. To make legal what was a de facto situation, a referendum would be held for the people to vote their assent. Everyone, that is, except the Jews.

"Are you going to vote?" Ruth asked Ulrich.

"Of course," Ulrich said. "I don't want to take any blame for this catastrophe. So it's going to be a no vote."

"Aren't you being a little foolish. They'll know how you vote."

"If these devils had allowed you to vote, how would you vote?

"You know how I would vote."

"Well, then, I'll be also voting for both of us."

The main polling station for the city's central ward was located in the City Hall. As Ulrich approached the grand neo-Gothic building, now festooned with huge black and red swastika banners, he gazed up at the Rathausmann, a statue in the form of a medieval knight, atop the high tower overlooking the park. 'How could the cultured people of Vienna,' he thought, 'allow themselves to be taken over by a gang of thugs?' He crossed the Arkadenhof, the large inner courtyard, and recalled a visit he had made as a schoolboy and being told by his teacher that it was comparable to the courtyard of the Doge's Palace in Venice. He followed the notices directing him to the hall where the voting booths were placed. All the officials wore uniforms, with swastika armbands. Ulrich signed the register, took his voting form and placed it in the ballot box.

There was a sudden commotion. Cardinal Kirschmann, resplendent in his red cassock, cloak and wide-brimmed tasselled hat, entered the room, surrounded by a retinue of fawning clergymen, followed by press reporters and photographers. He went up to the registration desk, took his voting form and voted, all the while being photographed.

"I've come here," he announced to the assembled group in a high moral tone, "to vote for the union of our country to that of the Greater Reich." The reporters scribbled in their notebooks. "Yesterday, I had a personal meeting with our dear Führer. I assured him of the allegiance and loyalty of myself, the bishops, the clergy, and Catholic faithful of Austria to him and the Nazi government and vowed him our full support and blessing. The Holy Father has expressed the firm view of the Church that godless Bolshevism is the greatest danger facing the Church. Bolshevism is the brainchild of the Jews, it is a movement run by Jews. In fighting that danger, the Church stands side by side with the Nazi government. In Spain and Italy, the Church has joined fascism in a holy crusade against the Jewish-Bolshevist forces ranged against us. As a token of our solidarity with Nazism, I have instructed all parish priests to fly swastika banners on the outside of their churches." His clerical attendants vigorously clapped. "The day has at last dawned," he solemnly intoned, "when the Jews, the Christ killers, will be made to pay the penalty for murdering our dear Lord and Saviour Jesus Christ." The red-clothed prelate, raising his arm in the Nazi salute, shouted '*Sieg Heil*' then swept out, looking neither left nor right.

The results showed, next day, that the overwhelming mass of the people had voted for the annexation or as the terms of the referendum put it 'do you pledge yourself to our Führer?' *Anschluss* was now a fait accompli. Austria as an independent state no longer existed. The Viennese newspapers described how all over Austria, exuberant crowds in the cities, towns and villages had voted to celebrate their new status as citizens of the Führer's greater Germany. A school holiday was declared. They printed page after page of pictures showing people dancing in the streets, flying swastika flags, of swastika banners hoisted in public buildings and workers' tenements, of flowers being handed to soldiers and members of the SS.

When Ulrich told his uncle Claus, about his experience at the town hall, he tersely remarked, 'Our dear cardinal has hitched the Catholic sail to the Nazi mast.'

* * *

Some days later, Ulrich went to a local Chinese dry-cleaners to collect a suit. Herr Tang came from Hong Kong, spoke poor German and some pidgin English. There was a strong odour of solvents and detergents.

"Madam Dreher, she no come today?" Herr Tang asked.

"She's not well."

"Too bloody bad. I velly solly." Tommy Tang, as he usually referred to himself, had picked up his English from British sailors. He fetched the suit.

"Herr Dreher, sir, why the people they make the Jews kneel down and clean the street? I no understand. I saw Jewish women on platform and people they cut the hair off. Why? They no criminals."

"Mister Tang, we have a new government. They don't like the Jews. So they harm them. Take them away."

"What they done?"

"Nothing. It's just that they're Jews. Many people Europe don't like the Jews. Some – here in this city – even hate them."

"Why so?"

"Because they're not Christians."

"I no Christian. They no come here to... to..." he was searching for the word.

"To harm you. No. It's just the Jews they want to harm.

"In Hong Kong many Jews. Good people, doctors, lawyers. Some they have the banks. Good people. Good people."

Tommy Tang shook his head and screwed his Mongolian features up into a huge question mark.

* * *

One day, several weeks later, there was a loud persistent knock on the door of the flat. It was a bedraggled and frightened looking Reuben.

"They've taken mother and father," he blurted out.

"What do you mean, taken them?" Ruth said, becoming quite agitated. "Who's taken them?"

"The Gestapo. They came this morning. I was out. I had gone to visit some members of our group at Albert Schoenfeld's place. The police had already cleared parts of the district. All sorts of rumours abound. I was going to propose we take some kind of action together. There was no one at his flat. In fact, the whole block seemed empty. I returned to our parents' apartment. When I got back, our parents had gone. A Christian neighbour told me what had happened."

"Oh my God," shrieked Ruth, who burst in to tears. She went to fetch her coat. "I must find them. I must find them."

"No, no," interjected Ulrich. He stepped forward, put his arms around her and stopped her from attempting to go out. "You mustn't go out. Don't do that. They'll pick you up. Your only safety is here." She put her head on his shoulder and sobbed hysterically. He held her tightly.

"Ulrich, you must do something," she pleaded, having regained some of her composure. She turned to Reuben, "Where is Rosa?"

"She's staying with a friend in Baden."

"My poor parents. What have they done with them? What have we done to deserve this? What is going to happen to us now? I won't allow them to take our children. They're treating us like cattle in a field. Ulrich we must do something." The words poured out of her. She started to cry once more. Aside from her sobs, there was a dreadful silence. Suddenly a cry came from the nursery. Ruth left the two men.

"Reuben, what are you going to do?" asked Ulrich. "Where are you going to stay? You'd better remain here for the present. You'll be safe here."

"I've phoned a friend and he's asked me to stay with him but nowhere is safe in this city. There are eyes and ears everywhere. People are being told to inform on their neighbours. We knew this was happening in Germany. But here? In Vienna? I sometimes thought that these things might happen but really didn't believe it. Christian lawyers I've known all my life are shunning me." He paused and shook his head trying to make sense of it all. "People are being arrested and hauled off to prison and worse. No warrants, no courts no explanations. They're being thrown out of their homes and being dispossessed of everything. The rule of law no longer exists."

A silence settled between the two men.

Reuben sat down and hid his face behind his hands. "To think," he said, "how much time I used to waste thinking that we'd be able to get out of this country. Go somewhere else. It was all talk. No action. How the devil did we allow this to happen."

"What do you mean?" Ulrich asked. "How could you possibly have prevented this? The Nazis are here because the Austrian people want them to be here. They want to be part of the Führer's so-called Greater Germany. The Austrians want to be ruled by the Nazis. In any case, it's what the Church wants. The Church is the Führer's most authoritative and staunchest supporter. When the Cardinal speaks the flock follow without question."

"I still think it could have been avoided. The Jews were – yes, very much past tense – a powerful force in this country. Banking, business, the professions. We could have, should have, put up greater resistance to the right-wing thugs who've taken over. If we'd been more concerned about our political and civil rights than talking about Zionism we may have been able to stop the rise of the Nazis in this country at least. We underestimated the anti-Semitism. We treated it like a cold, an inconvenience. Instead it's turned out to be a deadly cancer."

"I know someone at the British Embassy. He may be able to help us."

"What do you mean? Help who?"

"Help us. You, Ruth, the twins."

"You're behind the times, Ulrich. The embassy's closed. Didn't you know? Several weeks ago. The staff have all been recalled to England. Austria's no longer an independent country. We're merely a province of the Greater Reich." There was sarcasm in his voice. "Besides, the English are hardly likely to help Jews. They've got trouble with our people in Palestine."

"I must try to find out where your parents are."

"I feel so hopeless," said Reuben. "God knows what is going to happen to the hundreds of thousands of ordinary Jews who can't afford to escape out of the country. The better off have already gone. To survive, I'll have to leave. I can only hope that Rosa will be alright."

"Married to me, Ruth should be safe," Ulrich said. "Right now I'm ashamed of my own country. I'm not a Jew. Though I'm beginning to feel like one. I don't believe all that Nazi racist rubbish. The fact is it's here and it threatens my family." He paused. He began to speak with vehemence. "I'll go to see my parents. Even if it means getting down on my knees and begging then I'll beg. My mother can't refuse to hear me. Listen to me. Do something for us."

* * *

Memories came flooding back to Ulrich as he walked along the drive up to the house. The deep feelings of guilt and filial treachery that attached itself to his leaving had buried themselves in the inner recesses of his mind. He knew he no longer had to justify himself to anyone for what he had done. Loyalty to his ancestral family and religion had given way to love of his own small family. It was a Jewish family. He felt proud of being his own man now, his own person, that he had made the break. It had given him a freedom of mind and self-confidence he would otherwise have sacrificed to the will and whims of the Church. He changed his mind and was determined not to beg. He would not let his father humiliate him.

He rang the bell. He could hear the sound echoing through the house. A soberly dressed young man answered. Ulrich did not recognise him.

"I've come to see Frau Dreher," he said. Before the other could question him, he stepped into the hall and looked around.

"Mother," he shouted. "Mother, it's Ulrich."

After a short time, his mother appeared at the top of the main staircase. Ulrich looked up and spotted her.

"Mother, I've come to see you."

Elke had changed little. She was still a handsome middle-aged woman. It was as if the years had vanished like a mist on one of Austria's many lakes when the early sun rises in summer. For a split second he was a small carefree boy again, running up the French garden from the pavilion to meet his mother coming out of the orangery carrying a basket of flowers, the serious troubles that now beset him vanishing. His mother came down the stairs slowly, eyeing him fixedly. She approached him and held out her arms to embrace him.

"Ulrich how wonderful to see you." She took him by the arm and they went into the orangery. The chairs, the tables, the plants, the fragrance, the whole atmosphere was as he had known it. It was a place of contradiction for him. Here he had revelled in the warmth and care of his indulgent mother, here too the bitter battles with his father and the Monsignor had scarred him. For the instant, his mind was possessed by the past but the past was now lost in the present and the future was filled with fear and misgiving. His mother brought him back to earth.

"My dear Ulrich, what brings you home?"

Ulrich noticed a melancholy note to her voice. He was about to say that he had a home, his own home but suppressed the temptation.

"Mother I must speak with you. I'm in trouble."

"Trouble? What trouble? Money trouble?"

"No. Nothing like that. It's much more serious."

"I can't think of anything more serious than money." She gave a mild laugh.

"Mother please. It's what's happening. The police have taken Ruth's parents off to some kind of concentration camp. I'm afraid for Ruth and the children."

His mother sat silently looking at him. He tried to divine what his mother was thinking but his intuition failed him. He hoped she would not use words like 'loyalty' or 'duty'. He could not bear that.

"Ulrich when you left this family for the Jewish woman..."

"Mother, her name is Ruth, she is the mother of my children. They are your grandchildren."

"Alright, alright. I'm not going to quarrel with you about all that. However, I can't see what I can possibly do to help you."

"You could persuade father. He's must have a lot of influence with the people now running the country. He knows all the senior Nazis. He knows Colonel von Wartenberg."

"Ah. Him. He's been here a couple of times. He's trying to get the Jews to emigrate to Palestine. Is that where you want to go?"

"Mother, I'm not interested in Palestine. I just want to make sure these criminal Nazi thugs don't drag Ruth and the children off to a concentration camp. Ruth's done nothing wrong to anybody. She's a loving, caring wife and mother. What you were. What you were to us." His voice took on a pleading edge.

"Ulrich you must understand I don't have any influence over your father and his relations with these Nazi people. The lower ranks are just a bunch of working-class thugs. I don't like them any more than you do but they're here to stay. We've become part of Germany. The Nazis are determined to get rid of the Jews. I believe they're right. In any case, it's what the Church wants. The Cardinal gives his full approval to what the Nazis are doing to the Jews. The Jews as much the enemy of the Church as they are of the Nazis. As a Catholic, I'm bound to follow the Church."

"So it's come to this. If you help Ruth your daughter-in-law, you're helping an enemy of the state. Is that what you're saying? Excuse my language, mother, but I don't care a damn what the Pope or Cardinal or the rest of the Church thinks or says. I suppose they approve of these concentration camps where the Jews are being sent."

"I know nothing about such camps. It's probably just Jewish rumour."

"Mother, I never thought your hatred of Jews, because that's what it is, would turn you against your own flesh and blood. If you're not prepared to help then so be it."

"Ulrich you're being melodramatic. I don't hate Jews. I find them... I'm sorry I can't help you. If a choice has to be made and you left me no option, you must realise my loyalty is to your father."

"Where is father? Is he here? I really don't want to meet him."

"You won't. He's in Berlin just now. In fact, he seems to spend as much time there as he does here. He's opening a large factory there. When he's here, I spend a lot of my time entertaining army generals with red-striped trousers and pompous men in black uniforms. I dislike them. They're so arrogant." She pulled a small handkerchief from her sleeve and wiped her eyes. "This country's lost its way. People wanted change from the old empire. They went to war over it. Lost the war and now look what's replaced it."

Ulrich rose. He came and stood over his mother. He spoke softly.

"One day I shall return to this house. In the meantime I must care for my family."

He turned and left the room and the house.

* * *

Ulrich's next door neighbour was a middle-aged Jewish doctor called Aaron Tchirky, a Swiss ophthalmologist who had qualified at a world-famous eye hospital in Boston in the United States. After practising in Zurich, he had opened a clinic in Madrid where, at the beginning of the Civil War, he had sold up and come to Vienna. He and Ulrich sometimes played chess during which Ulrich found him a formidable opponent. The government interdict forbidding Jews to practise any profession had not yet been applied to Tchirky because he was a Swiss national with a diplomatic passport obtained, so he said, through his brother, a junior foreign minister in the Swiss government.

Late one evening at the beginning of November, a mere month after the German takeover of the Sudeten region of Czechoslovakia, there was a series of explosions that woke Ulrich and Ruth. There was a knock on the apartment door. It was Doctor Tchirky.

"I've just heard Goebbels on the radio encouraging people to revenge the killing of a German diplomat in Paris by a young Jewish man. He repeated the usual Nazi line that the German people are anti-Semitic and have no desire to have their rights restricted or to be provoked in the future by parasites of the Jewish race. Those explosions must be the revenge. I'm going to see what's happening. Will you come with me?"

"Certainly."

Ruth cautioned them to be careful. The two men made their way down to the street and into the city centre. There were crowds of people milling about, shouting and cursing Jews. Several lorries arrived, filled with men in stormtrooper uniforms, carrying axes, heavy hammers and long thick truncheons. Ulrich noticed the portly figure of Siedler directing operations. The troopers approached one of the city's main synagogues. Using the hammers they smashed down the doors and forced their entry. Soon they reappeared carrying the sacred Scrolls of the Jewish Law and threw them into the crowd of yelling bystanders, who took them and ripped up the fine coloured linen cloth and tore off the silver crowns, stamping them on the ground. The windows of the synagogue were smashed by the rowdy crowd, throwing stones and pieces of bricks provided by the troopers for this purpose. Flames leapt into the sky as the building took fire. The fire brigade arrived but made no effort to extinguish the fire, instead merely looked on, for it appeared to Ulrich that their presence was required solely to ensure that the adjacent buildings did not catch fire.

As they proceeded along other streets, they found rampaging crowds smashing the windows of Jewish shops, and carrying away the display goods. 'Theft has become an official act of revenge,' remarked Tchirky.

In one place they watched as the stormtroopers entered a block of flats and threw chairs, paintings, ornaments even violins on to the street where the awaiting crowds trampled on them and kicked them into the gutter. Other troopers appeared, escorting a group of men, women and children. They made them run the gauntlet of truncheons and whips before forcing them on to awaiting lorries. One elderly woman was too slow for the tormentors. She received a blow which knocked her to the ground. Two of them kicked her viciously in the head and back. Blood oozed from her mouth. They continued to beat her until she was dead.

Ulrich was about to run forward to stop the horror but was held back by Tchirky.

"Let us go home," Tchirky urged. "There's nothing we can do here." With difficulty, he dragged Ulrich back from the edge of the crowd. On their way back to their apartments they witnessed further episodes of savagery wreaked upon Jewish citizens.

"I don't know how you can stay in this country."

"Don't worry. I've already decided to go back to Switzerland. The Swiss are just as anti-Semitic as the Germans but they don't persecute us. At least not yet. I may yet return to the States. It's a much safer place."

Chapter 11

Vienna 1941

The warm rays of the early morning summer sun stroked the pavements as Ulrich, having an appointment in the town of St Polton, made his way to the Western railway station. He reflected on how the war had changed the life of Vienna: its wide boulevards – hence its name the Paris of the East – almost devoid of young men, most of whom had been conscripted into the *Wehrmacht* and dispatched to conquer and occupy Poland, France and other western European countries; at the railway stations, the endless coming and going of soldiers, glad to be free from the restraints of farming, factories and family hankering after action; the sound of troop trains echoing all night long; a growing black market; large noisy army vehicles of all kinds outnumbering buses, trams and private cars on the streets and avenues; the strictly enforced blackout curtailing any evening entertainment; a dearth of doctors and dentists, above all, the almost total decimation of the Jewish community. There was one noticeable change, the huge red swastika banners had long since been removed from outside Stephansdom and all other churches.

The general enthusiasm for the war had dimmed, when the quick victories at the beginning had turned into what seemed an endless conflict. It had been so different after the conquest of Poland. Why shouldn't they be gripped by war fever, greeting the Führer's blitzkrieg victories as if they were personally their own? His neighbours, overcome by bright-eyed self-congratulation and engulfed by a siren call of glory, told him with unquestioning certainty that the war would end before Christmas: that the British and the French would quickly agree a settlement, that their soldier husbands and sons would come home, that life would return to normal, back to fun-loving Vienna, celebrating with champagne and waltzes. Within the year and in a matter of a mere month, Norway, Denmark, Holland, little Belgium and an armed-to-the-teeth France fell like corn before a reaper. More recently it was the turn of Yugoslavia and Greece. Euphoria, however, had turned to doubt.

It's been a great illusion and they still don't see it, he thought to himself. Their teetotalling Führer is drunk on war and has become the new pied piper from Hameln. If this war continues, we'll all end up dead.

With time to spare, Ulrich stopped at a small cafe near the station. He ordered a coffee and looked around. At another table, a bald-headed man with a large paunch was reading the local morning paper. Ulrich caught sight of the bold headlines, 'German Forces Invade Russia'. For weeks there had been unconfirmed rumours – boosted by frenzied activity around the city's main railway stations – about a possible attack on Russia. Rumours, it would seem, no more. His mind was gripped by growing unease. As he sat anxiously sipping his coffee, the significance of this momentous news and its dire consequences for himself and his family intensified.

He decided to return home. On the journey back, he stopped at a kiosk and bought a paper. He recalled how, during his military service, in exercises in the Tyrolean Alps, he had always feared the sound of the thunder presaging a storm, catching unawares the young soldier marooned on a bare mountainside. He could hear that thunder now.

When he entered the apartment, he heard the singsong of '*aleph, bet, gimel, dalet*' as Gabel and Rahel chanted their way through the Hebrew alphabet. Ruth was trying everything possible to instill Jewish language and culture into the children.

"Why have you come back so soon?" she asked, on his sudden and unexpected reappearance.

He related his experience at the cafe and showed her the newspaper but she didn't want to read the news. Each day had brought further dread, and he knew her anxieties went much deeper than his.

"I'm almost certain to be called up now," he said. "We should've got out when we had the chance." He sounded irritated.

"That's not fair, Ulrich. You know I couldn't leave here not knowing where my parents were. As for Reuben and Rosa. I'm so confused. I live from day to day hoping to hear something."

"Ruth, darling, we've done everything possible. I've tried, Claus has tried time and time again through his contacts to find out where your parents are but to no avail. As for Reuben and Rosa. We just don't know."

"So what do you suggest?" Her tone suggested stress and deep fear. She began to weep.

He put his arms around her and held her close. He could feel her heart thumping and knew its cause. A number of Jews, some of their friends even, had killed their children before killing themselves rather than let them fall into the hands of the SS or Gestapo. He was determined that no harm would come to them or their children.

"Ulrich, I'm not concerned for my own safety or for my own life," she uttered between sobs. "I'm concerned for the children. These Nazi beasts kill Jewish children, even babies, without compunction. I'll do whatever is necessary to protect our own little ones. If you are called up, life here will become intolerable. Without you, we shall all end up in hell."

He tried to console her.

"I'll go and see Uncle Claus. He may be able to help us. Get us papers to cross the border. To do nothing will be fatal. They've invaded Russia with four and half million men. They're going to need more cannon fodder. Any day now they'll come for me. We must get out."

* * *

"I'm glad you've come," Claus greeted Ulrich.

"Why?"

"I leave for Berlin at the end of the week. A friend has got me a post in the Ministry for Foreign Affairs."

"You're working for the Nazis? I don't believe it!" The idea of his debonair uncle being in the service of the Nazi gang puzzled him.

"Working for is not exactly the words I would use. The opposite might be a more accurate description. I shall be a Trojan Horse in dandy's clothing. A mixed metaphor but that is how things are in this mad, mad world."

They sat for a moment in silence.

"The news about the invasion of Russia means I'm next in line to be drafted," Ulrich said. "In my absence Ruth and the children will be picked up and shipped off to a concentration camp. I've no option but to leave and take them with me."

"It won't be easy. You realise that you'll be considered a fugitive and traitor, don't you?"

"I'm no coward, Uncle Claus, but the army is gradually swallowing up each age group and I've every reason to worry, my cohort is next on the official register. How can I escape from the meticulous planning of the German military machine as it grinds its way through the list? I fear for Ruth and the children, for I won't be able to protect them. God only knows what will happen to them once I'm gone."

"Moloch is devouring his own children."

"Ruth is full of alarm and fear. And no wonder. The Jewish community has all but disappeared. When she goes shopping, I must go with her. I refuse to have her wear the obligatory yellow Star of David. She's cut off from her parents, family and friends, they've all vanished. She's not heard from Rosa nor from Reuben."

"I came up against a bureaucratic brick wall when I tried to find out. You know that. The SS are a law unto themselves, a state within the state."

"I'm not criticising you, Uncle Claus. Ruth continues to ask me, where are they? Hiding with friends? Taken by the Gestapo? Several of her friends managed to obtain visas from the Chinese consul here in Vienna and found refuge in Shanghai. But he left last year so that avenue is closed."

"Ah, Doctor Feng Shan Ho. I used to meet him at diplomatic evenings. A most kind and honourable man."

"Father Hahn used to regale us with harrowing tales of the wicked, so-called pagan Chinese. How ironic that a so-called pagan nation would bring succour to Jews being persecuted by their Christian fellow countrymen."

"Things are going to get worse for the Jewish community."

"Is that possible?"

"It is. I've heard tell from a friend high up in the Foreign Ministry that the SS are building camps in Poland. He says that these are not labour camps but death camps."

"That's unbelievable."

"Well, you'd better believe it. Given the casual and arbitrary murder of Jews on our own streets, I'm prepared to believe it. The Führer said only recently that the Jews should be exterminated."

"Uncle Claus I've really come to ask if you can help us to cross the border?"

"I'll do my best. You must give me a day or two. Ruth's passport will be marked with a J as soon as she tries to leave. Many countries, including Switzerland, won't allow her in."

Ulrich was silent for a moment.

"It's Ruth and the children I'm worried about. The close bond that tied her family together has been ripped apart. It's taken a terrible toll on her spirits. Her eyes have long since lost their glow, her voice carries an unspoken burden. She is restless and irritable. she easily gets ill-tempered. And I don't blame her." He sounded agitated. "I'll be candid. Our sex life has lost its fire and sparkle. She has become withdrawn. She refuses to venture out without me, she fears being picked up in some random sweep by the police, looking for deserters and spies. When we're on the trams or in cafes, you'd have to be deaf not to overhear young soldiers, on leave from Poland, relating personal stories of the horrors of the ghettos and concentration camps, of savage beatings and murders of Jews. For her, even the sight of a uniform is enough to bring fear."

"I don't know what's happened to this country," Claus said. "Some of the finest brains in Europe used to inhabit this city. Now ignorant numbskulls lead a flock of sheep. Just like the last time, this war won't solve any problems." He went silent. "Do you know what this war is all about?"

"I thought the Nazis wanted to build a European empire."

"I'm afraid you're wrong. The Führer's basic reason for waging this war is the extermination of the Jews. All other reasons are merely secondary to his main purpose. He has said often enough that this is his mission in life. He put it into writing. War is his means to comb Europe and purge it of its Jewish communities. The Nazis started in Germany, they came here, took Czechoslovakia, then Poland and the rest. The German army did the conquering, followed by the SS whose job is to flush out Jews wherever they can find them, and cart them off to Poland to the camps. Have no illusions. This war is not like any other war. It's about destroying a whole people."

"Then I must get Ruth and the children somewhere safe." Ulrich reflected for a moment. "Why hasn't the Church spoken out against all this?"

"The Church. You might well ask that. This has been its greatest moral failure since it refused to condemn seventeenth and eighteenth century slavery. If the Church really wanted to, it could have stopped this campaign of terror and murder. When we invaded Poland in thirty-nine, the Pope muttered pious words about both sides getting together and sorting out their problems. The same happened when the Führer's armies invaded France and the Low Countries. More sanctimonious claptrap. Yet a couple of years ago when the Bishops in Germany learned of the Nazis' secret so-called euthanasia action policy for the mentally handicapped, they were up in arms with fury. The Vatican was hostile to such a programme of the mass murder of the incurably sick. The violent reaction of the Church brought about the end of the whole affair. The Nazis were afraid that they would lose the support of the large Catholic population. However, when it comes to the Jews, to the murder of tens of thousands of Jews, the Church is silent." Claus stopped speaking for a moment.

"By the way, do you know the code name for this Russian exploit?" he added.

"No."

"Barbarossa. It's named after the Emperor Frederick Barbarossa our infamous Holy Roman Emperor. He was the leader of the Third Crusade in the 12th century. This is hubris. The Führer should study his history of Napoleon. He invaded Russia with an army of one-hundred-thousand and ended up with a handful of men. Winter defeated him. Sometimes the temperature went below thirty degrees. That's what's going to happen to our young men."

* * *

Next day, Claus came to the apartment.

"I think I may be able to help you," he said. "I've an old friend, we were students together and we've kept in touch from time to time over the years. His name is August von Grolman, he's now the general in charge of the southern Austrian area and northern Yugoslavia, with his headquarters at Klagenfurt. I've written this letter of introduction," he held up an envelope, "I'm sure he'll help you but you'll have to explain the situation yourself. *Quod scripta manet*, as the Romans wisely remarked, 'what is written, endures'."

"Can he really be trusted?" Ruth said. "It's known that the generals have sworn personal allegiance to the Führer. He's just as likely to hand us over to the police."

"I know him very well and I can assure you he'll do no such thing. He belongs to the old school of officers. One of his ancestors was a general who fought Napoleon at Waterloo. Ulrich, do you remember many years ago just before your twenty-first birthday, my telling you about one of my youthful exploits? The one where, on horseback, I jumped over a hearse during a funeral in the countryside. I had a friend with me and, of course, he did the same."

"Vaguely."

"Well, that friend was August von Grolman."

"You must have been very close friends."

"We were. He's been a soldier all his life. Served with distinction in Serbia during the first war, and took part in the invasion of France last year. He's highly decorated."

"There's one other problem," Ulrich said. "Money. We'll need foreign currency. The banks here won't provide me with any. I'm not some kind of international trader."

"You're in luck. The Führer's armies occupy half of Europe, so the German reichmark is now the new international European currency. It's easily convertible into Swiss francs or Italian lira. I've also thought of something else. One of the currencies which is used all over the Middle East is our own – no longer used by us I must admit – Maria Theresa thalers. It's where the American dollar got it's name from."

"That's news to me," Ulrich said.

"You never know where you might end up or pass through, so as a hedge against the future, I've brought along a couple dozen of these thalers. If you sew them in to your clothing they may very well come in handy."

"What are they worth?"

"I haven't the slightest idea. The fact is, they're silver-bullion coins. So they'll be worth what you can get for them. Even the British mint them. After gold, they're the best international currency I know of."

Ruth rushed forward and put her arms around Claus's neck.

"You're so good, Claus. If only the rest of this country were as kind as you are."

"Ruth, not everybody is a diehard Nazi. Ulrich here isn't and there are others. Precious few I must confess but they exist. You've one big advantage though."

"What's that?"

"The worldwide Jewish community. You'll find help from them. Faced with this Nazi onslaught against them, the Jews no longer have any borders. Not that they ever did. No matter what the Führer does, and he's determined to destroy European Jewry, he won't succeed. He's desperate to keep America out of the war." He hesitated for a moment. "That's why I'm going to Berlin. I shall be working, behind the scenes obviously, to make sure they do indeed come into the war. If they do, Adolf will lose. You must wish me as much luck as I wish you."

* * *

General von Grolman's headquarters were located in the sand-coloured Klagenfurt town hall, festooned with Swastika banners. A young soldier took Ulrich through an arcaded yard, up a stone flight of stairs to the general's offices, ushered him into a small room and told him to wait. He had left Ruth and the twins back at the hotel. Ruth had been in a state of nervous tension during the train journey from Vienna, but had suddenly found her calm self-assurance again on arriving at Klagenfurt. 'I feel relieved,' she told Ulrich. 'If only we can get to Italy, we shall be safe. The Italians are a friendly, cultured people. I can't believe that they would have concentration camps for Jews.'

After a short time, a young man in officer's uniform appeared. He wore tortoiseshell spectacles, which gave him a scholastic air.

"Herr Dreher," he said, "I'm General von Grolman's adjutant. Can you tell me what precisely is the nature of your business with the general?"

"I have a personal letter of introduction from an old friend of the general. He is my uncle. His name is Herr Claus von Juggardt."

"Perhaps, if I may take this letter to the general?"

Ulrich handed the letter over.

"Please wait here."

Ulrich did not have long to wait before the youthful adjutant reappeared and led him into the General's office. General von Grolman was tall, tanned and athletic looking, with a broad, deeply furrowed brow, strong chin, a Knight's Iron Cross with oak leaves hung around his neck and a heavy gold signet ring graced the third finger of his right hand. He was sitting behind a desk which had three telephones on it, two black and one red. There were also some neatly arranged papers and a thick green file. He stood up to greet Ulrich.

"Herr von Juggardt doesn't say much in his letter," said the General, as he sat down, "was that deliberate?" He spoke with a deep gravelly voice.

"Yes. He said it would be better if I explained my request in person."

"That's typical of him. Leave nothing in writing, he used to say. Of course, in those far-off days he was referring to love letters." A small smile played across the general's face.

"He thought it better that I give you my own explanation."

Von Grolman raised his eyebrows at this remark.

"Reading this letter, I formed the impression that you might have some important information for me. Perhaps in the field of intelligence. In which case I could put you in touch with my chief of military intelligence."

"It's not like that."

Von Grolman eyed him with a sharp, steely look.

"My wife, Ruth, is Jewish," Ulrich said. "I've two young children who are being brought up in the Jewish tradition. They face certain death if I'm not there to protect them."

The General held up his hand.

"Go no further. From your age, I take it you're about thirty. Is that correct?

"Yes, that's correct."

"So you're about to be called up? There's no need to answer that one. I'm acutely aware of the manpower situation of the army. I've the feeling that you're going to tell me something I don't really want to hear."

"General, I hope you're wrong."

"If it has to do with military matters, I'm rarely wrong. I've held command in the army too long not to be able to fathom the thoughts of young men."

"I hoped you would hear me out."

"For the sake of old friendship with your uncle, I shall certainly do that. More than that I can't guarantee. So young man, proceed."

Given what von Grolman had already said, Ulrich knew he had to proceed with circumspection.

"General, I wouldn't wish under any circumstance to compromise your position." He paused. "I need to get my wife and children out of this country before they can be taken off to some concentration camp. All I ask is that you could provide them with papers to ensure a safe passage across the frontier into Italy. I believe they will be safe there."

"For your wife and children there may be a possibility. Certainly not for you. There is no need for me to say why."

"Of course. I understand."

There was a pause in the exchange.

"You must realise, Herr Dreher, that this war is only just beginning. The *Wehrmacht* needs many more men. We occupy Europe from the Arctic to the Mediterranean and from the English Channel to Russia. Our incursion into the Balkans, part of which is under my command, is already swallowing up a huge amount of manpower. We've had to throw the English out of Greece, invade Crete and take over Yugoslavia."

"Sir, I'm thinking only of my wife and children."

"I'm surprised that you haven't turned to your father for help. He seems to be an influential figure in Berlin. His name is mentioned in the highest circles. I'm sure he would want to protect his daughter-in-law and his own grandchildren."

"I'm afraid not." Ulrich paused. "I shan't trouble you with the details, but because of my marriage to Ruth, there has been an unfortunate rupture between my family and myself."

"That's most regrettable. I knew your mother slightly through Claus. In fact, I was a guest at your parents' wedding, over thirty years ago."

"I, too, regret it. However, I can't stand by and allow the state to take my wife and children from me, as will inevitably happen, if, or rather when, I'm called up. One would have to be deaf and blind not to know what's happening. Her parents have been taken away without any judicial process whatsoever, the whereabouts of her brother and sister are unknown, all her friends have either fled or disappeared. I've seen with my own eyes the barbaric treatment of Jews on the streets of Vienna..."

Von Grolman cut in.

"Herr Dreher, I cannot and will not allow you to give me a lecture on the shortcomings of the German state. I serve that state. I'm not responsible for the decisions the state makes with regard to various peoples. I've a job to do and I shall carry it out. That is what soldiers do. We obey the orders of our political masters."

"General, I apologise for presuming to give you my views of what is happening."

"Apology accepted."

The general got up and walked across to the window where he stood looking out over the square with his back to Ulrich. He remained silent for several minutes as if he had forgotten Ulrich's presence. Ulrich knew it was a decisive moment that would determine his life.

"You're not the only one to have to make sacrifices, Herr Dreher," he said without turning around. "I've two sons. One is only twenty-three and is the commander of a U-boat. A U-boat is nothing more than a floating coffin. His life expectancy is minimal. My other son is serving as a tank commander in Russia. His chances of survival are also very limited. So you see, sorrow is widespread. I suffer and my wife suffers. I didn't start this war and neither did they." He paused, turned and walked back to his desk.

"Now, Herr Dreher, I'm a very busy man and this is what I propose. Tomorrow morning at six, my adjutant, Captain Brinkmann, will come to your hotel with a staff car. He will take you to the frontier and ensure the safe passage of your wife and children across the border into Italy. Italy is our ally and my relations with my Italian opposite number are most cordial. He will also ensure that you return here to Klagenfurt. After that, it's up to you what you do."

"General. I'm most grateful for your help. We'll be ready tomorrow."

"One more thing, Herr Dreher. I must remind you that failure to respond to call-up papers is a serious military offence. It will be interpreted as desertion, which is a capital crime. Desertion saps the moral fibre of an army. I've already had to order the death of two deserters under my command. A most unpleasant but necessary task. They were court-martialled and shot."

Ulrich remained silent.

Von Grolman stood up. He held out his hand.

"When next you see your uncle, please convey my kindest regards. Tell him, when this war is over, we must get together again."

As he crossed over the Alter Platz and made his way down Kammergasse, Ulrich walked dreamlike, heedless of the buildings and people he passed by. He faced a terrible dilemma. How to tell Ruth that he wouldn't be coming with her and the children. He came to a park where he sat down on one of the benches. Obsessed with the gloomiest of forebodings, he debated with himself in miserable indecision.

This news is not going to be easy. I wonder if that woman across there or that fat, podgy man know what it's like to lose a wife and children in order to save them. People just don't realise the terrible pain they've inflicted on their fellow citizens by allowing a madman to take over this country. The general says he didn't start the war, nor did his sons. Perhaps not but they damn well support it. Without the support of the army there would be no war. But he's right about one thing. If I try to cross the border with Ruth, they'll alert the Italian authorities who'll pick us up. We'll be brought back here. Ruth will be handed over to the SS and I'll be shot as a traitor, fleeing justice.

He made his tormented way back to the hotel while rehearsing the same arguments. It was so frustrating. He was in two minds whether to tell Ruth at once the ominous choices they faced or wait to tell her when they reached the frontier. The more he considered the matter the more tangled up he became in his own tormented deliberations. He was in for a surprise.

"How did the meeting go?" Ruth asked. She sounded composed.

"The general was most helpful. Thanks to Claus."

"Is that all?" From her tone of voice and looks, he knew she was reading his thoughts. He had no defensive barrier against her penetrating gaze.

"He's going to send a staff car tomorrow morning at six. It'll take us to the frontier and his adjutant will ensure a safe crossing."

"You don't sound the least pleased."

"Don't I?"

There was an awkward silence between them.

"Ulrich you're not telling me the whole truth, are you?"

Again a silence.

"Look Ulrich," Ruth said, "I know what's happened. Von Grolman has told you that you will not be allowed to cross over into Italy. Am I right?"

"As always," he said, without enthusiasm.

"Ulrich, darling, I'm just relieved we're leaving, putting distance between ourselves and the Nazis who are determined on our destruction."

"If you're relieved, I'm not. How do you think I feel, having to leave you and the twins? I don't like it the least bit. I feel I'm letting you down." He was now shouting. Showing his anger.

"Calm down, Ulrich. You made great sacrifices to marry me. I can't tell you how much I love you. You're everything to me. Whatever happens, that you must know. I've already worked out what we can do."

"I'm listening."

"When we cross the border tomorrow, I shall make my way to Venice. There's a large Jewish community there. I shall find friends and shelter. You can return here. Wait some days and then find some way to cross over. We'll be together again."

"You make it sound so easy that it frightens me."

"Don't be frightened. Remember those days when we were young? You said that if there are mountains to climb we'll climb them together. Well now, this is one more mountain."

Ulrich sat, not saying anything. He knew she was right. She had solved his dilemma. A burden had been – if only partially – lifted from his mind.

* * *

Promptly at six next morning, Captain Brinkmann turned up at the hotel with the staff car and a driver who put Ruth's case in the boot and helped her into the back seat with the children. Ulrich sat next to her. The adjutant, sitting in the front with the driver, turned around and faced his anxious passengers.

"This is the general's plan," he said in a coldly polite tone, "we'll drive to the frontier." He turned and faced Ruth. "When we get there, I'll escort you, Frau Dreher, and the two children through our military and customs barriers to ensure your passport is not stamped with a J, we'll then proceed to the Italian side where I shall engage with the Italian officer in charge. From there, you will be able to pick up the train to take you to wherever you intend to go. You, Herr Dreher, will remain in the car till I return. My instructions are that you must not attempt to cross the frontier." There was an unmistakable hint of threat in his voice.

Leaving Klagenfurt, the driver took the road to the north of the Worther See. A dark sheen came off the surface of the lake, lit up by the early morning summer sunshine. To the south lay the Karawanken range of wooded hills. The journey brought back to Ulrich memories of childhood, of summers, swimming and romping about with his younger sister Gerda in the astonishingly warm water of the lake, building sandcastles on the bathing beach, running along the shady avenues, enjoying ice creams. He could hear the tolerant chiding of his mother and her telling him that a famous composer, Beethoven, or was it Brahms, had fallen in love with this place and composed a symphony or violin concerto here. His family used to have a summer residence here but had sold it just after the Great War.

He held on to Ruth's hand. The early years of his marriage passed before his eyes, the honeymoon, the birth of the twins, the happy days taking the children for walks in the park, their first steps and their first words. Above all, the unfailing presence of Ruth in his life, cheering him up, joking with him, laughing with him, consoling him when he experienced difficulties, deflating him when he became pompous on his metaphorical soapbox. From her, he had learned to love books, to go to art exhibitions and concerts. His antipathy to art and music had dissipated under her encouraging tutelage. It was Brahms, he suddenly recalled, who wrote both his Second Symphony and the well-known Violin Concerto.

"We're approaching the frontier," announced the adjutant, sounding like the conductor on a tram.

Suddenly the sky seemed to darken for Ulrich. Among the few phrases of his scanty schoolboy French, one had stuck in his memory, *Partir c'est mourir un peu*, parting is a little bit like dying.

He felt as if he were part of a funeral cortege.

The car drew up in front of the frontier post and they all got out. An outsize red and black swastika banner hung limp from a flagpole. The adjutant, holding Ruth's passport, disappeared into the frontier post. Ulrich held Ruth tightly. She was weeping silently. He then picked up in turn Gabel and Rahel.

"You're going on holiday," he reassured them. "You go with mummy, for I must stay here to do some business and then I'll come to where you're going. We'll all be together then." The four-year-old twins looked at their father without saying a word. They seemed bewildered at what was happening.

The adjutant reappeared.

"Frau Dreher," he said, "your papers are now in order for you to be able to proceed to the Italian side. Please take the children and follow me."

Ruth, tears still in her eyes, grasped Ulrich tightly. She then lifted her heavy case.

"Children," she said, "stay close to mummy."

Captain Brinkmann made no move to help her with either the luggage or the children. Ulrich watched as the group passed around the wooden barrier and walked towards the Italian customs and passport control. When they had reached that point, they all disappeared into the wooden hut. After a time, they came out accompanied by an Italian in uniform. Ruth, on the other side of the Italian barrier, lifted her arm in a farewell gesture to Ulrich, who could see, even from that distance, that she was weeping profusely. As the adjutant walked back towards the German side of the border, Ulrich noticed that two Italian soldiers were accompanying Ruth and the children as they made their way to the railway station that could be seen a hundred metres or so further on. One soldier was carrying the case and, while Ruth took Rahel by the hand, the other Italian soldier took that of Gabel.

When the adjutant returned, he told Ulrich to get back into the car. As on the outward journey, no one spoke. Ulrich was lost in his own perplexities, racking his brains to think of some scheme or ruse to enable him to get to Italy. The seeds of silent hatred were sown in his heart as he realised that Ruth and the children were disappearing from his life. Captain Brinkmann must have divined his thoughts.

"Don't think of trying to cross over to Italy," he said, "I've made the Italian authorities aware of your military obligations."

"Your general is intractable," Ulrich retorted.

"Just be lucky he has helped you. I wouldn't help a Jew," he said with contempt in his voice.

"At least my family won't end up in some kind of death camp."

"I would watch my tongue if I were you, Herr Dreher. A careless word might cost you your life."

With that he made off in the staff car. Ulrich went into the hotel and up into his room where he sat down on the side of the bed, covered his face with his hands and wept like a child.

Chapter 12

Yugoslavia 1941

Ulrich, his spirit crushed, had a hunger for Ruth and a desire to see the children again. His grief, a bereavement almost, at her absence was yet offset by the relief that they were safe over the border in Italy. Was not exile better than a death camp? With them gone, a listless air of uncertainty hung heavily on his mind and the growing tedium of waiting heightened the suspense as he dwelt upon the unknown difficulties ahead. His plans to cross the frontier and rejoin them, making his life just bearable, appeared more futile and fanciful as each day passed.

This illusion became apparent when, not long after his return from Klagenfurt, he had been served with his call-up papers. He now considered himself a reluctant German soldier among the many recent recruits conscripted into the *Wehrmacht*. Well-known for its committed Nazi views, indoctrinated by drill and draconian severity, this was a highly disciplined and superior organisation which considered itself the main bastion of the Führer's regime. It was a totally different creature from the friendly, somewhat slipshod and easy-going Austrian army of his military service days.

Sitting on a bunk bed in a vast high-ceilinged room, in a run-down former cotton mill, turned into an ad hoc military barracks near the town of Eisenstadt, in southern Austria, he regarded with growing distaste the various pieces of his newly issued uniform. A field-grey woollen tunic, with its distinctive green collar, an eagle badge with swastika – *'the most abused religious symbol in history'* he had read somewhere, trousers, a cotton shirt, scarf, a brimless forage cap, a steel helmet, knee-high jack boots and finally an eight millimetre Mauser rifle but no ammunition. Except for the rifle, he associated the whole uniform with the wretched *Wehrmacht.*

He recalled with trepidation an unexpected and unwelcome encounter after his medical examination, some days previously in Vienna. The doctors had passed him fully fit: first-class sight, hearing and breathing.

"You've got nicely toned muscles," remarked the doctor, who was small and spoke with a faint Westphalian accent. "You'll make a good combat soldier!"

As he was about to leave the medical centre, a military official told him to report to an administrative office. On entering he saw two men in civilian dress sitting behind a table which had a yellow coloured manila file on it. The elder of the two was short, thickset, had the air of a typical minor functionary, balding, and wearing thick tortoiseshell spectacles. The stony-faced younger one with a broken nose and cauliflower ear, looked as if he had been a heavyweight wrestler.

"Herr Dreher," the older one said, "please sit down. We've called you in for a short chat."

"Who exactly are 'we'?" Ulrich asked.

"We're the state security police."

The Gestapo. Ulrich's immediate reaction was to think of Ruth. Had she been returned across the border? If the army is allowing these fiends to question me, he thought, it must be serious.

The older officer picked up the yellow file and opened it. He looked down at the opening page and read silently to himself. After a few minutes he spoke up.

"Your full name is Ulrich Ernst Dreher is it not?"

"Yes."

Ulrich never used his middle name except on official documents.

"It says here that you were married five years ago. Is that true?"

"Yes. Why are you questioning me, if you've already got the information?"

"Herr Dreher, we ask the questions. You answer them. Is that clear?" While polite, there was a sharp tone to the officer's voice.

"The record states here," he continued, "that your marriage was conducted in a synagogue. Now why was that? Are you a Jew? You don't have a Jewish name."

"I'm not a Jew. Is that an offence?"

"Herr Dreher, don't get fresh with me. You know perfectly well what I mean." There was anger now in the voice.

"I'm not sure if I do."

The inspector drummed the fingers of his right hand on the top of the table.

"Since you seem to be deliberately dumb, let me spell it out for you." More drumming of the fingers. "It's against the Nuremberg Laws for an Aryan to marry a Jew."

"I married my wife before these so-called laws applied in Austria. In any case, I don't go along with all this nonsense of being Aryan. I'm Austrian."

"Herr Dreher, you're incorrigibly stubborn and this is going to land you in serious trouble. Your wife is a Jewess, is she not? So your children are Jews. Two children according to the record."

He continued without waiting for Ulrich to reply. "Where's your wife at the present moment?"

"She's abroad."

"Where?"

"Switzerland or maybe Italy. I'm not sure."

"I think you're lying, Herr Dreher. That will not do. When did you last see your wife?"

"My wife is not a criminal. So what the hell has this to do with the police, with you? Oh, I see now. You want to arrest her, beat her up and knock the four-year-old children about," he said, his face twisted with disdain. "The Gestapo a have reputation for torturing unarmed women and young children. Why the devil don't you two get yourselves into the army and fight like real men."

The bruiser got up, went round to the side of the table where Ulrich was, took him by the shoulders, swung him around and landed a vicious blow to his stomach. Ulrich fell to the ground, feeling as if he had been hit by a charging bull. The pain was excruciating. He vomited on to the wooden floor. He lay for several minutes before he could raise himself on to his elbows.

"Get up you dirty Jew lover," he ordered. It was the first time he had spoken.

Gradually, and in great pain, Ulrich stood up. His legs felt wobbly and he slumped down on the chair.

"Now Herr Dreher," resumed the inquisitor, "I hope you'll answer my questions. They're quite simple and straightforward. Now, once again, tell me where your Jewess wife is and where your two Jew children are?"

It was some time before Ulrich answered. It gave him time to think of a way out of the hands of the Gestapo.

"It's possible they are with my parents."

"And who might your parents be?"

"My father is Dieter Dreher, the arms manufacturer. He's on speaking terms with the Führer and a close friend of the head of the SS General von Wartenberg. I myself have met the general."

The effect of this statement on both men was immediate.

The older one considered the matter for a little time. Suddenly snapping shut the yellow file, he said, "Herr Dreher, I shall investigate your claims. If I find you've been lying I shall return and personally make sure you're suitably punished." He stood up, the other doing likewise. They both walked to the door and left the room.

It had taken Ulrich a couple of days to recover from this ordeal but he reflected that, with a mixture of what Ruth called chutzpah and a half truth, he had been able to extricate himself from a potentially nasty situation. 'A half-truth is more difficult to disprove than a lie,' Claus had once remarked.

As he sat in the barrack-room, engrossed in his own thoughts, Ulrich was oblivious to the noisy sound of dozens of men, sitting about, quietly chatting and getting to know each other. The almost peaceful atmosphere was suddenly and violently shattered when the door at the far end of the room was flung open and a sergeant and a corporal strode in. A sharp whistle blast rent the air.

"Attention everybody. Stand in front of your beds," the order rang out. There was a rush to comply.

"Stand up straight."

The sergeant, accompanied by the corporal, marched slowly down the central aisle, scowling from side to side. When he came to the further end of the room he turned and faced the assembled men.

"My name is Faulhaber. Sergeant Faulhaber to you." He spoke in a strong Swabian accent. "I'm the worst bastard in the whole of the German army." He paused. "Let me make it very clear that if any one of you so much as hesitates to carry out any of my orders, you will be considered an even worse bastard than me and you'll be treated accordingly." He spoke with a bombastic steely-edged tone to his voice with curled upturned lip as he gazed dourly at the assembled recruits. Ulrich wondered what was in store.

The men were awakened next morning at five o'clock. By six, they had all been on the parade ground for half an hour, marching up and down, back and forth. Two hours later there was a short pause for breakfast. Then back to the parade ground. Stripping down to their underpants, they were then sent off on a ten kilometre run. Dressed again, the next task was Swedish exercises. After lunch, there was more parade ground marching followed by rifle practice. In the late afternoon, there was a forced route march, in which they each had to carry their rifle and a thirty kilo backpack. After the evening meal they were again ordered on to the parade ground for more marching. Finally, at ten o'clock they fell exhausted on to their bunks.

Day after day, they pursued the same regime of marching, training and gun practice. Faulhaber was true to his word. Any infringement of orders was immediately and severely punished, usually in the form of further forced marches even into the night. Ulrich knew that safety lay in not drawing attention to himself. It wasn't too difficult for he had done his military service and knew every wrinkle in the tripe, as another recruit, a small Bavarian sheep farmer, put it.

Each night as he lay on his bed, Ulrich's thoughts turned to Ruth and the children. Where were they, what were they doing and how were they coping? It was a relief to know that his beloved ones were not in danger of being dragged from the flat, or lifted off the street and taken away. He recalled the sound of her voice, and the movement of her clothes as she walked, remembered her smile and the fragrance of her perfume. He dreamed of their intimate moments together, the touch of her soft skin, felt her embrace, her kiss, the pressure of her breasts against his chest, their making love. The leave-taking at Klagenfurt seemed a long time ago and his present situation was full of questions and problems. Should he try to escape? Flee?

His fellow recruits were generally of his age group. Most were married with families, having ordinary jobs, as teachers, postmen, shopkeepers, bakers, waiters, tram drivers, musicians, minor officials. Others were dubious types, boasting of robberies, burglaries, of spells in prison. One rum character, named Kurt, told Ulrich how his prison had held some of Germany's worst criminals. 'When the war came these men were put in SS uniform and sent off to the East, forming *Einsatzgruppen* or killing squads.

Ulrich was gravely troubled as he lay looking up at the high white painted ceiling. He considered the situation. Rumours are rife that German soldiers have taken part in committing some of the worst atrocities in Poland, especially against Jews. Everyone knows the SS carry out such evil deeds. I wonder if these men in this barrack room are capable of shooting and killing the unarmed elderly, women and children? General von Grolman believed it his duty to carry out orders without question. What shall I do if I'm ordered to do the same? All the more reason, to get out before my moral scruples are put to the test.

* * *

One morning after breakfast, the post, accumulated over several days, was distributed. Cards, letters and parcels brought relief from the daily programme of training and marches. There was a letter for Ulrich. It had an Italian stamp, posted a fortnight previously in Venice. It had been forwarded from his apartment according to his instructions to the Vienna postal services.

"Italian girlfriend, then?" queried the soldier bringing the mail. Ulrich didn't reply. He tore open the envelope.

> *My dearest darling Ulrich,*
> *The children and myself are safe and well. Our friends here are looking after us. They are most kind and treat us as one of themselves. We occupy a small studio flat. The food is adequate and I'm learning to make pasta and pizzas. I'm also learning Italian and so are the children who find the unfamiliar sounds funny. For reasons you will understand, I cannot give you my address. I miss you more than I can express and each night I fall asleep thinking about you. I long for us to be together again. Our hearts are united forever. The children send all their love.*
> *Your loving Ruth.*

Ulrich read it over and over again. A warm sense of relief flooded through his body. They're safe, they're well, they're in good hands. He put the letter back in the envelope, folded it and put it into his trouser pocket.

"Good news?" A thickset man stood over him. His question sounded innocent enough.

"You could say that," replied Ulrich.

"The name's Wolfgang. Wolfgang Hirsch. I'm from Frankfurt."

"Ulrich Dreher. From what I've seen of you on the route marches you seem to be very fit."

"Thanks for the compliment. I used to train a local youth football team back home, then the war decimated the numbers and I was soon left with no one to train." He paused. "Where are you from? You sound Austrian."

"I'm from Vienna. Are you married?"

"I used to be but my wife died in childbirth."

"What a terrible tragedy. I'm sorry to hear that."

"In one way it was a blessing."

"How can you possibly say that?" There was a note of displeasure in Ulrich's voice.

"Well," Wolfgang hesitated, "and I hope you're not offended, but she was Jewish. With all the trouble that's been happening perhaps it is better that she's not alive to see what's happened to the large Jewish community in Frankfurt."

Ulrich realised that he had been put in an awkward position. He'd heard of these agents provocateurs paid by the Nazis to spy upon their neighbours and to denounce them to the authorities who put them in front of a kangaroo type of court which came to arbitrary verdicts condemning their victims to unspecified terms in a prison camp. Even schoolchildren were encouraged to incriminate their parents. Could he trust this man? All youth movements and organisations, all art, music and sport associations were tightly controlled by the Nazi Party who used them to instill party ideology, loyalty and anti-Semitism. He decided to say nothing about Ruth or the children.

Ulrich did not want to get inveigled into further conversation. "If this course lasts much longer maybe we'll get to know each other better."

It was a false hope. Late that afternoon the men were given an early meal after which they were ordered to line up in the parade ground, where they were put into different sections. After an endless hour, several army trucks appeared which some groups, but not all, were ordered to mount. A cold fear overtook Ulrich. I'm on my way to Russia, he thought. He inwardly berated himself for not having attempted to make an early escape from the barracks and make his way across to Italy. Each military order tied him more closely to the fate he was determined to avoid. Once the train went north through Germany and Poland his chances of freeing himself from his present fatal predicament would dwindle to nought. As the lorries left, filled with their complement of troops, Ulrich found himself in one of the remaining groups. As ever with the army, no explanations were given and no one dared ask for one. After a further interminable hour, the lorries reappeared, empty and ready for the remaining troops. Ulrich was one of the last to mount.

Large camouflaged canvas tarpaulins were drawn over the trucks so that no one could see in but, equally, the soldiers could not see out. The chatter and banter of the previous hours' waiting gave way to a palpably nervous silence. There was little comfort in the hard wooden benches as the trucks bumped along the road. Military vehicles, whose function was utility and not convenience, were not equipped with soft springs. No one smoked for they had been enjoined with dire consequences if anyone tried to light up. Ulrich had no idea where they were heading. All sorts of wild schemes passed through his mind, such as jumping off the truck, pretending to have become mad by using his rifle to threaten his companions, to faint or to be violently sick. Experience from his military service days had taught him that the army was well equipped to deal with such infantile ruses, young men trying such madcap ideas confined to a military prison and punished. Only now, if von Grolman were to be believed, it would be a firing squad.

The relative obscurity under the covering tarpaulin had now become total darkness. The only sound was that of the truck's noisy engine and its lurching, bumpy movement. During the journey, the initial silence between the men had gradually given way to the usual familiar soldiers' talk. A couple of hours later, Ulrich felt the paved road change to the much bumpier cobblestones associated with large towns and cities. He reckoned they had covered about fifty or sixty kilometres, in which case they must be in Vienna and heading for the western railway station, which would mean going to Germany. Finally the truck came to a stop. Ulrich heard the sounds of railway locomotives and the clanging of couplings. The acrid smell of train smoke caught his nostrils.

Having climbed down from the truck, the men were told to line up and await further orders. Looking about, Ulrich realised that they were not in the western main rail station at all but the southern one. It was from this station that the international lines went south to Italy, Hungary, Greece and the Balkans. We're going to Yugoslavia, Ulrich said to himself. Or Greece. Whatever, it's not Russia. A sense of release unshackled the bonds that held his mind bound to the idea that his fate had already been sealed. Over the previous weeks, his imagination had been filled with pictures of a vast, flat glacial landscape, where birds froze on the wing in winter. He felt his chances improving.

The warm summer night hummed with activity as army trucks disgorged their cargoes of soldiers. Military police were everywhere, eyeing the drawn-up ranks with disdain. The ordinary soldiers referred to these police as 'chained dogs' because of the distinctive steel gorgets they wore around their necks. Any attempt, Ulrich realised, to escape from this situation was doomed to failure. More trucks came and went. Trains filled up with soldiers and left. The night dragged on.

Finally the order was given to Ulrich's platoon to entrain. The train he was allocated was made up of fifteen carriages and two open freight cars with mounted flak guns. The men crowded on to the train where the lucky ones found themselves a seat while the others had to manage with standing or sitting on the corridor floor. Ulrich found himself with ten others squeezed into a compartment designed for eight: any vestiges of leisurely pre-war days had gone.

The compartment was lit with a single, dim, blue lightbulb. The window and corridor blinds had been already pulled down. As the men settled, one of the men produced two decks of playing cards and soon a game of canasta was under way. Although he had not played for several years, Ulrich joined in and managed a few good hands. Exhaustion overcame them and soon the compartment was full of sleeping and snoring soldiers.

Several times, the train stopped with a jolt, only to continue after a short wait. Finally several hours later, it stopped when one of the soldiers, sitting next to the window, raised the blind.

"We're in Zagreb. We're in Zagreb railway station," he said with great surprise, as if Zagreb were in some exotic far-off country.

"Where the hell's Zagreb?" asked another.

"It's in Yugoslavia," Ulrich said. "Croatia, actually."

"How the devil do you know that?" the man next to him asked.

Most of the men hailed from the western and northern parts of Germany.

"When I was at elementary school," Ulrich said, "during the last war, Croatia was part of the old Austrian-Hungarian empire. We used to have to learn the names of all the countries that belonged to the Empire."

"Oh, for God's sake leave out the history and geography lesson," the neighbour protested. "What I want to know is when are we going to have something to eat? I'm starving. I could do with a decent meal."

His wish was soon to be fulfilled. A sergeant came along the corridor shouting to everyone to get out of the train. Later, standing on the platform in the early summer dawn, with the sun already up, Ulrich felt a great relief from the confined space of the overcrowded sweat-smelling compartment, as he breathed in the fresh, cool air. Several buffet stands had been set up on the platform, providing hot coffee and snacks. The men swarmed around the counters, all shouting for attention. The air was soon filled with the sound of chatting and bantering laughter. The man who was Ulrich's neighbour in the same compartment, came up to him.

"You've been here before then?" he asked him.

"No," replied Ulrich. "I just happen to know that Zagreb is in Yugoslavia. So where are you from?"

"I'm from the Ruhrgebeite, near Dortmund. And yourself?"

"I'm from Vienna."

Before the conversation could be taken any further, a long train of sealed cattle wagons came alongside the other side of the platform. It came to a stop. In the middle of the train, between the cattle wagons, was a proper passenger carriage, from which a group of SS descended. They approached the buffet counters next to where

Ulrich and his companion were standing. The other soldiers made way for the newcomers.

Hearing human voices coming from the wagons, Ulrich wandered across to see what was going on. Built of heavy thick wooden planks, the wagons were constructed in such a manner as to prevent cattle and horses from breaking down the sides and escaping. In this case there was an added obstacle, namely, the open slats on the side of the wagon were criss-crossed with barbed wire. The openings were just high enough to allow Ulrich to see inside. The overpowering stench of urine and excrement was nauseating and made him retch. He could not understand what the people were saying. He called out if anyone spoke German. Not getting any reply in his own language, he tried English.

"What's going on? Why are you in there? Who are you?" he fired off his questions.

There was a sudden silence. Then someone spoke up in broken English.

"We're Greeks, from Athens and Thessaloníki. There are old people and small babies sick and dying in here. The Nazis are taking us to their camps. We've not eaten for several days. Can you get us food and water, please? You can have our jewellery, our necklaces, rings and bracelets," a voice pleaded.

Turning to go back to the buffet counter to get some water and food, Ulrich was accosted by a couple of SS men.

"What the hell do you think you're doing?" said one, in a threatening tone of voice.

"You've no bloody right to keep these poor people locked up like cattle," Ulrich snapped, hoping to sound as authoritative as possible.

"Don't get any big ideas, soldier," the other said. "What we're doing is what the Führer has ordered."

"So the Führer ordered you to transport defenceless old people, women, children and babies, deprive them of food and water and keep them in horrible foul conditions. Is that it?"

"Now that you mention it, the answer is yes. You're a German soldier so it's your duty to help us, not get in the way of what we're doing."

"Doing what exactly?"

"Taking these filthy Jews to labour camps, as ordered. We in the SS always carry out orders. In any case, we made them pay their own fares." Both men laughed at this.

"They're Greeks. They're not Germans. They need food, water and sanitation. Now if you stand aside, I'm going to get them food."

"Don't bother, soldier," said one. "If you attempt, to interfere with our prisoners, I won't hesitate to shoot you." His voice carried a note of menace.

A *Wehrmacht* officer, a lieutenant, was standing near one of the buffet stands. Ulrich approached him.

"Excuse me sir, but those cattle wagons are full of old people, women, children and babies. They've had no food or water for several days. I'm going to get some to take to them. That SS man has threatened to shoot me if I try."

"Your name is?"

"Dreher. Private Dreher."

"Private Dreher, I forbid you to go near those wagons. It's none of the army's business."

By now, a crowd of soldiers had gathered to watch the outcome of this minor military struggle. Tension rose as Ulrich, having bought bread and water, started to return to the cattle wagons. He had hardly got halfway when the lieutenant shouted at him to come back. Ulrich ignored him. He did not get far. The lieutenant ordered nearby soldiers to take hold of him and prevent him from getting anywhere near the wagons. Ulrich tried to resist.

"Let go of me," he screamed. "Are you going to refuse these women and children food and water? What kind of savages have we become?"

The lieutenant strode up to him and slapped him hard across the face.

"Put this man back on the train and make sure he doesn't get off again," he ordered. The soldiers, dragged a protesting Ulrich across the platform then pulled and pushed him up the steps on to the train. The others, their faces twisted with venom, yelled and shouted a whole glossary of lewd torment and low invective at the uncomprehending Jews in the wagons. Some made obscene gestures at their unseeing intended victims.

"You filthy snipcock swine, you scum of the earth, you shitbags, children of prostitutes..." So it went on and on. Each soldier seeming to have his own particular foul word or violent phrase.

From where he was standing in the corridor of the train, Ulrich heard this verbal onslaught. A loud whistle blew and the troops started back on to the train. Several of them, making their way to their respective compartments, hurled abuse at him, as they passed. One even spat at him. The members of his own compartment would not allow him to return to his seat. The train, gathering speed, made its way out of the station. Ulrich stood silent in the corridor, his neighbours not speaking to him, and began to reflect on the impulsiveness of his actions.

'How is it,' Ulrich said to himself, 'that these men, out of uniform, would never think of committing any kind of crime, men with families and children of their own, brought up in a Christian culture, would turn on their fellow human beings and show such devilish hatred? They couldn't possibly know any of the people in the cattle trucks. This war is not about an army fighting for justice and the rights of the people. It's a war against the Jews. So what are we doing here? Seeing those sealed cattle wagons, carrying hundreds of Jews to God knows what fate, it seems to me that we're here only to help the SS round up innocent people.'

Ulrich gazed out the corridor window at the passing landscape of forest and hills. The train passed through valleys where there was little habitation. The endless clackety-clack of the train's wheels over the gaps between the rails, emphasised the fact that he was being taken to a military action that he feared and strongly opposed. Through Ruth and the children, the Jews had become his own flesh and blood. In his own mind, in the innermost part of this soul he had become one of them.

Several times the train slowed down almost to a walking pace. The crowded compartments and corridors hummed with chatter and sing-song. It was just after midday when suddenly there was a massive explosion. The carriage rocked, shuddered and then turned on its side as it jumped the rails and rolled down a steep embankment, shattering and uprooting trees in its path, before coming to rest. Many of the men in the corridor had been knocked unconscious by the train's violent quaking and turbulence. Compartment doors jammed as their occupants tried in vain to get out. There was yelling and screaming as the men fought to escape.

Ulrich's carriage lay on its side and he found himself looking up at the blue sky. Unlike many of the others, he was still conscious. He took hold of a rifle that was lying near him and smashed a window. With great difficulty he crawled out, lifting himself on to what was now the topmost side of the train. He looked along towards where the locomotive lay on its side and saw that a fire had broken out and was rapidly spreading along the overturned carriages. Amid the chaos and noise he could see that unless he got down quickly he would soon be engulfed in flames. He jumped down and fell on some gorse bushes, breaking his fall. There were two or three others lying on the ground having been thrown out of the train. He could hear, coming from the train, the shrieks of the injured and dying and those trapped. There was a second blast as the ammunition from one of the freight cars carrying the flak guns exploded. The ensuing fierce fire added to the conflagration caused by the first explosion.

His instinct was to put distance between himself from the blazing scene, now staggering now limping away from the burning train into the adjoining forest. He tripped up several times. After a while, becoming aware of blood slowly dripping from his left hand, he stopped to examine his sleeve which was slashed in several places. His arm didn't appear broken because he could move it and his fingers, clasping and then unclasping his left hand. He carefully removed his military jacket and rolled up his sleeve to find that his arm had been deeply cut. This must have been caused by the jagged glass from the window he had smashed with the rifle, he reckoned. Not sure if an artery had been slashed, he ripped his jacket with the Swiss Army pocket knife that his former neighbour Aaron Tchirky had given him, and made a tourniquet to stanch the blood. As the hot summer afternoon turned to evening, he found himself walking along a single path. He could no longer hear the noise of the exploding ammunition. Instead the only sounds were those of the forest, the rustle of trees and the cooing of pigeons. He needed to reach a stream to quench his growing thirst. As it grew darker, he became weaker. The blood had stopped flowing down his arm. Finally he could go no further. He lay down and passed out.

Chapter 13

Yugoslavia 1941

Bright sunlight slanted across the hard earthen floor of the wooden hut where Ulrich lay. Waking up, he found himself on a hard straw mattress, on top of a wooden pallet. Where am I? How did I come to be here? What day is it? What time is it? He had no answers to his own questions. His injured arm had been crudely bandaged but had stopped bleeding and throbbing. He looked about the hut which had a corrugated iron roof and, to one side, a small window through which he could see the forest beyond. The hut contained a cast-iron stove, whose chimney went up through the roof, a small pile of kindling wood and a few logs, several rickety-looking wooden chairs and a kitchen table. Cooking pots hung from hooks on the wall as well as some ropes and chains and, on the floor, sat a basket containing potatoes and turnips. Desperately hungry and needing to relieve himself, he attempted to get up but found that he was tied to the pallet. Raising himself on his elbows, he bent over in an attempt to untie the knots that held the ropes firm. It was hard work.

Halfway through his task, he heard the sound of approaching voices and of the door being unlocked. Then, two young people, a man and a woman entered the hut and, at heel, a black Dobermann pinscher dog with red-brown markings. The man wore a check shirt, khaki trousers and an olive green beret with a hunting knife stuck into his belt, a rifle slung over one shoulder and a couple of dead rabbits strung together over the other. The woman had a coloured squared headscarf tied in a peasant-like fashion, and a belt around her green dress holding a holster and a pistol. The dog came across to Ulrich and sniffed his legs. The man shouted at it and made it squat under the table. Ulrich felt like a hobbled animal waiting unknowingly as to what might happen.

The man said something to Ulrich in a language that he did not understand. Ulrich pointed to his groin and said in German that he wanted to relieve himself. The man handed the rifle to the woman, said something and she kept it pointed at Ulrich as he untied the ropes. Slowly Ulrich stood up but felt unsteady on his feet. The man took the gun from the woman and led Ulrich outside. Prodding him in the back with the gun, the man indicated to Ulrich to go to the rear of the hut, where he was able to unburden himself.

Afterwards Ulrich turned to the man.

"I'm Ulrich," he blurted out.

The man took no heed but, prodding him with the gun, forced him back into the hut, made him sit on the chair and then tied his legs and his arms so that he could not move. The couple ignored him and continued to chat to each other.

"Can I have some water?" Ulrich pleaded in German. He stuck out his tongue and made what he thought were drinking sounds. The man spoke to the woman who went outside and returned with a tin cup which she put to Ulrich's lips.

The man came over and checked the ropes holding Ulrich to ensure they were secure. He spoke to the woman and taking the rifle, left the hut. When he had gone, the woman lit a fire in the stove and set about skinning, cleaning and cutting up the rabbits. She then peeled and chopped up the potatoes and turnips which, together with all the rabbit pieces – for no single part of the rabbit had been discarded – she put into a large cooking pot on top of the stove. She made no attempt to communicate with Ulrich who watched intently her every action and movement.

The bizarre, surreal situation in which he now found himself, the forest, the hut, the woman cooking the rabbit stew, brought back memories to Ulrich of the Brothers Grimm's tale of *Hänsel and Gretel*. He knew he was no child abandoned in the dark wood and left to starve to death. He felt his mind was wandering. Perhaps it was the hunger and loss of blood that were playing tricks on his mind.

After a short time, the aroma of the rabbit stew made Ulrich's stomach rumble. About an hour later, or so he reckoned, the man together with four others returned to the hut. All were dressed in a similar fashion and carried rifles. The group chatted among themselves. One of the men who looked older than the others came across to Ulrich and spoke to him in German.

"Who are you and what were you doing in the forest?"

"I escaped from the train when it was derailed."

"What's your name?"

"My name's Dreher. Ulrich Dreher."

"From the colour of your trousers you appear to be a German soldier. Are you a German soldier?"

"Yes. Did you bring me here?"

The man ignored his question.

"So what are you doing here in Yugoslavia?"

"I've no idea. I don't know why I'm here."

"Didn't your officers tell you where you were going?"

"No."

"I don't believe you."

"I'm from Vienna. I worked as an accountant. A few weeks ago I was called up, given some training, put aboard a train and sent to this part of the world. I'd no idea where we were going or why." He was beginning to get angry at the interrogation.

"The main railway line from this area leads back to Vienna through Zagreb. You must have known where you were when you passed through Zagreb station."

"Yes. Being an ordinary soldier, there was nothing that I could do about that."

"The German army illegally invaded this country, they've broken up Yugoslavia and declared Croatia an independent state. They're now in the process of helping the Croats to wipe out everybody else."

"What do you mean, wipe out everybody else?"

"I mean precisely that. Kill the Serbs and Jews and anyone else they fancy. Not if we can help it."

Just then, one of the other men came across and said something to the person questioning Ulrich.

"It's time for us to eat now," said the German-speaking man to Ulrich. "We'll finish this conversation afterwards."

The men sat around the table while the woman brought the stew pot and placed it in front of them. She filled a plate and brought it across to Ulrich. She put it on his knees while she untied the ropes around his wrists.

"Don't try any funny stuff," warned the man who had spoken to him in German, "we won't hesitate to shoot you."

The woman joined the others. Ulrich thought it the best meal he'd had since the night before Ruth and children left for Italy. He wondered how much he should reveal to these people. Army regulations demanded that when captured he give only his name, military number and rank. Not that, in his present position, he cared much for military rules but he didn't know who these people were. He'd heard about resistance groups in Poland. He deduced from what the man had told him that this was such a group.

When the meal was over the men lit up and soon the air reeked with tobacco smoke. They rearranged the chairs so that the five men and the woman were on one side of the table. Ulrich was ordered to place his chair to the other side. One of the younger men addressed Ulrich in German.

"Why didn't you stay with your comrades at the train?" he asked.

"Because I wanted to get away from a burning train. A natural thing to do, don't you think?"

"I would have thought it my duty to help save my comrades."

"Are you German? You don't sound German to me."

Like his companion previously, he ignored Ulrich's question.

"So why did you leave your comrades to burn and die," he taunted. "Hardly the act of a soldier. I'd say you're trying to desert. Were you attempting to desert?"

"There was ammunition on two of the freight cars carrying the flak guns. In any case I was injured. I'm not a hero nor martyr"

"Martyr. An odd word to use in the circumstances. I would call you a deserter. Fleeing from the action. None of your comrades tried to get away."

"Who are you people? Did you bring me here?"

"As a matter of fact we did. And we tended to your injuries."

"I'm grateful for that."

"We don't need nor want your gratitude. It's just we don't shoot people in cold blood. We leave that to the Germans and the Croats. They're expert at that, especially when it comes to unarmed women and children." There was bitterness and sarcasm in his voice.

"Look. I'm not German. I'm Austrian. I was one of the very few to oppose the annexation of my country by the Germans. I had no option when I was called up."

"So I'm right. You are trying to desert."

"I'm not a deserter."

"So, what are you?"

"I'm a fugitive. I'm fleeing the Nazi regime."

"So there's bad blood between you and the Führer?" The man smiled when he said this.

He waited a few moments before continuing.

"What are we going to do with you? If we leave you here and your German friends find you, you'll no doubt explain what happened. They're bound to send out a patrol when they discover that you're missing. If the Croats find you, they'll hand you over to the German army. In both cases our group could be threatened."

"I want to get to Italy. It's where my wife and children are."

"Is your wife Italian?"

"No. She's Jewish."

"You're a Jew? That's incredible. A Jew in the German Army? What next? The Führer converting to Judaism." The others laughed.

They all understand German, thought Ulrich.

"I'm not a Jew," Ulrich said.

He then went on briefly to relate the events that had led up to Ruth and the children fleeing across the border to Italy. They listened intently, questioning him when he mentioned von Grolman's name.

"He's the general in charge of the whole region of northern Yugoslavia," said one of the men. "We hold him responsible for the crimes committed by the German troops here. Even worse, he's done nothing to stop the Croatian atrocities against the Jews and Serbs who live here." He broke off speaking and conferred with the others. He then turned to Ulrich.

"We're leaving and you're coming with us. Be prepared for a couple of days hard walking. Joint German and Croat patrols are bound to come this way soon enough."

He untied Ulrich and the group prepared to leave. Ulrich wondered where they were going for they had not told him. He inwardly thanked these people for having saved him from his fate as a German soldier.

* * *

The single-file column wended its way along the narrow path and up a gradually steepening slope, the leader setting a quick pace. Ulrich was third in line behind two of the others, followed by the rest including the dog. They each carried a backpack and a rifle. A pervasive aroma of pine coming from the trees filled the air. Except for the rustle of a soft wind through the forest, the only sound came from their tramping feet.

Looking up, Ulrich reckoned, from the position of the midday sun, they were heading south-west. After a long hard pull upwards through a thickly wooded gully, they found the track zigzagging up to a ridge, where the trees had thinned out. It had been a long, brutal ascent for him but finally when they had reached the broad, grassy, bow-shaped ridge itself, clear of the trees, the landscape changed dramatically and Ulrich had a panoramic view to both east and west where long lines of low, pine-clad mountains stretched to the horizon. The luminous sky was a flurry of blue, white and pink tinged clouds. Below, he could see the railway snaking its way through the valley floor, in a north-south direction and, remembering the train derailment, he wondered what had become of his erstwhile comrades on the train. Reflecting on the incident at Zagreb station, he thought poetic justice had dealt his former fellow soldiers a fitting punishment.

Suddenly the leader held up his hand. They all came to a halt. The faint hum of a plane's engine could be heard growing louder as it approached.

"Take cover," he shouted.

Running down the slope, they came to a lower line of nearby trees and gorse bushes, where they took cover. They could hear the plane but not see it. It passed to the east, making a long sweep and returned over to where they were. From the slow drone of the engine Ulrich recognised it as a reconnaissance plane. It passed up and down the valley several times before finally making off. For the first time, Ulrich felt what his Uncle Claus had described as 'trench fear'.

The group retraced their steps to the ridge and continued their way. After several hours further travel, they descended from the ridge and found themselves in a deserted hamlet. The houses had been burned down and only the walls remained. There was no one about. The person Ulrich took to be the leader of this group led them to a building which was larger than the others, at the front of which was a large porch. From the charred remains of two octagonal towers and domes, Ulrich deduced that this was a church. The group entered through the vacant space where once the doors had hung. The floor was strewn with broken glass, icons, crosses and, to his disgust, even human excrement. The carcass of a dog, shot through the head, lay rotting and stinking in one corner.

"We can't stay here," the leader announced. "Let's find somewhere else."

It was not easy. Most of the houses were in a similar burnt-out, filthy and squalid state. They opted for one that was in a slightly better condition, the only one with a mainly intact roof. It was here they were going to spend the night. The leader spoke to one of the men who got up and went out, later returning with a bucket of water.

"Excuse me," Ulrich said, addressing the leader, "I've told you my name. Perhaps you could tell me yours."

"I could but until we know who you really are, you can call me Shlomo. That's a nickname but it'll do for the present."

"That's Jewish isn't it?"

"Correct. We're all Jewish. Now don't ask any more questions."

Ulrich once more found himself put aside from the others. He understood why they treated him with extreme caution. He would have done the same in their place. So far they had treated him courteously but coolly.

The others took bread, cheese and wine from their knapsacks and shared them with him. Before eating they formed a small circle and prayed in Hebrew. Ulrich recognised the sounds and the words for he had learned some of the language from Ruth. When he joined in they continued to pray, ignoring him. Afterwards, while they sat around eating and chatting, Shlomo and the young woman approached him.

"So you know how to pray in Hebrew?" the young woman said. It was the first time she had spoken to him. She appeared to be in her early twenties with large, deep-set brown eyes, hair centrally parted and falling behind her ears in a mass of curls, a long straight nose and high cheekbones.

"Only a little. My wife Ruth taught me. As I told your companion, she's Jewish."

"Did you want to learn Hebrew?"

"Not really. But she was teaching our two children Jewish songs, and the language, the alphabet that sort of thing. So I gradually picked it up. We used to celebrate the Shabbat meal." He paused, for the memory was a painful one. After a while he continued, "Tell me, for I'm curious to know, are you some kind of resistance group?"

"We can't tell you anything. Not yet," Shlomo said.

"What are we doing in this deserted village?" Ulrich asked.

"We're only passing through. We'll be on our way tomorrow."

"Do you know who or what caused all this destruction?"

"The Croats, not the Germans. This used to be a Serb settlement. That building we went into earlier was an Orthodox church. It was torched and desecrated by the Croats."

"Why would they want to do that?"

"That's a long story. As an Austrian you ought to know the history of this region. You clearly don't or you wouldn't ask such a careless question."

Ulrich was stung by this warranted rebuke.

The next day's journey repeated the pattern of the previous one, except that for the first few hours they made their way along the valley floor till they came to a wide stream flowing down from the mountains. After a while they crossed this by way of a narrow wooden suspension bridge held in place by steel cables, anchored to the river banks in concrete piers. Leaving the river behind, the group ascended a long and tortuous climb over a mountain that was steeper and more rugged than the previous they had climbed. They passed over the ridge summit to find themselves descending through a gully, strewn with stones, to a plateau of moorland and from there to a densely wooded valley. Following what appeared to be a well trodden path they finally came to a small inhabited village. Clustered around a square, the lower parts of the houses appeared to be made of mud and wattle while the upper parts were built of huge logs and planks of wood, with thatched roofs.

A number of people and some barking village dogs came out to greet the newcomers. Shlomo led Ulrich down one of the narrow alleys just off the square.

"This is my house, and this is where you'll be staying for the moment," he said to Ulrich, who noticed the mezuzah on the doorpost. They went inside. The ground floor consisted of one large room containing a cast-iron stove, a table and several chairs and against one wall, a small bookcase filled with books and papers. Shlomo took him up the narrow, wooden staircase and showed him into a small room.

"This is your room. Remain here until I come back. There is a latrine outside at the back. We call it the 'backhouse'." He smiled but did not explain further. Shlomo was a man of few words. With that he went off, leaving Ulrich wondering if he had been transferred back to a seventeenth century rural community.

As he sat on the narrow wooden bed, Ulrich thought long about Ruth and the children, about Vienna, his Uncle Claus, Reuben and the Jewish group, even about Doctor Tchirky. His previous life had disappeared, gone forever, he was cut off from all those he loved and dispossessed of all the things he cherished. He felt purged of every desire and want but one. I will survive and, whatever happens, find Ruth and the children.

After the mountain climbing exertions and the long trek through the forest, he lay back on the bed and drifted off to sleep.

He was aroused by Shlomo tugging at his shoulder.

"It's time to eat," he said.

"I've had some ideas," Ulrich said.

"I hope they're not just dreams."

"No, seriously, I think I may be able to help you."

"You have been dreaming!" he laughed. "Let's go downstairs. My wife doesn't like being kept waiting."

There were several adults and two children around the table. The room was lit by two oil lamps hanging from the ceiling. The lively chatter ceased when Ulrich came down the stairs behind Shlomo.

"This is Ulrich. He's a German soldier and is our prisoner for the time being."

"Gruss Gott, hello," Ulrich said, using the Austrian term rather the German one. "But I'm not German. I'm Austrian."

"It's the same thing these days," said one of the men. There was a tinge of hostility in his voice.

"Can we just have our meal without argument?" Shlomo said. He stood up and said a prayer in Hebrew.

"Have you ever attended a shabbat meal?" one of the men said, addressing Ulrich.

"Despite what you might think," Ulrich replied, "I do have a Jewish wife, and two Jewish children as I told your companions. I'm not Jewish but every Friday evening, strange as it might sound to you, I performed that same ritual as you have just done. I've never formally converted to Judaism. I'm not sure what to believe as far as religion is concerned but I do have faith and belief in my Jewish family."

"Good for you," one of the women said.

The meal, a chicken goulash, began uneasily. Only slowly did the conversation pick up.

"What's this idea you said you had?" Shlomo said, addressing Ulrich.

"Those rifles you and your friends were carrying. They're German army rifles if I'm not mistaken."

"That's right. We took them when we derailed your train. Why do you ask?"

"I know all about arms. I'm a precision engineer. My father owns an arms company in Austria."

"So how can you help us? Go back to Austria and return here with a train load of arms. That's sound an unlikely tale." He laughed and the others laughed with him.

"Please hear me out," Ulrich pleaded. "If you had to make a two day trip across mountains, derail a train to return with a few rifles, you must be short of arms. I once designed and produced a sub-machine gun which is now in use by the German army."

"So what do you intend to do? Build a factory in this village and produce sub-machine guns?" There was further laughter.

"Not quite. But if there's a blacksmith in the village and you can get hold of lengths of nine millimetre steel tubing I could put together a version of the gun I invented. Basically, it's a simple open bolt, blowback operated gun, firing pistol ammunition. It's not as simple as all that but with an accurate design to follow and a competent blacksmith I could manufacture a machine gun for you."

There was a stunned silence.

"How long would that take?" asked one of the men.

"I hoped you wouldn't ask that question. It all depends on the right type of tubing and getting sufficient steel for the various parts."

He had their interest. There were cracks in the ice and he felt a thaw setting in. He briefly recounted his time at the Technical Institute and described the sub-machine gun he had designed. He further explained the contract with the German government.

"So your father is manufacturing this gun for the Third Reich?" asked one.

"Yes. I regret that but I could make up for it by doing something for you."

"So what's in this for you?" asked another.

"You might help me to get to the Dalmatian coast where I can get a passage to Italy and meet up with my wife and children."

"That's asking a lot. Do you know how far the coast is? Two hundred kilometres across mountains and forests, occupied by the Croatian and Italian military. Then there's the language issue..."

"You mean the language you speak?"

"You wouldn't last five minutes if ever you found yourself alone," Shlomo said. "The Croats and Italians would hand you back to the Gestapo. And they wouldn't even give you a decent grave when they had finished with you."

"So I take it that you're Croats or maybe Serbs?"

"We're all Yugoslavs. Yes the language we speak is Serbo-Croat, which is the language of Yugoslavia. Even that is disputed by both Croats and Serbs. It's spoken by those who consider themselves Croats and those who consider themselves Serbs, except that the Croats use the Roman alphabet when they write, and the Serbs, the Cyrillic."

"Cyrillic that's Russian isn't it?"

"My friend, I think it better we don't go into this. It's complicated. All you have to know is that we're all Yugoslavs in this village."

"I thought you were Jews."

"Yugoslav Jews."

"So what brought you here?"

"We're all from this region – Croatia if you will. When the Germans invaded they gave the Croats their independence. The first thing the Croats did was to impose the Nazi laws against the Jews.

Most of us fled from Zagreb. In this village we have a teacher of literature, a nurse, a mathematician, and other workers."

"Fleeing for your lives, then?"

"Exactly. It was either that or a concentration camp. Not, I might add, a German concentration camp. Oh yes, the Croats have opened their own concentration camps. It's rumoured that they're even worse than the German ones. We need the rifles to protect ourselves."

"You wouldn't stand much chance against a well-armed German unit."

"The Germans hardly come anywhere near here. They're too occupied with the Serbian region. They guard the road and railway bridges."

"What about the Croat military?"

"They're mainly recruited from the towns and countryside and don't wander too far into the forest."

"What's happened to the original inhabitants of this village?"

"Before the Great War this was a woodcutters' village. Then after the war, it was deserted, it was too remote. We've made it ours for the time being."

"What are you aiming to do?"

"Stay alive and harass the enemy as much as we can. But it's not easy for we don't have proper arms."

With that the conversation gradually petered out.

"You must be tired," Shlomo said. "We're all tired. Tomorrow we'll go to see the blacksmith. Try to arrange something."

* * *

Ulrich did not get to meet the blacksmith the next day as proposed. Shlomo told him that he had gone on a mission. He didn't say where or why. In the meantime, he helped some of the men to haul logs in from the forest, saw them up and then split them. He realised it was the first time since his military service days that he had to do manual labour. Despite the fact that most of the villagers spoke German, some almost fluently, helped him to communicate.

He now wished he had taken more heed in his history classes at school. Previously, he had thought of Yugoslavia as one state, one people, one language. Now he was learning the hard way that it wasn't like that at all. Others appeared to take pleasure in telling him that Yugoslavia was a mixture of Catholic Croats, Orthodox Serbs, Muslim Bosnians, Herzegovinians and Montenegrins. Much of the population of the Croatian region were not Croatian, they were Serbs. Some Bosnians were Serbs. The Serbs had ruled it over the Croats. The Croats hated the Orthodox Serbs. They also hated the Jews and the Bosnian Muslims. Ulrich found the whole story most confusing.

"Serbo-Croat is a complicated language", the man who had been a schoolteacher told him, laughing as he said it, "and we can't agree what it should be called."

In the evening, they would gather in one house or the other and talk and argue well into the night. It reminded Ulrich of the lively meetings of the Jewish Action Group in his Vienna flat. Gradually he got to know them.

Finally the blacksmith returned. He arrived in the village with a donkey-drawn cart loaded with steel tubing. He was a small man broadly built with a mane of red hair and huge hands. Ulrich imagined that he could pick up his donkey, he looked so strong, which was very impressive since he appeared to be in his early fifties.

He introduced himself as Gaby and pointing to the tubes, with a guffawing laugh, said, "They're nine millimetre. It's what you wanted, isn't it?"

"Do you know anything about guns?" Ulrich asked.

"Of course! I served my apprenticeship as a gunsmith with the Skoda works in Pilsen. That was before the Great War when we were all part of the Austro-Hungarian Empire. Come, have a look at my smithy."

He proudly showed Ulrich the smithy, a large wooden structure at the bottom end of the village that housed a forge, an anvil, and, to Ulrich's surprise, a metalworking lathe. There was also a small manually operated milling machine and a tool grinder. In one corner was a large mound of charcoal.

"How did you acquire these machines?" asked Ulrich, pointing to the lathe and the milling machine.

"I once used to be the smith in a little town called Sisak. I didn't make guns but lots of folk had hunting rifles and I had to do repairs when they got damaged. I managed to bring the anvil and the other implements with me when we fled from the Germans." He gave Ulrich a knowing wink.

"What happens on your journeys when you get stopped by German or Croat patrol?"

"There's hardly any German patrols left in this region. As for the Croats, well, they're not the most intelligent of the population. The majority are from the farming areas and when they stop me and I tell them I'm a blacksmith they don't ask too many questions. Sometimes, I've even done cold shoeing on their horses."

"You're a wily fellow," Ulrich said.

"That's how I stay alive," Gaby said. "As for the guns, I need to know how many parts your gun requires, to work out the amount of steel that will be needed."

"I'll be able to give you a precise answer when I know how many guns you need or want. Allow me a few days to work on the drawings."

"Well, my friend, I must be getting on. I've got a lot of work to catch up on. When the ladies bring me their saucepans for repair they expect me to do the work as from yesterday." He laughed again.

Later that day Ulrich found Shlomo.

"Your smith is a competent man," he said. "Together we should be able to produce a sub-machine gun for you. But I need to reproduce the design. For that I'll need a good table which I can use as a drafting table. I'll also need a T-square and other drawing tools. Basic things like a pair of compasses and some pencils. The drawings have to be extremely accurate."

"I'll see what I can do," said Shlomo. "Nat, used to be a maths teacher in a high school in Zagreb. He may be able to help. It's possible he's got some of the instruments you need."

Chapter 14

Yugoslavia 1941

For several weeks Ulrich found himself working with Gaby, one of the few Serbs in the partisan village. Besides his native Serbo-Croat, the fifty-year-old spoke German, but also, so he said, English and some Russian.

"Under the old empire," he told Ulrich, "German was the language used in our elementary school. We spoke Serbo-Croat in the playground and at home. After the Great War, I happened to be in Istanbul, which was then occupied by the British, siding at the time with the White Russians fighting against the Red Bolsheviks. The British recruited me to work for them as a farrier. I was young and willing. The money was good."

They were sitting in Gaby's house eating a Hungarian stew prepared by Gaby's wife, Milena. She kept a cow, three goats and some chickens at the rear of their cottage in a small former stable. The cow gave milk which she churned into butter and, also, made into cheese.

"I remember setting off from Sebastopol," continued Gaby, "on an old freighter crowded with British soldiers, mainly Fusiliers, Royal Engineers and some cavalry troops. I picked up a fair amount of English from them. Later an officer told me that most of what I had learned would not be accepted in polite society. 'Too many obscene words,'." Gaby let out one of his fierce guffaws. "They were commanded by a young Captain Harrison who looked as if he had just left high school. Those British officers loved their drink and had greater respect for their horses than they did for the men under their charge. We landed at a place called Novorossiysk on the eastern side of the Black Sea. It was winter and everywhere was freezing. God it was cold. The men were fuelled by cheap Russian vodka, the only way to survive in that climate. We made our way across the mountains guided by Cossacks but like most of these military adventures it all ended in defeat. The Red Russian Army overwhelmed the White forces. When they saw that it was becoming a lost cause the British got out quickly. They were never really defeated. At least they would never admit defeat."

"How did you come to be here with this community?" Ulrich asked.

"When the Germans declared the break-up of Yugoslavia and made Croatia independent, the Croats, urged on by their priests, wanted to turn their country into a Catholic-Fascist state. The Catholic Croats hate the Orthodox Serbs. Well, I'm a Serb."

"Austria was a clerical fascist state," Ulrich said, "until the Nazis annexed it as part of the Greater Reich. History repeating itself."

"Not only did the Croats persecute and hound the Jews, they turned on the Serbs. My family's lived in these parts for God knows how many centuries. That didn't count, they couldn't get rid of us quickly enough. No place for the Orthodox. So besides burning down the synagogues, they destroyed the Orthodox churches and massacred our priests. They didn't try to hide what they were doing. The Catholic Archbishop of Zagreb issued a statement, published in the press, saying we Serbs had three choices. Go back to Serbia, be killed, or convert to Catholicism."

"Didn't you try to go to Serbia?"

"Not a chance. The Germans have their hands full stamping out Serbian insurrection. They're ruthless and would just as likely kill us as let us in. I came here because I had a number of Jewish friends. I've become part of the Jewish diaspora."

Gaby turned out to be a relentless taskmaster with a rapacious appetite for work that kept Ulrich busy designing the many parts that made up his sub-machine gun such as ratchets, recoil springs, bolts, ejectors, buttstocks and a host of other pieces. Because of the primitive working conditions, a fair amount of trial and error was involved. Things did not always go to plan. Having followed Ulrich's drawings, Gaby would sometimes discover that a part he had finely shaped on the metal lathe did not fit. After many arguments, heated words, trials and errors, they eventually came to an understanding which gradually eliminated the chances of a misfit.

The work on the gun took much longer than Ulrich had anticipated. His calculations had been based on the well-equipped Vienna Institute's workshops of a decade previously, with highly precise tools and electrically driven machines. Now he and Gaby were reduced to basic and not-so-accurate tools and manually driven machines. A simple function became hard labour. He learned to admire Gaby's resourcefulness, resilience and air of hope.

As summer turned to autumn, the first gun was ready. Shlomo had somehow or other acquired three large boxes of nine millimetre cartridges. Ulrich noticed that when the community needed something a group of men went off on what Shlomo termed 'a mission'. It was never revealed to anyone other than the participants the destination or aim of the 'mission'. They would return with all sorts of things, oil for the lamps, medicines for the village nurse, who also acted as an ad hoc dentist, teaching materials for the teacher, flour for baking, salt and other commodities the community could not make or grow themselves.

For a test firing, Ulrich set up a wooden target behind the smithy at about thirty metres distance. Gaby, Shlomo and several others were there to observe.

"Wish me luck," Ulrich said in a confident tone.

At the first firing the ejector spring failed. Adjustments were made. After several attempts, the gun worked perfectly, cutting the wooden target in half. One of the men produced a flagon of wine which he passed around the admiring group.

The next day, Gaby and Ulrich set about making more guns. It took nearly a week to make just one. Gaby was a chain smoker and, between lighting up and hammering an obdurate piece of metal into shape, he told Ulrich about Shlomo.

"I once worked in a large smithy in Zagreb. It's there I met him. He was the artistic director of the National Theatre. I'm not an opera or theatre man myself so I can't say how good he was but he did have a fine reputation, so I was told by those who knew him well. He kept a horse and that's how I got to know him. His troubles came with the Nazi invasion of Yugoslavia who turned Croatia over to the Ustasi."

"Who are they?"

"The worst bunch of nationalists you could ever imagine. Hate and violence were their two watchwords. They wanted to turn Croatia into a purely Catholic state. If you were a Catholic Croatian great but if you weren't, it was the chop. Literally. They sent their bully boys to his house, threw him and his family out and then imprisoned them. A sympathetic official managed to have him freed. He discovered that they had shot his wife in front of their three children and then shot the children. The poor man was devastated. He fled to the countryside where he met up with some fellow Jews and set up this community. I heard about this place, as I was in line for a death certificate I came here."

Ulrich thought about Shlomo's certain torment created by the grievous loss of his wife and children and the destruction of his creative life.

In late autumn the village, celebrated the Jewish feast of Succoth. Shlomo explained to Ulrich that the frail structure of the Tabernacle symbolised the dwellings of the Jews as they wandered in the wilderness after the Exodus from Egypt. Ulrich, thinking of Ruth, reflected on his own wanderings in the wilderness in which he found himself. He had great sympathy for Moses and his companions. They sang Jewish folk songs.

At the beginning of December three things happened. The first snow arrived, Shlomo acquired a shortwave wireless though Ulrich had no idea how he had acquired it, and the United States entered the war. They learned this latter piece of news from their newly acquired radio. Practically the whole village crowded into Shlomo's house to listen to President Roosevelt's speech, while the teacher of English interpreted it into Serbo-Croat for the anxious listeners.

The word that struck a chord in Ulrich's mind was Roosevelt's use of the word 'infamy' with regard to the Japanese attack on Pearl Harbour. He wondered why the President had not seen the infamy in the Führer's invasion of Czechoslovakia, Poland, France and other Western European countries and how he could stand by while a triumphant Nazi state, bombed massacred and slaughtered thousands. Although Roosevelt declared war against Japan he did not declare war on Germany. It was left to the Führer to do the declaring, out of sympathy for his Japanese ally. Such is the perfidy of politics, he thought.

A few days later, Shlomo invited Ulrich to one of his secret meetings.

"I've heard form reliable sources, who got it from the Jewish Agency, that the Nazis have held a secret meeting in Berlin and decided on what they term the final solution of the Jewish question. It seems they have put forward a plan to exterminate the Jewish people. We're not just at war with the Nazis – this is a fight for survival. If ever we fall into the hands of these people and their Croatian allies we can expect no mercy just death."

"So what can we do?" asked one of those present.

"We can't hope to defeat the German army by ourselves," Shlomo said. "What we do will hardly make any difference in the great scale of things. However, we can help our fellow Jews. That is why our next target is a railway bridge. The Germans are transporting Jews from the countries further south, mainly Serbia and Greece, to the death camps in Germany and Poland. If we can blow up a bridge here or there, it will slow down this traffic of death."

There were murmurs among the group of 'Death to the Führer' and 'save our people.'

Shlomo spread a map out on the table, around which they all gathered. It was a map dating back to the time of the Austro-Hungarian Empire when a double-track rail line had been constructed to join Vienna to Belgrade. He then placed a drawing of the bridge over the map.

"This is a massive wooden structure, fifty metres long, over a deep gorge. We have acquired nearly fifty kilos of high explosives. Our tactic is to lay the explosives at the base of the main supporting beams on one end of the bridge. This should cause the structure to collapse and catch fire. It seems before the war there was a proposal to replace this wooden structure with a steel and concrete one but war intervened and the plan didn't go ahead. If we can succeed in our endeavour it's possible that this railway line could be out of action for a long time. That's the plan."

"How well is it guarded?" one of the group asked.

"I don't know," Shlomo said. "The Germans have so many bridges and tunnels to guard in this region, it's possible that their forces are thinly spread."

"What about sending a reconnaissance party to find out?" Ulrich asked.

"I've thought about that, but in reality we cannot afford to lose any men as well as possibly alerting the Germans."

There was a long discussion about this point. At the end they agreed not to follow Ulrich's suggestion.

"We're much better equipped to attack the defenders at the bridge and, at the same time, defend ourselves if we come under attack, thanks to the efforts of Gaby and Ulrich. Ulrich you're coming along in case we have problems with the guns."

* * *

When the snow stopped falling, the seventeen-man sabotage group set out. Each one carried a heavy backpack, some had spades, one a pick, for digging holes, and one man carried a length of rope. The temperature was just below zero on a windless winter's day. Silence was maintained as the men trudged through the forest and over a mountain pass. Finally, at the end of the short day, they arrived at another deserted village. War had turned a sparsely populated area into a derelict land.

Notices in both German and Serbo-Croat had been nailed up in the burned out dwellings warning 'THE FOLLOWING WILL BE SHOT WITHOUT FURTHER WARNING!' The long list covered everyone who helped partisans, who possessed false documents, who carried arms, ammunition or explosives, and any who were culpable of a host of minor offences, and so it went on. For every German soldier insulted, attacked, wounded or killed, ten hostages would be taken and summarily shot. The decree carried the signature of General August von Grolman.

Ulrich recollected his image of the general, his immaculate clothes, erect posture and careful grooming, hinting at vanity and arrogance. However, it still required a leap of his imagination to associate the figure he had met with this chilling decree. He then recalled the general's words, 'I've a job to do and I shall carry it out. That is what soldiers do. We obey the orders of our political masters'. He wondered how an obviously intelligent man, as von Grolman was, had no scruples about carrying out his orders, his highest moral value appearing to offer blind obedience to his Führer's orders, even above his human conscience.

After a meal of bread, cheese and sausage, in the semi-darkness of an ill-lit cottage, Ulrich raised a more pressing problem.

"Aren't we putting the lives of innocent people at risk by what we're proposing to do?" he asked Shlomo, referring to the notice.

Shlomo eyed him gravely.

"My friend, people aren't made for war but they aren't made for servitude either. Behind the so-called friendly German soldier, asking his way down a street in some town, stands the Gestapo and the SS, rounding up our people and transporting them to the death camps. Our little group cannot expect to do more that irritate the occupier. Whatever we can do, we will do."

"Can you ignore these dire warnings?" Ulrich insisted.

"Of course not. Do you think I've not given this matter a lot of thought? The moral dilemma that faces us will not be solved by doing nothing. Remember your Hamlet? 'To be or not to be that is the question.' There are two kinds of people in this equation. Those who trim their loyalties and collaborate and those who resist. Because of our unique position, being Jews whose only fate, in any case, is death at the hands of the Germans and Croatians, we are inescapable resisters. These are times that try our souls. Unlike the Prince of Denmark, I don't have doubts."

Another day's march brought them to their destination. The bridge spanned a deep gorge at the foot of forested hills. Although the railway line was double track, it became a single line to cross the long but narrow bridge. The group halted and waited some way off as Shlomo sent a couple of scouts forward to ascertain whether it was guarded or not. They returned with bad news. There were guards, but they were unable to ascertain their number, for the guard picket was sheltered in a hut on the side of the bridge opposite to the sabotage group's present position. It was decided that the guards must be distracted or disposed of.

"I say we storm the bridge and kill the bastards," said one of the group. A sentiment echoed by a number of others.

"I'm not really interested in them," Shlomo said in a firm authoritative voice. "What is more important are the lives of those in this group and all of you are needed for this action. The loss of one or two of you could jeopardise the entire operation. We'll succeed if we use our brains and not be sidetracked by feelings of revenge. We're not here to settle scores."

The others nodded in mute agreement.

"The plan," Shlomo added, "is to set off a small explosion on this side of the gorge that will draw them over the bridge. If they get as far as this side we may be able to engage them. The element of surprise is on our side. Let's use it. Nathan is best placed to deal with this situation, and you, Ulrich can try out your new gun, so you go with Nathan."

Nathan was a heavy, thickset, reticent man who had worked as a mining engineer in coal mines in Bosnia. He carried a stick of dynamite. With him leading, both men made their way gingerly down the hill through the forest, avoiding stray tree roots.

"Be careful how you go and don't rush," he warned Ulrich. "Dynamite is highly unstable. It's the nitroglycerine. We don't want to blow ourselves up."

The steeply sloping ground, ice-covered fallen logs and branches made it a difficult descent and hindered their passage towards the rail line and the bridge. They came to a spot from where, down through the trees, the bridge and the small hut used by the guards were visible. The double track line came out of a tunnel and took a long turning to the right before crossing the bridge.

"You keep watch while I set the explosive charge," Nathan said.

"Why don't you place the charge on the railway line itself?" Ulrich asked.

"You'll see why later." This was said without further explanation.

Ulrich stepped further back into the cover of the trees while keeping an eye on the bridge and the hut on the other side. He felt very nervous and, despite the cold, realised that he was sweating. He remembered his time on manoeuvres in the Tyrolean mountains during his military service. That was mere simulation; this was the real thing.

Nathan came up the steep slope, waving his arms.

"Take cover, take cover," he shouted.

Ulrich crouched down behind a tree, when suddenly there was a small explosion whose echo ricocheted off the sides of the hills, but was muffled nonetheless by the thick forest.

When the sound had died down, Ulrich peered out from behind the tree. At that moment three guards, in German uniform, armed only with rifles, rushed out of the hut. They looked around for the source of the explosion. Moving cautiously and peering now and again over the side of the bridge into the gorge, they made their way across, one each side of the single track, alternately stopping then crouching. They brought their rifles up to their shoulders, swinging them from side to side as if ready to fire at an unseen enemy. When they came to the end of the bridge they stood for a moment, looking up at the hillside as if they did not know what to do. After what appeared a brief argument, one of them produced a packet and offered his colleagues a cigarette. They remained in this spot not venturing any further. They then turned and started to walk slowly back across the bridge, their rifles no longer at the ready.

At that moment, Ulrich and Nathan appeared out of the forest and ran towards the bridge. Ulrich stopped, knelt down and fired his sub-machine gun, felling all three men. Even at the sound of the gunfire, no one else came out of the hut.

Ulrich stood up and approached the three guards he had just killed. There was blood all over the railway sleepers. One had the back of his head blown away, the others had been cut in two by the machine-gun fire. He stood amazed and shocked at his handiwork.

"Don't waste your pity on them," Nathan said coming up from behind. "Is it your first time?" he asked.

Ulrich did not answer. He found that he was shaking and trembling all over, dismayed to see the three dead human beings lying there. They were alive only a few minutes ago, he told himself.

"Sentimentality has no place in war," Nathan said. He turned and made his way back to meet the others coming out of the forest.

Some of the group lifted the bodies of the three dead German soldiers and threw them down the side of the ravine. Two others attached the rope to the side of the massive wooden structure. When the rope had been secured, several of the party, carrying spades and the sole pick, slid down the great wooden pylons. The sticks of dynamite were then slowly and carefully lowered down to the demolition party. The other partisans including Ulrich remained on the bridge and on the tracks leading up to it to provide them with armed cover.

"Why are they digging holes?" Ulrich asked Shlomo. "Can't they just attach the explosives to the wooden beams?"

"If an explosive is confined in a hole in the ground it has a greater effect when it blows up. You'll see. Nathan knows what he's doing."

Ulrich peered over the side of the bridge and watched the demolition party at work. After a couple of hours, the party had dug deep holes at the base of four of the pylon's great wooden beams supporting the bridge. They placed dynamite in each of the holes and tamped it down with the earth that had been dug out. Detonators inserted in the explosives were then attached to wires that Nathan played out along to the end of the bridge to the hand plunger which would send an electric current to effect an explosion. When all was ready the demolition party regained the railway track and the whole party then made its way to a safe distance. There they waited for a train to appear.

An hour later a freight train came out of the tunnel and, slowly taking the long bend, approached the bridge. When it reached the middle, there was a huge explosion then the massive beams gave way. The locomotive, dragging its long wagons with it, plunged into the ravine. Further explosions occurred when the freight cars hit the bottom of the gorge. A huge fire started, slowly consuming the fatal wooden structure.

Shlomo gave the order and the partisan party started out on its way back home, their loads greatly lightened.

* * *

It was a painful and tiresome two-day trek back to the village. As they approached the first huts, it was obvious that something serious had occurred. The smell of burnt wood stung their nostrils, and a dead cow lay on the path into the village. The huts had been torched and looted. The anvil, the lathe and other tools and machinery in the burnt-out shell of the smithy had been taken away. Worst of all, there was not a soul to be seen. Rats skittered about.

"Maybe they've fled into the forest," Ulrich said.

Shlomo would have none of it.

"The Croatians have been here," he said, anger in his voice. "Where are our women and children?"

He crouched down as if burdened by his inconsolable grief. Ulrich went over to him and put his arm around his shoulder, not knowing what to say.

Shlomo stood up.

"This was bound to happen," he said in a voice filled with a mixture of distress and rancour. "They come in the middle of the night. No one escapes. Our families have all gone. Gone, I tell you. Gone to the hell created by these so-called civilised Christians."

"Perhaps," Ulrich said, "because we've destroyed the railway they won't be able to take them to the camps in Eastern Europe. Maybe we can find out where they are and rescue them."

It was some time before Shlomo spoke.

"My friend you're the only good German I've ever met," he said with tears streaming down his sorrow-stricken face.

Ulrich wanted to correct him. 'I'm Austrian not German' but didn't. His own mind was in turmoil. Filled with feelings of guilt at killing the three guards, of pity for the loss of the families. He was overwhelmed by a sense of angry despair.

Chapter 15

Yugoslavia 1942

It took three days of hard mountain trekking for the traumatised and bedraggled group, led by Shlomo, to arrive at another partisan village, a small group of wooden huts clustered at the foot of a forested hill. This was laid out in a similar pattern to the previous one they had occupied but much larger. Ulrich was surprised to see many of the partisans in this place wearing German army clothes and boots. He was informed that most of the partisan supplies of clothing, ammunition and explosives had been obtained in attacks against isolated German garrisons.

"The partisan leadership further south has been in touch with the British forces in North Africa," Shlomo said to Ulrich one day. "If all goes well we should soon have all the munitions we need. The British," he added, "will send some of their own people to assess our needs. They've promised to send us a shortwave transmitter."

"No need for me, then," Ulrich said. "Maybe now you'll fulfil your side of the bargain?"

"Bargain? What bargain?"

"Memory loss, Shlomo. Suffering from memory loss, are we?"

"I don't know what you're talking about."

"I know your mind has been on other things but you said you would help me to get to the Adriatic coast. I still want to join my wife and children in Venice. If that's where they are."

Shlomo did not answer immediately.

"It's not easy," he said, finally. "I'm not in charge here. I'll ask but you must realise the leadership here are busy fighting the

Germans and those other Yugoslavs who don't agree with them politically. My aim is to survive. If lucky, I might yet end up in Balfour's land for the Jews in Palestine."

"What do you mean, fighting among themselves? I never understood Austrian politics and I certainly don't understand theirs."

"There are two main groups here in Yugoslavia. Both want quite different outcomes from the war. The one we belong to is controlled by the communists, who want Yugoslavia to become a little soviet, Balkan-style, after the war. The other wants the opposite. They want the country to be like America or Britain or something similar."

"What a crazy situation. We're in the middle of an undeclared civil war in the middle of a world war."

Shlomo raised his eyebrows and shrugged.

"So I'll have to make my own plans," Ulrich said.

"I wouldn't try it. You're much safer here. Wait for a good opportunity to arise."

Listening to Shlomo he realised that every man had his own war to fight. He had his. They'll get their guns from the British, they don't need my help, he thought.

* * *

Ulrich shared the hut assigned to him with Karol, a Jew and a former dentist in the Polish army, a slightly-built man with a shock of black hair. Karol was usually sparing with words until one evening when Ulrich had been able to acquire a couple of bottles of beer.

Karol spoke English slowly. He drank slowly.

"Good beer," Karol said. "We have, or should I say had, a big brewing industry in Poland. They used to say the average Pole drinks a hundred litres a year."

"Two litres a week. Not bad."

"Good for my business. Beer rots teeth."

They both laughed.

"Where did you learn English?"

"I spent a year in England, in Bristol at a dental school. Besides pulling teeth, I used to go to watch Bristol Rovers the local football team. That was twenty years ago. Not long after the war against the

Soviets. Imagine, the Polish army beat the Red Army. Unbelievable." He sipped his beer.

"How did you come to be here?"

"When this war began, I found myself in a place called Łódź. That's in southern Poland. I was recruited into the army as a dentist. The condition of Polish teeth is appalling. I put it down to beer and sauerkraut. The officers boasted that we would easily beat the Germans. Our army was braver and tougher. We would beat the Russians. They should never have believed their own propaganda. Fatal. We had horses, the Germans had tanks. No competition. They cut through us like we were butter. All over in three weeks."

He gave Ulrich a melancholy look.

"To begin with," he continued, "I thought I might be able to get back home in northern Poland. But with German forces everywhere and hostile Poles only too willing to betrays Jews to the German authorities, I stayed in Łódź, in southern Poland. I soon found myself as a Jew confined to the ghetto. Conditions were horrible. Thousands packed into a small area, water was scarce and no electricity at night. The guards were ordered to shoot anyone trying to approach the barbed wire fence. It didn't stop them from shooting anyone when they were drunk. I set up a surgery and, to begin with, I had a number of patients. Many couldn't afford to pay so they brought food or goods such as rings, watches or cameras. Gradually conditions worsened. It wasn't unusual to see small children even frozen to death at the corner of the street. The grim reaper came in the form of frost and hunger."

He stopped speaking.

"Maybe the war won't last that long," Ulrich ventured.

"Don't count on it. The Germans have mobilised their whole nation. The rest of Europe lies in silent occupation. Only the Russians can defeat them. Eventually. In the meantime we try to survive."

"Karol isn't a Jewish name?"

"My real name is Aaron. I once made a pair of false teeth for this character who, he boasted to me, had been the best forger this side of Brest-Litovsk. He gave me a new identity in payment. Ironic isn't it, how the barter system works? You don't need money. We didn't in the ghetto. Shoes for potatoes, trousers for bread. Teeth for this, that and the other. With a new Polish identity, a passport and papers, a bribe to a venal guard and hey presto I was out of the ghetto, living on my wits. I was able to cross through Czechoslovakia and into Hungary. Ever been there?"

"No."

"If you think Slav languages difficult you should try Hungarian. It's a linguistic minefield. I was lucky. I looked up a fellow dentist, a Hungarian who'd done some training with me in Warsaw. He couldn't let me work as a dentist. The Hungarians are every bit anti-Semitic as the Poles. Got this law restricting the number of Jews in any profession. It's crazy. There you are. Got to earn the proverbial crust as the English say. So I helped out in his surgery as an assistant. Then I got to know this young woman. She spoke English. I felt lonely and cut off. My wife back in Poland. When her husband found out he threatened to inform the authorities. Believe it or not, this from a fellow Jew. Jealousy's one thing but betrayal? I came to Yugoslavia. My timing was wrong. The Germans arrived through the front door as I arrived by the back. Bad timing on my part. No way out."

* * *

A meeting had been called and the large wooden hut was crowded with partisans. The communist leadership's grip on the group was firm and disciplined, supervised by the political commissars. Although he had taken part in one or two excursions, mainly blowing up railways, Ulrich was still uncertain where he stood.

Three of the group leaders were seated behind a table in front of the gathering. One by the name of Zoran stood up. Middle-aged, a former trades union leader in a factory in Belgrade, he would have made a good singer, Ulrich thought, for he had a rich bass voice.

"I have some good news." There were loud cheers. "We've been in contact with the British in North Africa. They need our help." Further applause. "Most of the material that the Germans send to their forces there, comes through this region. We've been asked to increase our efforts to interrupt this flow. So we must increase the number of attacks on the railways."

"So what do we get in return?" someone asked.

"Guns, explosives and radio transmitters."

He looked around and then sat down. The meeting was supposed to be about strategy and tactics, Ulrich had been told, but it took a different turn.

Tomislav, or Tommy as he called himself, the leading commissar, rose to address the gathering. The commissars were the eyes and ears of the leadership of the whole partisan movement, somewhere to the south. Euphemism was their linguistic coinage. Words did not always mean what they meant. 'The people' was a word used to separate those supporting what the movement sought and 'enemies of people' for those who opposed its aims and objectives. No mention of Marx and Lenin. Shlomo told Ulrich that philosophy was confined to the political elite. Mustn't frighten ordinary folk with big words.

"The British," said Tommy, "are fighting the Germans. The Americans are fighting the Germans. The Russians are fighting the Germans. We're fighting the Germans. The present conflict rages over the whole globe. From Vladivostok in the east to London in the west, from Murmansk in the north to Cairo in the south. The British have an empire to protect. The Americans have their commercial interests to defend but Russia has its people to protect and defend. Most of the blood being spilt in this war on the allied side is Russian blood. They are our Slav brothers." He paused. "The American capitalists are fighting the German fascist capitalists. The American capitalists are also fighting the Japanese fascist capitalists. For them the war is about who runs the capitalist system. Our Soviet brothers are fighting not for money but for their people. They are fighting capitalism. We stand shoulder to shoulder with them. But we will not hesitate to sup with the British devil if necessary."

The men clapped.

The meeting proceeded in this manner. It lasted four hours. There was no further talk about strategy or tactics.

* * *

Spring had turned to summer when the partisan group were paid a visit by an Englishman. Nothing was secret in the partisan village and gossip just as rife. It was rumoured that he had been dropped off the Dalmatian coast by a submarine, and great applause greeted him as he arrived in the settlement. Two others came with him, both, it was said, former Yugoslav army officers, one of whom was weighed down with a large cumbersome radio transmitter. The Englishman was, in fact, a Scotsman, Major Lachlan Macpherson.

Ulrich, still resolved to get to the coast and thereafter Italy, was anxious to meet him. His vague plan however was going nowhere, for the occasion had not yet arisen. Were this newcomer to return the way he came, perhaps he would share his passage and contacts with him. The leadership, including the smooth-talking commissars, kept the newcomers away from most of the group.

Ulrich approached Zoran a few days later.

"I've Scottish ancestry," he said. "Any chance of meeting the newcomer. I've heard he's a Scotsman."

"For us he's British." There was a note of caution in his voice. "I'll see what I can do."

It proved unnecessary. Macpherson, a tall, slender man with fine, aristocratic features and smoking a pipe, had asked to see Ulrich.

"When I heard that you'd made a sub-machine gun I wanted to meet you," he told Ulrich. "I'm intrigued."

To Ulrich, his accent was that of Henderson and Jerrold, of embassy soirees and Pall Mall clubs. Relaxed and affable with a nonchalant air of self-confidence and stiff upper lip, he appeared to be the opposite of the rough-hewn commissars but was probably just as ruthless if not more so than the soviet political minders. Ulrich remembered his mother telling him that the British did not acquire their far flung empire without steel rods for spines.

"They, I mean your leader, has shown me one of your guns. I can't possibly believe you could have made such a gun in a smithy. Evidently you have. We've captured some German sub-machine guns during our retreat from Crete. Could've fooled me and damned close to a gun we British are manufacturing. I'm not a gun expert but I can tell a lookalike."

Ulrich explained his time at the Technical Institute in Vienna, his designs, the contract with the German government, his meeting with Henderson and Jerrold and his deal with them. He recounted how he had been taken by the partisans.

"I'm sure we'll be able to use your talents," said Macpherson, "but for the moment I'm not sure how. If you knew the disposition of German divisions, of troop movements such information would be priceless."

He didn't say much more. Before Ulrich had time to ask Macpherson to join in the trek back to the coast, one of the commissars approached and gently drew Macpherson away.

Not interested, Ulrich thought to himself.

"You look crestfallen," Shlomo said later.

"I didn't get the time to ask about joining his journey back to the Dalmatian coast." A dreary note in his voice.

"There are two wars going on here in Yugoslavia. The Allied war and ours. It's the same enemy, the Germans. Means are the same but different ends. You heard what that Tommy said. Well, it goes much deeper. The communists want British help and vice versa. However, the radio that Macpherson's brought, and the others that will be dropped by parachute later, are for more than telling his people back in Cairo what the partisans needs are. Besides giving the partisans weapons they want to know what the German army's strength is. There you have the problem. The partisans don't mind blowing up railway bridges and tunnels. In fact, enjoy it. Giving the British information about German troop movements is another matter. Our friendly commissars, it appears, are being tightlipped and reluctant to share that information with the British. Macpherson has a job on his hands."

"Job?"

"Of persuasion."

"Why? I don't understand these commissars. They're friendly, helpful and brave. What's the problem?"

"Politics. It's as simple as that. The British are thinking of defeating the enemy and finishing the war. Do anything for that end. The communist brethren take their cue from Moscow. Uncle Joe is a wily fellow. He knows that eventually he'll defeat the Führer. For although he's calling for a second front..."

"Second front, what on earth are you talking about Shlomo?"

"He wants the British to jump across the English Channel and draw vital divisions away from the Russian front, making it easier for Russia. He doesn't want the British and Americans to free central Europe. That's something he wants to do. Turn them into mini-Soviet Unions under his protection."

Several weeks later, during one of his sojourns at the camp, Macpherson got in touch with Ulrich.

"I've a proposition to make," he said.

"You're going to take me with you to the coast?" Ulrich asked. There was a buoyant note in his voice.

"Why would you want me to do that?"

Ulrich briefly explained his reasons.

"There's a problem. I'm not returning that way. However, if you were prepared to come back with me on my return journey, I'm sure the British authorities would listen sympathetically to any request you made."

"Your base is in North Africa, isn't it?"

"I'm not saying where it is."

"Wherever. Would I be able to get from there into Italy?"

"That depends. It wouldn't be easy. Difficult, in fact, but not impossible. It's been done before. It could be done again."

"I'll need to think about it."

"You'll have to think quickly as I leave in an hour."

"So what's your proposition?"

"I've been speaking to my people and they would like to see you. My proposition is to take you to see them. It's for them to explain what they want."

"Do you know what that is?"

"Sorry, old boy. I don't."

* * *

It wasn't a boat but a plane that Macpherson and Ulrich took for their journey.

The two-day trek through the mountains to the south ended up at a remote airstrip, where, under the ever-watchful eyes of the local partisans and after several attempts, radio contact was established and a small single-engined aircraft arrived. Besides the pilot it had room for only two passengers.

Once airborne, the small aircraft made its way over the forested mountains and then swung south, over the Adriatic, following the line of the Dalmatian coast, just visible in the dwindling twilight, and hence over the Mediterranean. The cramped cabin was unlit but for a number of small flickering red lights on the dashboard.

It was Ulrich's first ever flight and he wondered at the ability of the pilot to navigate in total darkness. Despite the deafening noise of the engine and the numbing cold, he attempted to look back over the events of the previous months. He saw a new side to the war. How the Jewish-communist partisans formed the steely backbone of the resistance to the German occupation. Their stubborn resolve, enduring courage and fierce bravery in the face of well-armed and highly trained *Wehrmacht* divisions, contrasted badly in his estimation, with the Austrian population who had so willingly and happily collaborated with the fascist invaders and conspired in the destruction of their country's independence.

He thought of the distraught, helpless creatures locked in the cattle trucks at Zagreb railway station, like animals to the slaughter that awaited them in some concentration camp run by Jew-hating, Jew-baiting madmen in black Nazi uniforms. Where are my Ruth and the children? he asked himself. Are they on their way to God knows what fate?'

He fell asleep thinking about their unknown fate.

He awoke to feel the plane on a steep decline as the pilot cut the engine power and made a gentle turn in the faint light of a summer dawn. He could make out a green arc-shaped form, resembling a lotus flower, of a wide river delta, guessing it to be the Nile. A sweeping vista of wheat fields, rice paddies and marshy swamplands fanning out from the great river's edge came into view.

* * *

A military car awaited them. The army driver saluted Macpherson and gave Ulrich a perfunctory glance. Macpherson sat in the front beside the driver, indicating to Ulrich to sit in the rear by himself.

"Have a good journey, Major?" the driver said, addressing Macpherson.

"Fair enough, sergeant. Fair enough."

Ulrich could not contain his curiosity.

"Where are we going?" he asked Macpherson.

"You'll soon find out."

As the car sped along the tarmacadamed road, they passed peasants on foot, wearing long white full length shirts or dresses.

Ulrich felt he had entered a strange world. He had but not in the way he thought.

"Any news, Stubbings, since I've been away?" Macpherson said addressing the sergeant.

"Nothing really, sir, except that Jerry's on our doorstep. A place called El Alamein."

"They won't take Cairo. Monty will see to that."

"The wogs have been rioting in Port Said, sir. Want higher pay to unload the ships."

"They're a troublesome lot the Arabs. If their leaders are anything to go by, they're all pro-German. Nazis the lot of them."

"We need them to do the donkey work, sir. If you can get them off their backsides, in a manner of speaking. Pity we couldn't use donkeys. Plenty of them about."

Both men laughed.

After about an hour's madcap drive they arrived at a military base. An armed guard with a red band around his arm and a surly look on his face, approached and demanded identity papers. He was not satisfied with Macpherson's explanation and, while he went into the guard hut, presumably to phone for instructions, a machine-gun placed in a nearby concrete pillbox remained trained on the car. The guard came out of his hut, raised the red entry pole and waved them through.

"It's good to see they're on their toes," Macpherson said.

The car stopped outside one of the camp's many long wooden structures, and both men got out, leaving Stubbings to drive away. Macpherson led Ulrich into the building, along a corridor and showed him into a room where a man in uniform sat behind a desk. He was absorbed in looking at some photographs. Behind him were several grey steel filing cabinets and, on the wall, three large maps.

"Brigadier, I've brought Ulrich Dreher, as you requested," Macpherson said.

He looked up. His face was familiar as Ulrich searched his memory. It was Jerrold. He rose and came round the desk to where Ulrich was standing.

"So, Herr Dreher, we meet again."

"Mr Jerrold. The Department of Ancient Monuments."

Jerrold smiled.

"Correct. Macpherson here radioed me he'd met you and mentioned your sub-machine gun. I knew it could only be you so I asked him to persuade you to return with him." He turned to Macpherson, "Damn good job, Macpherson."

Turning back to Ulrich, he said, "Now then, Herr Dreher, I'm sure you must be hungry. Major Macpherson will take you to the canteen. After that he'll bring you back here and we can have a little chat."

Jerrold's little chat turned out to be more than that.

"Your official status, Herr Dreher," Jerrold said, "is, to put it mildly, a bit odd."

"I don't think of myself as odd," Ulrich said. He gave Jerrold a wan smile.

"You're what we term an alien. No papers, a foreign name and a personal story to tell that you couldn't make up. No one to vouchsafe for you. The German authorities that do know you would shoot you on sight if they found you and no questions asked." He paused and gave Ulrich a searching look. Defiant too.

"But I have one," he continued. "Will you work for us?"

"Before I answer yes or no, is there a quid pro quo?" Ulrich replied.

"That depends what the quid is."

Ulrich repeated briefly what he had told Macpherson about his intention to get to Italy and find Ruth and the children.

"All those years ago, Mr Jerrold, in London you said you would help, if ever I needed it."

"We shall, Herr Dreher, we shall, as far as possible. But right at the present moment, we've much more pressing business to attend to. Unless we stop Jerry from taking over the Middle East with its precious oil fields and attacking Russia from its vulnerable underbelly, we'll lose this war. It's as simple as that. The desert fox, that's General Rommel to you Herr Dreher, and his Afrika Korps are just now hammering on our front door. They would kick it down but he lacks enough tanks, men and munitions. Now that's where you come in."

"Me?" Ulrich said with a sharp note of surprise in his voice and pointing his forefinger at his own chest.

"Yes, you, incredible as that might sound. Rommel's lines of communication are mightily stretched, all his reinforcements and material must come down through the Balkans. So far, the partisans there have done a stalwart job by blowing up railways and bridges."

"I know, I've actually done that myself."

"Jolly good. However, there's a problem. The partisans, for their own reason, are being selective with the information they pass on to us. They know a lot more than they say. What they don't say, we want to know. As I've said, that's where you come in, Herr Dreher. If you agree, we'll parachute you into Yugoslavia and your task will be to interrogate German prisoners, find out what military units are being sent to Rommel. You'll be under Macpherson's command and work with the partisans."

"What if the partisans refuse to cooperate with me? They may not allow me to interrogate prisoners. What then?"

"They will when we tell them that supplies of guns, ammunition and explosives depend on that cooperation. They need us for their reasons and we need them for ours."

"I know the arguments. I've already been harangued by their political commissars. It's a form of verbal torture."

Jerrold laughed.

Ulrich watched Jerrold and mentally considered his position.

If I accept his offer I shall be in a worse position than I was when I was the partisans' guest. They trusted me, sort of, now it will be under duress. On the other hand, if I refuse, Jerrold would wash his hands of me and I could find myself in a prisoner of war camp with Germans as companions.

"Well," Jerrold said , "what's your answer?"

"I really don't have much choice, do I?"

"That's it then."

Jerrold picked up another file and opened it.

"Macpherson here will take you to our camp where you'll get some specialised training. But before you embark on that there's the matter of your identity. From now on you'll be Lieutenant James Pendrick of Her Majesty's Royal Engineers. Given your background, I thought that regiment the most suitable. You can talk the language. In this folder," he pointed to another file, "you'll find your family history, your schools, past employment. Learn it, know it, memorise it. From now on you're an Englishman. So think English. Your life will depend on it. Forget your past, the lovely Vienna, Strauss, Beethoven, Goethe, Schiller the lot. Instead I recommend you learn the terminology of cricket and read past numbers of a magazine called *Punch*. Any questions?"

"Do I take it I've been granted British nationality?"

"Afraid not old boy. This is only a cover. If your cover had been a travelling salesman, it wouldn't make you one. When this is all over you could apply. No guarantees."

"What's all this about *Punch* and cricket?"

"If you get picked up by the Germans, you'll be on their list of British Officers. They keep lists like we keep lists. They'll interrogate you. Pump you for every scrap of information."

"It's a pity that I can't get in touch with my uncle. He must be able to give you all the information you require."

"You refer, of course to Claus von Juggardt?"

"Indeed. He left Vienna at the same time as I was called up. He went to Berlin to work for the Foreign Ministry."

Jerrold was silent for what seemed a long period.

"As I said to you all those years ago, I knew him at Cambridge. We've been in contact, well, in fact, ever since Adolf took over. A key man. Was."

"What do you mean, was?"

"Our intelligence lines to Berlin are dead at the present. I can't tell you any more." There was a note of finality to Jerrold's voice.

* * *

"Pendrick," shouted the drill sergeant.

"Pendrick," he repeated. He looked along the line of recruits up in front of him. His face screwed up in contempt.

Ulrich suddenly realised the sergeant was referring to him.

"Sir," he shouted out belatedly.

"Are you bloody deaf or what? And don't call me sir. To you I'm sergeant. Sir." The last was in arrogant deference to Ulrich's rank.

It was a British version of Eisenstadt. More, however, was added. Like the joys of parachute jumping. 'If your 'chute doesn't open, you're dead,' said the corporal in charge, without a trace of irony. Learning Morse code, cyphers and the intricacies of radio transmission. 'The Germans have broken the Partisans' codes, so any information you have for us you keep to yourself', the instructor warned him. 'Those who ignore the unforgiving laws of secret radio transmission pay a high price,' he was told in solemn terms. Yet without such transmissions, work behind enemy lines was a futile exercise.

He learned the art of personal survival, how to live off the land and, importantly, how to withstand harsh and protracted interrogation. He learned his part well and stuck by his story of his childhood in east Cornwall, his school and university in London. He was even cheeky. 'Come and visit me after you've lost the war,' he said to the unnamed who led the mock interrogation. He hoped he sounded condescending. He had received a mighty slap on the face. 'Don't patronise me you little English shit,' said the unnamed mock interrogator. They failed to break him. It was only a game after all.

Thinking he was still in Egypt, Ulrich discovered, much to his surprise, that the training camp was located in Palestine. Remembering the meeting of the Jewish Action Group in Vienna before the war, he inwardly smiled at the ironic transience of fate. The journey from Egypt in an army lorry together with British and French personnel, had been stiflingly hot, dusty and taken several hours. They ran into a sand-storm causing curses in various languages. To keep out the sand, someone closed the rear flaps of the canvas-covered lorry. Increasing the heat and making the lorry dark.

After five weeks at the camp, Ulrich and the other recruits were given weekend leave and he went to Jerusalem.

Jerusalem. Ulrich sat at a table outside a cafe in the modern part of the city. Conditioned by years of New Testament teaching, his mental picture was of people in Biblical garb, donkeys, sheep, goats, a nativity scene, or the Saviour of mankind carrying a cross, Ulrich found it difficult to accustom his mind to the sight of people in modern clothes, cars, lorries, army vehicles, telephone and electrical wires strung from high wooden poles.

"James," said his companion, a young woman by the name of Helen. She wore no make-up but was attractive. They used first names only. "Are you daydreaming?"

"Sorry my mind was miles away," he replied.

"That's fatal in this job. You could be taken by surprise. The Gestapo don't sleep on the job."

"So I believe."

"How did you get into this game?"

"Volunteered. I've known the chief for some years now. How did a young woman like yourself be recruited. I can't imagine you shooting your way out of a dangerous situation." He laughed.

"Never underestimate the female of the species. Actually, I can shoot. My father taught me to handle a gun."

"Shooting party on the Yorkshire Moors?"

"No. In Lebanon. He was English but we lived in Beirut, where I attended an English convent school. At weekends, my father would take my brother and myself up into the mountains. We would shoot wild goats."

"Are your parents still in Lebanon?"

"No. My father died about five years ago and my mother moved back to France. I went with her but after a couple of years when the war broke out I returned to the Lebanon."

"Didn't you like France? All that lovely food and wine so they tell me."

"After Lebanon, I found it too anti-Semitic. I was a member of a Jewish group at the Sorbonne. The young thugs from the Action Française used to gatecrash our meetings and attack us. It was nasty and brutish. Authors, such as George Bernanos, were openly hateful of Jews. The right-wing press encouraged hatred of Jews. Balzac was right when he called the French newspapers 'intellectual brothels'."

"You must be afraid for your mother."

"I am. I've not heard from her for some time. The right-wing Vichy government took over the Lebanon after the fall of France. Communications with France were still possible. Now I hear that the Vichy authorities are rounding up Jews in France, depriving them of their citizenship and handing them over to the Germans." She began to weep. "I'm sorry, but it's terrible to think what might have become of her."

"Perhaps she may have been able to escape to Spain." Ulrich thought she looked even more attractive with the tears running down her smooth cheeks. There was no consoling her.

Chapter 16

Yugoslavia 1943

As the Handley Page Halifax neared the drop zone, Ulrich, shaking nervously, tried but failed to remember the instructions of his parachute instructor, a phlegmatic Yorkshireman, by the name of Foster who spoke with a slight stutter. The deafening throb of the plane made thinking impossible. It was pitch black, then a red light came on. He clipped his parachute's static line to the overhead cable running the length of the fuselage and heard the order to check equipment. He looked down through the black hole in the floor, held his breath for a moment, and jumped. The mighty rush of cold air hit him like a punch taking his breath away. He tumbled over and over when suddenly the parachute opened, jerking him into a vertical position. Bending his knees slightly to break his fall and full of fear, he floated down through total darkness towards the unseen ground. The sound of the aircraft became fainter till there was absolute silence, except the rippling of the air through the parachute. His mind, for no reason, was inexplicably filled with the words of the young nun who taught him his catechism, '*never forget the Angel of Death is always at your shoulder*'. It was overcast with no moon. A night when an Angel of Death might come calling

Suddenly he hit the ground or rather a thicket of bushes which cushioned his landing. Picking himself up, he looked around wondering where the partisan reception party could be. As his eyes became accustomed to the darkness, he could see a number of men coming towards him. He didn't know whether they were Croats, Germans or partisans. It was too late to worry.

They shouted out, first in a language he vaguely remembered, then in English. Partisans.

After some hours scouring the nearby ground for the containers that held the arms, explosives and a promised radio transmitter, the welcoming party escorted Ulrich to their headquarters. He was introduced to the leader called Petrovic. His tall, greying good looks, bass voice and sharp eyes combined to give him an air of authority.

"What's your name?" he asked in thickly-accented English.

"Captain James Pendrick of the Royal Engineers." He liked the word 'captain'. It had a certain ring about it.

"We don't have the comforts of the officers' club in Cairo," he said, "but you're welcome to share what we have."

Later that day, in the quarters that the partisans allocated to him, Ulrich reviewed his last meeting with Jerrold in Cairo.

'Now we've got Jerry on the run,' Jerrold had said, 'it's even more important than ever to learn what forces the German High Command are sending to Rommel, and do everything we can to stop them. The partisans have captured a German general, by the name of von Schwenke, on his way to North Africa from headquarters in Berlin where he was in charge of troop dispositions. He possesses information we urgently need. It's going to be your job to interrogate him.'

'Why me? I thought you would have sent Major Macpherson.'

'That was the original intention but I've sent him on another more urgent mission.'

Ulrich had thought for a moment.

'Why can't you bring von Schwenke here,' he said, 'like I was?'

'Good question. Von Schwenke is the partisan's prisoner not ours. The Germans and Croats shoot any partisans they capture. By keeping this general in their hands they will be able to trade him for their own people when they're captured by the enemy. So they're not going to hand him over to us. Hence your mission. We've promoted you to captain because the general would not deal with some lower rank or any old civilian. For radio communication, we've assigned the general a code name. Enyalius. He's a minor Greek god of war,' Jerrold explained. 'You'll probably remember he's mentioned several times in Homer's *Iliad*.' He paused. 'There's one more thing.'

'What's that?'

'This chap's a general. Forget any films you may have seen about James Cagney, Chicago mobsters, G-Men and American police third-degree methods. Third-degree is just another word for torture. Torture in whatever form is useless and self-defeating. Military officers such as von Schwenke are not criminals and must not be treated as such. The key is tact and finesse. We've discovered that it works with people like him. So don't let our partisan friends rough him up.'

After a few days familiarising himself with the situation at the partisans' quarters and in discussions with Petrovic related to his mission, Ulrich set out with a small detachment of partisans for the cave in the mountains, where the German general was being held. The trek took several hours across a rough mountainous terrain. The partisans proved hardy companions and he found it difficult to keep up. On his arrival, he was confronted with armed guards, hanging around the entrance, smoking and chatting. The cave, lit by three oil lamps, was about half the size of a tennis court, with straw covering the ground and a pile of logs to one side. The acrid reek of wood-fire smoke stung his eyes.

Unshaven, dirty and giving off a strong body odour, von Schwenke, was sitting in a hunched position on the floor near the back of the cave, his ankles bound with thick rope and his arms tied around his back. He reminded Ulrich of Kate in the *Taming of the Shrew*, cutting a forlorn figure in her ruined wedding dress. This, however, was no comedy. His uniform had lost all its dignity. Gone was the shine on the braided gold shoulder boards and the tunic's six silver buttons. The left breast pocket was torn where highly prized medals had once been attached. His crumpled field-grey breeches, with their theatrical red stripes down the sides of each leg, had not seen a batman's iron for weeks. His black leather belt with its motto of 'God is with Us' on the buckle was missing. God, it appeared, had deserted the general.

Wouldn't a humiliated, cold and probably hungry senior officer of the mighty *Wehrmacht* resent being interrogated? Ulrich thought. Before setting out for the general's place of captivity, he had made it clear to Petrovic that he alone would carry out the interrogation and not brook any interference from the partisans during the questioning.

Petrovic had given him an interpreter to ease his dealings with the general's guards.

"Tell the guards to untie the prisoner," Ulrich ordered the interpreter. "Then get us a couple of chairs. I can't do this work standing up." He felt self-assured.

When the general had been untied, the chairs, rough wooden structures, were brought from the rear of the cave. Ulrich invited von Schwenke to sit down.

"I'm a British officer," Ulrich said, introducing himself. "I've been sent by the British authorities to speak to you."

He then produced a flask, opened it and offered it to the General.

"A drop of schnapps might help our conversation," Ulrich said in German.

The flask was Jerrold's idea. 'That usually contains a fine malt when I go fishing in Altnaharra, in the Scottish Highlands,' he had remarked. 'Happy days.'

It was a risk. Von Shwenke did not know him or why he was there and could possibly think he was trying to poison him.

Von Schwenke eyed him suspiciously, yet he took the flask nonetheless. When he had taken a drink, he handed the flask back to Ulrich.

"If you're a British officer," von Schwenke said, "then you might tell this lot of swine, I'm a German general, and I insist that they treat me as a prisoner of war under the Geneva Conventions. The German government treats Allied prisoners according to those Conventions. Look at these conditions." There was fury in his voice and his eyes blazed with fire as he gestured to his place of captivity. "What kind of place is this to hold a German officer? A cave, and a damned cold one at that. I'm shackled like a wild animal, there's no privacy, I'm given little to eat and I'm allowed to wash only once a week."

"General, there's no use berating me," Ulrich responded, "I'm afraid there's little I can do about this. You're not a prisoner in the hands of the British authorities. These partisans holding you don't form part of our forces. We've little if any control over them. They're fighting their own war, if you like."

"What war would that be?" There was scorn in the voice.

"I'm not going to go into all that. I'm not here to give you a history lesson on the recent past. Though I might, just might, be able to help you."

"How can you do that?"

"First, I shall try to persuade the leader of the partisans to give you better living conditions. I can't promise results. However, if you cooperate with me, the British authorities would guarantee your life."

"Life? What do you mean, guarantee my life? How can they do that if they don't have any authority over these criminals." His voice held a mixture of arrogance and contempt.

"These partisans won't hesitate to kill you if they don't get their way. They made it clear to me that, when you invaded their country, illegally in their view, you set the rules. Summary executions, bloody reprisals against civilians, torture, an arbitrary rule of law. The Gestapo. The SS and Concentration camps. The partisans are playing by your rules, General. If your presence here threatens them, they'll shoot you."

Von Schwenke remained silent.

"If you give me the information I seek," Ulrich continued, "the British government could make the partisans hand you over to us." Ulrich realised that he was stepping well outside his remit but felt he had to say something to convince a sceptical enemy.

"What information would that be?" He glowered at Ulrich.

"The dispositions of the *Wehrmacht* divisions being sent to North Africa."

Another long silence.

"That I refuse to do. I'm many things but traitor is not one of them. I've sworn an oath of allegiance to the Führer. As a British officer you demean yourself by supposing that I might renege on that oath."

"General, I'm not asking you to become a traitor. I admire your loyalty but you don't seem to realise that you're losing the war. After Alamein, you're losing North Africa, after Stalingrad, where your Field Marshall von Paulus surrendered, you're losing Russia."

"If I have a choice between treachery and loyalty, I choose loyalty. Have no fear, right at this minute there are German and Croatian units searching this region for me. I have the consolation that if I'm shot, my people will have no mercy on these people. We wiped out whole areas in Russia and we'll do it again here. Allied bombers do not hesitate to drop their lethal loads killing innocent German women and children. So why should we be different?"

"Is that your final word?"

"Yes." He fell silent for a moment before adding, "I'm intrigued to know how you speak such excellent German, I would say with native speaker competence. Also, I think, with a slight Austrian accent."

"My teacher was Austrian."

If only he knew.

* * *

Radio links with Macpherson's headquarters were cut off for several weeks as the partisans tried to fix the generator which supplied the electricity for the radio. Ulrich's report had to wait. He wondered what Jerrold's reaction would be when told about von Schwenke's refusal to cooperate. Despite several visits to the cave, his efforts were thwarted by the even more bedraggled, intransigent general.

When Ulrich did re-establish the radio link, Jerrold had other plans for him. A British agent in Switzerland had made contact with Cairo. His message was that a senior German officer, based in Zagreb, wished to cooperate with the allies. It would be Ulrich's job to meet this officer in secret and liaise with him. Detailed information would be given him in the next drop. He had to leave Enyalius alone for the moment and try again later.

Ulrich was surprised when he open the package sent by courier from Macpherson. An Irish passport in the name of Brian Prenderville! What the devil does Jerrold think I am? A Shakespearean actor? The adjoining note required him to find his way to Zagreb, posing as an Irish dealer in metals working for a Venezuelan import-export company based in Dublin, on his way from Istanbul to Zurich. His contact in Zagreb was one, Anton Vogel, a clerk in the Zagreb branch of a Swiss investment bank with headquarters in Zurich. The story appeared so far-fetched as to be wholly incredible until he realised that the bank in question was a branch of the same Swiss bank which held his own account, the one opened for him by Jerrold those several years ago. The British octopus had its tentacles spread very widely.

* * *

The main railway station in Zagreb awakened painful memories for Ulrich. He wondered what had become of the pitiful Greek Jews herded into sealed cattle carriages that fateful day when the real purpose of the war was once more confirmed for him. He made his way to the Palace Hotel, a four-storey art nouveau building on Strossmayer Square. There was a scattering of SS and senior German Army officers in the dining room that evening. Ulrich wondered if one of them was his potential informant. In the eyes of these his fellow diners – if only they knew – he was a deserter turned traitor. In this web of intrigue no-one ever knew who his neighbour really was. A smile broke out on his nervous face. Jerrold the puppet master was several steps ahead of everyone else, scheming, hatching plots, planning, arranging, prearranging. Ulrich felt he himself was scarcely half a step ahead, if that.

The next day he found the Zurich bank on Varsavska Street. The war did not exist inside the bank. The odour was of Swiss neutrality, secrecy and money. 'Creosus wasn't Greek', his Uncle Claus had once remarked, 'he was Swiss.' He approached one of the desks and asked to see Herr Vogel, explaining that he had an appointment. The young clerk gave Ulrich a wary look, told him to wait, got up and went off. He returned accompanied by another man. Was this Herr Vogel?

"I understand you have an appointment with Herr Vogel," he said. "May I ask who you are?"

"The name's Prenderville," Ulrich said in German. "I have an appointment with Herr Vogel."

"I'm sorry to disappoint you, Herr Prenderville, but Herr Vogel is no longer here. You've missed him by a day. He was recalled to Zurich only yesterday. He is not expected to return. Can I possibly be of assistance?"

"That's kind of you but no thank you."

As he left the bank, a police car raced down the street, its bell clanging. He could hear a similar sound inside his head.

What now Mr Jerrold? Ulrich asked himself.

There would be no answer to that question. Or any other question that he asked himself. Where to go now? How to contact Jerrold who had not given him an alternative plan? He felt Jerrold had been remiss. The ice on the espionage lake was thin and cracking. As he walked back to the hotel, a plan began to form in his mind that would be, he hoped, in his own interest. He had a new name, new identity, neutral passport. Now he would get a train to Trieste and thence to Venice. To Ruth. The ice began to harden under his feet.

"There are two gentlemen wishing to speak to you, Mr Prenderville," said the concierge at the hotel reception desk, when he arrived back. He pointed across the foyer to where the two were sitting smoking.

A shiver went through him.

He approached them.

"I'm Prenderville," he said in English, addressing the older of the two. "I understand you want to see me."

They stood up. Both were of medium height and well-dressed in dark grey suits.

"We're from the Ministry of the Interior, Security Service," said the younger of the two, giving Ulrich a sharp look. "We would like to ask you a few questions." He spoke in halting English. The older man said nothing.

"Before you ask any questions," Ulrich said, "I would like to remind you that I'm an Irish citizen, and the Irish Free State is neutral."

"We'll deal with that matter later. We would like to know what your business is with Herr Vogel of the Investment Bank of Zurich?"

"That's a private business matter, if I may say so," said Ulrich, "but since you ask, I've had business relations with this bank for several years. I'm on my way from Istanbul to Venice and when I learned that Herr Vogel was here I dropped off to renew our acquaintance. That's not a crime I hope." He smiled at his own creative thinking.

"The fact is Herr Prenderville, your friend Herr Vogel has been expelled from this country and sent back to Switzerland for indulging in unlawful activities."

A staid Swiss banker indulging in unlawful activities? Tax evasion, perhaps, hiding South American military junta's plundering of the state coffers, maybe. The Swiss don't consider these as illegal.

"What's that got to do with me?"

"On the surface nothing. Curious timing though, for Herr Vogel has been, how shall we put it, allegedly bribing a member of the government of the independent state of Croatia. Had he been a Croatian citizen he would have been charged with a very serious offence. We're dealing here with the matters of state secrecy and security. Now suddenly, you turn up asking for him."

"I'm not responsible for what Herr Vogel has been up to. I know nothing about that. Is that all?"

"For the moment. We must ask you to remain in Zagreb until we have finished our inquiries."

"For heaven's sake, how long is that going to take? I'm due in Venice in the next few days."

"Herr Prenderville, if you attempt to leave this city without our express permission you will be arrested. Do I make myself clear?"

He watched the two men walk away.

They were waiting for me, said Ulrich to himself. They knew my name and where I was staying. How did they know?

He went up to his room and lay down in the bed. He watched a fly trying vainly to escape. It went up and down the windowpane, it flew around the room, buzzed over him, went back to the window. Rising up, he took the towel off the wooden towel rail and, after two attempts, swatted it.

They'll be watching the entrance to the hotel and the railway station, he mused. Who's to say they haven't enlisted the hotel reception desk clerk. Eyes and ears everywhere. He knew he was an amateur fallen into the company of worldly-wise and agile craftsmen, whose fundamental virtue was a lack of any scruple. The few skills he had learned in the camp in Palestine did not cover the slippery cul-de-sac in which he now found himself. He considered several avenues of escape but each one proved even less plausible than the previous one. He felt his confidence being sorely tried.

He decided to stay one more night in the hotel. Recalling Jerrold telling him to think himself in to his role, his resolve returned.

Next morning he picked up *Der Rheinische Merkur,* the only German newspaper available on the breakfast room stand. It reported that General Jürgen Stroop, had been transferred to Warsaw to crush a revolt by Jewish gangsters and thugs in the Jewish Ghetto. Ulrich thought about Ruth and the twins.

"Herr Prendeville." The two security officers had returned.

"Yes? What do you want?" Ulrich's voice sounded petulant. "Just remember I'm an Irish citizen."

He glared at the two officers

"You must come with us. Certain matters have arisen. We have questions to ask you."

They ushered him out of the hotel and put him in the rear seat of a Citroën car. The journey was made in silence. They did not even look at him. The car pulled up outside what looked like a grand building with high windows, pillars, a former bank maybe. He was taken into the main hall and then led down stairs to a corridor with doors leading off on both sides. As they escorted him along, a man wearing a long, thick rubber apron which reached down almost to the floor, came towards them in the opposite direction. In his right hand was a revolver. The apron dripped with blood. As he passed Ulrich's little group he muttered something. The two security officers laughed. Ulrich felt a chill run down his spine. The unknown terrorised him. Stopping in front of a thick steel door, the older of the two knocked. The door was opened from the inside. The security officers pushed Ulrich into the room.

The room, stinking of stale urine and blood, was shrouded in semi-darkness with a single seat in the middle facing a table with chairs behind it. They sat him down in the seat and shackled his legs with leg irons, and secured his arms by tying them to the arms of the metal chair with thick wires. Thus restrained and his stomach knotted with fear, he felt he was going to vomit. A single blazing light was turned on, the beam catching Ulrich full on the face, hurting his eyes and blinding him to the rest of his surroundings.

"What the bloody hell's going on?" he protested. "You'll pay for this. I demand to be freed."

"Now, Mister Prenderville," said a soft voice in English, "if that really is your name. What are you doing in this country? Why did you want to see Herr Vogel?"

"Can you turn that light off my face," Ulrich said.

"Feeling a little pain, are we? This is only a foretaste of what's to come unless you cooperate with us." The interrogator paused. There was a long silence.

"Tell me, Mister Prenderville, where did you start your journey?"

"Istanbul. Look I've already told you. Why do you persist in asking me questions to which you already know the answers?"

"So your train came overnight from Istanbul on Monday? Arriving in Zagreb on Tuesday morning."

"That's correct."

"Not correct." The voice took on a harsh edge. "The train from Istanbul was derailed south of Belgrade. So where did you begin your journey?"

Ulrich remained silent while he thought out the implications of this news.

"You can save us a great deal of trouble and yourself a great deal of pain if you just tell us the truth. You see, Mister Prenderville, we have every reason to believe that you've been working for the partisans and that your proposed meeting with Herr Vogel was related to that. Is that not the case?"

"I don't know what you're talking about," said Ulrich.

"Answer the question!"

Ulrich could hear his heart beating hard against his rib cage. Sweat ran down inside his shirt. Just then he felt an electric shock pulsate through his whole body. His breath came in spurts. He leaned forward and vomited, the hot acid-smelling fluid soaking his trousers and seeping down his legs.

"A little reminder of what we can do," said the voice. There was another pause.

"I repeat, we know that you've been working with the partisans. Since you're obviously not from this part of the world, let me tell you the partisans are the enemy of the independent state of Croatia. This state is no longer part of the corrupt regime of warmongers and their Orthodox Church bedfellows in Belgrade. We're now free. It's our duty to ensure that it remains free. It was the British who engineered the *coup d'état* which opposed our freedom. So if you're working for the British, which we believe you are, the sooner you tell us, the better."

Another stronger electric shock.

"I don't know anything about all that," Ulrich muttered. "You're wasting your time."

Still another and still stronger shock.

He closed his eyes and the vision of himself with Ruth walking in the Vienna Woods passed before his eyes. Ruth and the twins playing games in their flat in Vienna.

A third and very strong shock. He fainted. Someone threw a bucket of water over him, then grabbing his hair, yanked his head back.

"For the last time, tell us what you know about the partisans. Where they're getting their guns and radios from. Where are the British agents? Answer stupid, stubborn man."

There was no answer, for Ulrich had lost consciousness and no number of buckets of water could revive him.

* * *

Ulrich lay on the floor of a dark cell lit only by a single green bulb which gave the place an air of floating in space. The foetid reek of his own excrement and urine assailed his nostrils, every bone and muscle in his body burned, his eyes ached and had lost their focus, his temple throbbed, and his mouth felt as if it was caked with hard mud. He had difficulty forming the simplest of thoughts. Gradually his mind cleared and his vision began to return. He waggled his toes to make sure they were working, closed his fists then opened them and looked at the palms of his hands which bore burning marks. Every position he tried merely increased the lancinating pain flowing though his body.

He thought of von Schwenke in the partisans' cave. That too had a foul stench about it. It seemed easy then to take the moral high ground with the general who, faced with a choice, did not give way.

I did not give in. To tell a little is to tell everything. To whom do I owe loyalty? Austria? No. The Greater Reich? Certainly not. To the British, to Jerrold? Perhaps. To Ruth? Yes. But I don't trust these Ustasi security people. They must have learned their trade from the Gestapo. If I tell them what they want to know they will have done with me.

Time passed. It was impossible to know how it passed. Here, seconds, minutes, hours became meaningless. Except for the incessant hurt wracking his body, he felt in a dreamworld.

It was no dream. The door suddenly opened and two men entered.

"You need some fresh air, Mister Prendereville. We thought you should take a short break to revive your memory. You'll spend a little time in one of the camps we've established here in Croatia, where you'll learn to appreciate your present surroundings."

* * *

Coming out of the prison block where he had been assigned the lower of a three-tier bunk bed, Ulrich could see a high wall into which several concrete bunkers and guard towers had been built. In front of the wall were lines of tangled barbed wire. A fellow prisoner told him that this part of the camp was a prison for inmates specially selected by the Ustasi security service. It was a warm late summer's evening, and he noticed the swallows swooping, diving and performing aerial acrobatics. But the camp was no pastoral scene.

Except for newcomers, the majority of inmates were walking skeletons, whose ravaged bodies were witness to a regime of starvation and physical punishment. The camp inflicted terrible indignities upon its hapless inmates. Squalor reigned, prisoners were obliged to relieve themselves at an open latrine, which consisted of a long, wide and deep pit covered by planks. Ulrich was shocked to see several bodies which had fallen, or been pushed or thrown in. Washing meant sharing a bucket of foul smelling filthy water with about twenty others. There was no soap or towels. An almost total lack of drinking water added to Ulrich's woes, and he learned that if he wanted a drink he would have to walk a couple of miles to a stream which was also used as a latrine. His diet was one small bowl of turnip soup, which as the days passed was served sometimes in the morning, sometimes at night. As he lined up for his first meal he noticed several very young boys, skinny, stark naked and shivering despite the warm weather, standing in the meal queue, holding small bowls in their hands. A guard approached and chased them away, using a long whip. One child fell and was brutally kicked by the guard. He cried out but the guard continued to kick him in the head until there was no life left in him. The guard then shouted to some inmate to pick the child up and throw him into the latrine pit.

After the morning meal, the shabby, rag-clothed and emaciated prisoners lined up to be assigned to labour groups. Ulrich's group was assigned to empty the barracks of the corpses of those who had died in the night. And there were many, from young children to old men. The stench of blood, vomit and bodies pervaded the large ill-lit rooms where hundreds lived, sharing crowded bunks. With three other inmates, he carried the dead bodies out and placed them on two-wheeled carts. When the carts were full, each taking about twelve corpses, they then pushed them several hundred metres to where other prisoners had dug long deep pits. To bring some dignity to this work, Ulrich, at first, tried to place the bodies on the carts. A guard thrashed him. 'Throw them on. They're scum Serbs and Jews.' Resistance was futile. The sick and dying, weakened and enfeebled, were dragged from their beds and clubbed or kicked to death by the guards. No bullets were wasted. Some guards seemed to take pleasure in stabbing the children in particular. Each time before they carried out a killing, they would shout *'One less Jew, one less Serb'*. They laughed and joked as they carried out these murders with total impunity. Any prisoner who slackened in his work was summarily executed. In the middle of the afternoon, Ulrich began to tire. The gruesome and grisly work made his head swim with fear and anxiety. But the thought of sudden, unexpected death at the hands of some guard, made him bear the burden of his work.

One evening later, he lay exhausted, his mind filled with the horrors he had witnessed.

"Are you a Serb?" The deep voice was that of a young man, flowing black beard, thick eyebrows, a prematurely-wrinkled forehead and sad brown eyes. He spoke in whispers in German.

"No," Ulrich replied, "I'm Irish. My name's Brian Prenderville. The Ustasi security police have sent me here as a punishment to get me to talk. But I've nothing to say."

"Some of the prisoners think that you may be a spy for the police. Are you a police spy?"

"No. I don't speak any of this Serbo-Croat language." There was a silence.

"My name is Avnar Meisel.

"Can you speak English?"

"Actually, yes. I spent a couple of years teaching the subject at a high school in Belgrade."

"Why are the Croats murdering their fellow Yugoslavs?" Although he knew the answer, the question was prompted by his recently acquired Irish alter ago.

"That my friend is a long story. It's to do with religion. Things were not too bad under the old Austrian regime, which was a bulwark of the Catholic Church. I'm sure you must have heard of the Holy Roman Empire even in Catholic Ireland."

"Sort of," Ulrich said.

"Well, then, Orthodox people were considered second-class citizens. A bit like the Jews really. Tolerated. After the Great War, when Austria lost its empire and the Jugoslav Republic was created, Croatia lost its high and mighty position. This meant that the Catholic Croats were now ruled by the Serbs in Belgrade. They didn't like it. The Catholic Church schemed to get Croatian independence. But that was never going to happen. When the Germans invaded Yugoslavia, the Vatican put pressure on the Führer to make Croatia independent. They've got what they wanted. They're close allies now. It's time for revenge. The Ustasi government sent its people to Germany to see how they run their death camps and have brought the system here to rid Croatia of its Serbs and Jews."

"The Führer seems to export only German vice."

"Not exactly. The Croats have got their own version of evil."

"It looks the same to me. You put your enemy in a camp and kill him."

"There's a difference. The camps may belong to the state but this camp and others are run by members of the Catholic clergy."

"I don't believe you."

"It's not a matter of belief. You'll see on Saturday."

"Why Saturday?"

"It's the Jewish Shabat. It's the day when they kill the Jews en masse."

"Are you a believer?" asked Ulrich.

"I used to be a teacher then I studied to become a rabbi, but this war stopped my studies. When the Germans invaded I came back up here thinking it would be safer. I'm a Serb and a Jew. I soon realised that being a Jew was like carrying a death sentence over your head. I tried to escape from my village, where I had taken refuge, a place called Glina but was caught."

"So you've landed up here. Have you thought of trying to escape?"

"Of course but it's very difficult. The walls are well guarded and the fences are electrified. I've not been here long so I'm still reasonably fit. In another few weeks I won't have the strength. I would like to escape if only to alert the rest of the world about this Croat concentration camp."

The next day Ulrich was assigned to a labour group, constructing a dyke that ran along the bank of the nearby river. The dyke ran parallel to the river about fifty metres from the bank and in between the two was a high fence topped by rolls of barbed wire. While he worked on the top of the dyke, laying heavy stones brought by carts pulled by prisoners, one of the inmates suddenly ran down the side of the dyke and made for the fence which he started to climb. He had reached the top of the fence when a guard opened fired and shot him. He lay where he had fallen. To Ulrich it meant the fence at that point was not electrified.

On the way to the dyke and near to a huge brick factory, Ulrich had noticed that there was a blacksmith's shed. Two nights later, it was midnight when he crept out of his barrack room. The guard at the door had disappeared. This was not an unusual occurrence: many of the guards took the opportunity during the night and darkness to visit the women's part of the camp where they would regularly rape women and girls. They would openly boast to the male prisoners how many times they had 'punished' a woman or girl in one night.

Silently, Ulrich worked his way past several blocks, hearing the nightmarish groans shouts and screams of the prisoners. Arriving at the blacksmith's shed, he discovered that, while the large front door was firmly locked, there was a side door held closed on a latch. Lifting the latch he entered and, guided by the glow from the permanent fire, he searched for what he was certain to find among the many tools being forged in the smithy. It took a little time but eventually he found what he was looking for. Luckily, the guard was still missing from his post when Ulrich arrived back at his barrack room. He knew he was taking a fatal risk when he hid the newly-acquired wire cutters in his thin mattress.

Shabat. All the male prisoners were obliged to gather in silent lines facing a fence which separated their compound from that of the women, girls and children. The guards on both sides had their rifles and sub-machine guns trained on the prisoners. Ulrich then saw the first group of women appear, naked, some carrying toddlers and babies. When a couple of hundred had assembled, they were ordered to lie face down on the ground. There was confusion as mothers struggled to hold their children close. There was wailing and crying. Other guards appeared armed with long steel bars, thick wooden staves, axes and mallets. Three of them were wearing the robes of the religious order of Franciscans.

"That friar in the middle is the camp commandant, he's called Father Filipovic," Avnar whispered to Ulrich.

Father Filipovic was carrying a megaphone. He turned to where the male prisoners stood on their side of the long fence.

"Today is the Sabbath. It is the day appointed for the Jews to receive their punishment for killing Our Lord Jesus Christ, our Saviour. We the representatives of the Church are the sacred instruments chosen to carry out the long-awaited judgment. The archbishop knows of our work. We act in God's name." He waved his arms towards the prostrated women. "May these Jews die and rot in the hell prepared for them."

A woman suddenly stood up, holding a baby in her arms.

"The butcher is here," she screamed out.

Father Filipovic, a big towering man, came across and brutally snatching the child from her, took it by its legs and smashed its head on the ground, its brains soaking into the earth. Taking hold of the woman, he stabbed her to death using a knife which was strapped to his hand by a leather type glove. Ulrich watched in horror as the clerical and lay butchers set about flaying, clubbing and bludgeoning the women and children, raping the young girls and digging out eyes with specially constructed hooks. The friar, having watched three guards sexually abuse a woman, took hold of her and throttled her, throwing her limp body to the ground.

The horrific butchery continued all day long. The shrill screams and ear-piercing shrieks of the hapless victims jarred and jangled in Ulrich's head as if he were in some kind of madhouse. He felt like a voyeur in an abattoir. The place of slaughter at the end of the day was literally a charnel house.

The brown habits of Father Filipovic and the two other friars as well as the uniforms of the guards were dripping with blood. Groups of male prisoners arrived to take away the corpses to the brick kilns which had been turned into a crematorium. The stench of death hung over the camp.

Finally in the late afternoon, the camp commandant took up his bullhorn.

"Let all know that we have done the Lord's work today. The Jews have paid for their sins. God bless Croatia."

Chapter 17

Yugoslavia 1943

Ulrich and Avnar took turns rowing the boat. They needed to keep it mid-river far enough away from either bank to avoid being spotted by a random night patrol. Avnar a strong rower, said he knew the river well. They were helped by an ambiguous full moon. It could guide their passage but also disclose their whereabouts.

The escape from the camp was easier than Ulrich had anticipated. He had persuaded a not-too-reluctant Avnar to take part in the breakout.

Avnar had objected at first. "What about the electric fence?"

"There's a stretch, just below the new dyke that isn't," insisted Ulrich. He related what he had witnessed only the week before.

"One other thing," continued Ulrich, showing he had scouted out the area, "there's a small rowing boat tied to a stave on the bank. I saw a couple of guards use it. If we can just get through the fence we should be able to take advantage of it."

"You make it sound as if it were some kind of summer outing instead of a desperate bid to escape certain death."

Having left the prison block in the middle of the night, they avoided the searchlights from the guard towers on the far wall. They crawled over the newly constructed high, wide dyke down to the fence where Ulrich, using his cutters, cut a hole at the bottom, enabling them to squeeze through and make their way to where the boat was tied. Luckily, a pair of oars had been conveniently left in the boat.

"We used to own one of these what we called flat-bottomed skiffs," Avnar remarked, as he took up the oars and guided the small vessel into the middle of the river. Given their dangerous circumstances, a nervous Ulrich thought his remark pointless. Ulrich worked out that by rowing at around five kilometres an hour and the river flow being a similar speed, they should cover around a hundred kilometres in ten hours. It would be some days before their absence was discovered for it was rumoured the camp guards kept no daily tally of the number of inmates present in the camp, arbitrarily killing so many of them and failing to record the deaths. The boat was another problem. Were the guards to discover its absence they would start a search. This was a dangerous risk which the two men were willing to take.

"If we can get about hundred kilometres further south, we should be in Serbia," Avnar said.

"I don't really care where we go," Ulrich said, "as long as we can put as much distance between ourselves and that horrible hell-hole."

As the river took them further and further away from the camp, Ulrich reflected on his short time at his place of punishment. His Jesuit schoolmasters had preached that life was a journey, a pilgrimage, at the end of which lay Heaven and God. It was the 'City of God' where all the popes reside and reign. It was in Holy Week that the priests subjected the impressionable, adolescent boys to sermons on hell and its torments. The words echoed in his head: lust, greed, envy, anger. The list was long. The emphasis of course, they being young boys, was on lust. The celibate priests took great care to stress this point. Father Hahn rhapsodised: 'if you listen you can hear the wailing voices of the lustful being punished for their sins – they are whirled about in dark stormy winds.' Then came the moment when he described how Christ after His death descended into hell, where the evil ones who, falling victim to their passions, are being punished for their bestial deeds. 'These souls turned devils are mired in filthy muck and assailed forever by eternal fire. The stench of everlasting death and the horrible noise of the damned souls are the signs of hell.'

I've just seen hell and it has been created by the priests of Church. How can men convince themselves that they are doing God's will by killing their fellow human beings? A kind and just God would hold back their hands, if such a God existed.

A much traumatised Ulrich attempted to excise the vivid and bloody scenes from his mind, but in vain.

The hours passed. Each took it in turns to row. Ulrich began to realise that Avnar was doing most of the rowing, his contribution was to drift in and out of sleep. The only sounds were those of the boat, the water, and an occasional owl and nightjar. At length, the first glimmer of dawn streaked the eastern horizon. A light cool wind came across the river from its western side.

"We must lay up somewhere," suggested Avnar. "We can't take any chances in the daylight."

"How far do you think we've come?"

"About forty kilometres or so."

They came to a bend in the river, where a thick wood came down to the water's edge, the branches of trees reaching over its surface. The daylight was upon them. Ulrich, at the oars, steered the little craft into the bank, where they both got out and hauled it into bushes, out of sight. They alternated at keeping watch and sleeping. At one point, Ulrich woke to find that Avnar had been into the woods and returned with handfuls of wild strawberries.

"You're a genius," he told Avnar.

Ulrich began to look upon this friendly aspirant rabbi as a younger version of Rabbi Levitansky. Suddenly before his unbidden eyes there paraded the faces of those whose fate he knew nothing. The Rabbi and his wife, Reuben, Rosa, Ruth's parents, the members of the Jewish Group, his own Ruth and children. Where were they all?

At dusk the two men dragged the boat down to the river's edge and into the water. Midstream was reached once more and soon they were making progress. Another early dawn found them much further along their river course.

"I remember coming to this place a couple of years ago with my father," Avnar said. "He knew some of the Jewish farmers around here. We may yet be in luck.

"If they've not been taken away by the Croats or Germans," Ulrich said.

"I hope you're wrong."

They approached the left riverbank and hauled the little craft out of the water and hid it in some bushes. They climbed to the top of the embankment. In front of them lay fields in which were sheaves of corn stacked up into shocks to dry.

"I know where we are," Avnar said. "More or less," he added in a cautious tone of voice.

"Where?"

"This side of the river is Serbia and that other side is Bosnia-Herzegovina. I reckon we're not more than a hundred kilometres from Belgrade."

"More or less?"

"I was never much good at geography."

Ulrich laughed.

The two, cautiously skirting along the side of the field, made their way to a farmhouse which was located on the far side of a field of barley. It was a small single storey building with an open barn to one side. In front of the barn was a young woman, sitting on a three-legged stool milking a cow. She was wearing a white linen blouse with embroidered sleeves and a full length multi-coloured skirt. She looked up on their approach. Avnar spoke to her in a gentle, calming voice. Ulrich was unable to follow their conversation, but whatever Avnar said, it made the young woman stop her milking and stand up. She led them into the house where they were greeted by a middle-aged women who eyed them suspiciously. The young woman spoke to her, which seemed to mollify her. Avnar turned to Ulrich.

"At first they thought we might be German agents or secret police," he explained. "The older lady remembers my father. I've briefly told them we've escaped from the Croatian prison. In any case, I speak native Serb, something no German soldier could do. They said they fear the Germans who send patrols around here looking for partisans."

"Ask them about the partisans," Ulrich said. "Joining a partisan group would be better than falling into the hands of the Germans."

"That wouldn't be wise. We don't want to endanger them. I've asked her for some food and perhaps they might give us some clothes. This prison garb is not helpful in our situation."

The older woman went off and returned with some old clothes. Ulrich found it difficult to fit into the short baggy, dark green trousers. "I'm a Serbian peasant now," he said to Avnar, as he put on the black waistcoat and black socks with red colouring. She then made them sit and served them bread, milk, sour cream and a piece of hard cheese. After their meal, the young woman took them into the barn where they stayed for the remainder of the day.

"Have you any plans," Ulrich asked Avnar, "what our next move might be?"

"I know the Swedish consul in Belgrade. He's Jewish. If he's still there, I'm sure he would help us."

That evening, under a threatening sunset sky, they returned to where they had hidden the boat and again took to the water. Eventually they arrived at a large swamp-forest area on the left bank of the river. By a moonlit gloom Ulrich saw egrets and storks, the only birds that he recognised.

"This area is called the Obedska pond," Avnar said. "It used to be hunting ground reserved for the Austrian Imperial family."

As they progressed further south towards Belgrade, there were several horseshoe bends and, as they rounded one, they could see lights ahead.

"That's a railway bridge," Avnar said. "It's bound to be guarded. We must reach the eastern bank for that is where the city is. I know my way about this city. The Swedish consulate is not far from the main cathedral, in the same street where my uncle had his jeweller's shop"

* * *

The consulate was located in a commercial part of Belgrade. Avnar led the way up a flight of stairs in a dismal looking building. On the second landing there were two doors. Outside one were four separate brass plates announcing the presence of the consulates for Ireland, Spain, Portugal and Sweden.

"How odd," Ulrich remarked, "they must all share the same office."

An attractive-looking young woman sitting in front of a typewriter looked up when they entered.

"Can I help you?" she asked in Serbo-Croat, eyeing them up and down disdainfully.

"We would like to see the Swedish consul," Avnar said.

"You mean Herr Nyström?" the secretary said. "What name shall I give?"

"Avnar Meisel. Herr Nyström knows me."

She stood up and, disappearing through the door behind her, left Ulrich and Avnar looking like a couple of workmen holding their peasant caps in their hands. A minute later she reappeared accompanied by Herr Nyström, who greeted Avnar warmly.

To Ulrich, Swedishness meant tall and blond. Herr Nyström was small and rotund with dark brown eyes and wore steel-rimmed glasses.

Avnar and the consul engaged in an animated conversation in which Ulrich heard his Irish name mentioned more than once. He realised that they must be discussing him in the manner people discuss a cripple in a wheelchair, in the third person. 'Does he do this, does he want that?'

With his self-esteem wearing thin, Ulrich abruptly intervened.

"Herr Nyström, do you speak English?" he asked.

"Of course."

"I need help."

He then went on to relate the events of the previous several weeks, still insisting on his Irish alias as Prenderville. Herr Nyström was a good listener.

" I can help Avnar," the consul finally said, "but unfortunately I can't see how I can legally help you."

"What do you mean?" His tone was a mixture of entreaty and frustration. "I'm a fugitive. It's true I've no proof of identity but if the Germans arrest me, my fate is certain. Concentration camp, only German this time, and death. I need a passport and money. I'll repay the money."

Nyström sat down in his swivel chair, placed his hands joined prayer-like under his chin.

"You must understand, Mister Prenderville, I'm only an honorary consul and have limited diplomatic powers." He stopped for a moment as if to consider the situation. "However, the Swedish government, unlike Spanish, Portuguese and Irish, all of whom I represent, has given me special authority to assist people of Jewish persons of whatever nationality. In that way, I've helped more than a thousand to get away." He sounded proud of himself. "So I can help Avnar here but not you. In any case, the Irish government has been somewhat parsimonious in giving me any blank passports so I don't have any of these at the present moment."

"My wife is Jewish," Ulrich said. "She's an Austrian Jew. My two children are Jewish."

Nyström gave him a searching look.

"From where I sit, Mister Prenderville, it is impossible for me to check up on your story. You certainly weave a most plausible tale which leads me to suspect that you have kissed the Blarney Stone and are therefore Irish. I repeat, I don't possess any blank Irish passports. I am prepared to take a risk – having done so in the past – so I suggest the following. You will spend the night at a local hotel run by a Swedish friend of mine whose wife is Serbian. That way you might avoid being apprehended by the ever-vigilant Germans. Return here tomorrow and I shall have your passports and travel forms ready."

* * *

Sitting in a First Class compartment of the Istanbul train, Ulrich had time to reflect on the unpredictable fortunes of war, controlling the fragile thread of his own life. He was alone, for the consul had advised the two men to travel separately, and wondered how long it would be before fate took yet another turn.

The further I travel the more I think about the wretched death camp with its blood-stained friars. In my mind's eye I have, no, I retain – for it will always be with me – a vivid picture of wild-eyed priests holding obscene batons beating the brains out of innocent Jewish women and children, their wails and cries echoing in my head. How can priests whose hands were anointed to perform the sacred rituals of the mass, use them as instruments of assault against innocent women and children, the very perfection of mankind, the very core of our humanity? I feel crushed with fear, pain and sorrow. I feel lonely and overcome with a profound sense of utter loss and bewilderment.

Ulrich drifted off into sleep. He was in a great cathedral, made of red bricks, narrow with a high vaulted roof, and as he advanced slowly down the central aisle he became aware of the heaps of skeletons and corpses, of rats gnawing at the bones, of gallows, of whips and knives. Proceeding down the aisle towards him were clergy dressed in red cassocks carrying an immense crucifix on which hung not the dead form of Christ but a huge swastika. He heard the drumbeat of death, the screams of the dying and the tortured. To his surprise a river of blood came down the aisle towards him and he found himself drowning.

Awaking, he found himself covered with a cold sweat. He looked out of the window but it was night. *'Who am I?'* he asked himself. At all times Ulrich, then James, then Brian now Erling Holmbeck, a false Swedish citizen, his own question went unanswered.

* * *

Arriving in Istanbul at the Sirkesi station, Ulrich checked into a small run-down hotel near the docks. On the following day, he went to the British Consulate, in a tidy villa overlooking the Bosphorus. In the middle of the front lawn, from a defiant flagpole hung a limp Union Jack.

"So what can we do for you?" said a tall youngish man, who introduced himself as deputy-consul. He gave Ulrich a guarded look.

Ulrich briefly related his experience of the previous months, stressing his work for British intelligence and mentioning Jerrold's name. He produced his Swedish passport, which the deputy-consul examined carefully.

"Your present legal status is that of a citizen of a neutral country, so why have you come here?"

"I must try to find my wife and children who are in Italy. Only the British can help me. Can you give me British identity papers?"

"Why? You've already got a passport." There was layered disdain in the voice. "You've turned up here unannounced, spun an unproven yarn a mile long and expect me to believe it. Istanbul's a honeypot for enemy agents. You could be one for all I know."

"Look I know first hand, having been part of it, what the British are up to in Yugoslavia. Don't you want to protect your own sources? I think you should have a word with your Intelligence people and see what their reaction is."

Three days later, a rebuffed and uncertain Ulrich found himself en route to Alexandria on board the *Namel,* a Turkish owned freighter. This rusting vessel had, before the war according to the captain, plied its trade around the Mediterranean but was now confined to the Black Sea and the occasional voyage to Egypt. It reeked of a mixture of rotten fish and diesel oil and, when it achieved even a leisured speed, groaned like a pig in an abattoir. The captain, a Greek of great girth, strode around the ship, smoking a foul-smelling meerschaum pipe and relentlessly bullying his sullen, mainly bearded, crew who looked as if they had escaped from a prison for pirates.

At dinner on the first evening, Ulrich shared the captain's table with the only two other passengers, Bulgarian Jews hoping to get into Palestine. Ulrich found the meal, grilled octopus in vinegar together with a beetroot salad, unappetisingly exotic. The captain produced a bottle of ouzo and pronounced, 'This is the very best. It comes from Lesbos.' Having consumed several glasses himself, he stood up and recited one of the poems in Greek to his bemused audience. He then gave a detailed description in broken English of the poems of Sappho, highlighting their lesbian content. One of the Bulgarians who understood some English translated the captain's explanation for the benefit of his companion

Later, as Ulrich lay on his bunk suffering from a mild bout of seasickness, romantic childhood fantasies about three-masted sailing galleons, with cannons blazing and cutlass-waving crew gave way to feelings of extreme misery. The Mediterranean can be a cruel sea, he thought.

At Izmir, the ship put into port and remained there for a couple of days before setting sail again. The first evening out at sea, Ulrich looking pale and wan, left his cabin and sought some fresh air on deck. Hung with lights everywhere to indicate that it was registered in a neutral country, the little freighter ploughed a wake through a calm sea. Somewhat unsteadily balanced against the deck rail, he looked up at the Milky Way, arched across the sky in a hazy bank of light. He thought of Ruth. Would he ever see her again? Is she still in Venice with the twins.

"Herr Dreher?" spoke a voice behind him.

Startled, Ulrich turned around. A host of fears invaded his mind. A German agent sent to kill me? He gripped the railing.

"Remember me?"

"No."

"The name's Bethell. We met when you came to London to sell your project for a sub-machine gun."

Bethell had an amused look on his face. Ulrich looked at the older and now slightly greying man who had been privy to his erstwhile secret mission. The voice, long forgotten, evoked memories of an event that had caused him mixed feelings with its overtones of perfidy.

"Yes, now I remember. You were with Mr Jerrold."

"I'm now stationed in the Embassy in Ankara where I received an urgent message from our deputy consul in Istanbul. I came to Izmir where I boarded. I've been in touch with Jerrold and he has a task for you."

"I'm no longer working for the British government."

"My dear boy, once you've joined this trade you never leave. Once in, never out. Your head carries too many things of military importance. Think about it. If you were captured by your former comrades in arms, our dear Gestapo would soon make you squeal."

Bethell smiled, giving Ulrich a searching look but spoke with a firmity of purpose.

"I hardly think that's possible," Ulrich said. "I'll have no truck with the Germans or Italians. All I want is to find my wife and family, who crossed the border two years ago. If you agree to help me I'd be willing to help you."

"You might very well believe we can help you do that, old boy. The fact is, the situation is very fluid. You're probably unaware but Italy recently surrendered to the Allies. The Italian government has halted all ships, trains and vehicles carrying German troops. We always reckoned the Italians were quite useless when it came to fighting but they've overpowered the German forces on Corsica. The mind boggles. The Italians freeing French territory from the Nazis. The latest news is that Italy has declared war on Germany."

"Then Ruth and the children could still be in Venice."

"Perhaps. We can try to find out for you." He questioned Ulrich about his time in Yugoslavia. Ulrich related his story, but found it a straining endeavour. Bethel was, like most of his kind, a good listener. He said that Jerrold was now back in Britain.

Later, Ulrich spent the rest of the night in his tiny cabin thinking about Ruth and the children. His mind wandered back to his honeymoon. Sitting in the swaying gondola, holding tightly to Ruth, aware of her subtle perfume, as she quoted from a copy of Ruskin's *Stones of Venice*, the visit to the original ghetto. Is that where she is at this moment? The sight of the Milky Way portends better things to come, he thought, as he drifted off.

The next morning, he arose early to find Bethell doing gymnastic exercises on deck. Arms up, touching toes, stretching, running on the spot. Great vivid flashes of lightning lit up the far sky on the western horizon, followed several moments later by the sound of distant thunder.

"Don't worry about the storm," Bethell remarked to Ulrich, "it's moving further west." More exercises. "You should try this. I did this at school. We Wykehamists are a hardy lot you know." Bethell put both hands on his knees and with much effort tried to regain his breath. "Ever been in the scouts?"

"No. In any case, the Führer abolished the scouts in Germany and replaced them with the Hitler Youth, who were formed to promote the Nazi movement and its nasty racist theories. Nothing like the scouts."

"I was a scout when I was a boy. Camping, woodcraft, hiking. It was great fun. Funny thing though, you might not believe it but originally the swastika used to be part of the scout badge." He went on in this vein referring to BP - 'that's Baden Powell, for scouts'.

Ulrich had stopped listening.

"You said Jerrold has a task for me."

"So I did. Yes, well, it's not exactly exciting. He wants you to give lessons in spoken German to some of our army officers, to prepare them for interrogation and liaison purposes. Many did German at school but are rusty or not really up to speed. It'll give them a chance to hone their foreign language skills. God only knows, many need it. What do you think?"

"I think that he should keep his word and help me to get to Italy."

"You're asking a lot. We've invaded Italy, and making good progress. Be patient and you might find yourself there sooner than expected."

"When it suited them, the British dropped me into Yugoslavia to interrogate a German general. I ended up in a Croatian concentration camp. It's no thanks to the British I'm here. So why can't I be dropped directly into Italy?"

"If life were that simple, old fellow. If only." He stopped speaking. He went across to the deck rail and looked over the sea.

Several minutes passed in silence. Ulrich could hear the throb of the ship's engines and the occasional shout from below deck.

"Well, do I get an answer?"

"I don't have any other road to go down. So, yes, I accept your offer."

"Jolly good. You won't regret it."

Chapter 18

Italy 1944

Rome was bathed in an Egyptian heatwave. Ulrich, a glass of white wine in his hand, relaxed in a deckchair on the rear veranda of the Villa Bellina, a town house on a quiet cul-de-sac off the Via Aurelia. In the background, he could hear music coming from a gramophone. Someone liked Elgar. Leaving Cairo the previous day, he had flown to Rome in a Lancaster by way of Benghazi in Libya and Bari in southern Italy into a military aerodrome just south of the city. Despite the quiet of the veranda, the throb of the plane's engines still reverberated in his head. A Major Hargreaves had met him off the plane and brought him to this elegant house, with its cool marble floors and alabaster statues, that had once, according to the major, belonged to the Italian ambassador to Argentina and now been requisitioned by the occupying Allied Forces.

Ulrich did not regret leaving the British Council language centre in Cairo, where he had spent the previous several months improving the German language skills of his students, composed mainly of junior, but also some senior, officers. In an atmosphere where security was pinned to the wall in the form of a poster reading *'Careless talk costs lives',* one young lieutenant, whose German made Ulrich wonder if the English would ever speak German without using public school vowels, had indiscreetly whispered to him, 'We're off to Blighty tomorrow, old cock'. The reason became clear when the Allied Forces landed on the beaches of Normandy. Later, Jerrold in London radioed Cairo directing him to Rome.

"May I join you?" It was Major Hargreaves.

"Of course," Ulrich said.

"I find this Roman heat impossible." Hargreaves took out a handkerchief and wiped his face and neck. Ulrich noticed he had a small mole on the side of his nose.

"Next winter," Ulrich remarked, "when you're perishing in the cold, back in Blighty – as you British call it – you can take comfort from the memory of these blue skies, the sunshine and a glass of white wine. From this veranda, the war seems so far away."

"Sorry to intrude on your dreams but the front line isn't all that far from here. Just north of Florence, actually. Didn't you read the papers in Cairo?"

"I was speaking metaphorically."

"We're attacking the German defence line which they call the Gothic line. Very Prussian. I must admit they're giving the Yanks a run for their money. They've got some really clever commanders who know all about strategy and their soldiers are no walkover."

"Haven't you read the news from Russia? Atrocities committed by your highly praised *Wehrmacht*. It's no better than the Vandal hordes who butchered the inhabitants of this very city all those centuries ago."

"Been reading up on your history then?"

"No. Just the newspapers."

"Touché." Hargreaves smiled. "All being well we should see the end of hostilities before the end of this year."

"Aren't you being rather optimistic. If the Germans fight as ferociously as they've been doing in Russia, how much more so when they've got to defend their own homeland? The Führer has bred a race of fanatics."

Both men sipped their wine.

"Do you mind if I ask you a personal question?"

"Go ahead."

"How do you, as an Austrian I mean, feel about working for us? Reading about your own fellow countrymen being killed in air raids and at the battle front?"

"To be frank, I've never had any qualms of conscience. You might well think I ought to have feelings of guilt. Well, I don't."

"Why is that?"

Ulrich related his experience at the railway station in Zagreb, and General von Grolman's terrifying edict threatening death and reprisals against the civilian population.

"An army that carries out orders to help in the wholesale destruction and systematic elimination of European Jewry is not a legitimate army. The government that gives the orders are mass-murderers. For me there never was a choice. So given the opportunity, I joined you."

"I don't blame the German people as a whole for what has happened," Hargreaves said. "It's the Führer and his gang that I hold responsible for this whole catastrophe. You can't really blame the ordinary foot soldier. After all when you consider it, even the generals are merely carrying out orders from their political masters.

He lit a cigarette and blew rings into the air. Ulrich regarded him with curiosity. He still had difficulty in understanding the English. Their dry sense of humour, their obsession with class, their mad habit of understatement, their patron saint an odd romantic figure slaying a mythological creature.

"I disagree," Ulrich said. "There's no moral equivalence between the Germans and the Allies. The Allies took up arms to defend themselves. The Führer set out deliberately to eliminate the Jewish race. The war, the invasions, the conquest of Europe were all expressly undertaken to accomplish his main aim. Anti-Semitism is a moral evil. By focussing on the Nazi leaders alone you divert attention from the millions of Germans and others who support the Führer's aims and objectives. Your argument absolves the individual of his moral responsibility. Everyone has to be responsible for his actions, whether it's putting the bayonet into the enemy or dropping bombs on his cities."

"Very philosophical, I'm sure." Hargreaves paused. "What you're saying is every soldier, sailor and airman is a criminal?"

"That's not what I'm saying. That misses the fundamental principle."

"Which is?"

"That if an action is criminal the person who carries out that action is a criminal. Germany right now is fighting for its very survival, yet the Führer can still find the huge manpower, the trains, the resources to deport Jews from the furthest ends of Europe to the death camps in the east. For him that is precisely what this war is all about. Every German who takes part is complicit. The rounding up of Jews in Greece and France or wherever is only the first step in a criminal act. The *Wehrmacht* officers and even the ordinary soldiers know perfectly well what the aim of these roundups are."

"We've got anti-Semitism in England but it hasn't led to murder or concentration camps. In any case I've always been led to believe that the Führer went to war to create what the Germans described as *Lebensraum*, in plain English, to create more room for an over crowded Germany."

"England, Belgium and Holland have greater densities of populations than Germany but they didn't think to invade the rest of Europe to find space. That reason is a convenient myth for the unpalatable truth that the root cause of this war is anti-Semitism."

"Not all Germans are anti-Semitic."

"That's true, but the vast majority are. They supported the legislation that deprived the Jews of their civil rights, excluded doctors, scientists, lawyers, university professors, orchestral players from their professions and jobs, confiscated their property, and reduced whole families to penury and destitution. They supported the social practices that cut Jews off from their fellow citizens. Once this had become acceptable it was only a short step to condoning violence against Jews and then actually taking part in it."

"How do you know all this?"

"Because I saw it happening all around me in Vienna. When the majority of ordinary people at the behest of a government use violence against their fellow citizens, women cheering as Jews were beaten senseless, those people can't hide in the shadow of the leaders. Each one is responsible for his or her actions."

"It could be argued that all those who support the Führer were deceiving themselves."

"Not so. They didn't choose to deceive themselves for the simple reason that they were and still are in their hearts and minds anti-Jewish. They know what they're doing and they want to do it. Anti-Semitism is a crime, just as much as slavery is a crime, or the lynching of blacks in the southern states of the United States. A person faced with a moral choice must be held individually responsible for their actions. It's as simple as that."

He was talking to himself for Major Hargreaves had stopped listening. His eyes were closed, his head had fallen on his chest and he was emitting a gentle English snore.

* * *

Next morning, holding a pre-war map of Rome in his hand, Ulrich, in uniform, made his way down the Via Aurelia and soon found himself walking beneath the high wall marking the boundary of the Vatican City. Following Bernini's colonnade, through which he could see, in St Peter's Square, nuns in a variety of habits and priests in cassocks and wide-brimmed clerical hats, he proceeded down a side street, past a large hospital, and on to a main thoroughfare. Along the narrow side streets were American and British soldiers strolling about, army lorries and jeeps drawn up. Coming to the Tiber, he crossed a wide bridge and followed the river downstream. His mind on Ruth and the children, he was not interested in the glories of the Eternal City, he was looking for the Jewish Ghetto.

He had been given the location of the main Roman synagogue which was on the left bank of the Tiber, whose summer flow was brown, shallow and slow. Walking along the riverbank, he felt his spirits beginning to rise, the rows of plane trees offering welcome shelter from the fierce sun. A few anglers were languidly fishing, but, given the condition of the water, Ulrich wondered whether it was out of hope rather than expectation. After a short time, he arrived at a spot where there was an island in the middle of the river. He passed a weir linking the island to the left bank and, a little further on, the Great Synagogue of Rome rose up in front of him. Surrounded by palm trees, its high square dome overlooked the river and the ghetto area. Unlike the vandalised synagogues of Vienna, it looked unscathed. The huge front door was locked, so he went to a side door which also was locked. He stood waiting and wondering what to do next.

He heard a voice behind him say something in a language which he took to be Italian.

"I'm sorry," Ulrich said in English, turning to the speaker. "I don't speak Italian."

"Can I help you?" the man responded in English.

"I'm looking for the rabbi, or someone who can tell me where I might find the offices of the Jewish Agency."

"Why do you want to do that? Are you from the military authorities?"

"No. I want to know about my wife and children. They're Jewish and fled Austria to escape persecution and sought refuge in Venice."

"Our rabbi was taken away by the Germans some months ago and there's no office of the Jewish Agency here. In the meantime, I've become the caretaker of the synagogue. Are you Jewish?"

"No. It's just that..."

He held out his hand.

"My name is Ricci, Doctor Ricci."

Doctor Ricci was a small, squat man with a brush moustache, swept back black hair and bushy eyebrows. He reminded Ulrich of a shaggy dog his family once owned when he was young.

"Let's go somewhere," Ulrich suggested, "where we can talk."

When they were seated outside a cafe, under a huge yellow awning, Ricci gave Ulrich a quizzical look.

"How is it you're British with an Austrian-Jewish wife?"

"That's rather a long story but it's a fact." Ulrich was reluctant to give this stranger any more information than was necessary. "How do you speak English so well?"

"After qualifying here, I did a postgraduate year in Scotland at the Edinburgh medical school."

"How, as an Italian, do you feel about being occupied by British and American forces?"

"I think you're wrong, my friend. We're not occupied, we've been liberated. When Italy declared war on Germany last October and joined the Allies, Rome was then truly occupied. Except it was the German Army that was doing the occupying. The German generals were so angry against the Italian government for deserting them that they allowed their so-called iron-disciplined soldiers to run amok here in Rome. They spent their days pillaging, stealing Old Masters, priceless manuscripts and art treasures." He stopped speaking.

"Well?"

"Before your armies freed us, this place was hell. The German Army and SS rounded up and deported nearly all the Jews. My family and myself were lucky. We were sheltered by some friends of ours. They took great risks for us."

Ulrich looked at Doctor Ricci, and wondered what suffering he might have undergone, waiting in fear of being caught.

"So the Germans rounded up all the Jews in Italy including Venice?"

Doctor Ricci lifted his shoulders and extended his arms in a classic Italian gesture.

"I don't know. It's more than likely."

Ulrich was taken aback by this news. He buried his head in his hands for a moment.

"It's possible your wife and children could be safe. A number of families here in Rome were saved by good Christian neighbours. I know one or two priests who helped shelter Jewish families. Even convents. You mustn't despair."

Ulrich looked at his untouched coffee. It is strange, he thought, how in moments of great concern your mind can be distracted by some trivial thing.

"You must understand that we Italians never really wanted the war. Some did but most didn't. When the Führer asked Mussolini to put Jews in camps, Il Duce agreed, probably knowing that it would never happen. The Germans don't know or understand the Italian mind. They could never fathom the spirit of disorder and disobedience that is buried deep in Italian society. Two words sum us up. *La busterella,* bribery, which is almost a national sport, and *menefreghismo,* which means I don't care a damn about rules and regulations. So one way or another, everyone from army generals and senior officials down subverted the government's policy."

"What about your own family? Have they all escaped deportation?"

"No. My parents, my two brothers and their families were deported last January. We learned through the Jewish community in Zurich that sealed cattle trains with Jews on board were being transported through Switzerland to Germany via the St Gotthard pass with the knowledge and consent of the Swiss government. One witness, a Swiss railway supervisor, himself a Jew, seemingly witnessed harrowing scenes in the middle of the night at Zurich's main railway station."

"I can only hope for the safety of my wife and children," Ulrich said in a slow low voice.

"You must not give up hope. I nearly did when Il Duce made the error of declaring war against the Allies in June 1940. He was too influenced by the Führer and became increasingly anti-Jewish.

However, like most of what he said, it was rarely followed by any action. Here in Rome, the Jewish community were somewhat fearful but we could go about our lives without much difficulty. Until the Nazis arrived and started the deportations. Then a real hell opened up for us."

After some moments, Doctor Ricci stood up.

"I'm sorry that I must leave you now. I must get back home. My wife will be anxious. This past year has left us all very nervous. Good luck with your quest."

Ulrich, watching Doctor Ricci disappear down the street, was filled with foreboding about Ruth and the children. He rose and made his way back to the Villa Bellini. As he walked along the Borgo Santo Spiritu, near the Vatican, he saw coming towards him two Franciscan friars, dressed in their brown habits, tied round their waists with the distinctive brown rope-cincture. Inside his head he could hear again the shrieks and screams of the Jewish women and children as they were dragged naked across the camp's parade ground to be brutally dispatched by men in similar religious dress. He felt sick and weakly, he wanted to yell out at them but his lips were paralysed, he wanted to attack them but his legs became lead. He lay back against the wall of the building. They passed him by without so much as a glance. He staggered across to the gutter and vomited.

* * *

Immaculately dressed in a brigadier's uniform, Jerrold arrived at the Villa Bellini the next day. Ulrich's hope rose. He speculated that Jerrold might be able to help him find Ruth and the children, for he seemed to have unlimited powers over men and materials.

After a solitary lunch, not knowing where the others were, Ulrich went out on to the veranda. The encounter with the two friars the previous day had shaken him and now preyed on his mind. Doctor Ricci's tale of the fate of Rome's Jewish community had undermined his complacency. He thought about Ruth and the children, hunted and forsaken, left to a horrible doom at the hands of SS butchers. Or brown-clothed friars. God forbid. The sights and sounds of the cattle trucks on Zagreb railway station returned, containing not Greek Jews pleading for food and water, but his own beloved ones pleading for his help.

He started to read Scott's *Ivanhoe* but fell asleep.

"Fancy a swim?"

It was Jerrold. Ulrich sat up.

"I've a jeep at my disposal, so I thought I might take a trip out to Lake Albano."

"Where's that?"

"It's about thirty kilometres south of here. You want to come?"

Under a high milky-blue sky, Jerrold drove through the village of Castel Gandolfo, remarking 'this is where the Pope spends his summer holiday', and turned the car off on to a rough path skirting the side of the lake. He proved to be a strong swimmer, going far out into the middle. Ulrich splashed about near the shore, his thoughts on Ruth and the children, wondering what plans Jerrold might have for him.

Later, as they sat in the sun, Jerrold produced a bottle of wine and a couple of glasses from a wicker hamper.

"Sunshine, blue skies and good wine," Jerrold said. "Not commodities you'll find in England these days." He paused for a moment. "I've got some news for you."

"Is it about my wife and children?"

"No. I've no news about them."

"I was hoping you might have news for me about Ruth and the children." There was a note of vexation in his voice. He was thinking about what Doctor Ricci had told him.

"I'm sorry about that. As I told you, we've no news."

"So why did you bring me to Italy?" Ulrich said.

"One of General von Culmann's deputies has escaped the clutches of the Gestapo and wants to talk to us. He crossed over the German lines and surrendered himself to our forces."

"Who is General von Culmann?"

"He was head of German Intelligence Service until he was implicated in the plot to assassinate the Führer and executed. I need a native speaker of German to be at his interrogation. My own German is passible but I need someone who will help me to avoid misunderstandings. I've decided you're the best candidate for the job. I can't oblige you but you could be doing yourself a favour."

"What favour would that be?"

"I've been able to obtain British naturalisation papers for you. If you accept, it means that from now on you're a British citizen."

"Can I refuse?"

"I thought you might say that. As British, you may choose to go to Palestine with your wife and children, if you find them. In that case I would be able to get immigration certificates for you and your family. As you probably know the British authorities are none too keen to let Jews into Palestine. The offer is there. Oh, by the way, I took the liberty of keeping the name Pendrick."

"I'll think about it."

The drive back to the Villa Bellina was made in silence but Ulrich knew his decision. It took a leap of will to reject his Austrianness but he knew that he could never again associate himself with a country that had prostituted itself at the hands of its favourite son, the little corporal from the town of Linz. Doctor Ricci had survived. Ruth and the children must have survived, he told himself. Jerrold's offer could not be rejected.

When they had arrived back at the villa, Jerrold parked the jeep.

"We're making an early start tomorrow for Florence," he said, in a breezy, laconic manner.

Chapter 19

Florence 1944

It was early morning when Jerrold stopped the jeep on a hillside road some miles south of Florence, the sun rising like a searing disc into the deep-blue Tuscan sky. On the hillsides around them were deserted vineyards. It had taken two days to cover the three-hundred kilometres or so from Rome. Ulrich jumped down and looked over the valley towards the west and the sea. The road to Florence was littered with dozens of wrecked German and British army trucks, half tracks, heavy artillery and other pieces of ordnance. Disabled tanks lay on their sides, guns pointing obscenely to the heavens. Ulrich was shocked at the sight of a blasted landscape, pulverised towns and villages, beleaguered and impoverished people wandering about bewildered at what had happened to their homes, razed to the ground as two armies fought bitter bloody battles for control of this once land of beauty and loveliness.

"I came here when I was a student," Jerrold remarked. "I recall lovely trattoria, friendly people, wine, church bells. It's heartbreaking to see some of these medieval hill towns reduced to rubble. War destroys souls as well as bodies."

Later, they were passing what appeared to be a makeshift cemetery, when Jerrold brought the jeep to a sudden halt with a screech of brakes. He got down and Ulrich followed. There, alongside the road, was a small patch of ground, several mounds of earth and a number of hastily erected crosses. Someone had put up a board and roughly painted in English:

Look among the mountains in the mud and rain
You'll see the wooden crosses,

The graves without a name,
Heartbreak and toil and suffering gone,
The boys beneath them slumber on.

Both men stood hatless, gazing at the nameless graves. Neither spoke. In the midst of a war which had devoured the lives of millions, Ulrich felt touched by this rough roadside graveyard. He wondered at how many young men had left their homelands and come to this foreign land to give their lives to defeat an evil enemy.

Arriving in Florence, they could hear the sound of distant guns from the nearby warfront to the north. Jerrold steered the jeep carefully through the narrow streets and alleyways of the medieval city crowded with tanks, guns, army trucks.

The British had taken over the Hotel Medici. Ulrich noticed how British officers always knew how to pamper themselves. He thought that at least he had one thing in common with these men in uniform. He had seen brutal death at close quarters.

The next morning he went with Jerrold to the local prison, where the Germans to be interrogated were being held. It was a grim building, now empty of its usual population of petty criminals. An army major and a couple of privates led them down a high, wide corridor, with rooms on either side. They stopped in front of one. On the door was a brass plate indicating it had been the prison governor's office.

"You can use this room, brigadier," the major said. He unlocked the door and, standing to one side, ushered Jerrold and Ulrich in. "If you'll kindly wait in here, sir, we'll fetch General Ortmann." He then withdrew, closing the door behind him.

Stripped of any sign of the previous occupier, the room had a gloomy air. The sole pieces of furniture were a table and several chairs. Jerrold opened his briefcase and took out some papers.

"If General Ortmann is prepared to talk to us," Jerrold said, placing the papers on the table, "he might reveal matters of the greatest importance. What you may hear inside this room could determine what happens after this war is over." He stopped and picked up a sheet of paper. "For that reason I must ask you to sign what we call the Official Secrets Act. This covers all matters of State that the British government considers to be secret."

"What matters are they?"

"Anything, really. That means the government can define what it likes to be secret."

"That sounds very English."

"It is. It's English law. It's not a contract, it's a law, so you're bound by it whether you sign it or not."

"So why have I to sign it?"

"Because it will prove that you were present at this time and this place when certain matters were discussed."

Ulrich reflected for a moment. He wondered if the general, by some remote chance, could tell him about the whereabouts of Ruth and the children. So he signed. Jerrold then handed him a fountain pen and a legal notepad and instructed him to make notes of the interrogation.

There was a knock on the door. The major had returned accompanied by the two privates and a bareheaded, man dressed in a German general's uniform from which the epaulettes and collar tabs had been removed. The usual holster, cross-arm belts and ribbons were also missing.

'Another von Schwenke' thought Ulrich. Ortmann, who appeared to be late middle-aged, was of medium height, broad-shouldered, with well-chiselled features, beetle-browed, sharp, intelligent eyes and wisps of grey showing through his dark brown, swept-back hair. His rigid bearing suggested a brittle character.

Jerrold motioned Ortmann to sit on one side of the table while he and Ulrich sat on the other. Ortmann fixed his steely eyes on Jerrold, who took a red file from his briefcase.

"Can I have your name and rank, please?" he asked, in a mild tone of voice.

"I am Colonel-General Hans-Jurgen Ortmann." The strong baritone voice hinted at a tenacity of purpose.

Reading from the file, Jerrold then recited the facts of Ortmann's family, his early life, education and military career. During this recital, Ulrich hoped to read the general's expression but his face reminded him of the cryptic features carved on the sphinxes he had seen outside Cairo. Jerrold closed the file when he had finished. With precise movements, he took a briar pipe from his tunic top pocket and carefully filled it with tobacco from a leather pouch. Producing a box of matches, he struck one, moved the flame in circles above the tobacco while he slowly puffed, drawing the flame into the bowl. Ignoring the presence of Ortmann, he gave the pipe serious consideration as if he were relaxing back in his Pall Mall club. He leaned back on his chair, eyes half-closed with a contemplative look on his face, like a monk meditating.

"General," he asked in a slow, casual manner, "why did you surrender yourself to the Allied forces?"

Ortmann did not reply immediately. Instead, he fixed Jerrold with a cool regard.

"The game is up," he eventually said. "We appear to be losing the war." He paused for a moment. "In surrendering myself, I believe I may be in a position to help to bring it to a speedy end and perhaps spare more lives and further suffering."

"That's most laudable, General, but would it not have been better achieved if you had remained in your position as Deputy Chief of the German Intelligence?" Jerrold was all English courtesy and calm restraint. "Besides, I'm certain your erstwhile fellow generals, to say nothing of the Führer himself, will consider what you have done as treachery."

"I took no part in the July plot against the Führer," Ortmann said sharply in an offended tone, "but because I was General von Culmann's deputy, I was a prime suspect, marked out as a traitor by the Gestapo. It was only a matter of time before they came for me."

"That plot was only hatched," Jerrold continued, "because the more intelligent generals realised, as you've just said, the game was up. Indeed, the game has been up for the past two years ever since you lost at Stalingrad. It would seem that your Führer's 'folie de grandeur' has come to an end. He should have read von Clausewitz. If he had, he would never have started his 'total war'." Jerrold paused and sucked on his pipe. "The truth of the matter, as I see it, is that the plot to remove the Führer did not spring from a desire on the part of some generals to end the war but rather to put in place a leader who would come to a peaceful agreement with the Allies in order jointly to stop the Russians from taking over your almighty Reich? Is that not so?"

"That's speculation," Ortmann said with a dismissive wave of his hand.

"It's reality. The Allies insistence on the unconditional surrender of the German forces made many of your generals realise that they may be indicted for war crimes. They had imagined themselves as part of a Greek chorus, observing the cataclysm as if they themselves were not participants. Getting rid of your intransigent Führer was the first step to saving their own necks."

The two men eyed each other across the table. There was tension in Ortmann's eyes but Jerrold, relaxed, continued to puff on his pipe.

"My own inference," Jerrold continued, waving the stem of his pipe at Ortmann, "is that those senior officers and civilians who have not been implicated in this plot, will show even greater loyalty to the Führer. So, when this war comes to an end, which it will within the next twelve months or so, can you tell me whom can the Allies rely upon to take up the reins of civil government?"

Ortmann took some moments before answering.

"I cannot give you a name or names. Those who supported the plot were a very tiny, albeit powerful, group of people. They and their families have been executed. You must understand that the whole German people, the military, the industrialists, the civilian population and, of course, the churches, in particular the Catholic Church, are solidly behind the person of the Führer and his aim to defeat the Jewish-Bolshevik conspiracy. That is the sole reason we have fought this war. I would have thought that the English would want to join us in defeating this conspiracy."

There was defiance in his voice.

"I'm afraid you've misunderstood what the Allied position is," Jerrold said. "As far as we are concerned there's no such conspiracy. It's a myth dreamed up by the Führer to justify his so-called struggle. A piece of Nazi propaganda. A pity you let your unblinking patriotism swallow it."

Ulrich thought Jerrold's tone was Olympian. The words steel and spine came to his mind.

There was another long pause while Jerrold played with his pipe.

"You mentioned the Catholic Church," Jerrold persisted, "are you a Catholic?"

"No. I was brought up a Lutheran." He paused. "That was not in your otherwise faultless red file." A strained smile broke over the general's face.

"Are you telling me that the Catholic Church, the self-proclaimed most powerful moral voice in Europe supported the Führer?"

"Yes."

Jerrold remained silent.

"It's not just moral support the Church gives the Führer, it's legal. By the concordat signed a decade ago by the present pontiff, who was then the Vatican's Cardinal Secretary of State, and the Reich, Catholic bishops swore an oath of allegiance to the German state which obliged them to make their clergy honour it. It surprises me that you, as an intelligence officer, and I'm presuming that's what you are, wouldn't know that."

"The Catholic bishops and priests in England support our cause."

"Perhaps so but the official institution called the Catholic Church has always supported the struggle, the Führer's crusade against Jewish-Bolshevism. When we invaded Poland, a Catholic country, the Pope remained silent. When we invaded the Soviet Union he rejoiced. When we imprisoned priests for supporting local resistance groups in Poland, France or Belgium did the Holy Father intervene?"

"Well, did he?" Jerrold cut in sharply.

"No. He considered that supporting the Führer's campaign took precedence."

"That's a highly dubious moral stance to take, don't you think? Jerrold said in a nonchalant way.

"I hardly think that the British can talk about morality." Ortmann paused for a long moment. "In July last year, my wife, daughter and our three grandchildren were killed or should I say murdered when British and American planes dropped thousands of tons of blockbuster bombs on Hamburg, creating a firestorm, a huge inferno which incinerated tens of thousands the greater number civilians. I call that mass murder."

"What about your murderous killing of Jews?" snapped Ulrich in a voice grim with anger, interrupting the interrogation dialogue between the other two men. "Scouring the whole of Europe, filling your hated concentration camps with millions of innocent men, women and children. What did this Holy Father have to say?"

Jerrold and Ortmann both looked at him in surprise.

"I can't answer for the Pope," Ortmann replied. "He's always supported our side in this war. Besides, he was always kind and considerate to our generals and troops when they went to visit him at the Vatican. There is anger in Berlin that he so quickly changed sides when the Allies turned up on his doorstep. I've no doubt your American and English generals and troops are at this moment lining up to kiss his Pontifical ring." His voice vibrated with sarcasm.

"You say the Pope has always supported your side in this war." Jerrold was clearly not going to be sidelined by the idea of Allied Generals kissing the papal ring. "What exactly do you mean?"

"I can only speak from the point of view of our Intelligence Services. Our relations with the present Pope have always been the friendliest possible. He's known all along about our efforts to eliminate the Jews throughout Europe. He, his cardinals and bishops in Germany, welcomed that. The Church didn't much like some of the Führer's racial policies. However, the greatest enemy of western civilisation is the Jew. In that, the Führer and the Pope spoke with one voice."

Ulrich turned to Jerrold and spoke in English.

"Can you ask him about my wife and children and about my Uncle Claus."

Before Jerrold could answer, Ortmann intervened.

"I speak English," he said in English. "Who is this Uncle Claus, you refer to."

Jerrold nodded to Ulrich.

"Go on, tell him," he said.

"My uncle's name is Claus von Juggardt. I believe he worked in the Foreign Ministry in Berlin."

"Yes, I know of him," said Ortmann. "So you're his nephew. How is it that you're working for the British?"

"General," Jerrold said, "I'll ask the questions. My interpreter here just wants to know what has became of his uncle."

Ortmann remained silent for some time. He looked at Jerrold then, slowly he turned his gaze to Ulrich. He sat back and folded his arms.

"Claus von Juggardt," he said, "is dead. He was found guilty of passing information to a foreign power and hanged."

Once as a young man Ulrich, skiing off-piste down the high and difficult run on the Zweitausender in the Austrian Tyrol, had suddenly fallen against a large rock hidden by the snow. He thought he was going to die. For a split second his life passed before him. As Ortmanns's icy voice pronounced the fatal words about his Uncle Claus, a procession of past events swiftly paraded before his mind's eye: Claus, wearing a coloured yarmulke, turning up in the synagogue at his marriage to Ruth, dancing the horah with Ruth and the other ladies and being loved by all; putting him in touch with the British Embassy, which had brought him into contact with Jerrold the man sitting next to him; his vital help, enabling Ruth and the children to escape to Italy instead of being locked up in a sealed cattle truck and dispatched to a death camp. Ulrich was filled with a deep grief. Inwardly, he recalled John Donne's words:

'any man's death diminishes me, because I am involved in Mankind;
And therefore never send to know for whom the bells tolls;
It tolls for thee.'

"Claus von Juggardt was well known to our Intelligence Services," continued Ortmann. "He belonged to what we called the 'Elgar Orchestra'."

Jerrold sat up alertly from his langurous position. It was as if Ortmann had slapped his face.

"The 'Elgar Orchestra', what on earth are you talking about?" he said. There was instant concern in his voice.

"Ah! So our famous British Intelligence is not so all-knowing after all." There was a roguish grin on his face.

Ortmann pushed his two hands against the table and smiled at Jerrold.

"I seem to have struck a sensitive chord. If you want me to tell you what I know there has to be a quid pro quo."

Jerrold eyed Ortmann as if he were a cobra. He sat sucking on his pipe.

"I've seen a list of possible war criminals," he said slowly. "Your name's on it. Your cooperation now could help me remove it."

Ortmann sat silent for several minutes.

"Our people coined the word 'orchestra'" he said, "to refer to any enemy espionage ring. So the Soviet ring was given the name of the 'Red Orchestra', then there was the Paris orchestra, and so on. A 'piano' is the name given to a short-wave transmitter, a 'pianist' is a radio operator, 'conductor' is an organiser." He turned to face Ulrich. "Your uncle was a conductor. Of the Elgar Orchestra. British. He was betrayed by one of his own people. Even in the hands of our Gestapo he refused to talk. He was tried and executed. That's what happens to traitors."

There was a long silence.

"My interpreter," resumed Jerrold, " would also like to know if you have any knowledge of his wife and children. They are Jewish and were living in Venice, their last known whereabouts."

"I can't say specifically what's happened to anyone. If she's Jewish, then the SS will have probably transferred her to captivity in Germany. When the Italians were our ally, and a pretty useless ally at that, they always refused to hand over their Jews as demanded by the Führer. When they changed sides and turned against us, we took charge. Our forces and the SS rounded up as many Jews as they could find. Even the Holy Father, so I was reliably informed, watched from his window as the Gestapo and the SS rounded up the Jews of Rome. My own intelligence was that they were taken by train through Switzerland and are working in the factories in the Reich."

"So my wife and children could be among those poor victims?" Ulrich snapped.

"Possibly," Ortmann said. "I really don't know."

"Let me get this correct," intervened Jerrold, "are you saying the Swiss authorities, allowed your people to transport Jews through Switzerland to imprisonment in Germany?"

"Yes. They've been most helpful to us all during this war, providing us with vital chemicals, rare minerals and financial loans necessary for our war industry."

"They were supposed to be neutral."

"So were the Americans during the first years of the war but that didn't prevent Roosevelt from providing Britain with actual war materials such as guns, trucks and tanks."

"What did Germany give the Swiss in return?"

Ortmann was silent for a few moments.

"Gold. Not German gold, for by this time we didn't have any."

"So whose gold was it?"

A further silence.

"Jewish gold."

"You mean looted gold, stolen gold?"

"Sort of. They were dead Jews. Gold teeth and jewellery."

"Victims from your camps?"

"I presume so."

"So the specialist smelting companies would know the provenance of this gold." Jerrold stopped at this point. He relit his pipe, once again going through the same almost religious ritual.

"What numbers are involved in this trade?"

"Several hundreds of tons."

"My God! You mean there were hundreds of thousands of victims?" intervened Ulrich in an angry tone.

"Probably many more. Millions more likely. They were only Jews." Ortmann spoke the words in a cold and dispassionate way.

Jerrold sat back in his chair. Ulrich looked at the general to see if there was a spark of emotion in his face.

"I can read surprise in your face," Ortmann continued. "You still don't understand it. Yes, millions of Jews have died in our labour camps. As I've been trying to tell you, this war has been fought with the sole purpose of eliminating the Jewish scourge from our midst. Every German citizen knows this and that is why we have sacrificed so much to achieve it. We don't consider the death of Jews as a bad thing. On the contrary, it was what we have been aiming for during the past decade. That is why everyone including the Catholic Church, which you seem to be so interested in, gave and is giving the Führer their full support. Everyone knows what is happening, from the railwaymen who take the Jews to the camps in their trains to the insurance companies who insure the camps and everyone else in between."

Jerrold suddenly stood up, collected his papers, put them in the file, and indicating with a nod of his head to Ulrich to follow, went to the door, opened it and called in the two soldiers on guard outside.

"Take the general back to his cell," he ordered the guards in an abrupt manner.

* * *

Outside the prison, Ulrich turned to Jerrold.

"Are you going to have Ortmann taken off the list?"

"There never was a list." Jerrold gave Ulrich a tantalising glance. "Our game is not played by normal rules. I was surprised that a senior intelligence officer of the Reich would fall for the oldest trick in the trade."

The two men walked towards Jerrold's jeep.

"Is there something you're not telling me about Claus?" Ulrich asked.

"I shouldn't by rights be telling you this but since you're his family you might just as well know since the poor man's dead. He was working for us. Had been ever since the Nazis came to power. He was our man in Berlin. His intelligence information was pure gold. He warned us about the invasion of Russia which confirmed reports we had from other sources. We passed it on to the Kremlin but foolishly they ignored it. The Gestapo had him under surveillance for some time. He told us that but still continued his secret work."

Several minutes went by, during which neither spoke.

"He was another father to me when I was a child," Ulrich said. "Looking back I owe him a lot. He was a staunch ally when I wanted to marry Ruth against my parents' wishes and those of the Church. My mother, his sister loved him dearly whereas my father used to refer to him as a dandy, a wealthy fop, a poseur. He was none of these things."

* * *

While a vicious Italian winter had brought stalemate to the front in the north, Ulrich remained in Florence learning Italian and paying visits to the several art galleries. Wandering through the galleries, engaging himself to understand the paintings and sculptures, guided by Ruth's spirit, his interest and understanding of art and artists grew.

One morning, with a high filmy cloud obscuring a leaden sun, Ulrich, wearing a long army greatcoat against the raw cold, crossed the Ponte Vecchio, over an Arno running at flood. He went to the Pitti Palace, where he went up to the Palatine Gallery on the first floor. The grand rooms, decorated in high baroque style, reminded him of his meeting with Smith in the equally baroque ornamented Stephansdom. 'It's too papist', had remarked the enigmatic Smith.

Confronted with Caravaggio's *Sleeping Cupid,* Ulrich's face lit up with a wistful smile. *That's hardly papist*, he said to himself.

As he entered one of the rooms, he noticed another visitor, dressed in the uniform of a British army officer, his face sideways to him, looking at *The Allegory of War* by Rubens. Ulrich could not but marvel at the coincidence of names for the visitor he recognised was Ruth's brother, Reuben.

"Reuben," he shouted, his voice reverberating around the large room.

Reuben turned to face him. For a brief moment his features were full of puzzlement. Then, as his intense interest in the painting yielded to recognition of his brother-in-law, his eyes widened like balls of fire and his face broke into an unrestrained expression of delight.

"Ulrich." Reuben's voice sounded rapturous. "Is Ruth with you?"

"No, I'm afraid not."

"Is she here in Florence?"

Approaching, he took Reuben by the arm.

"The news about Ruth is not good," he said. There was solace in his voice. "However, it isn't all bad," he added. "Let's go where we can talk."

The bar on the Piazza della Signoria was crowded with Allied military personnel.

"Let's speak English," Ulrich said to Reuben. "Our neighbours would get the wrong idea if we speak German."

As he slowly drank his red wine, Ulrich gave Reuben a detailed account of his family's tragic separation but only a redacted chronicle of his own experiences, omitting the painful horrors he had witnessed and being circumspect about his work with Jerrold. The fountain of Neptune in the middle of square, as he well knew, was decorated with the figures of Scylla and Charybdis. In discussing his own part in the ongoing war, he was resolved to steer a prudent course.

"I've been talking too much," he said finally.

Reuben smiled. His brown weather-beaten face and callused hands told a story different from that told by the once soft gentle features and hands of the dedicated Viennese lawyer. He remained silent for some moments before he spoke.

"Do you think Ruth is still alive?"

"Deep inside me, I hear a constant voice telling me she is. I battle with myself to make it grow louder but it doesn't. Only death is final, I tell myself. I don't feel the pain of a bereaved, I feel the pain of separation. When I saw people being taken away by the Nazis, it was the same as a death sentence for them. Ruth wasn't taken away. Some people have survived. You did. So, I hope. I cling to that."

" The Nazi takeover was so sudden, so absolute," said Reuben. "I felt I was living in a Vienna surrounded by enemies. When my parents were taken away, I fed on anger and thoughts of revenge. These proved hopeless. To help my parents, I knew I had to survive. When I left Ruth and yourself that tragic evening, I took refuge with a close friend. I didn't have a plan. My only concern was escape and to avoid being taken into the Nazis' so-called protective custody. It was only when I crossed the border into Greece that I found friendly, helpful people. The Jewish community in Athens fed, clothed, housed me and found me work."

"So what work did you do? As a lawyer?"

"No, I worked behind a bar. It earned me enough to buy a passage to Cyprus and then on to Palestine."

Ulrich recalled Jerrold's strictures about allowing Jews into Palestine.

"How did you get an entry permit?"

"I didn't. I was an illegal person in the land of my forebears."

"So you fulfilled the Zionist dream."

"It was hardly a dream. I joined a kibbutz."

"What's a kibbutz?"

"A sort of community farm. Everything was held in common."

"Sounds just like a monastery."

"The one I was in was very secular, though we did celebrate Shabbat and other holy days. It was hard work. I found I was working in the fields twelve hours a day planting trees, growing vegetables. In one sense it was, and is, a great way of life. If you like communal life that is."

"So how have you ended up wearing a British uniform?"

"There's a sobering irony in all this. From the time they took over Palestine, the British cultivated the favour of the Arabs. British officials would openly tell you that if they had to offend one side they would rather it be the Jews than the Arabs. Yet when the war came, they discovered that most senior Arabs were actively pro-Nazis. To help their war effort the British formed the Jewish Brigade which I joined together with thousands of other Palestinian Jews. I saw action in Libya and now here in Italy."

They drank up the wine and ordered coffee.

"Shall we be able to meet again?" Ulrich asked.

"You mean here in Florence?"

"Yes."

"Probably not. Tomorrow my unit is off to the front on the east coast. Don't ask me where. I don't know."

Reuben sounded dispirited.

"You mustn't give up hope," Ulrich said. "Our hope is not forlorn. We shall find Ruth."

"I wish I could share your optimism."

Ulrich was not to see Reuben again. Some weeks later he read in an army bulletin that Lieutenant Reuben Gitelmann had been killed in action, burned to death trying to save colleagues from a tank that had caught fire. This time he did feel the pain of bereavement. He could not pray, for his faith did not stretch that far. He did weep, for his stoicism did not stretch that far either.

Chapter 20

Venice 1945

It was late spring. 'THE WAR IS OVER' boldly proclaimed the posters outside newspaper kiosks on the narrow streets of Venice. When the Allies broke through the German fortified Gothic line, Ulrich, calling on Jerrold's influence, had attached himself to a New Zealand brigade whose aim was to liberate Venice. The other officers only knew him as Captain Pendrick of the Intelligence Corps and gave him a respectful wide berth.

He found a hotel on the Calle de Mezo. It had a run-down, neglected air, frayed carpets, worn out furnishings, here and there peeling wallpaper, and a menu limited by rationing. Even the wine at his evening meal had a slightly acidy taste. The few ageing waiters eyed him with wary looks. Captain Pendrick could afford to ignore looks. His mind was on the more serious matter of finding Ruth and the children.

The morning after his arrival, he made his uncertain way to the Jewish Ghetto district through a damp and drizzly city, crossing St Mark's Square on duckboards, flooded by the spring high tide. A gloomy mood filled his spirit, for he did not know where to start looking. The few people he accosted and inquired for directions in Italian, gave him suspicious looks but no directions. He was sympathetic to their plight, knowing they had had to put up with a domineering fascist regime and then, in the previous year, a resented Nazi rule. Little wonder they were distrustful.

He walked up the Calle del Forno and found himself in front of a two-storey yellow stone building. He recognised the Levantine Synagogue. Recalling the day Ruth had guided him around, he approached through hopeful tears. Like the synagogue in Rome, it was intact and locked. His optimism diminishing with every step, he wandered about until he came across a small bar and went in.

"Ah," muttered the elderly waiter, coming up to him, eyeing his uniform. "British officer, no?" He spoke in English.

"Yes," Ulrich replied.

"I learn English in Glasgow for five year. My brother he has fish and chip restaurant there. Nice people but they no speak English in Glasgow. Very strange dialect. You from Glasgow?"

"No. My people originally came from the Highlands."

"I give you special coffee. On the house, as you say. Also I bring a small *spuntino*, I not know the word in English. This one is crab fried in egg."

"The word I think is snack. You're most kind."

"Is nothing. You save us from the Germans."

He went off whistling to himself. A number of other people came into the bar. Some looked at Ulrich strangely, others nodded and smiled. After a while, the waiter returned with the coffee and the *spuntino*. He put the dish down in front of Ulrich.

"This we call *moeche. Buon apetito*."

Later, after he had served the other customers, the waiter returned and sat opposite Ulrich.

"I no speak English for years. You like Venice?"

"Yes." After a pause he said, "I'm looking for my wife and children."

"How so? Your wife, she Venetian?"

"No. She is Jewish and fled Austria at the beginning of the war and came here to Venice for safety. I want to know where she is and what's happened to her."

The waiter gave him a rueful look.

"My friend, it has been a terrible time for us all. I work here years. Many Jews were my customers and friends. During the time of Mussolini they were bullied. He gave them how you say, the Glasgow kiss." He laughed. "You cannot do this, you cannot do that. But they still free to come and go. We Italians like the Jews. Then last year Italy joined the Allies and the Germans came. They very angry at Italians. The *Tedeschi*, the Germans, they acted in bad, bad ways. The Gestapo and SS came hunting for Jews. We Italians hid the Jews. They are our friends. The sisters in the convents and some priests sheltered Jews. If the Nazi found you hiding a Jew," at this he drew his forefinger across his throat, "they kill you. They took hundreds away in trains. The Germans, they very bad people."

"Can you tell me where the convents are?"

"Wait, I ask my wife. Cecilia," he shouted.

A stout woman, wearing a long multicoloured pinafore, appeared from a room at the rear. The waiter spoke to her in very rapid Italian, which Ulrich could not follow. He turned to Ulrich.

"She speak a little English but not so well. She say there are two convents. The Sisters of Mercy and the Sisters of the Good Shepherd."

Cecilia nodded her head and smiled at Ulrich.

"I write down the address and draw a map if you have paper and pencil."

Ulrich produced a small notebook and pencil and handed both to the waiter.

"You have been most kind to me," Ulrich said.

As he left, he pushed an American dollar note into the waiter's hand. Hope began to return.

It took Ulrich some time to locate the two convents. The Sisters of Mercy told him they had clandestinely harboured a number of Jewish children but none with the names of Gabel or Rahel. He came away disappointed but not disheartened. The convent of the Sisters of the Good Shepherd was on the Calle Cavalli not far from the Rialto Bridge. Following the directions sketched out by the elderly waiter, he found himself outside a massive oak door, which had a brass plate fixed to the wall on one side describing it as the Convent of Sant'Apollonia. Using the large metal knocker, he banged on the door. After a few minutes, a small flap was opened to reveal the head of a white-coifed nun peering at him.

"What do you want?" she said in a soft voice.

"My name is Captain Pendrick. I'm a British Officer and I would like to speak to the Mother Superior."

"Wait here."

With that the nun closed the flap. Ulrich waited several uncertain minutes, then the door was opened and the same nun ushered him in.

"Follow me," she instructed.

As he walked behind the nun, catching the swishing sound of her black habit on the stone flooring, he could hear high voices of children away in the deep recesses of the building, the sound raising his hope. At the same time, his mind was harassed by the persistent torment that reality might prove to be a mirage. He steeled himself for disappointment.

On the walls of the corridor were paintings of saints and framed photographs of groups of nuns. A strong aroma of beeswax polish and cleanliness filling the air brought back memories of visits to his sister's boarding school. Opening a door, she ushered him into a room and told him to wait. Presently the door opened and two other nuns came in, one much older than the other.

"I am the Mother Superior," the elder of the two nuns said in Italian. "What is it you want to see me about?"

The younger nun quickly translated into English what the other had said. "Mother Superior does not speak English," she explained.

"I've come to inquire whether you have in your care my wife Ruth who is Jewish as well as my two children," Ulrich said.

The Mother Superior gave him an inquisitive look.

"I understand that several Jewish families sought refuge in convents here in Venice," Ulrich continued. "I was hoping you might be able to help me."

"The Gestapo came here searching for Jewish people but I sent them away," the Mother Superior said in a firm but calm voice. "Our religious order cares for vulnerable young women who get themselves into trouble. The bishop told us not to cooperate with the German policy of hunting for Jews. I threatened to call upon his help if the Gestapo or German soldiers tried to enter this place of refuge."

Ulrich could not tell the age of the Mother Superior, but her kindly, swarthy features had the word tribulation etched on them. As a child, the nuns he had met were strict teachers of religion, who tended to harangue their young charges. This religious belonged to that silent band he had heard about who took care of the poorest of the poor, nursed those with disgusting diseases and sheltered victims of abuse.

Ulrich related the story of Ruth and the children, and their flight to Venice to escape the Nazis and explained his change of name.

"Now that the war is over," the Mother Superior said, "I can reveal we don't have any Jewish adults here but we have been sheltering Jewish children for the past eighteen months. Their parents left them in our care and they are still here. We don't know what has happened to their parents but we do know that the Nazis took many Jews away. God help those poor creatures."

She fingered the rosary hanging from her woollen belt.

"Perhaps if I told you my children's names you might be able to identify them," Ulrich said.

"That's a possibility."

Ulrich gave her the names of his two children. She turned to the younger nun and spoke rapidly. Without translating what the Mother Superior had said, the two nuns left the room.

When they had gone, Ulrich wandered round the room ignoring the art work displayed on the walls. They are much older now. Shall I recognise them? What if I don't? Panic overtook him and he gripped the back of a chair to steady his nerves. He tried to excise any thought that his dream of being reunited with his children would be shattered.

The door opened again. This time the Mother Superior and the younger nun entered followed by a third nun who was holding the hands of two children, a boy and girl aged about eight years old. When they saw Ulrich they both drew back as if frightened. Ulrich's heart sank for he did not recognise them.

"Are these your children?" asked the Mother Superior.

"No," replied Ulrich. "I'm sorry but these two are not my children." His voice carried the disillusion of reality, of hope being dashed.

The Mother Superior nodded to the nun holding on to the children, who then left the room.

"You are right," she said, "those are not your children Gabel and Rahel but I had to be certain. We do shelter two children of those names. I shall fetch them myself."

She soon returned holding the hands of two other children. When they came into the room, Ulrich did not recognise them immediately. The picture he had carried in his memory through the years of war-torn separation was of two children several years younger than the two who now stood before him looking like two waifs and strays with sallow complexions and wearing what appeared to be second-hand clothes. The children's unmistakable features of their mother removed any lingering doubt. It was Gabel and Rahel.

A gentle wave of relief and joy suffused his whole being.

'*Shalom*' he greeted them. He was about to step forward and take them in his arms, but the two children gave him a frightened look and the girl, visibly alarmed, hid behind the Mother Superior's generous religious habit.

It took several minutes before the Mother Superior persuaded the reluctant children who the tall man in military uniform was. As Ulrich tried to ply them with questions in German about their mother and their daily lives, they refused to answer him and remained sullenly silent. Not comprehending the children's reluctance, exasperation overtook him.

"My dear Captain," explained the Mother Superior, seeing his frowned and anxious looks, "your children don't reject you. You're just a stranger in a strange uniform. Even we adults have had reason to fear military uniforms. All the Jewish children have suffered much in the last few years. Since they came here, they've not been able to venture outside the confines of the convent. Your children are old enough to understand why they're here. However, it isn't natural for children to live in a convent. For too long now, our little friends have all been deprived of normal family life. We've done our best but it's a poor substitute for the love their parents would give them." She paused and smiled. "One of our great poets, Giacomo Leopardi, wrote, *'amor nasci corragio.'* Courage is born of love. Captain, you will learn to know and love your children through your present suffering."

"I must find their mother. Do you know what became of her?" he asked.

"I'm sorry I don't. She left the children here at the time the Gestapo were going round the houses and other buildings, even churches, hunting for Jewish people. She didn't give her name but she was in an evident state of terror, afraid of what might happen to the two children. The day after she brought them here she came to visit them and left them crying. Naturally, they didn't want to stay here. She never came again. Once the English had defeated the Germans I expected her to come to take them but she didn't."

"I'll have to arrange for them to be looked after while I search for their mother."

"I don't think that's a good idea," the Mother Superior said. "If I may say, from a long experience in such matters, a change of location and other people to care for them will only bring further distress. It's going to take months if not years to mend their broken lives. Children are nonetheless resilient and, given time, they will recover from their trauma. This convent is a sanctuary, we have peace and calm here. I'm prepared to offer them a haven of safety until you can find their mother."

Chapter 21

Vienna 1945

Ulrich opened the door to Claus's apartment. It did not appear to have been lived in since his uncle's death. A musty odour filled the air and a thick layer of fine dust lay on tables, chairs, lampshades, display cabinets and the cello case. He felt an unexpected, what was it? ...chill as if the dwelling itself harboured a death wish. The concierge, now a wizened old man with wrinkles and a limp – 'the result of a piece of shrapnel' – had recognised him, despite his British officer's uniform, and given him the spare key, as well as the uncollected mail from the postbox. Ulrich was obliged to use the staircase since the lift was not working, there being no electricity – it came on only irregularly. Cautiously entering the elegant drawing room, he noticed its Dürer woodcut prints and Impressionist paintings still in place which pleased him for, as he had been told, looting was widespread in the city. He wandered through the dining room, the kitchen, the bedrooms, opening windows until he finally arrived in the study.

Glass-fronted oak bookcases and silver-framed photographs covered the walls. He examined the photographs with grave interest. The young child Claus outside Stephansdom's great West Door, after his First Communion, surrounded by his parents, senior clergy and members of the von Juggardt family, the ladies in fashionable fin-de-siecle dresses, the men in very stiff and formal looking imperial suits. A youthful Claus and another man in student uniforms, both on horseback. He peered closely. For some time the recognition eluded him. It was von Grolman. 'He's been indicted as a war criminal by the Yugoslav Authorities,' Jerrold had informed him. The student Claus with his sister Elke, both in ski wear, somewhere in the Tyrol. A group outside the synagogue that day of Ulrich's wedding.

Using a handkerchief, he wiped the dust from the top of the rosewood writing desk and the fan-back Windsor chair, then sat down. There was nothing on the desk except a bronze Tiffany table lamp which Claus had brought back from New York. The two sets of the four-tiered desk drawers were all locked. He then recalled his uncle confiding in him that the ornate Bureau Mazarin desk contained a secret compartment. He gingerly felt the edge of the desk all the way round but found no button or lever. Lying on the floor, he crawled underneath the left side but found nothing. Under the right set of drawers however, he detected a long steel rod which reached up beyond the rear of the drawers. He pushed it up but nothing happened. When he pulled it down there was a clicking sound. Getting to his feet, he found that the topmost right-hand drawer had unlocked. He opened it.

Among the several papers was a sealed envelope with the words 'Last Testament' written on the front. Ulrich hesitated for some minutes before taking a penknife out of his pocket and cutting it open. It contained a single page written in elegant handwritten Gothic script.

This is the last testament of me Claus August von Juggardt.

The law will dictate how my estate will be apportioned. I write this in the knowledge that my clandestine actions and activities are now known to those who consider it their duty to uphold what I consider an aberration of the principles and practice of natural justice. I believe in universal justice. This can only be achieved through suffering, as Aeschylus in his Oresteia has the old men of Argos remind us, 'Zeus lays it down as law that we must suffer unto truth.'

With growing incredulity and bewilderment, I have watched over this past decade as a miasma of evil took hold of my fellow countrymen, twisting their minds, persuading them to commit unspeakable crimes in the name of justice. In truth, what they really sought was not justice but revenge and retribution. The descent from a civilised society to savagery has been swift. Men who committed atrocities, gassed and murdered the innocent in their millions, also worshipped and prayed to God, received His Body in Holy Communion, were forgiven their sins by his appointed clergy, wiping away – so they believed – their guilt.

I have worked to prevent this tragedy or rather to mitigate its worst excesses. I am proud of what I have done but ashamed of the little I have achieved. Nemo judex in propria causa, no one is his own judge. So I shall leave it for others to judge what I have done. I can only hope that from the ashes of the empty desolation now surrounding us, a phoenix will arise to produce a new civilization.

It ended with Claus's signature.

His elbows placed on the top of the desk and his face cupped in his hands, Ulrich wept. It was some time before he could compose himself and gather up his thoughts.

I love you Uncle Claus. I shall miss you dearly. You were a good friend, such gentleness of manner, so intelligent. In repose your face was suffused with a certain melancholy but when you began to speak it was filled with kindness and care. Yet... no family to console you during your last agonising hours. Ortmann revealed that they didn't use a rope but piano wire. What sadistic barbarians.

He gazed out through the wide bay window and recalled his visit to the Dreher house the previous day. Walking up the driveway and seeing his former home surrounded and occupied by Russian troops was a cathartic moment. All that remained of his childhood and youth spent in that house were the memories hidden away in the deeper recesses of his mind. He considered himself no longer Austrian or Christian or Dreher.

The clanging of a fire engine's bell could be heard in the distance. Which god is brooding over the city? Nemesis perhaps? He rose up, closed the windows and left Claus's apartment, determined to find Ruth.

* * *

On his arrival in Vienna from Venice, Ulrich had presented himself at the British offices of the Allied Control Commission only to be confronted with an irate colonel, whose walrus moustache reminded Ulrich of Archduke Franz Ferdinand. He demanded to know what the devil he was doing wandering about Europe without proper military authority. 'You Intelligence people are a deuced law unto yourself,' the colonel had said. 'Loose canons and dangerous to boot.' Ulrich recounted his time in Yugoslavia and Italy and showed him his papers attesting his temporary ad hoc commission in the British Army, citing Jerrold's authority. The colonel was eventually mollified enough to acknowledge his army status and give him an officer's pass.

Next day, he set out for the office for the resettlement of displaced persons. The early summer sun gave the near-empty and ravaged streets an unreal air. Ulrich felt the unreality. In his mind was the picture of a pre-war Vienna, a city of Hapsburg splendour and beauty, embellished with a stunning array of brilliant architectural forms, of a people endowed with a fun-loving spirit inspired by the music of Beethoven, Mozart and Strauss.

What confronted him, as he carefully picked his way along the broken pavements, was a pathetic reality. In Florence, an American officer from Texas had told him, 'now our boys can reach Vienna, they're bombing the shit out of the old place.' The city had an ugly, ramshackle air. The empty gutted churches no longer echoed to the sound of a *Te Deum* rejoicing at great military victories, nor vibrated to Brahms' great chords telling the congregation '*wie lieblich sind deine Wohnungen*', how lovely are thy dwellings. Where once stood Baroque buildings, the pride of Europe – the Paris of the East was the boast – were either gaping holes and mountains of rubble or massive walls leaning at drunken angles with gaunt blackened timber beams and fire-scarred oak roof trusses. These tragic stone and wooden carcasses all bore grim witness to relentless Allied bombing and savage street fighting against battle-hardened Soviet troops.

Barely disguised expressions of shock and bewilderment were etched on the forlorn and dejected faces of the benighted citizens.

Their glorious leader has committed cowardly suicide, Ulrich reflected, and they just can't accept they've been defeated. The destruction of their homes and city is the reward for their blind support. Where now those obscene larger-than-life pictures of the Führer and the parade of truculent goose-stepping troops, singing Nazi songs? Gone are the days of heady rallies, roused by the triumphant sound of trumpets from Tannhauser. Their worst nightmare has come about. Occupied, ravaged and looted by the Red Army.

The office for the resettlement of displaced persons was housed in a partially damaged baroque building on the Getreidemarkt, just around the corner from the badly damaged, golden-domed Secession museum. Ulrich entered with the same hope and anxiety he had on knocking on the door of the convents in Venice. The receptionist manning the desk in the main lobby directed him up a staircase to a large room filled with makeshift tables, each marked with a separate letter of the alphabet. A number of raggedly dressed, haggard and starved-looking people were waiting around.

"I would like to speak to the person in charge," Ulrich asked a middle-aged man staffing one of the desks.

"That would be Doctor Friedman," the other replied.

He pointed to a small adjoining room where Ulrich found Doctor Friedman, a man in his late thirties, small with a hairbrush moustache. He peered at Ulrich through thick glasses, regarding the British uniform with a certain quizzical suspicion.

"How can I help you?" he asked Ulrich.

"I want to trace my wife."

"Everyone wants to find someone. So what brings a British officer here? I don't understand."

Once again, Ulrich had briefly to retell his story.

"Please come with me," Doctor Friedman said, and, going back into the main room, took him to the desk marked with the letter D. There were a number of files on the desk but the name Dreher could not be found anywhere. At Ulrich's suggestion they went to the desk marked G.

"You must understand," Friedman explained, "that Europe is filled with millions of displaced and missing persons of every nationality. It's not even possible with our limited records to know who is displaced and who is missing. The good news is that the war has not destroyed all the population records kept by government and municipal councils. Besides which, the Germans kept meticulous records of all those they took away and sent to the camps. All the files in this room are Austrian, mainly covering Vienna. Each day our agents get their hands on many more documents but, given the financial restraints under which we work, the process is slow."

He picked up one of the files, and quickly leafed through it. There were a number of Gitelmanns recorded as been taken by the Gestapo, whereabouts unknown, but none with the name Ruth.

"If, as you say, your wife left Vienna four years ago," Friedman said, "she will not be among these records."

Later Ulrich wandered the broken streets, his tormented mind wondering who controlled his fate and why he was being tantalised.

* * *

Ulrich returned to the Allied Control Commission offices the next day. The uniformed receptionist handed him an envelope with his name on it. It was addressed to 'Captain James Pendrick' but, on opening it, he found a short note written in English but headed 'to Herr Ulrich Dreher'. It asked him to go to a certain cafe on the Annagasse that afternoon. It gave a time. It was not signed.

"Who handed this in?" he asked the young soldier behind the reception desk.

"I can't say, sir. A young lady, if I remember correctly, but she didn't leave her name."

"When was it delivered?"

"First thing this morning."

Ulrich was slightly disturbed but intrigued. Why the cloak and dagger approach? His experience, however, had taught him that in matters of Intelligence, there was no other way.

The Krafft café on the Annagasse had a wooden board where once there was a large window. It looked like some forgotten relic from the Great Depression of the thirties. Despite the sunshine outside, it was dim and ill-lit on the inside. There was only a couple of other customers present when he entered.

The waiter who came to serve him, gave him a surly look but Ulrich, waving him away, told him he would order later. He waited.

Why the subterfuge? All I want to know is the whereabouts of my wife. What information has this young woman that justifies such furtiveness? He ordered a coffee and drank it slowly.

A young woman entered and, seeing Ulrich, came across to his table. She was small, carrying a brown leather handbag, slung over her right shoulder and wearing a green gingham dress with white polka dots.

"Captain Pendrick?" she asked in English.

"Are you the young lady who delivered the note?"

She did not reply to his question.

"Let's go for walk," she said. "It's safer to talk outside."

She appeared too young for subterfuge. His perception was wrong. He was aware that war had destroyed all social distinctions of age and gender. Women flew planes, wore workman's trousers, smoked in the street, were part of partisan bands and used guns.

"Before we go any further," he said, "might I ask who you are. You have me at a disadvantage."

"What do you mean?"

"You obviously know who I am but I don't know who you are."

"I'm from the Jewish Agency."

"And your name?"

"Talia."

"How do you know about me?"

"We have friends everywhere."

"So it seems." He looked around. "Look why don't we go to the Stadtpark, it's near here. We don't want one of the Allied commission jeeps stopping to ask us what we are doing."

They walked down Fichtegasse, crossed Schubertring, passed Beethoven's brooding statue and went into the Stadtpark. Music could be heard coming from the Kursalon. The full-leafed trees, the flower beds and the birdsong offset the background of the devastated city. An old man sat on a makeshift chair playing a violin. Ulrich put a dollar bill into the hat at his feet.

"You're looking for your wife. Her maiden name is Gitelmann. Is that right?"

"Did Doctor Friedman tell you about me?"

"A mutual friend. Here in Austria, the authorities are reluctant to help in tracing missing Jews. That's why the Agency has set up its own organisation here. We might be able to help you."

"How can you do that?"

She opened the brown leather bag she was carrying and took out a pencil and a small pad.

"Only if you can give me some kind of description of your wife. Do you have any photos, for example?"

Ulrich looked at her with disbelief. Where has this young woman been for the past five years?

"I've lost everything I ever had," he said. "Everything. Look around, Europe lies ruined before our very eyes. And you ask me for photos. Well, I don't have any." He felt and sounded frustrated and angry.

"Captain Pendrick, you're not the only one to have lost everything," she snapped back. "I'm Czech and Jewish. I've lost my whole family. My father and mother were both doctors. Their sole mission in life was to help sick and dying people. They died in Treblinka. I've seen every kind of human horror, I also don't have any photos for I was lucky to get away with my life."

She gave him a defiant stare. From the taut expression on her face, Ulrich knew that it was not going to be easy to placate her. They continued to walk through the public gardens. There was a long silence before he spoke.

"I apologise. I'm forgetting my manners. Perhaps we can find somewhere to sit and I'll try to give you as much information about my wife as I can."

A couple of squirrels in jerky jumping movements raced across the path in front of them.

"At least they've not killed off the wildlife," he said jocularly.

She laughed.

"I need your help," she said, "and you need mine otherwise we wouldn't be here. Squabbling won't do any good."

He told her the story of Ruth and the two children, of his visit to the convents in Venice. She took notes.

"I shall pass on the information about the other children in Venice to my colleagues," she said. "All of us in the Agency are anxious to trace every missing Jewish man, woman and child, the victims of Nazi persecution."

"How are you going to do that?"

"With help from people like you. My job is to track down as many as possible of the Jewish survivors of the mass-killings that have taken place over the past decade. The Agency's plan is to help these people to settle in Palestine which we hope will become their homeland and a place safe for a Jew in which to live."

"Aren't you making a large assumption. How do you know they'll want to go to Palestine? They might very well want to return to their homes."

"I think, with respect, you don't realise that most of the surviving victims of the camps don't have homes or families any longer. Those we've taken under our protection told us they don't want to return. Their urgent wish is to get away as far as possible from the people who betrayed them and caused them so much horrific suffering. Not only the Germans but also their collaborators the Austrians."

At her mention of the word 'Austrian', Ulrich's mind conjured up the image of Cardinal Kirchmann, resplendent in his red robes giving the Nazi salute. If anyone in high authority was a Nazi collaborator it was his Eminence.

They came to a lake in the middle of the park. It appeared that the ducks had gone. Eaten, no doubt by the hungry citizens, thought Ulrich.

"I used to come here often with Ruth and the children," Ulrich said. "We'd feed the ducks, have picnics, play games, laugh and have fun." He was silent for a moment. "Can you really help me to find my wife?"

"I hope so. I seemed to have forgotten the reason why I contacted you. It's about your wife really. Our information is that many Jews taken from Italy were transported to Germany. In which case I can give you the name and address of a contact in Berlin who may, and I stress the word *may*, be able to help you find your wife. Unlike other agencies, we're primarily concerned with our Jewish brothers and sisters. Berlin has become the main focus of the Agency's activities."

Ulrich took the piece of paper she handed him.

"I must leave you now," she said.

He held out his hand, but she grasped him by his arms and kissed him on the cheek. She made off, towards the wooden bridge that crossed the Wien.

He looked at the paper she had just given him as if he had just been given the key to his future. How strange, he thought, it is in our human existence, hope can be based on such a small thing like a piece of paper.

* * *

The twin-engined Dakota flew low over Berlin heading for the RAF base at Gatow on the western side of the city. With ever-growing incredulity, Ulrich watched a completely ruined city pass beneath. The terrible destruction in Italy and Vienna had shocked him but this pulverised and devastated urban sprawl stupefied and terrified him. Berlin was no Nazi Valhalla, instead it was a Dantesque horror, a fitting epitaph for the boasted thousand-year Reich. As if beholding the vengeful ashes of a huge funeral pyre of hubristic Germanic dreams, he wondered what curses had been cleansed from the German people. Wagner himself could not possibly have envisioned such a literal *Götterdämmerung*.

Mesmerised by this desolate vision, it took him some time to collect his thoughts together. He had been lucky to get this flight. After his meeting with Talia, he had gone back to the offices of the Allied Control Commission, where he had offered the once irate colonel a bottle of malt whisky from Claus's reserves. 'I've been in touch with London and Jerrold vouchsafes for you,' confided the now emollient senior officer, who had directed him to an office which arranged for him to get one of the RAF flights to Berlin.

From the Gatow base, he solicited a lift into the city from a British Army lorry which dropped him in the centre near the Brandenburg Gate. 'If you stand on a chair,' the chirpy cockney driver quipped, 'you'll see the whole of Berlin. It's full of vistas and views.' He laughed. Ulrich passed large groups of women, most wearing headscarves, some without shoes, pathetic figures huddled together - there were few men about – clearing with their bare hands great piles of building rubble from the bombed out and shelled buildings. He had been told they were called *trummerfrau* or rubble women. Drawn up along the streets were rows of Russian tanks. Berlin was a corpse inhabited by walking wraiths.

After several fruitless quests of passersby, he finally found himself outside the address Talia had given him. In a city where practically every building had been destroyed, it was one of the few semi-intact buildings left standing.

Making his way up the war-damaged staircase, he found himself facing a door on which was pinned a roughly written notice with the words 'Jewish Resettlement Office'. He knocked and, without waiting for an answer, entered. On one side was a throng of poorly dressed people, mostly emaciated and skeletal, either standing about or restlessly sitting on chairs, their haunting expressions a mixture of resignation and anxiety. On the other were several tables behind which sat men and women anxiously looking at files or engaging with persons in front of the table. All eyes turned on him as he came in and an alarmed silence suddenly descended on the room.

A short, thickset man, seeing Ulrich, got up from his desk and strode towards him. He had a distressed but determined look about him.

He cast an uneasy eye at Ulrich's uniform. "We've permission from the Allied Control Commission to be here," he said in a combative tone of voice.

"Please ignore my uniform," Ulrich said. "I'm not here on any kind of official business. I'm looking for a David Günzburg."

"I'm David Günzburg. What do you want?" The tone had not softened.

Instinct alerted Ulrich to tiptoe through the feelings of these people, knowing why they were all there.

"I've just come from Vienna," Ulrich said in a soothing voice, "where Talia from the Jewish Agency gave me your name. I'm looking for my wife."

Günzburg gave him a quizzical look.

"She's Jewish, and was taken by the Germans from Venice where she had sought refuge."

This brief explanation appeared to appease Günzburg somewhat.

"I'm afraid," Günzburg said, "you may have come to the wrong place. Our work here is to help the Jewish survivors of the camps to resettle in Palestine. We could not possibly start to track down missing people. That task is well beyond our means so we've limited ourselves to aiding those who come here seeking help."

Ulrich rubbed his chin in disappointment. He felt frustrated.

"I thought that if she were alive, she may have come here for help," Ulrich said anxiously.

He gave Günzburg Ruth's name. Günzburg returned after a fruitless search of the records.

"You could try the Allied Commission. They've opened centres where people can trace missing relatives. You're a British Officer and you don't know that?"

"I only arrived here this morning. I was hoping that you might be able to help."

"I regret I can't do more for you. We're overwhelmed here by the numbers who come to us."

Günzburg waved his arm in a gesture taking in the room.

"These people want to get to Palestine," he said. "Despite the several million Jews massacred by the Germans, few countries want to give the Jewish survivors a refuge. It is true the Jews from France, Holland and Belgium can return home but German Jews don't want to stay here any more. And Polish Jews... they're trying to escape Poland not go back there. Why do you think the Führer placed all his extermination camps on Polish soil? Even now after this terrible war, a few Poles still hate the Jews and are killing them. I listen every day to stories of horrors still being committed against our people."

"Why are you telling me this?" Ulrich said. "I'm not unaware of what has happened to the Jewish people these past ten years. I'm married to one. My children are Jews." His voice contained a note of prickliness. "I've also been fighting against the Nazi evil."

Günzburg hesitated before he spoke.

"You're a British officer. I'm trying desperately to get Entry Certificates for as many of these unfortunate people as possible to enter Palestine. Yet despite the many Palestinian Jews who have fought for Britain in the Jewish Brigade, the British authorities in Palestine have severely restricted entry." He paused. "Perhaps you might convince your superiors of the desperate need for them to show a little more compassion."

"I'll try my best," he said with doubtful conviction, knowing he was a a tiny cog in a giant political Ferris wheel.

* * *

With single-minded purpose, Ulrich trudged daily around the devastated city, looking for Ruth in the various make-do centres caring for camp survivors and displaced people who, with frightened and dazed expressions, wandered about in aimless fashion. At each centre, he talked to some of those who formed this transient populace, but the name 'Ruth Gitelmann' did not evoke any response. In the concentration camps, they told him, human beings did not have names only numbers. The Nazis dehumanised their victims before killing them. These witnesses of mass-murder and inhuman torture related such tales of personal loss and tragedy his own quest began to appear almost nugatory. His spirits, like the sun, rose in the morning and set in the evening.

One morning, leaving his quarters in the British military compound, he saw an American Army jeep parked outside the press hut and sitting at the driving wheel was his old acquaintance Bill Thompson, wearing the distinctive dark olive-drab American Army officer's uniform.

"Gee whizz," said Thompson. "Well, I'll be damned."

He jumped out of the jeep and came towards Ulrich, his face wrapped in smiles.

"Ulrich Dreher. In a British Army uniform. Tell me I'm seeing an apparition."

"It's no apparition," Ulrich replied.

After first greetings, Thompson persuaded Ulrich to go back with him to the American military base. In the officers' mess and over coffee, Ulrich briefly related his own war experiences, explaining why he had come to be wearing a British officer's uniform and his search for Ruth, seized by the Nazis.

"I'll not give up," Ulrich said. "I must know what's happened to her and I owe it to my children."

"It's going to be difficult," Thompson said. "The true scale of the massacres of Jews is only now being revealed. The figures we've already collated at the American Army news agency here in Berlin defy human understanding. Six million slaughtered, among whom at least two million were children. It's beyond belief. Some of our most hardened troops report they were reduced to tears when they liberated the concentration camps. We now know that besides concentration camps, there were specific death camps. Can you believe it?"

"Actually, I can," Ulrich said in a calm way. He went on to relate what he had witnessed in the death camp in Yugoslavia.

Thompson looked at him gravely.

"It's ironic. At the news agency we're receiving press releases from the Catholic Church explaining how the cardinals and bishops here in Germany secretly and in some cases openly defied the Führer, encouraging the faithful not to take part in the Nazi campaign against the Jews. As if the Church had not trucked with the Nazis as soon as they came into power. As head of the agency, I refuse to distribute this lying rubbish to the press. Before America entered the war and I could still operate here, I interviewed at least one cardinal and several bishops and they all supported the Führer's campaign against the Jews. You add the fact that the Vatican signed a concordat with the Nazi regime ensuring, among other things, the Church's support for the Nazi regime. These prelates all tell you the Church was against the Nazi's racial policies. Maybe. But the evidence is beyond question that the Catholic Church knowingly and compliantly turned a blind eye to the Führer's systematic destruction of European Jewry. Now they're trying to wipe the blood off their priestly hands. All very convenient."

There was a further long silence. Thompson suddenly got up and went across to fetch another two cups of coffee.

"I'm sorry to say," Thompson said when he returned, "I've some rather unpleasant news for you. One of my major assignments is to file reports for the major American press about the whereabouts of the top Nazis. A large number have already been captured and are in prison awaiting trial. Most charged with war crimes. Now, and this is the difficult part for me to tell you, among those already arrested are a number of major industrial figures who are alleged to have used slave labour in their factories."

At this point, Ulrich already surmised what Thompson was about to say. A deep unease overtook him.

"My father?" Ulrich said in a calm and grave tone. It was as much a statement as a question.

"Afraid so."

There was an uneasy silence between the two men.

"He's in Spandau prison." Thompson paused. "Do you want to see him?"

"No. Not particularly."

"He may be able to tell you about your mother."

Ulrich considered Thompson's remark. To the surface of his mind came the image of himself as a small boy being carried on his mother's shoulders around the French garden at their home in Vienna. She used to hold up his two outstretched arms and made him pretend he was a jockey, while she repeated loudly, 'We'll win the Derby.'

"You can't bring back the past," Ulrich said.

"Too many ghosts, eh?"

"No. Too many tragedies." Ulrich paused. "My father chose to support and follow the Führer. No one forced him. My mother accepted his decision."

"Had she any choice?"

"Not really. But she could have accepted Ruth." Ulrich hesitated. "The whole matter is in the past and too tangled to be unravelled. I can't afford to spend my limited emotions on rebuilding fractured relationships. I must spend my energies looking for Ruth."

There was a long thoughtful silence.

"Look," Thompson said, "I've got a jeep and some spare time. I'd like to help you in your search for your Ruth. The Red Cross have set up a temporary field hospital not far from here. Let's start there."

Thompson drove at reckless speed, overtaking American and Russian military vehicles, and arrived at what appeared to be an extended tented village located in the extensive Volkpark in the centre of the city. There was row upon row of white tents, each with a large red cross painted on two sides. A military-style caravan was being used as a reception office. Having introduced himself, Ulrich briefly explained his quest to a white-coated attendant who had a harassed, careworn expression on her face.

"Our records," she explained, "are very far from complete. When we first opened, we registered everyone coming here but it soon became impossible. There are nearly two thousand patients now and we're accepting only the more serious cases. Most when they arrived were too ill or traumatised to be able even to give us their names. Many are just walking corpses." She advised Ulrich to make inquiries at every tent.

By mutual agreement, Ulrich and Thompson split up to search different areas. Each tent comprised a dozen or so army cots, on which lay or sat wraithlike creatures who, eyes sunk deep into their bony sockets, stared at Ulrich as he entered. Their stern stares held a terrified history of unspeakable pain and horror. He could almost taste the powerful odour of carbolic and the latent fear that pervaded the atmosphere. The eerie silence was broken only by the groans and bronchial coughs of the seriously ill and dying.

Further into the tented complex, he was stopped by a doctor, a stethoscope dangling around his neck.

"I would avoid those," he said, indicating a certain row, "infectious diseases, cholera, typhoid, typhus that sort of thing."

Ulrich ignored the warning. He had come too far to care about his own safety. He continued his search.

Near the end of one row he went into a tent, his mind blotting out any feelings of failure of his self-imposed mission. He looked around and, as if drawn by some hidden power, his eyes came to rest on her. She was sitting on the side of her bed. There could be no mistake. He did not see the emaciated and haggard features, the greying hair and uncomprehending stare. Spellbound he saw only the raven-haired and golden brown-eyed beauty he had stumbled into all those years ago in the Institute, scattering the books on the floor.

"Ruth, Ruth," he cried out, "it's me Ulrich."

As he bent over, he looked deep into her eyes, he touched her face, and taking her hard, calloused hands into his own, kissed them. Acknowledging his presence, she silently raised her thin arms and, placing them around his neck, burst into uncontrollable tears.

After a time, he spoke.

"The twins have survived," he whispered, his voice holding a manly warm glow, "Gabel and Rahel are safe and in Venice."

Just at that moment Thompson came into the tent.

"Your odyssey is over," he said to Ulrich.